Rachel Lee was hooked on writing by the age of twelve and practised her craft as she moved from place to place all over the United States. This *New York Times* bestselling author now resides in Florida and has the joy of writing full-time.

Nicole Helm grew up with her nose in a book and the dream of one day becoming a writer. Luckily, after a few failed career choices, she gets to follow that dream – writing down-to-earth contemporary romance and romantic suspense. From farmers to cowboys, Midwest to *the* West, Nicole writes stories about people finding themselves and finding love in the process. She lives in Missouri with her husband and two sons, and dreams of someday owning a barn.

Also by Rachel Lee

Also by Nicole Helm

Discover more at millsandboon.co.uk

CONARD COUNTY: K-9 DETECTIVES

RACHEL LEE

ONE NIGHT STANDOFF

NICOLE HELM

MILLS & BOON

First Published in Great Britain 2023
by Mills & Boon, an imprint of HarperCollins*Publishers* Ltd
1 London Bridge Street, London, SE1 9GF

www.harpercollins.co.uk

HarperCollins*Publishers*
Macken House, 39/40 Mayor Street Upper,
Dublin 1, D01 C9W8, Ireland

Conard County: K-9 Detectives © 2023 Susan Civil-Brown
One Night Standoff © 2023 Nicole Helm

ISBN: 978-0-263-30712-2

0223

Printed and Bound in Spain using 100% Renewable Electricity at
CPI Black Print, Barcelona

CONARD COUNTY: K-9 DETECTIVES

RACHEL LEE

Prologue

Dear Vince,

I know it's been over ten years since you saw me, but you kept sending me birthday presents, so I'm sure you give a damn about me. I need to tell you what happened after the last time I saw you.

My stepfather, Aloysius Bund, pastor of the Church of the Well-Lived in Conard City, started abusing me when I was ten years old. I was terrified and ashamed, but I didn't know he was the one who was wrong.

It wasn't until I was fifteen that I heard something at school about another girl and realized it wasn't right. I told the Elders, Miss Hassen and Mr. Zeb, they didn't believe me. They told me I was lying, that the pastor was a holy man who would never do such a thing. They warned me not to tell my lies again and called me sinful.

Because the Elders didn't believe me, I thought no one would believe me.

I took the only escape I could see. I joined the Army because it would take me beyond reach. I thought I would be safe there.

I wasn't. Some guy sexually assaulted me on

*the third date. It didn't count, they said, because I
was dating him.*

*I need someone I trust to know why I killed my-
self.*

There is no safe place for me anywhere.
Love,
Celia.

The fingers holding the letter tightened, then relaxed, allowing the sheets of paper to fall onto a desk.

Vince's hands clenched into fists so tight that his
knuckles turned white.

He then typed a note and printed it on a sheet of paper.

A few minutes later, Vince rose and went to the outer
office to speak to his assistant, a woman he had trusted
with his life on more than one occasion.

"Send this anonymously to this guy." She knew what
anonymous meant and would make sure no trail returned
to him.

Then, back in his office, he stared down at Celia's
letter. Time to get some intel from an old friend in the
Conard County Sheriff's Office. He needed to know
whatever there was to know about that church.

His deep, furious voice spoke one word: "Payback."

Chapter One

The war was over. For some. Jenna Blair stood on the porch of her aunt's house and dropped her duffel on the wood planking while she stuffed her hand into her camo pocket and pulled out a key ring. One key. The key to her aunt's door.

A key to her past. To a girl she doubted she could recognize anymore.

A heavy sigh escaped her. Pointless to think that way. Pointless because the intervening years always changed people. Her change might have been faster or harder than that of some, but change was the order of life. A natural progression, however painful and abrupt it had been.

She had chosen this path, she reminded herself as her hand hovered near the door's lock. Funny, though, how that path had come in a full circle right back to her aunt's door.

The door she had exited, the one she was about to enter. Past meet future.

Oh, hell, she thought. Time to get on with it. No point in mordant ramblings or philosophical thoughts that probably didn't have an original smidgeon in them. Self-indulgence.

She squared her shoulders, twisted the key in the lock and pushed the door open. Slinging her duffel over her shoulder, she stepped inside, closing the door and her eyes at the same time.

She smelled the faint odors and aromas of her childhood here, but time had changed those, too, and right now the house smelled a bit musty. It certainly sounded empty, lacking even the ticktock of the grandfather clock.

Aunt Bernice had set off on her round-the-world cruise four weeks ago. A cruise that Bernice had dreamed of forever. Jenna remembered all the times she and her aunt had pored over brochures and maps, planning together.

Bernice had finally saved the money, only to set sail just before Jenna returned home. They'd always planned to take this cruise together, but Jenna had changed her mind. The Army had shown her more than enough of the world for a while. She had been a military nurse, sometimes in field hospitals in combat areas. The memory of wounded and torn bodies would follow her into the afterlife.

Climbing the wooden stairs at one side of the entry hall, she headed straight for her bedroom. That hadn't changed, either. The rather sober dark blue-and-white decor she'd chosen for her college self was still there. She dropped her duffel on the made-up bed and felt almost surprised when dust didn't rise in a cloud. Bernice had apparently never stopped caring for it.

Then she opened the folding doors of her closet and found her old clothes still there. But mostly she noted the scent of lilac her aunt so loved. In an instant, Jenna's eyes prickled with tears. God, how she loved Bernice.

Stiffening herself, she reached for an old pair of jeans and a green T-shirt emblazoned in gold with the word ARMY. She'd had her mind made up that long ago, but she didn't want to wear it now. Instead she pawed around for something less triggering and found it.

The clothes were somewhat looser now, but it didn't matter. What mattered was the comfort she felt wearing them. Old training shoes were still good enough to wear. Jenna now reaching for Jenna then.

She opened the dark blue curtains, looked out briefly at the summer sunshine and the side of Old Lady Hassen's house, which needed a coat of paint. Hardly surprising, given that the woman was in her nineties and barely nodded to her neighbors. If she depended on her church, the Church of the Well-Lived, she might wait forever for the help or the money to do it.

Then Jenna remembered her primary task.

Bernice's dog was at the vet's. She needed to go get Mistral. A fancy name that Bernice had loved but that had inevitably become Misty.

On the way out, Jenna stopped to wind the grandfather clock and set the time from the military-issue watch on her wrist. The ticking resumed and the house felt closer to normal.

Grabbing her aunt's keys from the hook just inside the kitchen, she got her aunt's car and set out on her mission to recover Misty. She'd seriously missed that dog. Bernice had adopted her as a puppy shortly after Jenna had joined the Army, and the two had become friends when Jenna was home on leave.

The fur-face had a way of worming herself into hearts. Jenna wondered if Misty would even remember her, then wondered why she should. The dog had never failed to remember her when she came back on leave. It was Jenna who was trying to leave memories behind.

Misty had been boarded for the past month with the vet who maintained his office and kennels just outside of town along a narrow county road. Mike Windwalker, his face revealing his Indigenous ancestry, greeted Jenna warmly and told her right off that Mistral was fine.

"She sure loves her walks, though. She'll keep you busy, Jenna."

The mixed-breed dappled dog with striking mismatched eyes of gold and blue, jumped up at the sight of her and started barking. Her feathery tail wagged so hard that Jenna had to laugh, and when she squatted down to greet her, Mistral just about knocked her over. Slobbery kisses, lots of them, and it took a couple of minutes to calm her down.

"Yes, sweetie, you're coming home." Jenna laughed. "Home with me."

Dragging the leash Bernice had left behind, Misty ran to the car and jumped into the back seat the instant Jenna opened the door.

"I guess she knows where she's going," Mike Windwalker chuckled. "Have fun, you two."

The countryside remained familiar to Jenna. Slightly rolling spaces between mountain ranges, dry and dusty in the August heat. No sense of homecoming commingled with the familiarity of the thousands of acres of ranch land.

She saw some cattle and some tumbleweeds caught on fences. This area certainly hadn't changed.

The minute Jenna and the dog were in the house, Misty dashed wildly to every room, taking a few minutes to sniff, but finally returning happy and panting to the kitchen, where Jenna waited for her with crunchy biscuits.

After a supper of canned pea soup, Jenna took the dog out to the large front porch and sank into one of the Adirondack chairs, enjoying the warm evening and its gentle breeze. Misty had been trained to stay on the porch, so no worries there. She *did* intently watch anyone who strolled by and offered some wags of her tail.

She hardly noticed the friendly waves. To Jenna's relief, no one stopped to chat. She wasn't ready for that yet. She needed some time to let the change to her life soak in.

She was home to stay. No worrying about what lay right around the next corner. Days without plans or duties, other than a dog. Time to make the biggest transition of her life, excepting only the death of her parents and her entry into the Army. Even nursing school hadn't felt this momentous.

Now lazy days awaited her, a chance to recover and get her feet under her in this new life. She wondered how she'd adapt to filling her own hours with whatever she chose. She was hardly used to those choices anymore.

But she didn't worry about it one way or another. She felt detached in so many ways now. As if only anger remained.

She sighed and stroked Misty's head. The dog tried to lean into her, a difficult task given the width of the arms on the chair.

"We'll go for a long walk in a little while," she promised Misty.

Those amazing mismatched eyes looked up, that feathery tail sweeping the porch. She would never know if Misty had only picked out the word *walk* from that sentence or if she'd caught it all. Jenna believed that dogs understood a whole lot more than most people thought.

She caught sight of a man approaching. He was tall and lean, wearing old jeans with a chambray shirt and hiking boots. Almost black hair, cut short. He walked a dog, what appeared to be a large brown-and-black Malinois. Misty rose, taking instant interest. A chuff escaped her.

The man and dog halted on the sidewalk in front of the porch. Something about him rang a distant bell in Jenna's memory, but she couldn't identify him.

"Hi," he said, his voice warm. "You must be Jenna. You probably don't remember me, but I'm Kell McLaren. This pooch is Bradley, and he and Misty like to romp together in the front yard. Okay by you?"

Misty had already made up her mind. She leaped down the porch steps in a flash, barking happily, and Bradley answered. Kell bent and unhooked his dog's leash.

Decision made, Jenna thought with faint amusement. The two dogs began running in circles, taking turns chasing each other in the large yard. They were about the same size, so neither won the chase, not that either appeared to care.

Kell mounted the steps as if he had done so many times and didn't need an invitation. He settled in the chair at an angle to Jenna's. "Bernice said you were coming home to stay. I did that nearly a year ago."

That's when her memory snapped back. Sergeant McLaren, the Marine recruiter who'd come to her high school when she'd been a junior. The years had treated him well, she thought. He still had that strong jaw and nose, but his face had been weathered some by wind and sun.

"I haven't had any time to settle in," she remarked.

"It takes a while." He smiled, his gray eyes crinkling a bit in the corners. Totally attractive, something she was in no mood to recognize. "It did me. Bet it won't be long before you'll be looking around for some way to get busy again."

"At the moment, I'm planning on learning to drift for a change. What did you do?"

"Got myself involved in contract work once in a

while." His smile turned into a grin. "Once an adrenaline addict, always an adrenaline addict. Wait and see."

"I don't know that I want that kind of adrenaline again."

"There are different kinds. But I know exactly what you mean."

He probably did.

The dogs had run themselves ragged and climbed onto the porch, panting and grinning.

"I'll get them some water," Jenna said, glad of a brief escape. Kell disturbed her in some odd way. As if she couldn't quite breathe.

When she brought the big bowl of water back to the porch, she carried biscuits for the dogs. Between them, they lapped up almost the entire bowl of water, then sat politely waiting for the treats they could no doubt smell.

Jenna had to smile at those hopeful furry faces, then handed them each a biscuit. "I wonder how they can enjoy anything when they gulp it down so fast."

"Ask them. Maybe the smell's enough." Kell rose, leash in hand. Bradley sat straight up and waited for the clip.

"I always feel like I'm separating Romeo and Juliet when I take Bradley home." Kell flashed another smile. "I've intruded long enough. See you."

Jenna watched man and dog stroll away and wished she'd been hospitable enough to offer some lemonade or other soft drink. But she hadn't really wanted to socialize, not with a man, any man.

Or had she?

KELL MCLAREN WALKED Bradley another mile or so around town before heading home. His K-9 walked right beside him, as he always had.

Jenna Blair was back. Bernice had told him she was coming home as if it would be a joyous experience.

Kell had his doubts about that. Jenna had been a nurse in the Army, and nurses got to see some of the worst of it when they dealt with casualties.

He also had some idea, from his own experience, of just how much adaptation was required for this transition. Coming home was harder than going to foreign places to begin with. He had no idea why, but he knew that almost everyone he had talked to had come back from the war feeling as if they had stepped onto a different planet. Everything seemed strange. Uncomfortable.

Becoming comfortable took a while. Switching from the rigid military to a more relaxed civilian life took a while, too. Switching from an existence full of threat to one with few threats was another difficult journey.

For a while, a hair trigger would remain.

Regardless, he thought Jenna was an attractive woman with her bright green eyes and auburn hair. He also thought she wouldn't appreciate him noticing that, though he couldn't say why.

He and Bradley reached the small house he rented in exchange for doing repairs. The owners wanted to sell it eventually, but in its present state, they didn't have a chance.

He and the dog settled into their late dinners. Sometimes Kell wished he enjoyed food as much as Bradley apparently did. He ate only for fuel. When that had begun, he had no idea.

So he ate a heaping plate of instant mashed potatoes along with two fried hamburgers and a whole package of frozen broccoli and didn't taste much of it. Bradley sat beside him looking hopeful, waiting for the plate he knew he would get to lick.

How many times had he shared his chow with that dog? Probably hundreds if not more. Dog food might be healthier, but there were plenty of times no kibble had been available. Kell tried to be more careful of Bradley's diet now, but that didn't break old habits. Two buddies who shared everything, good and bad.

"Green beans in a little while," Kell promised the dog as he licked the plate clean. Bradley loved frozen green beans second only to peanut butter. Of course, he'd scarf down green peppers, frozen broccoli and sliced apples, too.

"Is there anything you won't eat?" he asked Bradley as he carried his plate to the sink. But he knew there was. Things he didn't like to think about.

Chapter Two

From the farthest end of the continent, a letter was sent anonymously to the Church of the Well-Lived in Conard County, Wyoming. It reached Pastor Bund of course, without being opened. It was a rule never to be broken.

He glanced at it, debating whether to open it. He occasionally got junk mail, but this looked different in some way. At last he reached for his letter opener and sliced along the fold. Inside was a single sheet of paper.

I KNOW WHAT YOU DID TO CELIA. YOU'RE GOING TO PAY.

Bund's hands trembled as he stared at the paper. Only two other people knew besides Celia, and Celia was dead. That left Miss Hassen and Mr. Zeb. Blackmail? He crumpled the paper and thought about how he would handle this.

WHEN JENNA STEPPED out into the morning a few days later, she knew it was going to be an uncomfortable day. Not only had the temperature risen, but the humidity had soared to unpleasant levels, which it rarely did in these parts.

Misty, on the leash beside her, sniffed the air and didn't exactly look happy.

"I know," Jenna said. "But we both need a bit of a jog before it gets any hotter."

Five days and already she felt as if her body was demanding attention. Fitness levels decreased rapidly, and that was not something she wanted to let happen. Besides, anger was beginning to pierce her detachment, and exercise would help with that.

She set out at a slow jog in deference to the dog, but knew she herself was going to need a decent, long run before too many more days passed.

Misty seemed happy enough, however, and trotted along except for occasional pauses to smell a post or an especially green and tall clump of grass.

"I'll never know how you like the smell of dog doo and pee," Jenna said. "I guess it's your pee-mail, huh?"

Finally, Misty paused to do her business, then waited patiently while Jenna used a poop bag to clean up after her. "You know, kiddo, this is the part I *don't* like."

She came around a corner and saw Kell, wearing shorts, and Bradley heading her way at a fair clip. She made no effort to change course. Kell had become familiar from his daily visits to her front porch to let the two dogs play. She didn't feel as edgy around him anymore.

Misty pulled at the leash trying to get to Bradley. Bradley, however, stayed at heel beside Kell, although the dog's tail began to wag rapidly. Two friends meeting.

Misty gave a small leap when Bradly got near, but Bradley remained almost stolid, other than his tail.

"How do you get him to do that?" Jenna asked in amazement.

Kell half shrugged. "He's a trained Marine K-9."

Jenna's interest perked. "Oh, wow. What type?"

"Scout."

Jenna looked at Bradley with new respect. "That's a tough job."

"It sure is. Mind if we walk with you?"

"I was just about to turn around. I'm not sure at this point how much Misty is used to."

"We'll go with you. Bradley is getting close to the end of his two miles."

Jenna was surprised again. "He goes that far?"

"Well, he likes to rest a couple of times, though not always."

"Misty needs more rest than that," she answered wryly.

"Yeah, but sometimes Bradley just wants to sniff around. We take an easy stroll for that."

Companionably, the four of them walked back toward Aunt Bernice's house.

"Not going to be a very nice day," Kell remarked. He pointed to the western mountains, where dark clouds wrapped the peaks. "God knows we need some rain, though."

"Good for grazing," Jenna agreed.

They came around the corner on the street where Jenna lived and saw paramedics parked out front of the Hassen house. When they reached Jenna's house, they paused as a stretcher was wheeled out, the body and face completely shrouded by a blanket.

"Oh, my God," Jenna murmured. "Miss Hassen?"

The stretcher was followed by a middle-aged woman in loose drab gray fabric, her face almost as gray as the dress. She was one of the church's ladies who came frequently to look in on the old woman. Sometimes a group of them would come, according to her aunt, probably to socialize. And the pastor, of course. Two or three times a week.

"Apparently so," Kell answered. "Has to be Miss Hassen."

They watched the stretcher pass, and as it did, Kell said quietly, "Oh, hell."

Jenna looked at him. "What?"

He pointed down, and she saw Bradley crouched on his stomach, his tail raised straight up and not moving.

"He's alerting. Something is wrong."

Jenna stared back at the stretcher. "What?"

"I don't know. He's never alerted to a corpse that didn't smell like explosives. But he's got a scent now that he doesn't like."

Jenna looked at the dog again, then said, "Let's go inside." It wasn't an invitation she'd made to anyone yet and felt uneasy even as she offered it.

"Bradley, up. Beside me."

The dog obeyed at once, and Kell bent to praise him and scratch him behind the ears. Bradley's tail returned to wagging.

"Yeah, let's go inside," Kell agreed. "Something triggered him, and I don't want him exposed for long."

Once they were inside, Jenna gave the dogs a bowl of water. Belatedly, she remembered her manners, and though it made her feel even more uneasy, she offered coffee.

"Sounds great. Thanks." Kell sat in one of the kitchen chairs while Jenna moved around slowly, starting the coffee. She could feel his gaze on her, making the muscles between her shoulder blades twitch a tiny bit. What the hell was she doing? The question, however, didn't stop her from giving the dogs a cookie.

At last, coffee poured, Jenna sat across the table from

Kell. Distance. She needed to keep a distance. Anger rumbled deep inside her, and she tried to suppress it. "So, no idea why Bradley alerted?"

"Only that something's wrong. He doesn't like things that are wrong."

"But what could it be?"

Kell shook his head. "I wish I knew. I keep him in practice with targets, but nothing that has anything to do with a body."

"I doubt you could practice with many of them," Jenna replied dryly.

Kell smiled faintly. "Wouldn't that be a big deal?"

"It'd make the headline on our local newspaper, which isn't much of one."

"Only the police blotter report and plenty of advertising," he agreed.

Jenna felt an unfamiliar smile tug the corners of her mouth.

"So are you settling into freedom okay?"

She hadn't thought of it that way, but maybe that's what it was. "I'm feeling the lack of exercise, for sure."

"I take Bradley out to the vet's agility course a few times a week. Bernice used to let me take Misty sometimes." He cocked a brow at her. "You could come, too. You can get a surprising amount of exercise running with a fast dog around an agility course."

Jenna thought about it, the surprising urge to go along growing in her. "Does Misty do the obstacles, too?"

"A few of them when she feels like it. I don't push her on the training, but she loves to get out there and run until she's exhausted."

"We'll do that, then." Again discomfort began to rise in her, but she smothered it, seeking her self-control. A free run would be good for Misty, and maybe good for herself as well, to play some long-distance fetch. Even use a Frisbee with her. *Activity*, as the first Duke of Wellington had once said. *That's the key.*

"Good," Kell answered as if it were settled. "Soon, if you can. Just let me know."

As if her days were too crowded to fit it in. She had to do something about these empty days. All they did was allow her to brood and suffer from bouts of fury. She shook herself.

"Something wrong?" Kell asked.

She didn't want to speak of it to anyone. Not a single person. She'd done her speaking, and it hadn't done her a bit of good. "I'm fine." A bald lie.

Just then, thunder cracked loudly, announcing the arrival of the storm. Then she heard the skittering of claws on the floor. She turned at once and saw Bradley cowering in a corner and shaking.

"What's wrong with him?"

"PTSD," Kell answered.

"Can't you do something for him? Comfort him?"

"No." Then Kell sighed. "He's already reacted. If I try to comfort him, I'll reinforce his behavior. I just have to make him endure it for a short while."

"But you *must* be able to do *something*!" Jenna couldn't believe he was being so cold about this.

Kell leaned forward, resting his forearms on the table. "I'm doing everything I can, but it may take years to get him past this. I can't predict."

"But…"

He shook his head. "I can't encourage this response. But we work on immersion therapy. Little by little I expose him to the sounds that frighten him and offer him a treat when he remains calm. Unfortunately, I can't control the volume of the thunder."

"But then how do you do it?"

"I start from very quiet and work our way up to loud. He's gotten better about gunfire, for example. I take him out to the firing range. We started at a long distance where we could barely hear the crack of the guns, then worked our way steadily closer. We've still got a ways to go, but when he reacts like this, I don't give him a treat or any attention at all for a short while. It's called extinguishing an unwanted behavior."

He shrugged one shoulder. "Sudden explosions of thunder, I can't help. I try to work on it at home with a recording at very low volume, but I'm beginning to wonder if he can tell the difference between recorded and real."

"Maybe." Jenna looked at Bradley and so much wanted to comfort him, but what Kell was saying made so much sense. Even *she* had trouble with thunder. It was too much like a big explosion or a barrage. "I feel so sorry for him."

"I do, too. One of my major preoccupations is to help him. My God, how many times did he warn us of a sniper or an ambush? Or roadside bombs? I couldn't count them. Anyway, this problem apparently started when I was wounded in a firefight. These K-9s are wedded to their handlers. Hell, I feel the same attachment."

Jenna nodded. She had some PTSD, too. She was lucky because, for the most part, it only gave her nightmares. During the day, she was able to manage it. So far.

"PTSD. You, too?" she asked presently.

"A bit. Well, maybe more than a bit, but I was lucky. Therapy helped a lot. Bradley wasn't so lucky. We were separated for a few months while I recovered and rehabbed. He refused to work with another handler or go into intense situations. When the Corps was done with us both, we got sent home together."

Jenna nodded, feeling a surge of sympathy. She had

all-too-vivid memories of her time in a field hospital, images and sounds that persisted. Kell and the dog must have them, too.

"God," she said finally. "The war really isn't over."

"Not for all of us." He leaned back, apparently lost in thought, but his face revealed nothing.

Then he sighed again. "Anyway, I can't take him home until the thunder moderates quite a bit. I hope you don't mind?"

"Not if it'll help Bradley."

He smiled faintly. "Thanks."

Just then, thunder rumbled again and, along with it, came a sharp crack of nearby lightning. Jenna looked at Bradley again. The poor animal was shaking even harder.

"What have we done?" she asked.

There was no answer.

WITH EVERY OUNCE of his being, Kell felt acutely aware of the dog's misery. He made himself turn to another issue. He couldn't pay attention to Bradley just then. Immersion. Too fast, but still immersion.

He spoke eventually. "I'm concerned about him alerting to the corpse."

"Now I am, too. I wish either of us could tell what it was that bothered him."

"He's a scout, finely tuned into some things. I can't be certain, but something sure as hell troubled him about that body if it made him alert. Something was wrong with it, maybe something only he could detect."

"That would be my guess."

Kell studied her. Jenna was attractive, albeit a bit too thin, but she seemed standoffish in some way. Distant. Detached. The only real emotion she'd displayed had been about Bradley. What had happened to her?

Something must have. Bernice had talked about her often, always in a bright way. Not only did she love her niece, but evidently the last time Jenna had been home, Bernice had seen or felt nothing unusual. Insofar as Kell knew, anyway. Something must have happened in the meantime, but there was no way he could ask.

He looked at Bradley, who was shivering less, and decided it was time to distract him.

"Jenna? Do you mind sharing some dog biscuits?"

She jumped up and got the bag out of the cupboard. Misty immediately leaped up, her nose following the bag.

"Let's do this together," Kell suggested. "Some training time will help distract Bradley from his fear, and Misty sure won't mind."

"Absolutely," Jenna agreed. "Maybe Misty can be sort of a role model."

Thunder rumbled again. *Damn storm*, Kell thought. He rose and made the *Come* sign to Bradley, swinging his bent arm to his chest.

At once, the dog focused on him, a good sign. When Bradley didn't move, Kell motioned again. This time, Bradley slunk toward him. "Good boy!" Then he offered a treat. Bradley chomped it down, another good sign. The dog's eyes remained focused on him at last.

"Now you," he said to Jenna.

"I always say it to Misty. Why the gesture?"

"Dogs understand body language, and in dangerous situations, you have to be silent." He watched Jenna make the sign while saying the command.

Misty, who had been sniffing at the tabletop, immediately answered, coming to Jenna. A treat for the dog, too, followed by praise.

He smiled. Maybe this would distract Jenna from her problems, too. He hoped so.

Bradley still shivered, but he remained intent on Kell, a very good sign. Next was the *Sit* command, followed by *Stay* when Kell walked from the room. Bradley didn't follow. Then *Down-Stay.* Bradley was beginning to come back. His heart lightened.

Jenna repeated every exercise with Misty, who was having a grand old time, grinning a doggy grin and waving her tail rapidly.

Eventually, a small laugh escaped Jenna. "She's having a blast!"

Kell smiled. "It's a good thing, isn't it? I have another one for you, but not right now."

She looked at him, her green eyes clearer and her face more relaxed. Pretty, with her short auburn hair and gentle chin. "What's that?"

"I can't do it here for obvious reasons, but Bradley loves to seek. I make him stay while I sprinkle kibble all over the house. At the *seek* command, he rockets all over the place sniffing out the kibble."

"That sounds like such fun. Like an Easter egg hunt."

"It sure tickles him." Since Jenna appeared so interested, he added, "Training isn't a drag for the dogs. For them, it's a great thing. They please their owners, get treats or hugs and plenty of pets. Good thing for the owners, too. They get a kick out of a well-behaved dog and probably enjoy the affection as much as the animals do."

Jenna looked at Misty. "We're headed for a whole new world, girl."

When Kell judged the thunder had grown distant enough, and, serendipitously, the rain had stopped, he and the dog headed home, with only a few pauses for training, each exercise a step forward.

He was intensely aware of Bradley's every movement, every hesitation. His dog was still unnerved by the distant thunder, but not terrified. Kell often felt that the two of them nearly shared a mind, the connection was so close.

But his attention was also focused on Jenna. She was so tense, although it had eased somewhat since he started visiting with Bradley every day. But still. Even with PTSD, she shouldn't tense up over an ordinary conversation. Could it be something about him in particular?

That didn't seem likely when they hardly knew each other, and he was positive that he couldn't have given her any reason to distrust him.

So why was she reacting as if she were responding to a potential threat? Man, she should have had enough buddies during her time in service to know that the threat didn't come from Americans. So why was she reacting to him this way?

Or maybe she reacted to *all* men this way. The notion nearly stunned him. Could that be it? But why?

Then he had some ugly ideas he didn't like at all.

Rain began to fall again.

JENNA STOOD AT the living room window, staring out at the gray day. Misty had plopped herself on her big red doggie pillow in front of the seldom-used fireplace.

What next? she asked herself. She couldn't keep doing nothing without going mad. But she wasn't ready to look for a nursing job, not by a long shot. Stirring those memories seemed dangerous right now. While the work wouldn't be as awful, she still wasn't ready to look into the jaws of hell again, however rare it might be around here.

She sighed, then heard Misty stir. Looking over at her, Jenna saw the dog had raised her head and cocked it to one side.

"I'm okay, Misty."

The dog wagged her tail a few times, then resumed her nap.

Boy did she envy that dog. A simpler life, mostly one of happiness and love. Which immediately brought Bradley to mind. Well, that dog didn't have only happiness. Far from it.

In Bradley's reaction to the thunder, she saw herself but with different triggers. God! Men were her triggers now. Any man. She was grateful, however, that she no longer felt that way about Kell. He was easygoing. Friendly. Nothing about him seemed threatening except his sex.

And maybe the idea that she felt stirrings she hadn't felt in a long time.

She sighed again. Matters were growing steadily more complicated. Her mind. Her life. Kell. Bradley.

She'd heard quite a bit about scout dogs when she was over there in the midst of hell. Stories told by soldiers who were both impressed and grateful. Man's best friend, indeed, unless you were on the wrong side with bad intentions.

But she ached for him. How awful to have PTSD and no one to talk to about it. Relying on your handler to read you well enough to help, able to express only through your body.

Kell seemed to have a handle on it, though. Any handle he could get. But it had to be awful for him, too. To see his buddy broken like this, to feel the extreme empathy that could only be born between two soldiers who relied completely on each other.

Sometimes life was a bitch.

She remembered the image of poor Miss Hassen being carried out of her house, her life over. In her nineties, to be sure, but so completely isolated except for her small church, except for a woman who came to visit and take care of her needs. Except for her pastor, who visited two or three times a week, always at night. Bernice had told her all about it, shaking her head disapprovingly. "An old woman needs more," she had said.

A natural death. Except for Bradley. A scout dog was trained to alert only to certain things. Kell was probably right when he said the dog must have detected something wrong about the body.

But not one of the things he was trained to alert to.

Of course, she'd heard stories of scout dogs and patrol dogs exercising their own initiative at times out of the bounds of their training. Like when they charged for help when their handler was wounded. Things like that.

Had Bradley been exercising his K-9 intelligence? Or just a dog's intelligence? Did it matter?

It had bothered Kell, and it bothered her. She wished that dog could talk with more than his body language.

A vain wish, just like so many of her wishes that had been dashed. Her dreams. Crushed.

Again she sighed and, this time, shook herself. She was giving in to self-pity, and she loathed self-pity. She needed to get out of the mire of her own thoughts to turn them to something more productive.

But how? She honestly didn't feel like socializing yet, even though it was good for the mind and the heart. She couldn't possibly go back to work, either, although she was going to have to face it sooner or later. Reading? Maybe she should distract herself with good novels. Escape into another world just for a few hours.

Internally, she sometimes felt like seething, boiling lava. At other times, she felt almost hopeless. No novel could cure that.

Chapter Three

The day dawned with clear skies, more common in August than the heavy rain of a few days before. Jenna had finished breakfast and was starting to sip her second cup of coffee when Misty stood up, tail wagging, and looked at the front door.

Then came the knock. Amused at the way the dog had sensed a person outside before she had, Jenna went to answer the door.

Kell and Bradley stood there, Bradley sitting tall. Misty had other ideas, barking so excitedly she nearly lifted her paws from the ground.

"Misty, settle." Sometimes the dog listened and sometimes not, Jenna thought with amusement. Misty grew quieter, but she was far from settling.

Kell wished her a good morning. "Bradley and I are about to leave for the agility course. Would you like to join us? Or I can just take Misty with me if that's all right by you."

She considered the options surprisingly quickly. "I'll go along." A run around with Misty would probably make her feel a whole lot better.

"Want to come with us? Or drive yourself?"

"I'll follow." No question about it. Closed in a car, there was no means of escape.

"Great. I'm parked out front, so mount your steed. We'll wait for you."

As if she didn't know the way to the vet. She kept silent about it, though, and was soon following Kell's pickup through town and out into the countryside. Another beautiful August day, the sky a deep blue despite the dust in the air. The rain had greened some patches, though.

At the vet's, Mike Windwalker greeted them.

"How are my pals doing?" he asked, squatting to scratch behind their ears. "No sickness, I hope."

"None," Kell answered. "Just the agility course."

"I'll put it on your tab, then." The vet stood.

"Misty, too," Kell answered. "I'm hoping to persuade Jenna this is fun. Misty already knows that." He looked at Jenna and winked.

What did he mean? That he knew Jenna had plenty of experience with obstacle and agility courses? Perhaps.

As they walked toward a fenced area full of bright tunnels, ladders and hurdles, Jenna asked, "How much is the charge? I'll pay you back. And you run a tab?"

"The cost is five dollars per dog, no biggie. Don't pay me back. And yeah, I run a tab. Mike thinks it would be ridiculous for me to have to bring five bucks every time, so I have an account I pay once a month."

When they reached the gate, Kell opened the latch. Bradley, amazingly calm, waited. Misty began barking again and rising to her hind feet.

Jenna spoke. "I guess she *does* like it out here."

"What dog wouldn't?" With the gate open, he said to Bradley, "Run."

The dog took off with Misty right on his heels. Jenna felt one corner of her mouth tip up as they raced around the enclosure, clearly happy to be free and running.

Jenna spoke. "It must cost Mike a lot to maintain this place."

"Probably more than he's charging. All the equipment must start wearing out sooner or later."

Before long, Kell called Bradley to heel, then started leading him through the course. The dog enjoyed himself while Misty watched, occasionally running around, but mostly watching.

Jenna did the same, noting that Kell never spoke a word, guiding Bradley around with hand signals only. Well, except for the praise. Jenna couldn't imagine getting Misty to that point. Then she wondered why she should even try. Misty seemed happy enough. Once she crawled on her belly through a tunnel, and another time she climbed the ladder, perching on top for a few seconds before leaping down the other side.

Kell got a bit of a workout, too, running through the hurdles with Bradley, taking each leap beside the dog. Oh, man, did that look great to her. When was the last time she'd taken a hurdle? Overall, Kell was right about the workout you could get with a fast dog.

Part of the course involved snaking through a long line of yellow posts. Bradley waited to start until he received a hand signal from Kell.

Jenna looked at Misty. "Would you like to do all this?"

The dog, of course, could only look quizzical.

"Yeah, I know. I don't ask you that often." But then she had a thought. There was one command she was sure Misty knew.

"Misty, go."

Misty took off like a shot. She headed for those hurdles as if she'd been hoping.

"Incoming dog," Jenna called to Kell.

"Got it." He jumped out of the way but didn't tell Bradley to stop. The dogs took those hurdles together, leaping gleefully over each one.

"Wow," Jenna said as Kell came to stand beside her.

"They're both young and enjoy using their bodies. Sort of like us."

He didn't look at her as he spoke, but Jenna felt those words to her core. She'd been missing it, hadn't she?

She glanced at Kell. "Mind training a person?"

He faced her, chuckling. "We probably need to be trained more than they do, at least when we start. Sure, training Misty would be fun. How trained do you want her?"

"Kinda like Bradley is," she said. "Well, mostly, if you know what I mean."

"I do. No more than obedience. That's useful enough for any dog and owner. She'll get a kick out of it."

"I already think she understands every word I say. Sometimes she just ignores me."

He laughed again. "Okay, next time we're out here, we'll work on getting her to pay attention *every* time you want her to."

BACK AT JENNA'S house with two happy but tired dogs, she surprised herself by inviting Kell in for some lemonade. She was almost as surprised by his acceptance. He ought to be growing tired of her by now.

Because the dogs wanted to flop on the cool kitchen floor rather than a rug, they once again sat at the small table to enjoy the lemonade Jenna had made the day before, out of a can naturally. The tart, cold liquid tasted like ambrosia to Jenna.

"I don't remember ever seeing you when I was growing up," she remarked. Surprising to her, too, was that she wanted to know something about him. Another stirring of a desire to socialize? She hadn't felt one in a while, except once before with Kell.

"You wouldn't have seen me," he answered. "I grew up at the far end of the county. You know that little town, Martha's Creek?"

She nodded. "I've heard of it but never been there."

"I'd be surprised if you had. Population around six hundred. There was enough to get by there, in part because of the ranches. A small grocery store that sold necessaries besides food. A hardware store. A tiny church. A bar, of course. A few other things."

"But school?"

"One room. The teacher was a tough old bird who never let us get away with anything. She'd even upbraid us outside of school if she saw any of us getting into mischief."

"And your family?" she asked.

"Just me and my dad. He ran a repair shop and a two-pump gas station."

"That must have seemed very limited to you when you were young."

He shrugged. "Not when I was a kid. Not until I was sixteen and seriously started thinking about the wider world. When I turned eighteen, I made my dad drive me to the nearest recruiting station. A few weeks later I was on my way to training at Parris Island. Dad was disappointed. He wanted me to take over his shop. I didn't want to. I'd already spent years working there, and it just wasn't my thing."

Jenna nodded. "I guess the Marines *were* your thing."

"You could say that. I only left under duress."

"Your wounding?"

"I think I mentioned that."

She hesitated, wondering how well she really wanted to know this man, then asked, "How bad was it?"

"I still have shrapnel near my spine."

He shrugged it off, but Jenna didn't. The shrapnel probably meant he'd had other wounds as well. She'd seen plenty of them. "No paralysis, I take it."

"Only a bit at first. Rehab got me past it. What about you? You joined the Army for a reason, right?"

A snort escaped her. "You don't just fall into something like that. I don't know exactly why, but while I was in nursing school, I started thinking I could do more to help in the Army. Hardly surprising since I'd thought about it a few times after you came to our school as a recruiter. I guess the seed was planted then."

"It sometimes is. You lived with Bernice, though?"

"Since I was four."

"That's a young age to lose your parents. At least, I think that's what happened?"

Jenna just shook her head. The story no longer disturbed her. "Dad loved the rodeo and went on the road riding bucking broncos and the occasional bull. My mom wanted more than sitting here waiting for him to show up on the rare occasions he felt like it. She gave me over to Bernice and took off to greener pastures. I barely remember her. After that, Dad apparently couldn't find any reason to come back here, so that was that."

"You never hear from them?"

"Not since I was left with Bernice."

"Hell." He drummed his fingers on the tabletop.

Jenna shook her head. She didn't need any sympathy. "Bernice loves me. I think I got the better deal out of it."

"Maybe so."

Apparently rested, the dogs stirred. She heard them trot into the living room.

"You don't mind?" Kell asked.

"This house is dog-proof unless they decide to chew on a chair leg. They can wander or sleep anywhere they choose."

KELL FINISHED HIS second glass of lemonade, then rose. "Time to move on. I enjoyed your company today, Jenna."

Which was true. He'd enjoyed every minute of it. He noticed, though, that she didn't return the sentiment. He was willing to bet she hadn't always been so detached, so withdrawn inside herself. Not growing up with Bernice, who was a real pistol.

Outside, he and Bradley began a mission. Since Bradley had alerted to the body of Miss Hassen, Kell couldn't shake the feeling that it was important, not just an odd reaction. The dog might not have been trained to alert to a wide variety of things, but Bradley was often far more aware than his human. Something had bothered him, and that was not a matter to be ignored.

Kell looked down at his K-9 and wished, as he had so many times before, that Bradley could talk. Often enough, they seemed to read one another's minds but this time the connection was opaque.

"What did you sense, big guy?" Something abnormal had gotten the dog's attention.

Bradley glanced up at him but continued his steady trot beside Kell.

"You have amazing powers of recuperation, pal." And he did. The dog could exhaust himself, then sleep for a short while and be once again in top form. Now here he was ready to go again after tiring himself at the agility training.

Three blocks later, they were downtown. They passed the Courthouse Square, where some older men engaged in games of checkers and chess at concrete tables and benches that had the game board carved into the granite tops. The lawn in front of the courthouse building was spacious and had greened up from the recent rain. A familiar scene, weather permitting.

He and Bradley entered the sheriff's office, and Kell spoke to the deputy, Cal Murchison, who sat at the front desk. "I was wondering if Gage could spare me a minute or two, Cal."

Cal picked up his desk phone, punched in a number, then spoke almost immediately. "Kell McLaren and Bradley are here to see you."

Then Cal looked up with a smile. "You know where his office is, Kell. Head on back."

Kell found the sheriff sitting at his desk with a stack of papers on one side and a computer on the other. Half of Gage Dalton's face was marred by a burn scar that gave him a crooked smile. He leaned back in his creaky chair and winced as he did so. Pain from a long-ago car bomb when Gage had been in the DEA.

Gage waved Kell to a chair, then looked at Bradley. "How's his PTSD?"

"Slowly improving."

Gage nodded. "It'll take a while. Damn shame what we do to these dogs."

"They also save a lot of lives."

"Can't argue that. So what can I help you with, Kell?"

"Miss Hassen."

One of Gage's brows lifted. "How so? Did you know her?"

"Did anybody?"

"She was definitely one to keep to herself except for that church of hers. So what's up?"

"Bradley alerted when the body passed him."

With another wince, Gage straightened, placing his elbows on his desk. He looked at the dog. "He did?"

"Absolutely."

Gage's attention returned to Kell. "Must have surprised you."

"It did. Look, Gage, I may be making a mountain out of a molehill—wouldn't be the first time—but Bradley's training is still good. I keep it that way. Although I have to admit he's never alerted to a corpse before unless it had explosives attached or nearby."

Gage nodded thoughtfully. "But Miss Hassen's death was from natural causes, according to the doctor." Then he looked at the dog again. "Alerted, huh?"

"No mistaking it."

Gage rubbed his chin, then reached for a pencil and began to tap the eraser end on his desk. A steady beat, that pencil tap being one of the sheriff's trademarks when he was thinking. He then made a swift change in direction.

"I hear you're visiting Jenna Blair."

Kell half smiled. "The grapevine's running again? I'm just seeing her because of the dogs." Which wasn't strictly true, but Kell didn't want anything more going around the rumor mill, especially since it wasn't exactly more than that. "Bradley and Misty get on like a house on fire. Seems only right to give them play time."

Gage's gaze strayed back to Bradley, who was sitting at attention taking in everything, though exactly what mattered to the dog just then was anyone's guess. Then he repeated himself. "So he alerted."

"Yup."

The pencil dropped to the desk as Gage rubbed his chin. "Well..." He drew the word out, apparently thinking. At last, he stirred and winced as he did so. "I worked with K-9s when I was in the DEA. They're reliable. *Very* reliable. You sure it's not his PTSD?"

"Positive. It would be the first time he's alerted outside of his training since we got here."

"Well, hell," Gage said. "I've seen enough of these dogs to know they sometimes get out of their boxes. In a good way. Too damn intelligent not to think for themselves sometimes."

Kell nodded, feeling a bit of relief that Gage wasn't dismissing the issue. Then he was surprised he'd gotten even a little tense over this. Maybe because of Bradley. He didn't want his buddy treated as if he were broken.

"Something was wrong with that body," Gage said after a minute or so. "I'll take Bradley's word for it. Only problem is what."

"He hasn't learned to talk yet."

At that, Gage smiled. "Except with his body. He sent kind of a big signal."

"He sure did." Kell reached to scratch Bradley behind one ear. "Anyway, I don't know what anyone can do about it now. I just felt it was important for you to know, although I can't say why the hell I did. It just kept bothering me."

"I can see why." Gage reached for his pencil and started tapping it again. "The body's still in the morgue. I'll need to rustle up a good reason to require an autopsy, and Bradley won't be enough. Sadly."

"There's probably nothing to actually *see* there, or it would have been found immediately." Kell sighed. "Okay, I've done my duty. I let you know." He started to rise when Gage stopped him.

"You know, Miss Hassen doesn't have any relatives, at least none we can find. No one's going to claim her body as far as I can tell. Certainly not her church. Why would they want to pay for her funeral? That's a lot of money even at the bare minimum. The county will have to deal with her remains."

Kell waited, sensing the sheriff had thought of something. He was right.

Gage leaned back, pencil forgotten. "I know one thing I can justify. We'll screen her for toxins. Claim an anonymous informant. Judge Carter will approve that. Although I can't begin to imagine why anyone would want to kill her. Dang woman didn't know anyone outside her church."

"They're all like that, I hear," Kell answered. "I don't know much about them."

"Nobody does, except that the gospel they preach isn't traditional. And that they're more of a personality cult around their pastor, Aloysius Bund. But they mind their own business well enough that nobody has a problem with them."

Kell shook his head, not liking the sound of it at all. "That kind could turn bad in a single minute from what I hear. Like Jonestown."

"Or Waco. Anyway, it hasn't happened. It might take a few days for an order from the judge, and I'm not sure how long it will take the hospital to do the tox screen. I just might mention the results to you."

Kell laughed. "And I won't hear them. Fair enough?"

Gage looked at Bradley. "He's one fellow who deserves to be listened to. But there's another thing. If we find something, I'm not sure what we can do about it."

FEELING BETTER, Kell took Bradley toward their own home just three blocks from Jenna's. It was coming on the time he had been taking Bradley over there to play with Misty. He wondered if that might be too much for Jenna in one day.

He was concerned about her. As far as he could tell from what she wasn't saying, she hadn't gotten in touch with her old friends around here, and there must be some who hadn't moved away.

But there was a lot that woman wasn't saying. That worried him. She ought to be able to understand that she could talk with another vet about even the most horrible things she'd experienced. But she wasn't talking. Not really talking at all, just skimming the surface in any conversation.

Then he looked at Bradley. "What do you say, Bradley? Is it time to be a little forward with the pretty lady? We could take her some dinner."

Bradley continued to wag his tail gently. He was mostly a happy dog when he was with Kell.

"Yeah, I agree. Let's go to Maude's and get her to pack us some dinner. What do you think she'd like to eat?"

Kell almost laughed at himself. That dog was not the best reference on food. He'd eat anything on Maude's menu, including the plates.

JENNA HAD STARTED to grow hungry, and Misty had as well. The dog had begun poking at the pantry door with her nose. Kibble time.

Jenna loved watching that dog. Remarkably communicative when you paid attention. The world from a dog's viewpoint must be a very different place.

Jenna couldn't imagine it, although she'd tried a little while ago. A world that depended on smells and sounds more than vision, she surmised. Although maybe not. Misty's body sure had some stories to tell about her moods and desires.

Tuning in to Misty made her feel better. So did all the hugs and sloppy kisses. A dog's love was reliable. Trustworthy. And Misty didn't play any power games or sexual games. No pretense in a single bone of her body. With her, what you saw is what you got. Happy with her own dogginess.

Man, Jenna thought. Were these good thoughts or crazy thoughts? She couldn't always tell anymore.

She still wished she could be more like Misty, though. Very much in the moment, very aware of her needs and feelings and disturbed by none of them.

Sighing, Jenna rose to get the kibble, then heard a knock at the door. From Misty's suddenly wildly wagging tail, Jenna guessed it was Kell and Bradley. For the second time today?

She didn't know whether to feel good about it or scared. Was she letting him get too close? But the dogs…

Giving up, she went to the door with Misty.

Misty exploded out the door into the front yard and waited, bowing toward Bradley: *Come play*.

"Play," Kell said with a motion of his hand. Bradley took off, and the fun began.

Kell smiled at Jenna and lifted a couple bags from the porch. "I bring dinner unless you want to tell me to get lost."

Astonishingly, she didn't want to. She opened the screen door until she could hook the latch on a little screw sticking out of the siding. "Come on in. I'll stay out here and watch the dogs."

"We'll eat when they wear themselves out," he said firmly. "I'll just take these into the kitchen."

Jenna slid into an Adirondack chair and gave herself up to the warm, breezy evening and two dogs romping joyously. Yep, she wished she could be like them.

Kell returned and sat. "Fun to watch, aren't they?"

"Hugely fun."

"I could tell Bradley was pining again."

Surprisingly, Jenna felt amusement bubble up inside her. "How could you tell that?"

"His head kept turning in this direction while we walked."

"I thought he was better behaved than that," she said, teasing him and astonishing herself. She hadn't felt like teasing anyone in a long time.

"Well, it depends. Like I said the other day, he gets his time just to be a dog. We were taking a stroll back from the sheriff's office…"

Jenna sat up straight, curiosity extinguishing everything else. "The sheriff's office? Is something wrong?"

"Not yet anyway." He gave a whistle, and Bradley stopped sharply just before he ran into the street. "Boundaries," Kell said.

Amazingly, Bradley listened and trotted back into the yard. Misty followed him, just because she always followed Bradley.

"Boundaries? He understands that?"

"Absolutely. Necessary training. Sometimes he needs to be corralled off-lead. That's one word I use. Now he'll stay within five meters of me. Less if I give him a different command."

"I learn something new every day," Jenna remarked. "But what about the sheriff?"

"Yeah. Well, I couldn't let go of the way Bradley alerted to the corpse. So I told Gage. He understands enough about K-9s to agree it shouldn't be ignored. He's going to get some toxicology tests done."

"Wow," Jenna breathed. "I thought the alerting would be the end of it."

"It might be." Kell shrugged. "Maybe Bradley was wrong. I need to be settled about that in my own mind." He turned his head toward Jenna. "Part of the reason that dog and I get along so well is because I understand him. If there's something new, I need to understand that, too."

"I can see that. But the tox screen. Couldn't someone object?"

"Nobody's claiming the body. Anyway, Gage is going to get a court order citing an anonymous source."

A small laugh bubbled out of Jenna, the first in a long time. So long it felt strange. "I hardly think Bradley is anonymous."

"He'd agree with you. Still, imagine going to the judge and saying, 'Well, this dog had a feeling…'"

Jenna laughed again. God, she couldn't remember the last time she'd felt this good or this comfortable. Kell did that for her. Liking him was getting easier and easier.

A dangerous thing? Probably, but just then, she didn't care.

Chapter Four

Two days later, after giving Jenna a breather, Kell arrived in the early morning to suggest they take Bradley and Misty on an easy walk together. "You know, a dog walk, where they get to stop as often as they want to sniff all those things we can't stand."

Jenna managed a smile. "That's the only kind Misty gets, but she never tires of them. I think she'd like it even more if Bradley came along."

"Maybe she will. I know I'll enjoy walking with you."

Jenna felt an immediate recoil but suppressed it. Kell. This was Kell, who, beyond all reason, had crossed her barriers. At least to this extent. It had only been a friendly remark anyway. Not a threat of any sort.

She leashed Misty and they set out, she remarked on the way Bradley stayed at Kell's left knee. "Does he even need a leash?"

"No. I use it because it makes people feel easier when they see him. Besides, I think Bradley likes it."

"But why would he?"

"Security. Ownership of the leash? I'm not sure, for obvious reasons, but have you ever taken Misty's collar off?"

"Never needed to try."

"Well, if you do, you'll see how possessive she is of it.

Ownership? A security in belonging?" He shrugged, then asked, "How much do you know about Miss Hassen?"

"Almost nothing. Only what Aunt Bernice told me."

Kell ruminated a minute. "I wonder why she didn't live on the compound with the rest of them. Especially after she grew frail."

"Beats me. Maybe she loved her home. Maybe she didn't want to be surrounded by people all the time. It's not as if she never had company. Bernice said small groups of women from the church would come visit a few times a week. They came to drive her to the service on Sunday morning. Then there was Pastor Bund. Bernice said he visited two or three times a week in the evening. She wasn't alone all the time."

"That's good. No one should be alone like that."

Jenna wondered if he was making a sideways comment about her own isolation, then decided he wasn't. At this point, as far as she could tell, with Kell, you got exactly what you saw. Like Misty.

"Do you live in the moment?" she asked suddenly.

Kell looked at her. "Meaning?"

"That you don't worry about tomorrow or live in the past."

His jaw tightened. "The past has a way of creeping up on you. You probably know that. As for tomorrow?" He returned his gaze to the dogs who'd evidently found something fascinating in a bush. "What's the point of worrying, Jenna? You can make plans, they'll probably fall apart, and all you can do is—in golf terms—*play it as it lies.*"

"I didn't know that was from golf."

He flashed her a smile. "A useful saying, don't you think?"

Misty suddenly pulled hard at the end of her leash.

Jenna focused on her. "I think there's something she wants to smell that she can't reach."

"Bradley wants to follow her." But Bradley was better trained and simply stood beside Kell, his entire body pointed toward Misty.

They moved in the direction Misty was pulling and she shoved her head right into some bushes, returning almost immediately with a yellow tennis ball in her mouth.

"Now that *is* important," Kell chuckled. "Nothing wrong with *her* priorities."

Bradley *woofed* once with approval.

Kell laughed. "I see a game of fetch in the near future."

Then Misty dropped the ball right in front of Bradley, who snatched it up, then bowed in the universal dog sign of a desire to play.

"Oh yeah," Jenna said. "Play time is coming. But not here."

"Nope. Bradley, leave it."

The dog immediately dropped the ball. Misty cocked her head, clearly not understanding. Jenna knelt. "Bring it to me, Misty."

Well, thought Jenna a bit smugly, Misty wasn't *untrained*, just not as highly trained as Bradley. Nor did she need to be.

"You know," Kell said as they approached her house, "I hear that church is weird. Like a cult."

"They might be. I don't have a measuring stick for that. But I *do* wonder about all those people living together in that old farmhouse. They've given up everything, as far as I can tell."

They climbed the porch, set the dogs loose to run and play with the tennis ball.

"Do any of the members of that church work?" he asked.

"I have no idea."

"So how do they get by?"

"Good question. Bernice saw two or three of the women in town shopping occasionally. Other than that?" She shrugged. "Maybe they grow something they can trade. Goats for milk and cheese, eventually meat. They must do *something* with those goats. I'm just spitballing here."

He snorted. "Wouldn't it be something to find a field of marijuana growing out there? Good cash crop."

"What a picture, those hyper-religionists growing pot."

"Who knows what they're being taught out there? Maybe religion according Pastor Bund."

"That wouldn't be the first time."

"No." He sighed. "Indoctrination can be dangerous sometimes."

She looked at him. "Don't all churches indoctrinate?"

"You've got me there. Okay, personality cults can be dangerous. However, I've never seen anyone react to this group except with a raised eyebrow or a roll of eyes. Harmless, evidently."

"They *did* look after Miss Hassen."

"True." But he shook his head. "Maybe I'm biased, but I don't trust them."

"Any idea why you feel that way?"

He thought for a couple of moments. "Maybe I don't trust groups that live in closed-off compounds and operate in total secrecy. I always think there must be something they need to hide."

She raised an eyebrow. "You mean like military black budgets or black ops?"

That pulled a laugh from him. "Got me again."

"There's a difference, though. Supervision. A command structure, not just one person."

She had to choke out that last. Command structure? A pox on it, as Aunt Bernice would say.

"Didn't leave us much room, did it?"

"No."

She felt him looking at her as she turned to watch the dogs. She'd let something slip to him. He'd picked up on it. Not good. "The dogs are getting tired. I'll go get them a bowl of water and some treats."

"I'll take care of it," Kell said as he rose. "You just relax."

Relax? Hah. She'd been *relaxing* since her return home and was beginning to think it wasn't healthy. Not at all. She needed more things to do, to think about. Better things than the memories that wouldn't lie down and die. A distraction from the anger that still burned in her gut. She *needed* to move past that somehow, because there'd never be a resolution. Never.

Both dogs were flopped on the porch, panting and grinning, when Kell returned with the big bowl of water and biscuits. The dogs both looked torn between treats and water, but that didn't last long. They dove into the water first.

Kell spoke when both dogs had sated themselves and returned to lying down.

"Bernice said she named the dog Mistral first?"

"Yup. Beautiful name, but in the way of dogs, nicknames developed. Misty was the enduring one."

"Some other ones?"

"My favorite of the others was Ms. Super Genius Wonderdog."

A laugh burst out of Kell. "I love that. What brought it on?"

"Misty was always trying to cadge corn chips. One day she heard me rustling the bag and came running—

right past one that had fallen on the floor. The words just burst out of me."

"I love it."

Out of nowhere, the feeling overwhelmed her, dizziness that made the world spin. "I'm sorry, I need to go inside and take some medicine."

She rose shakily, and at once, Kell was on his feet, steadying her with one hand beneath her elbow. "Jenna? What's going on?"

She closed her eyes to avoid seeing the spinning world, but that didn't help. Oh, God, it was so bad nausea was rising within her. He was helping her to the door, and she knew she'd have fallen without him.

"Dizziness. Bad. Concussive injury."

"Well, you're in good company. Think of all those football players."

She could barely manage a smile.

"Bed or somewhere else? And where is the medication?"

"The living room recliner please. I can't lie down right now."

He guided her carefully and held on to her until she was safely seated. "Meds?" he repeated.

"Bathroom cabinet. The only prescription bottle."

KELL WENT TO get the pills and a glass of water for her. Now he understood even more clearly what she'd been through. A field hospital right near the action. And how did she deal with these episodes when she was alone? Crawl?

He hated to think. She could be a danger to herself, weaving around this house, nearly falling over with every movement.

After she took the meds, he sat across from her. Now he could see how her eyes were twitching back and forth.

"It's not this bad very often," she said. "Honestly. Usually, it's much milder and I can deal with it. This one's just worse than most."

"Do you have vertigo very often?"

"No, not even the minor episodes, but the mind's an amazing thing. It can adapt. It *is* adapting. When the mild ones happen now, I hardly notice anymore. It has to get really bad for me to stop."

He thought he could understand that. "You served in a field hospital?"

"Unfortunately."

He'd been inside them, once as a patient, other times to check on his Marines. He'd seen what was going on in there, particularly after a bloody encounter. It was as bad as any battlefield, and the hospitals were often under attack. He could easily believe she'd had a concussive trauma.

"I can't leave you like this, Jenna. You can barely stand up."

She could hardly look at him, the way her eyes were dancing around. Her voice was tart. "How do you think I managed before? I don't need rescuing."

He sighed. "I'm not talking about rescuing you. I'm talking about helping you to avoid an injury. What's so bad about that?"

"You can go. I'll be fine."

He doubted that, but further argument seemed pointless if she was going to react this way. He'd half expected she would get to this point, as tightly locked in as she seemed to be, given the way she avoided looking at people. "Okay, but I'll be back to check on you later. You can't deny me that."

At least she didn't argue this time. Rising reluctantly, he said only, "Anything I need to leave for Misty besides water?"

"Just water. No food until morning."

Misty was sitting right beside her, watching her intently. Dogs knew. Somehow they knew.

"See you in a couple of hours."

"If you must."

"I must," he said firmly. "Just let me be a good neighbor. Misty will need a walk anyway."

"I'd forgotten about that."

"So Misty needs me even if you don't. I'll go now."

Outside, with Bradley walking beside him off-lead despite his usual concern that people not get frightened, Kell wondered how to deal with such a stubborn woman. Well, he'd done the best he could. At least Misty's needs had quieted her down.

Something more had to be goading Jenna than her tour in field hospitals. Something that made her standoffish. Hell, she still hadn't gotten in touch with her old friends, who must remain around here.

Hell's bells.

As he was approaching his house three blocks away, he saw the swirling lights of an ambulance again. He hardly knew the guy. Another standoffish person. The world seemed to be full of them. And this guy, unlike Miss Hassen, had to be hardly more than fifty. Probably a heart attack.

But he was dead, Kell saw that when they rolled the stretcher out and the guy's face was covered. Grief was about to come to someone.

A day that had begun so brightly had darkened emotionally for him.

He turned toward his house when he suddenly realized Bradley wasn't beside him. Turning around to find the dog, his heart plunged.

Bradley had moved closer to the stretcher and was alerting.

Damn it all! Again? What is going on with that dog?

He gave a quiet command, and Bradley rose, returning to Kell's side.

Another mystery.

"What's going on, pal?"

Of course, there was no answer. All he could do was wonder if Bradley was getting nervous about something else.

Double damn it.

Chapter Five

In the morning, Jenna felt a lot better. She still needed to move carefully but was able to get around to feeding herself. Feeding Misty was more difficult since she needed to bend over to get the kibble and put both water and food on the floor. Clinging to the edge of the counter, she managed.

Breakfast for her was a slice of buttered bread. She could manage that without too much turning around.

No shower, though. If she'd had any thought of attempting it, that evaporated when she went to the bathroom. Too much, just yet.

She took another dose of her medicine and prepared for a day of sitting on her butt again. She hated this. Well, these days she seemed to have a whole lot to hate, some of it nearly overpowering. Did she want to think about that? Not today. Problems were growing like weeds.

But her eyes were still jerking around too much to read a book. Maybe the TV would have something to distract her.

The front door opened just as she settled into the recliner with the TV remote in hand.

"Good morning," Kell said pleasantly. "I dare to enter where I'm not wanted. Had to check on you and Misty, though. I know *you* don't want anything, but does she need a walk? Bradley is outside looking brokenhearted."

Well, that pulled a smile out of her. "I'm sure she does. The most I could manage was to let her out the back door."

"Looks like she's eager. If that tail wagged any faster, she'd be flying like a helicopter. We'll be back in forty-five minutes or so."

"Thank you, Kell."

"I'm a dog lover, if you haven't noticed. Come on, Misty, before the two of you die on opposite sides of a screen door."

Jenna heard them leave and felt a moment's embarrassment about the way she'd reacted to Kell last night. Even when he'd returned last night to walk Misty, she'd barely said a word to him.

Why? She guessed she hated to reveal weakness of any kind. Maybe that was a weakness in itself?

God, if there was one thing she'd learned in the military, it was how much a soldier had to rely on comrades.

Until that reliance turned into a nightmare.

She had to stop thinking about it. It couldn't be dealt with any longer, so she needed to let go of the scalding scar. The burning memory. But there was nothing quite like betrayal. Nothing. She wondered how much she'd ever trust again.

Nearly an hour later, Kell and two dogs burst into the house, clearly happy.

"It was a sniffing walk," Kell told her after he filled the water bowl for the two of them and returned to sit across from her. "I doubt Misty has as much stamina as Bradley. She isn't trained to it."

Her curiosity piqued. "Are scout dogs trained to have more?"

"To their physical limits. Which is not to say they don't need to be rested. But I know for sure that Bradley will push himself further than he should. Under some circumstances that can be good, but under others not so much."

Being afraid to move her head too much, she couldn't nod her understanding. "What happens if they do too much?"

"They collapse. Or they stop being as alert as they should be. Gotta watch out for it, if it's possible. K-9s are very task-driven. And I do mean driven."

"Like soldiers."

"They *are* soldiers."

"And Marines," she added with a faint smile. "I know you guys are particular about that."

He laughed. "You bet. I was lucky to get Bradley. He'd trained with another guy, one who got killed in a road accident. It doesn't always happen, but Bradley was willing to train with me. My second K-9." His face darkened then.

"Second?" she prodded gently.

"Second," he repeated grimly. "My first, Junior, got too close when he was sniffing out a roadside bomb." His eyes closed.

"That must have been awful." She ached for him, which should have been a warning sign about how much she was becoming involved, but the warning passed her by with merely a thought.

"It leaves a hole in you when a buddy dies, whether he's furred or not." His eyes snapped open. "To be honest with you, I didn't want another K-9, not ever. But then they tossed Bradley in on me while I was refusing to continue. Good handlers can be hard to find, and they didn't want me to quit. Anyway, they brought Bradley into my barracks room, and that, as they say, was that." One corner of his mouth lifted in a half smile. "Couldn't resist that dog."

"I can see why."

Both dogs had come to join them and were sharing Misty's large pillow bed, snoozing happily.

Kell startled her. "Bradley alerted again last night. At a corpse."

"What?" She nearly sat up, but her vertigo reminded her that might be a mistake.

"Exactly. What? Second time he's alerted to a corpse. I hope he's not developing a new problem. Anyway, they were carrying out this guy from across my street. Not that old, but he lived alone and hardly talked to anyone. I've been there a year and I don't even know his name, which tells you something. Hard not to know everyone around here."

She remembered that to be true, at least while she'd grown up here. "That's sad. The man, I mean. As for Bradley…"

"Yeah, as for Bradley. This is so unlike him, at least unlike his training."

She drummed her fingers, one of her few safe movements at the moment. "Are you losing your trust in Bradley?" She saw the dog's ears perk as he heard his name, but he never opened his eyes.

"No, I'm not. It's not a matter of trust. I've trusted that K-9 with my life and the lives of many others. But this is different. He might be developing a new fear. Or he might be sensing something he hasn't been trained to do. Something his mind is recognizing all on its own. I think I mentioned once before that these guys can act on their own intelligence outside their training. As if once they know their regular targets, they can recognize other things."

"It's possible. I've never thought extensively about K-9 intelligence."

"I've had plenty of reason to." Kell sighed, looking at his dog. "Bradley, you worry me. Too often lately."

Jenna saw the grooves of concern on Kell's face and wished she could help in some way. Any way.

Kell stirred. "What next?"

Jenna bit her lip before answering. "I'm not sure, but I suggest we treat these alerts on Bradley's part as being valid. As yet, there's no reason to think otherwise."

"All I can do," Kell agreed. "Time will tell. I guess I should tell Gage Dalton about this. He can at least do another screening for toxins. Then I'll know."

Jenna realized her vertigo was beginning to settle down, which was a relief. A long way from being gone, and she'd have to be careful for a few days, but it was improving. Almost cause for celebration. Almost, but not quite. She knew how fast these episodes could resume.

"You know," Kell said a while later, "I've been thinking, what if there could be a link between these two deaths, something that Bradley might have sensed?"

"A link? How is that possible? Did they even know each other?"

He shrugged. "Damned if I know. No, I was just thinking that they were both recluses. Speaking to almost no one. They couldn't possibly have any enemies if they didn't go around anywhere to make them. So it must be natural causes. Certainly in the case of Miss Hassen. The other guy...well, I don't know. I guess I could try to learn a little about him."

Jenna closed her eyes, a big mistake, because without her jumpy eyes to tell her approximately where she was in space, her messed-up head took over and made her feel even more like she was spinning. She snapped them open immediately. "What good will that do? Especially when there's no evidence of any wrongdoing."

After a moment, Kell laughed quietly. "I'm going over the top here, huh?"

"Only because of Bradley," she said. "I get it. You want answers and you don't want to wait."

"Seems like I won't have another choice. I need to get back to repairing that damn house I rented. You wouldn't believe how many things deteriorate when a house is left empty for a few years. Anyway…" He rose. "Anything you need before I leave? Water? Coffee? Some kind of food or snacks?"

Bradley was already rising, stretching from head to foot, recognizing the signs that he and Kell would soon be on the move.

Jenna accepted the offer of water gratefully, and a box of whole grain crackers would come in handy, too.

"See you later. I'm off to walk Misty," Kell said on his way out the door. "Call me if you need anything."

What a nice man, she thought after he left.

Then, *Have you lost your mind, girl?*

She stared at the bottle of meds Kell had left right beside her and decided not to take them. They always made her sleepy and she didn't want that.

Instead, she wanted think about two recluses who had died within days of each other. She wasn't one to believe in coincidences, especially when Bradley had alerted.

That troubled her.

KELL WAS THINKING about that, too. Coincidence? He didn't much believe in coincidence. He had to find out more about these two people. There might be no connection of any kind, but Bradley had alerted. That had to mean something, even if the answer caused him more worry about his dog.

He looked down at his K-9. "You know, pooch, you've

got enough trouble to deal with without adding more to the pile. I honestly hope you were right."

But right about what? He headed once more to the sheriff's office.

Facing Gage Dalton across his desk, Kell wondered if he was just wasting the sheriff's time.

Dalton looked at Bradley, who had parked himself at attention beside Kell.

"Okay," Gage said. "I get the whole thing about K-9s, but twice? Are you sure he's okay?"

"That's what I need to find out," Kell admitted. "Has he got a new problem, or is there a good reason for his reaction?"

Gage nodded slowly, his pencil once again tapping the desk. "Heard you were working on training him for rescue work. Maybe that's what's happening. Search and rescue dogs alert to the dead as well."

Gage had been checking him out, Kell realized. "Yeah, I am. Bradley needs to work. But we haven't gotten that far along yet. First, I need to get him over his fear of sudden loud sounds. In the meantime, the only searches we're working on is finding a live human." He smiled faintly. "Your deputies are willing to help out with that."

"I heard. The guys kinda like it." Gage sighed. "Doctor said Mr. Zeb's death was a heart attack. Seems he's been having a heart problem for some time."

"And maybe that's all it was."

Gage sighed. "Okay, for your peace of mind, I'll get another toxicology done. But that's the only reason. Neither death is suspicious, you know. Fits right in with prior health problems."

"Anything on Miss Hassen?"

"Low blood sugar. Very low, which isn't unheard of in

a diabetic. Too much insulin, maybe not eating enough. Dangerous recipe."

"It's possible," Kell acknowledged. "Maybe that's all Bradley was sensing."

A few minutes later, he was heading back home with his dog, unsatisfied in a way he couldn't explain to himself. Worried about Bradley.

And frankly worried about Jenna.

Today, he decided, he'd bring her some lunch. She oughtn't be teetering around her house to feed herself, and crackers weren't enough.

For now, he could look at tearing out that rotted floor beneath the bathtub at his place and start toting up what he'd need. At least the property owners were paying for the supplies. Of course, when you thought about it, labor was a hell of a lot more expensive than the parts.

And tonight he was going to start a few conversations with his neighbors about the late Mr. Zeb. Kell had only been here a year, but they'd been here a lot longer. They must know *something* about the guy.

JENNA WAS ACTUALLY glad when Kell and Bradley showed up around one in the afternoon.

"I hope you like burgers," he said. "Bradley has a passion for them. He could hardly keep his nose away from the bag."

Jenna arched an amused eyebrow. "Failed training?"

Kell laughed. "Nope. I just didn't command him to leave it."

Misty was hopping all over the place around Bradley.

"No walk yet," Kell said. "We need to eat while it's still hot. Jenna? Bring it to you here?"

"If you wouldn't mind." The swimmy feeling still hadn't entirely lifted, and her one trip to the bathroom had been a challenge. Soon it would pass, she promised herself. This wasn't going to last forever. Unlike other things.

A few minutes later, Kell handed her a plate covered with a large burger and fries, as well as a napkin.

"Dig in," he said cheerfully as he went to get his own meal.

Seated across from each other in the living room, they ate for a while in silence while the dogs' eyes begged from the pillow.

Jenna spoke. "It always makes me feel cruel, the way Misty looks at me when I'm eating."

"How do you think dogs have survived for so many thousands of years? Excellent beggars. And of course, there's that grin and wagging tail."

"And the love. They've got that down, too."

"Loyalty," he added.

"In short, people should be more like dogs."

"Absolutely. It would be a wonderful world, all right."

After cleaning up from lunch and eating Jenna's left-over fries—with one or two making their way to the dogs—Kell said, "I'm going to talk to my neighbors later. At least as many as I can find. I want to know more about this guy who died. I gather his name was Mr. Zeb."

Jenna straightened in her chair. "Mr. Zeb? I know who he is."

Kell's expression was first surprise, followed by intensity. "What do you know?"

"He's involved in that Church of the Well-Lived, just like Miss Hassen. I seem to have heard at one time or another that they were both elders or something."

"Yet another one who doesn't live at the compound. What do we make of that?"

Jenna shrugged. "I wish I knew. I don't see any need

for a connection, except that maybe they were both such introverts they couldn't stand to be crowded like that."

"Then how did they both become designated elders?"

"Something changed since they were?"

"That could explain it. A good reason to talk to the neighbors. When did the guy move in? How long has he been there?"

"I don't know. I never met him."

Kell frowned faintly. "That's a problem right there. I gotta see if my neighbors know any more about this guy. Anything at all. He's clearly not fitting the church profile."

"Maybe that's a flag or maybe not. Miss Hassen sure seemed to have a lot of contact with them."

He raised a corner of his mouth disapprovingly. "Surrounded, more like. Didn't you say those women were always visiting? And that their pastor came over a few nights a week?"

"As far as I know."

"Given how recently my neighbor died, folks will probably want to talk."

Jenna sat up at last and didn't feel as if she might fall over. "I want to go with you."

"But your vertigo."

"You have a strong arm to lean on, and I'm getting better. Not up to walking Misty yet, unfortunately."

"I don't mind. And they remember my promise to take them out. So I'll go do that now and be back for you this evening."

He thought that Jenna looked as if she were glad to have something to look forward to. Boy, did he understand that. On his way out, he saw some of those gray-dressed women carting things out of the Hassen house.

Like buzzards, he thought, *swirling around a rotting corpse.* He just shook his head.

It took all kinds.

Chapter Six

It was a very pleasant evening as Jenna and Kell walked to Kell's street with the two dogs. Neighbors were sitting on their front porches or lawns, enjoying themselves and chatting with others. Pitchers of iced tea and lemonade sat on a lot of folding tables with plastic cups stacked nearby. *Sort of a block party,* Jenna thought.

She was still a little unstable, but she hadn't been wrong about Kell's powerful arm. It steadied her as little else could have. At least the world had mostly stopped spinning.

People greeted Kell warmly and invited him to help himself to a beverage. They kindly invited Jenna to take a lawn chair and join them.

They knew Bradley already, but they showered a lot of attention on Misty, her blue and gold eyes captivating them.

One woman, identified as Mrs. Mardella, said, "She looks like her name, Misty. The way her dappling blends with itself."

Jenna didn't quite see it, but she wasn't about to disagree. Misty appeared delighted by all the attention, traveling from one hand and cooing voice to another. No leash.

The dogs brought everyone together, and chairs moved

from houses around to join in the Mardellas' yard. Now it was definitely a block party.

It didn't take long for Kell to edge the conversation around to Mr. Zeb, nor did it take long for the gathered people to share what little they knew.

"Weird bird," James Jones said, after introducing himself to Jenna. "Hardly ever saw him in the ten years he lived here. Barely waved if you said howdy to him."

"It was, I don't know…" Mrs. Mardella's voice trailed off but only briefly. "Always made me uneasy the way he couldn't be the least bit neighborly."

"I know," said another woman. "But what do you expect from them folks? When those women come into town, they won't even look at you."

Heads all around nodded.

"And the way they dress!" Mrs. Mardella said disapprovingly. "Those washed-out gray sacks. They look like washerwomen more than a hundred years ago."

"Maybe they just don't know how to sew," another woman said, unleashing laughter among the group.

"Anyway," said a man, "I figure Zeb must be important in that group. The pastor was always visiting him, like they had important meetings. Couldn't have been nothing else, considering that Zeb was off to the commune several times a week."

"Private meetings?" Kell suggested.

"Must've been, although you'd wonder what kind of secrets they'd have, living all close like that. I always worried about them kids, though. Being raised like that away from the rest of the human race. Guess the dang church wouldn't want their minds to get polluted."

Mrs. Mardella laughed loudly. "Any pollutin' is going on inside that place."

"Makes you wonder what they're up to," James Jones said darkly.

"Indeed," Kell answered. "I'm sorry, but I need to get Jenna home. She's feeling a little peaked."

Sympathies were voiced, but in truth, Jenna was glad to escape. Too many people all at once. Too many men. Her skin had been crawling the entire time.

Only when they rounded a corner, away from all those eyes, did she start to relax. Count on Kell to miss nothing.

"The crowd bothered you, huh?"

"It'll take some getting used to." If ever she wanted to again.

"We learned one interesting thing, though."

"You mean about the kids? Yeah. That bothered me. Not just that they're cut off, but…" she hesitated.

"But what might be happening to them out there?"

Jenna's stomach rolled over. "I can't bear to think about it."

"But we both have. And now we've got to learn more about what might be going on inside that compound."

Jenna had to agree. If those children were being mistreated, someone needed to know about it. And no one, as near as she could tell, had even looked.

She spoke. "Sometimes *live and let live* isn't a good guide."

"You read my mind."

A SHORT WHILE LATER, Kell insisted on running out to get them a meal from Maude's diner. Officially titled City Café, the place had been known at Maude's diner for as long as Jenna knew, and probably before that.

The same way the Conard City Bakery had become known as Melinda's bakery. If folks knew you around here, you might as well not bother hanging a sign. People would call your establishment by your name. It was one of those little quirks about this town that amused Jenna.

Like the city police that existed only to satisfy the egos of the city council. The Sheriff's Office had managed it all since this place was founded but was responsible to the county, especially since the sheriff was an elected official. Then a small federal grant, and presto, the city police were born. All eight of them. The best part, Jenna supposed, was that the council had been able to choose their own chief of police, Jake Madison, rather than have him elected. A minimal exercise of control.

It was, she had learned early, another pull and tug on the reins of power around here. There were many others. Politics affected quite a lot.

But she didn't want to think about politics, because it might lead her back to the military, where plenty of politics played out. It was a relief when Kell returned with large bags redolent of wonderful food.

Both dogs decided they wanted a share and waited patiently in their politest poses near the table. Amazing how they always managed to raise Jenna's spirits.

"I was thinking," Kell said as he opened containers of steaks, fries and broccoli, along with a huge salad, "about that church. Those folks are so isolated and so determined to remain that way, I can't imagine how anyone could learn anything about them."

"It would be difficult," Jenna answered as she sliced into a thick steak. It was so tender it nearly melted in her mouth. "I need to remember how to cook," she remarked.

"Why? Maude already knows how."

Jenna laughed quietly. How did Kell do that? She'd been convinced a man would never make her laugh or smile again. Not ever.

"How is your Aunt Bernice enjoying her cruise?"

Guilt speared her. "I don't know. I haven't checked my email yet." A terrible oversight to be blamed, she thought, by her drowning in self-pity. *God, I'm turning into a terrible person*, she thought.

"Let me know when you find out. She told me that you two used to plan on taking the trip together."

"I bailed on it a while back. Round-the-world cruises take a lot longer than any military leave would allow."

He raised an eyebrow. "Time isn't stopping you now. I bet you could buy a plane ticket and join the cruise at one of its ports."

She looked down at her half-eaten steak. "I suppose. But the Army showed me enough of the world for a while." And cruises would be full of crowds, crowds that contained men. If her skin had crawled during the gathering in the front yard earlier, how much worse would it be if she were *trapped* among strangers? She didn't want to find out.

"You saw some of the worst of it," he ventured.

She didn't reply. She'd never tell anyone what had happened. Anger kept her silent. The idea that she wouldn't be believed had already been learned the hard way. Shame…even though she should feel none, she did anyway. Some things couldn't be rooted out by logic.

"You should talk about it," he said gently.

Her meal turned to sawdust. "Why?" she demanded. "Why would I want to talk about it?"

"Because you're thinking about it all the time."

"So? You'll never understand what happened to me. You're a *man*!"

The look on Kell's face made her want to run from the room right now. But she refused to give ground.

Instead, she forced herself to spear a piece of broccoli. "The church," she said, deliberately blocking that line of conversation.

"What about it?"

"As you said, they're too insular to get inside and find out what's going on. Ideas?"

"Only that I could check police records going back to the dawn of time. Maybe one of them got into trouble. We might learn something about them."

That caught her attention. Suddenly her meal didn't look quite as unappetizing, which was unfortunate for Misty, who'd been close to getting a huge heap of left-overs. "You think there might be something?"

"There might be a wedge. Those people don't want anyone to know anything about them. What if we found a way to get one of them to talk?"

"I like that idea." She paused, thinking about it. "But it would have to be something really embarrassing. A fifteen-year-old drunk-driving ticket wouldn't do it."

"We can hope. But there's only one way to find out."

Later, after Kell and Bradley departed, Jenna headed for bed. Misty followed her and jumped up beside her, lying close. Jenna wrapped her arm around the dog and buried her face in soft fur.

Misty didn't need to know the who, what and why. She only needed to know Jenna's feelings, and she curled even closer.

Those men grabbing her…

"God," she murmured, as tears started to fall. "Oh, God."

No justice.

No reprieve.

KELL WALKED HOME unable to enjoy the night. The al-ways-faithful Bradley trotted beside him. "What do you think, buddy? Did Jenna just tell us a whole lot? Or nothing at all."

Bradley chuffed quietly, his only answer.

"I agree. She told us a whole lot. Men? Yeah, men. I sensed it in her when we first met. I think you're the only reason she lets me hang around so much. Your romance with Misty, I mean."

Bradley's ears perked at the sound of Misty's name.

"Tomorrow, pal. You'll see her tomorrow. Sometimes ya just gotta wait."

Just like he was going to wait until Jenna trusted him enough to tell him what had happened to her. He suspected it was far more than concussive trauma. Far more.

He hated what he was thinking. Absolutely *loathed* it. Unconsciously, his hands tightened into fists. Bradley felt the tension, whether through the leash or some change in Kell's scent. He nudged his leg.

Kell squatted immediately and grabbed Bradley's head in both hands to give him a serious scratching. He honestly didn't know what he'd have done without this dog. Joined at the hip, joined emotionally. Joined mentally.

"Bet you never thought you'd be a therapy dog, did you, guy." But that's what Bradley had become in his own unique way.

Rising, Kell resumed the trip home, deeply troubled. He wished there was a way he could help Jenna.

Maybe the church thing would help her get out of the worst of her funk. Though the connection between the two deaths and the church was coincidental, there just might be something more.

It would keep them both busy for a while, anyway.

And keep them together. Spending time with Jenna was rapidly becoming a craving.

"I better be careful, huh, Bradley?"

A chuff of agreement answered him.

Chapter Seven

Another bright morning dawned, though with what promise Jenna couldn't imagine. Far from escaping her problems, she seemed to be sinking ever more deeply into the mire. Maybe Kell was right about her needing to talk to someone.

Except, she absolutely couldn't imagine stripping herself so psychologically bare. Exposing herself in such an emotional way. Revealing her anger and all the scars that had come with it.

Better to rediscover the detachment that had served her so well in the past months while she had waited for her discharge. Better to just pull back from any contact to protect herself.

Then she looked at Misty, who was happily gobbling her bowl of kibble. Well, she couldn't separate that dog from Bradley. That had become obvious. But along with Bradley came Kell, who was slipping dangerously past her guard. Little by little, she felt the chink in her armor growing larger. She had to prevent it from bursting wide open, exposing her to more pain.

The need for action propelled her to pull on shorts and a T-shirt and to get Misty's leash. They always took a short walk before the dog's breakfast, and Misty usually napped afterward, but when she saw the leash, she gave one bark of happiness at the prospect of an extra walk. Jenna suspected the dog could use a brisk walk, too, while the morning was still cool.

Dry air carrying the night's lower temperatures greeted them. It was a beautiful day. Jenna had always loved days like this. Until now. Now she didn't much care.

Just as her legs began to feel pleasantly stretched and her anxiety began to ease, she saw Misty suddenly perk up and start wagging her tail wildly. Bradley must be around. The relationship between the two dogs was amazing. Maybe they had it right, judging only in the present despite whatever might have happened in the past.

Look at Bradley. If ever a dog had reason to be distrustful, it was Bradley. No such thing.

Sure enough, coming around a corner ahead were Kell and Bradley, the two trotting along together. Kell was smiling when he reached them. The two dogs butted noses, signaling pleasure with their tails.

"They've got it bad," Kell remarked. "Thank goodness they're both neutered."

"Amen to that."

"How about letting them romp in your yard?" he asked.

Jenna nodded and turned around. Misty never hesitated, walking beside Bradley as close as she could get.

Before long, however, the silence between Jenna and Kell began to feel uncomfortable to her. Had he started to pull back from her after what she'd said yesterday? Part of her hoped he was yet another part didn't want that. Regardless, he was a smart man and had probably thought he was included among the group she'd disparaged. Well, he was, although not quite.

Mixed up much? she asked herself.

"How's the immersion therapy going?" she asked as they neared her house.

"A little at a time. Say, have you heard from Bernice?"

An image of her aunt's laptop sitting on the little desk in the bedroom suddenly appeared in her mind. "Oh, God, I'm awful. I'm sure she's been emailing, and I still haven't even looked."

"Better get to it," he said pleasantly. "Next thing you know, she'll be making one of those expensive ship-to-shore calls to find out if you're still alive."

Aunt Bernice would definitely do that, Jenna thought glumly. God, had she become thoughtless, too? Angry or not, she didn't want to despise herself. "I'll do that when we get back."

As they reached the porch of her house, Kell asked, "Am I going over the top with this whole church thing? Might be coincidence. Might be natural deaths."

Jenna glanced at him. "Bradley alerted to both."

"Yeah, but sometimes I wonder. I'm still trying to help him get all the pieces together. This could be something more left over."

She couldn't deny that. She didn't know enough about Bradley's condition. Then she surprised herself by saying, "How long have you trusted that dog? Maybe you should trust him now."

The dogs both wanted water and biscuits rather than outdoor play. In the way of tired dogs, they then flopped and closed their eyes.

Jenna asked Kell if he wanted coffee or something else to drink. She didn't want to be rude again to this man.

"Coffee would be great, if you don't mind. Thanks."

He leaned against a counter while she started the pot.

A thought occurred to her. "Did you ever hear anything from the sheriff about that tox screen?"

"Oh yeah, I meant to tell you. Miss Hassen's blood sugar level was way too low. As Gage said, too much insulin or failing to eat enough could have caused that. It's the cause of death in a lot of diabetics, I guess."

"That would make sense. Especially the not eating part. She was so old and didn't get around very well from what I could tell."

"So maybe that's all that Bradley detected."

The pot gave a blast of steam, signifying it was about done brewing. Kell turned and pulled two mugs from the cupboard.

Rather than going to the living room, they sat facing one another across the kitchen table.

"Aunt Bernice preferred sitting here to the living room," Jenna remarked. "She always said that room was the relic of the age of dinosaurs."

Kell laughed. "I knew she liked sitting here, but never why."

"She talked about redoing it, but never did. Probably because she was saving for this cruise."

"She got her priorities straight, I guess."

Jenna smiled faintly. "I never thought the room was that bad, but it sure annoyed her."

Kell finished his coffee and rose to carry the cup to the sink. "Bradley and I need to go home. I've got some more renovation to work on."

"And I need to read some emails."

"See you later," Kell said as he left.

He would? Jenna wondered, then realized it was something to look forward to. Little enough of that at the moment. Anyway, she told herself, it was just because of the dogs. She didn't quite believe it.

Jenna had her own email account on Bernice's computer, and she went to power up the laptop. No password protected it. Bernice had always said that if anyone wanted to look at her computer, they were welcome and would probably die of boredom.

So it was that Jenna opened her own email and found a flurry from Aunt Bernice, a veritable travelogue that entertained her and gave her the wisp of a desire to be there. But only a wisp. She had some problems to sort out before she went gallivanting off on a pleasure trip.

The most recent email from Bernice expressed concern about not hearing from Jenna. At once, Jenna began typing a response, feeling horrid about not considering her aunt sooner.

Once that was done, she headed back to the kitchen to refill her mug. A glance into the living room told her Misty was still zonked out. Poor doggie had certainly gotten her workout that morning.

But as she sat drinking more coffee, which she didn't really need, she started once again thinking about Miss Hassen and Mr. Zeb and their connection to that church. Undeniably odd that both had died within such a short time of one another.

But possibly coincidental. Possibly. The niggling feeling wouldn't leave her that she and Kell had invented some kind of conspiracy theory, although Kell was right that he needed to find out if Bradley had another problem.

But maybe someone had a grudge against that church? Someone who had once been a member? Someone who had grown up behind those closed doors? Murder two people for that?

The notion made her stomach turn over. Sickened, she dumped her coffee and began to pace. She supposed, at this point, the only thing left to do was wait and see if anyone else from the church died.

Mordant thought. Angry though she might be, she

wouldn't wish death on anyone. She'd seen enough death to last a lifetime, and it was an ugly thing. Few people simply went to sleep and never woke up.

Life was rarely that kind.

She thought about going over to Kell's house just to have some distraction. Someone else who might understand these feelings, if not the cause of them.

But then she feared she might say too much. Might expose too much of her dark secrets and thoughts.

To a man, no less.

Right. No chance she would drop in on Kell. Sighing, she continued to pace and wished she could share Misty's uncomplicated life. Wishing she could be like the snoozing dog who could forgive and forget just about any unpleasantness that might come her way.

Then she thought of Bradley, all twisted in knots by his experience as a scout dog. She could identify with that, totally. What she could not imagine was that anyone would devote themselves to trying to help her cope the way Kell was doing with Bradley.

No, she had to find a way to cope all by herself. There was no other choice.

KELL, MEANWHILE, had taken Bradley to the firing range. Only one man had been engaged in target practice, but it was enough to cause the dog to tense.

Still, between them, they had managed another ten feet before Bradley refused to take another step. Kell squatted and rubbed the dog's ruff, getting Bradley to focus intently on him and not the gunfire.

"You're a good boy, Bradley. A champ. Brave beyond words."

Until experience had broken him.

Kell rose and turned around, the dog at his side, and

inevitably thought about Jenna. She was broken, too, just like Bradley. Just like so many vets. And if she wouldn't talk, there was little he could do to help her deal.

Man, that woman made him sigh. He forgot all about renovations and headed himself and Bradley to her house as he'd promised earlier. Whatever had ripped Jenna up, he was certain she had never told Bernice about it. She wouldn't want to upset her aunt.

Bernice was lucky to be far away on her cruise, unaware of how damaged her niece had become.

Well, hell, he thought. There *had* to be something more than self-isolation.

JENNA WAS UNSURPRISED to find Kell and Bradley at her door even though it hadn't been all that long since they'd left.

"I figured the pups were going to die of separation," Kell said with a smile.

"Hardly," Jenna answered while opening the door to let man and dog enter. "Misty is zonked out."

"Not anymore," he answered.

Jenna turned to see Misty eagerly looking at Bradley. Those two dogs were something else.

"Bradley might need a nap, too," Kell said. "We just went out to the firing range."

Stepping inside, he unleashed his dog and watched the two pals meet with a nose-to-nose greeting.

"How'd it go?" Jenna asked, feeling some concern for Bradley.

"Quite well, actually. He got ten feet closer than the last time. Then I could feel the anxiety start, so I squatted down and got his full attention. When the dog becomes focused on you, you've made a great stride."

The dogs were apparently both tired. They took up position on Misty's bed, snuggled close, then shut their eyes.

Half smiling, Jenna looked at Kell. "I'm afraid I don't have anything to offer you except coffee."

"You're avoiding the grocery store, too, huh?"

She hesitated, then reluctantly admitted, "I guess so."

He shook his head a little. "Okay, that's bad. How are you planning to eat?"

The truth was she was beginning to run out of canned and dried foods. Bernice liked to cook and always had fresh ingredients around. Jenna had no idea if she gave a damn about cooking and hadn't been much interested in food for a while.

"Tell you what," Kell said. "I'll take you to the grocery store tomorrow. Maybe you'll feel more comfortable with me."

She would, she realized with some uneasiness. She was also disturbed by how much he appeared to have sensed about her. But he was right, she needed to buy food. "Thank you."

"No problem. I need to do some shopping, too." His face gentled in the most pleasant way. "Bradley will kill me if I run out of canned food. Dried kibble is a last resort for him."

"But what about his teeth? Doesn't he need to chew?"

"Gnawing is what he needs most. Pig hide rolls are his favorite, and better for him than rawhide. Anyway, I have to order those online. Meantime, I gotta keep him happy."

"You certainly do."

"As for dinner tonight, I'll hit Maude's again. If you don't mind."

"I can't keep imposing on you."

He chuckled. "If you think you're imposing, I got

news for you. It's nice to have company besides a drooling dog."

That drew a quiet laugh from her. He made her laugh when she didn't feel like laughing at all, and she supposed that was a point in his favor. But maybe it was dangerous, too.

"Jenna? If you feel like I'm crowding you, just let me know."

"You think I want to be responsible for canine heartbreak?" No, she didn't feel crowded, not by him. "I don't mind you coming over." And she really didn't. Where the devil was this going? Where was he taking her?

Or maybe it was all about his dog. She already loved Bradley.

"Well, we can't stand here by the door," she said, taking her courage in her hands. "Coffee? About all I have left."

"Coffee," he agreed. "I learned over my years in uniform to never let a decent cup pass me by. Man, did I get sick of instant, no matter how much they claimed to have improved it."

"I fully understand. Instant was bad, but so was that stuff brewed in those big urns. I couldn't tell why."

"Me neither. Maybe it was that metallic taste. Or maybe the fact that they probably cleaned those things once a year."

"I'd believe that." Contractor food would never get five stars. Or even one.

Once again, they faced each other over the table. Conversation lagged until Jenna, with trepidation, finally bared a part of herself. "I need to get out more. Pacing this place between walks with Misty isn't enough."

"Probably not. You reading much?"

"I can't seem to concentrate on it." She'd been a reader

from way back, and it troubled her that she could open a book and simply stare unseeingly at the page. Well, a lot of things bothered her now. Why not that as well?

"Maybe something else will work. Music? I don't know. Anyway, I'm thinking about taking Bradley to the agility course again. Day after tomorrow? You and Misty, too?"

She didn't have to think for long. "That sounds good. Maybe you can help me teach Misty to do more things."

"I'm sure she'd love that. Dogs are happiest when they're challenged, and pleasing their handlers is icing on the cake."

"I don't think of myself as Misty's handler."

"Maybe you should." He shrugged. "Doesn't matter. I've been a K-9 handler for a long time. Wrong word for you, maybe."

Not for him, she thought. He must have found it gut-wrenching at times to send Bradley into dangerous situations. "How did you stand it, knowing Bradley could get hurt when you sent him out to do his job?"

"I was doing mine. So were the men and women he protected. He was a Marine. You think I never got orders to risk my neck?"

He had a point.

"Sure, it was hard to see my buddies walk into it, too. K-9s have a lot of guts."

As did the Marines and soldiers who walked right into the thick of it, many relying on K-9s to help them through.

Their only conversation, she realized, was about the dogs. The dogs kept bringing them together, but they discussed little else, and that, she admitted to herself, was because of her. All the places she didn't want to tread, all the scars, hardly healed, that she didn't want to re-open. At some point, she *had* to find her way around this.

But she didn't know how. She felt so bruised. Every emotional touch hurt her. So what else could she talk about? A future she couldn't begin to see?

So many of her dreams had been crushed. All of them, in fact. Where did she go from there?

The man sitting patiently across from her respected her silences. He didn't press her. He just let her be and appeared to accept the broken person she'd become.

"This church thing," he said after a while. "I'm wondering if I'm leaping to conclusions. Maybe we should just let it ride until we find out about this Zeb guy, why he died. That'll give me information about Bradley, and I need it. Later we can decide if there's anything to pursue."

"I was wondering myself. You *did* say earlier that you needed to know if he was broken in some other way. Or possibly he just detected something unusual about those bodies. Like Miss Hassen. Maybe he sensed her low blood sugar."

"Maybe." Kell shook his head slightly. "I may still be alive because of that dog. He was never supposed to leave my side unless I told him to. Then I was wounded and he tore off, eventually finding a medic and insisting he follow. The guy did, maybe because he had respect for our K-9s. Anyway, Bradley wasn't under orders *then*."

"Smart, too." And around to the dogs once again. She moved away. "Like you, I don't trust the insularity of that church. Most churches are open and welcoming. Always seeking new converts. This one isn't. At the rate it's going, it'll die out." Then she remembered. "Except for the children."

Kell nodded. "Except for the kids. They're probably expected to continue with it."

"Hope for the future of the place."

"Or victims. As we discussed, there's no way for anyone to know."

"That," she said firmly, "truly concerns me."

"For a number of reasons, we have to keep sniffing around. See what we can find out about those people. Anyone they might have had contact with outside the church."

Jenna snorted. "How likely is that? We've got two dead people who didn't even live at the compound. As far as I know, they've had no contact with anyone else. It bugs me that they didn't live out there. And despite that, the church still wrapped them up, always coming to visit them, taking them nowhere but the church."

He didn't answer immediately, going instead to get himself more coffee. "This stuff you brew is wonderful. Thanks."

Then he sat again, staring past her into some thought of his own.

"You know," he said presently, "it occurs to me to wonder, rather late, how those two were getting medical care if they never saw anyone else. Someone had to prescribe that insulin. And if Zeb had a heart problem, he must have been seeing someone. How else would anyone know?"

"Good point. Maybe we should try to find out if they have a licensed doctor out there."

He nodded. "Maybe that would be our way in. A way to learn something. Someone must be caring for health problems. And if that person isn't a member of the church, it would help to know that, too."

"Help how?" she asked. "No doctor will discuss a patient without permission."

Kell nodded. "Unless the sheriff has a reason to find out and maybe gets another warrant for information."

She almost laughed. "You mean like he took those blood tests? With an anonymous source. How far do you think he wants to go with this?"

Kell sighed. "At some point, I'm sure he'll mention the separation of church and state. If he didn't already. I honestly don't remember. I was too concerned about Bradley's alert."

"Understandable." All right. They had *two* topics of conversation. All her fault. Back to the dogs. "What kind of future do you see for Bradley?"

"Search and rescue. He's already got the search part down, and he loves it when some of the deputies play the game with him."

"And the rest? I hear the dogs get depressed if they don't find many living people, only dead ones."

"Games are played with live persons crawling under debris to give the dogs a positive experience. Apparently it perks them right up."

"And you think this would help Bradley?"

Kell regarded her across the table. "Yes. He's a working dog, has been for a few years now. Most dogs, I gather, prefer to have jobs. It makes them happier."

"So they need a reason for their existence, too." A reason she didn't have, at least not yet. Sometimes she wished she had died during the repeated shellings the field hospital had undergone. The red cross stamped on the roofs of the hospitals had become meaningless since Vietnam, making them targets like any other.

He spoke, startling her with what he said. "You got that concussive brain trauma at a field hospital, didn't you?"

She didn't want to answer, didn't want to summon those images. "Yes," she answered flatly. "I was lucky, getting only headaches and vertigo. Can we not go there?"

"Since you don't want to, we won't. But sooner or later, you'll need to, Jenna. For your own sake."

"Talking about it won't change anything."

"Unless it loosens your past enough to allow you to start moving forward again." He rose. "I'll go get dinner now. Can Bradley stay here?"

"Absolutely. He's never any trouble at all."

She watched him leave and wished she could open up the way he wanted her to. But it would serve no purpose, and she sure as hell didn't want his pity. Or to find out he thought she had gone too far.

Grimly, she stared into her cold cup of coffee, hearing the coffee pot tick quietly. Hearing the grandfather clock tick even more loudly. A familiar sound that should have soothed her and made her feel at home again.

Except this place no longer felt like home. It was becoming laced with her sorrow and anger. Her fury had begun to fill it.

Thank God Bernice was half a world away.

Chapter Eight

Kell had plenty to think about while he walked to Maude's. It felt odd not to have Bradley beside him. Strange. Lonely.

He wondered if Jenna would understand that the K-9 was his comfort. His own therapy dog. When Bradley was there, he focused on little but the dog.

And lately on Jenna. Her reactions were disturbing him more and more. Did she think she was the only one who had survived with trauma? Or that no one else would understand her? There were few things in life that no one else could understand. You just had to find the right person to listen.

Any number of vets in this county could understand the blood, the gore, the shellings, the bombs. The terror and the fear. The ugliness of the black humor, the dehumanization of the enemy that kept them going through atrocities.

Hell, he knew of one guy hereabouts who couldn't drive down an open road without going on high alert because of the possibility of a roadside bomb. Even after all this time. The guy dealt with it by gritting his teeth and forcing himself to keep going. Immersion didn't seem to be working too well for him.

But maybe the guy had immersed himself too fast, unlike the careful stages Kell was following with Bradley.

And now that Bradley was getting better about gunfire, perhaps it was time to introduce him to other sharp sounds. Like a nail gun. A hammer. Other things. But so far they were getting nowhere with thunder.

What if it wasn't the sound at all that bothered Bradley. What if it was the concussion? The sudden change in air pressure that accompanied a shockwave. That might explain why Bradley didn't react to those CDs of thunder he'd bought.

Hearing the distant rumble of thunder might sound like artillery, but did lightning cause a shockwave? And what about the thunder itself?

He'd have to look into that.

Meanwhile, he had two puzzles on his plate, and thinking and talking about dogs wasn't going to solve one of them. Jenna kept deflecting one way or the other, but she *was* deflecting. He didn't see how he could put an end to that. Not without arousing her ire. And he sensed she had plenty of ire to go around.

"Hell," he muttered to himself as he stepped into Maude's. Evidently, the dinner crowd had started to drift out. He nodded to some, smiled and offered a greeting to others he knew better.

Soon this town was going to start whispering about Jenna, because where there was a vacuum, unpleasantness could fill it up. He didn't want that to happen.

He stepped up to the counter to place his order, wondering why he couldn't escape the feeling that something was beginning to coalesce. Something dark.

BRADLEY GREETED HIM with glee and Misty wasn't far behind. Kell was amused by Misty. Apparently he won her favor by being the guy who brought all things good, namely Bradley.

Jenna greeted him with a smile, too, an unusual expression for her. Maybe she was taking a step forward, at least with him.

"Bradley is pathetically well behaved," she told him as they carried the bags into the kitchen.

"Pathetic?"

"If he knows how to make any kind of mischief, I sure didn't see it."

Together, they got out plates and utensils. It seemed Jenna didn't want to eat out of a box tonight, and he couldn't blame her. He'd also brought some lattes, which really pleased her.

Tonight, they ate breaded pork chops, some fried chicken wings, salad, mashed potatoes and even dessert in the form of Maude's famous peach pie.

"I thought peaches were out of season," Jenna remarked.

"Ah, Maude has a secret and she shared it when I asked."

"Which is?"

"She buys peaches by the bushel, removes the pits, cuts them up and freezes them. No peeling involved, but when she thaws them, the skins slide right off."

"I never would have imagined that! Maude's a genius."

"When it comes to food, she sure is."

Another silence fell, but Kell didn't want to say anything that might ruin dinner. Let her enjoy eating, then he was going to risk getting thrown out. He'd have to trust Bradley and Misty to change that. In the meantime...

"Any idea what you might want from the grocery store tomorrow?"

She shook her head. "I'm going to fly by the seat of my pants."

"I'm getting a hankering for strawberry shortcake."

She raised her head. "Wrong time of year. I'm sure of that. Or does Maude have another secret? Anyway, I have no idea how to make it."

"I do. I'd gladly be the chef. But here, please, Jenna. My rental is a wreck, in the midst of renovations."

"Here is fine," she answered. She sounded as if she meant it.

A relief. But he had to find another little step to take with her. God knew what. Any possible way to get her talking apart from the dogs and the cult. Two subjects weren't going to carry them along forever.

As they sat eating peach pie, he asked casually, "What made you decide to join the Army? You may have told me, but I don't recall." He made a face. "My recall isn't always good anymore."

"The war?"

"Maybe. Or maybe just advancing years."

She shook her head. "Yeah, right."

"Anyway, the Army?"

"I don't exactly know. Maybe I wanted to help more when life was truly on the line. The average emergency room doesn't always provide that."

He nodded, ate another mouthful of pie, then asked as casually as he could manage, "Field hospital?"

"Sometimes. Maybe most of the time."

"God, that had to be stressful. I visited one a few times and was a patient once. I don't know how any of the medical personal stuck it out."

Her eyes closed, and he wondered if he pressed too far. At last she spoke.

"Sometimes the floor was covered with gore. After a

really bad incident. We couldn't keep up with it. As long as I live, I'll never forget the terror, the groans and cries. The times we couldn't help except with morphine and had to move on to a patient we had a better chance of saving. Triaging. Life and death decisions. I never want to make another one."

"But more troops survived than ever before, thanks to you."

Her eyes snapped open. "Is that good? Really? We send them home with severe brain trauma, with missing limbs, paralysis. With all kinds of disabilities. I began to wonder if we were doing a good thing at all."

His chest tightened with sorrow for her. "You guys saved me and I'm glad of it."

"Maybe some are. I spent some time at Walter Reed. A lot of those vets were very angry and depressed. Looking forward to limited futures. Or not wanting to look forward at all. There were always some who took it in stride. Stiff upper lip and all that. But there were too many others…" She shook her head. "I saw a lot of marriages blow up, too. Wives and husbands who couldn't handle the idea of taking care of an invalid for many years to come. Who simply couldn't stand the changes in someone they'd loved."

"I hate to say it, but I can understand."

"I understand, too, but you wanna talk about a body blow to people who'd already had one? Not helpful."

He shook his head, having nothing at all to say to that. He cleared his throat after a few minutes. "I guess you took a lot of shelling at the field hospitals."

"Of course. God bless the RPG. Not." She sighed and pushed away her barely touched pie. "We had to be near the front lines, such as they were, to be of any real help. Hey, did you guys ever find those front lines?"

He spoke flatly. "They don't exist in guerilla warfare."

"Hence the need for Bradley." She looked to one side and saw both dogs sitting patiently, practically drooling as they waited for something to fall from the plates. Or to lick them.

"Can Bradley eat any of this?"

"He'll eat anything. He used to share my rations. Dog has an iron stomach, I swear. Even I couldn't eat some of that stuff."

She smiled faintly. "Bet he didn't get any instant coffee."

"Well, not that for sure. Peaches might be a bit acidic for him, though. Orange juice is a total waste on him."

Back to the dogs, he thought. Well, at least he'd gotten a little more out of her. A horror story. He'd seen it from a different perspective, but he knew it.

She cut up bits of her leftover chop and handed them one-by-one to each dog. "So what exactly did Bradley do?"

"Like I said, he was a scout, or a patrol dog if you prefer. Except that patrols tended to take several dogs with them. Bradley's job was a bit different. He went out alone. Surreptitiously. Creeping along until he found something. Might be explosives. Might be a sniper. Might be an ambush. I'd wait for him to come back. He'd alert, his entire body pointing. Or he'd come back prancing along, wagging his tail. No threat. At least not within his range."

"Could he tell you what kind of threat?"

"Yeah, as we moved forward. He'd nose at the ground pointing out a bomb. Or look at both cliff faces, signaling an ambush. Or in just one direction signaling a sniper or two. Point is, we never went in totally blind."

"That's important."

"Very." And back to the dogs again. He'd given her

an opening wide enough to drive a truck through, but he felt he hadn't reached the core of what had caused her to become so detached.

He suppressed a sigh and wondered if he ever would. Regardless, he had to admit he'd been allowed further into her life than anyone else he could see. Maybe she'd eventually come to trust him enough to tell him the story that had locked her inside herself. Because it was more than the shocks of combat nursing. Of that he was convinced.

After cleaning up dinner, he suggested the dogs get their last walk of the night. "I'll take them both if you want. If you're still having some vertigo."

"I'm fine now," she insisted. "I need the walk, too, as much as Misty does."

"You gonna mark every shrub, too?"

At least that dragged a reluctant laugh from her.

"Don't tempt me," she said.

THE EVENING HAD cooled enough that Jenna grabbed a sweater. Kell seemed impervious.

Seeking some kind of safe conversation as they walked, she asked, "How did you get the name Kell? It's unusual."

"Ah. I was lucky."

"How so?"

"My mom wanted to give me her family name of Kelstrom. Dad put his foot down, said I'd be teased mercilessly. Hence Kell."

"She didn't get anything to say about it?"

"Do I hear a feminist? Well, of course you are. No, she got some say or I wouldn't be Kell. I could be Harvey Jackson McLaren, Junior. Being a junior would have been a curse. Do I look like a junior to you?"

Another small laugh escaped her. "Nope. Not at all."

"Well, that's all that I would have heard while I was growing up. Junior this and Junior that. I'm pretty sure I'd have come to hate it."

"And the other kids would have used it against you somehow?"

"Bet on it. That's kids. But some of them teased me about my strange name."

She saw him shrug, as if it didn't matter. But maybe it had. How would she know? Or did she even want to know?

He spoke. "We all grow up eventually. If we're lucky, we don't carry many scars from childhood teasing."

"True." No, the real scars came later. "I was teased after my mother left town. Some of my classmates told me it was *my* fault she'd run away. At least Bernice was squarely on my side. She always insisted that I couldn't possibly be to blame for the irresponsibility of my parents. As she liked to say, they were the adults making the decisions."

"She was right, obviously. But it still had to hurt."

"Lots of things hurt. We have to move past them somehow."

Another hint. God, she had to stop dropping them, or Kell would open her like a can of sardines. He was beginning to ask too many questions as is. She ought to keep him away.

But then she looked at the dogs and cussed inwardly. She couldn't hurt Misty that way. The pooch didn't deserve it.

She was relieved, though, when the walk ended and she was at last alone in the house with Misty.

Her sanctuary. Bernice had always made this her sanctuary. Had even dissed her own sister for skipping town and roundly blamed her son-in-law for abandoning his daughter.

When Jenna had become older, Bernice had once said, "I wonder how many other kids that bum has left scattered around the rodeo circuit? He ought to be up to his eyeballs in paternity suits. Hah! He wouldn't be able to ride enough bulls or bust enough broncos to survive financially."

The image seemed to please Bernice. Jenna merely wondered how many siblings she had that she'd never meet. Pointless question.

Whatever had brought her here, good decisions or bad, she was here now. In her safe home, one Bernice had created for her with constant love.

God bless Bernice.

Chapter Nine

Jenna joined Kell and the dogs for the trip to Mike Wind-walker's agility course. It was for Misty's sake, she told herself. She didn't want to admit she was there for Kell's company, which she had begun to crave. Maybe she was coming out of her shell a bit? Or maybe she was freaking nuts to keep exposing herself to a man.

Regardless, Kell had brought along a bag of small treats. "Low cal," he assured Jenna. "The way Bradley loves to eat, he'd become a blimp in no time. So here's how you do the weaving around the pylons."

While he told Bradley to stay, he led Misty around the pylons, getting her to zigzag with treats on the ground. Misty's tail kept wagging fast enough to lift her from the ground.

"She's a smart dog," Kell said as he straightened up. "Do this with her a few more times, then slow down on the treats. One every other pylon, and only if she does it right. If not, no treat, then take her back to the beginning of the course. She'll get it. Eventually, you'll only have to give her a treat at the end of the run."

Misty looked longingly at Bradley, but only until the first treat caught her attention. Then she became laser-focused.

Jenna enjoyed watching Misty cock her head as if she

were trying to figure it all out. Once, she even tried to outsmart the trick by dashing past all the pylons to the end. Which didn't get her a single treat, of course.

But then Misty got the picture, and by the time the exercise ended at Kell's suggestion, she was down to a treat at every other pylon.

"She's doing good," he said. "But time to give her a break. That kind of focus is tiring."

"And Bradley?"

"He's got more endurance for this kind of attention. Maybe because he realized it wasn't a game during training, at least eventually. Or maybe that's just the way he is. Anyway, you don't want Misty getting bored or tired, because she might not be as cooperative next time."

That made sense to Jenna. "I've got my limits, too."

"Always let them rest," Kell said with a smile.

AFTERWARD, JENNA WENT home with Misty, feeling the emptiness of the house stronger than ever. She longed for her Aunt Bernice's company. Worse, she yearned for Kell's.

"God," she said aloud as she gave Misty a fresh bowl of water. "What's wrong with you, girl?"

Misty gave her a quizzical look.

"Not you, girl. Never you. You're a good girl."

No, just herself. Feeling her barriers starting to crack. Risking herself, even if it was with only one man. A man who seemed nice in every way.

But appearances could be deceiving as she'd learned the hard way. *Thank you, Army.*

Telling herself that they weren't all that way didn't help. She'd run up hard against the brick wall of authority and male privilege. Hard enough to shatter everything inside her.

Trust was gone now, for one thing. Shame and guilt and anger had become her constant companions. Her anger was justified, but the rest? She kept trying to talk herself out of the shame and guilt. What had happened to her had *not* been her fault. But shame and guilt plagued her anyway.

Sighing, she considered what to do with the rest of her day. Nothing occurred to her. Nothing ever did. She'd promised herself time to heal, but she didn't seem to be healing at all.

Pacing was all that seemed to ease any of her anxiety. The only thing. Climbing the stairs again and again until she was sure she'd wear out the carpeting Bernice had covered them with. Movement. She had to keep moving, even without direction.

Memories tried to rise and she squashed them ruthlessly. They'd do no good except to increase the boiling in her blood, a boil that never dropped below a simmer.

Worst of all, she had become useless. Pointless. Achieving nothing and going nowhere. She *had* to find a way out of this mire.

Early in the evening, when she was standing in the pantry trying to decide which can to open, her phone rang. It was Kell.

"Grocery store tomorrow?" he asked.

"I guess."

"Hey, a little more enthusiasm than that, please. Think of all the delicious frozen food you can buy to tempt yourself with. How happy Misty will be to have something good to lick off your plate."

Once again he managed to pull a faint smile from her. "I wasn't thinking of Misty when you said 'grocery store.'"

"I figured you weren't." He paused. "I heard from the sheriff."

Her heart quickened, her hand tightening on her phone. "So fast?"

"He expedited the tox screen, apparently. I told him you were curious, too, because of Bradley. He wants us to come to the office tomorrow."

Which left her wondering what was coming next. That was another question she'd lived with for too long: What was next?

"Anyway, I'll pick you up at ten, if that's okay. We can do the grocery store after. Sound good?"

For the first time, she considered getting into a car with Kell. "Sure." She *had* to know if she could. "The dogs?"

"They'll be happy curled up at your house. You know that."

She did. They had before. "Okay."

"Ten it is."

After the call, she resumed her pacing. Getting in a car with a man? But her curiosity about what Gage Dalton might have to say overwhelmed her fears. He wanted them to come to the office?

That didn't sound good at all.

FOR HIS PART, Kell did his own pacing. Bradley had alerted. Yes, he trusted his dog, but he also had a good idea of just how broken Bradley was right now.

Maybe that alerting wasn't a good enough reason to respond to two deaths that had only one connection: that cult outside of town. Coincidence? He looked at Bradley, who was happily chewing on a baked pork rind.

Coincidences happened. Maybe it was amazing that Gage was willing to take the dog's alert as a sign he needed to look deeper into the two deaths.

But Miss Hassen's passing could be easily explained.

Apparently Zeb had a heart condition. Two older people died. Nothing mysterious about that.

Except for Bradley. The dog had detected something.

"Jeez, Bradley," he said to the contented dog. "What were you trying to say?"

No mind reading occurred. The instant Bradley heard his name, he'd wagged his tail a few times, then continue gnawing.

Life should be like these moments right now. For everyone.

Except it wasn't.

Look at Jenna. She seriously troubled him because he didn't believe it was her time as a nurse that had left her like this. No, there was more to it.

And he was being a damn fool. Growing attracted to a woman who was sealed up like a safety deposit box in a bank.

There could only be trouble from that. But then he remembered her pretty but sad face. He even remembered, in the way of a man, stupidly enough, the way her jeans cased her bottom. The way her loose shirts tried to hide her other attributes.

She was definitely buried in some private hell, and he wished he could dig her out.

Chapter Ten

Ten in the morning came fast, depending on perspective. For Kell, it seemed like a short time. For Jenna, the hours had felt endless.

Anxiety hit her hard as she opened the door of Kell's pickup truck. She hesitated, then used the strength that had carried her through hospitals to carry her inside. Her heart wouldn't stop hammering, though.

He was close. She could detect the scent of man—not good—and the scent of his soap. Better. She tried to focus on that.

Today he wore old jeans with faded patches on the knees and butt. They suited him, as did the blue western shirt with its snap closures.

She sought a safe subject. "So you want Bradley to become a search and rescue dog? Not just retire?"

"He's had a job and a purpose all his life. He still needs one. Running around with Misty isn't going to satisfy him forever."

She wondered if it would suit Misty. Bernice had kept her as a mostly indoor dog, but Misty was showing a definite taste for the outside world. She wondered if she might be making a problem for Bernice when she returned from her trip.

"You must miss Bernice a whole lot," Kell remarked

as he pulled into a parking place near the Sheriff's Office front door.

"I do. More than I expected since I was home so rarely. Maybe it's being in the empty house."

When they entered the sheriff's department, they were immediately ushered back to his office. He didn't rise to greet them, merely waved them to chairs, giving them his crooked half smile.

"No dog today?" Gage asked.

"Bradley is sacked out with Jenna's dog, Misty."

Gage nodded. "Okay, straight to the point. I told you about Miss Hassen. An overdose of insulin might be easy for a woman her age. So would forgetting to eat."

He leaned forward, wincing as he did so. "Now, Mr. Zeb. Also related to that cult. Or should I say 'church' to be politically correct? Doesn't matter. Point is, the man had a heart condition. Congestive heart failure. Shouldn't be unusual to find a prescription drug in him. digoxin, or something like that. Anyway, the amount in his system was way too high. Enough to cause a fatal arrhythmia."

Jenna held her breath and looked at Kell. His expression was as grim as a severe storm.

Gage reached for a pencil and began to tap the eraser end on his desk. "So Bradley was right. Something was wrong. Can't tell if it was some kind of mess-up or something more."

"What can be done about it?" Kell asked.

"Nothing on my end. I don't have any proof a crime was committed."

"Hell," Kell said.

"Even if I suspected that church group might somehow be involved, I can't investigate a church. First Amendment protection. I'd need something more to go on. Proof there was a murder and it was connected to that damn compound. Assuming it was murder, which is a big assumption right now."

Jenna nodded. "I get it. So what now?"

Gage rapped his pencil a few more times, then dropped it. "No official investigation." He looked straight at Kell. "That K-9 of yours might suss something out. Or private individuals might learn something."

He looked at both of them. "But I don't want to know anything about it unless you find something. What's more, if you decide to start looking, this could be seriously dangerous."

ON THE WAY to the grocery store, Jenna spoke. "What the hell do we do about this? He's right. It just might be coincidental. Regardless, I don't think anyone is going to get inside that group to sniff around. And what if it's only one person, anyway? How would we find them?"

"I'm thinking," Kell answered. "So far, no good ideas."

"Except one thing," she said. "Those two people didn't live at the compound. Why not?"

"It'd be nice to have an answer to that." He shook his head a bit as they pulled into the grocery store parking lot. "Maybe check property records and find out when those two moved out of there."

Jenna unhooked her seat belt. "I like that better than trying to ransack the county archives for any arrest records. Those people keep a low profile. Bet not one of them has ever gotten drunk."

Kell flashed her a smile. "Their loss."

As they walked into the store, he made a surprising proposal. "How about we take the dogs on a picnic?"

The dogs again, apparently the only unbreakable tie between them. She thought about it. "Where would we do that?"

"I know a rancher just outside of town who wouldn't mind at all. We served together."

Jenna tensed, then let go of it. The dogs. A picnic. She could probably survive that.

KELL WATCHED THE emotions flicker across her face, though he couldn't exactly read them. She'd done a great job at developing an impassivity he suspected hadn't always been a part of her. He had just begun to expect her dismissal of the picnic when she surprised him.

"That sounds like a good idea, Kell. Thanks for thinking of it."

Relieved, he followed her into the store. Of course, they had to do some regular shopping, but they finally settled on some sub sandwiches, potato salad and bottles of unsweetened iced tea for the picnic. Then they bought a small cooler and ice to top it off.

"We're going to have to fight the dogs for these sandwiches," Kell said. "But look, I'll drop you off at your place to put your groceries away. I'll do the same, then come back with a blanket to sit on. Dried grasses are prickly."

TWO HOURS LATER, they sat on a blanket beneath the warm sun. Kell had been right about the dogs wanting the sandwiches, but both were polite enough to wait patiently. When their patience ran out, they dashed around the open spaces, enjoying their freedom.

A gentle, warm breeze blew like a caress. Jenna tilted her head back, enjoying the sun on her face, allowing an unusual relaxation to fill her. If she could just stay like this forever.

She glanced over at Kell. He was sitting with one

knee bent up and his elbow resting on it. And he was looking at her.

She quickly diverted her gaze to the dogs, part of her frightened, part of her wanting to reach out. Wanting his attention.

She was losing her mind. She knew better, far better than to think that way.

"Penny?" he said after a while.

"Not much in the way of thoughts." Untrue. Thoughts were beginning to plague her in a new way. Just what she needed, a fresh concern.

"Heard anything from Bernice?"

"She hasn't responded to my email yet. Knowing her, she's probably having a ton of fun. Busy. Happy." *Happy.* She'd like to know that feeling again.

"Bet she is," Kell said. "That woman is a firecracker."

"A great way to describe her. Bernice always had a dozen irons in the fire, and any time, there was a chance to have fun, she was right in the center. And I loved how she always spoke her mind. You never had to wonder where Bernice stood."

"That's true. So you like outspoken people?"

"It's better than wondering what's hiding behind the words."

"Good point." He dropped his knee and sat cross-legged, facing her. "I only got to know her after I moved here a year ago. Because of Misty, obviously. But I liked the way she spoke her mind, devil be damned."

Jenna sat up, too, feeling safer. "What brought you back here? I thought you were in a rush to get away."

"I was when I was eighteen. But this area had always been home anyway, and Bradley needed a much quieter environment. Seemed like as good a place as any."

She nodded, agreeing with that. Quiet. People on the

streets who weren't perfect strangers, although she hadn't gone out of her way to meet any of them. Still, her childhood here had given her a sense of security. Security that had been ripped from her, except here.

The dogs finally wore themselves out and came back panting to lie beside them. Jenna took the remains of her sandwich, broke it into small pieces and fed the pups. Kell poured water into a collapsible bowl for them.

Kell spoke. "I don't know about you, but it's so nice out here I don't want to go back."

She agreed with him wholeheartedly. "It's peaceful."

"One of the best things, and maybe the hardest to find."

Silence fell except for the chirruping of a few crickets, which must be getting hungry around here, and the occasional squawk of a large bird. Overhead, a bald eagle soared on rising thermals.

Jenna watched it, then said, "I'd like to be free like that eagle. Soaring above everything."

He opened his mouth as if to say something, then closed it. After a bit he said, "I guess we're all prisoners of ourselves."

The truth of that struck her hard. Prisoner of herself? So true. Nobody else was paying for what had happened to her, so why should she keep paying the price over and over? She needed to find a way to move on. She needed to *force* herself out of this anger and pain. People had suffered far worse than she had. They had overcome.

But she still didn't want to talk about it. Sometimes the shame overwhelmed her anger. And she still couldn't imagine why she felt guilty when she had done nothing wrong.

She turned her head up to look for the eagle again, but

it had moved on, leaving an unblemished blue sky above. Not even the wisp of a cloud.

"Let's go home," Jenna said. She needed to escape suddenly, although from what she couldn't say. "Maybe we can figure out what to do with property information. If we can get it."

"Oh, it'll be in the clerk's office, possibly even on their website. Maybe it'll amount to a hill of beans, but at some time or other, the ownership of those two houses had to change. Even if it was some kind of inheritance."

But she could feel him looking at her, gauging why she suddenly wanted to go. Embarrassment filled her. He looked like he knew something was wrong with her but didn't know what. And she sensed he was determined to find out.

Except for the dogs, she'd probably have cut off all communication with him.

As they loaded up his truck with dogs and picnic remains, Kell asked the question she'd feared.

"Something more than your time in field hospitals has you upset, Jenna. What happened?"

"None of your business!"

Silence accompanied them all the way home.

KELL DROPPED MISTY and Jenna at her home, hating himself. He'd put his foot in it, asking a blunt question he'd been trying to avoid.

"Damn," he said under his breath. Bradley slipped between the front bucket seats from the back of the king cab. The dog lay down on the passenger seat and stretched to put his head on Kell's thigh.

"Yeah, Bradley, I did it. Big-time. She'll probably never speak to us again. The worst of it is that she's

right. It *is* none of my business. I can worry about her all
I want, but I don't have the right to know."

Bradley answered with a quiet chuff. Kell took one
hand off the wheel and scratched him behind the ears.

As he turned onto his own street, he braked quickly.
What the hell?

Women in faded gray were coming out of the Zeb
house carrying items and putting them into the back of a
pickup. Why? Had Zeb left his belongings to the church?
The house, perhaps? He'd heard something about people
who turned everything over to Bund's organization. Well,
it was Zeb's property to do with as he wished, and those
women were certainly making no secret of their activi-
ties. But then he remembered seeing the same thing at
the Hassen house. Odd? Probably not.

Nonetheless, as soon as he pulled into his own drive-
way, he jumped out and headed across the street with
Bradley.

"Can I help you ladies?"

None of them answered him, although they shot sur-
reptitious glances his way. Strange. He watched them
for a few moments, then headed back across the street
to his own place.

Weirdness prickled the base of his neck. Something
was wrong with this. He promised himself that he was
going to find a way to get into that house that very night.

KELL WAS BREAKING the law and he knew it. If he jim-
mied a door or window, it would be even worse, leaving
traces of his presence that could get him into some serious trouble. Gage wouldn't look kindly on it and probably wouldn't cut him any slack.

Nevertheless, he waited until every house on the street
was out, long after the women of the church had departed.

Long past midnight. He told Bradley to stay. Then he dressed in black, pulled on a black ski mask and headed out with a tactical flashlight, a hooded one with a very narrow beam. Those women were in a hurry to get stuff out of that house. But what stuff? Maybe they'd already taken it.

Only one way to find out.

Gaining entrance was far easier than he expected. The back door into the mudroom was unlocked.

Once inside, he had to figure out where to look, not an easy task given that he had no idea what he was looking for. Some valuable item? A scrap of paper? Church records maybe?

Great plan, he told himself. The absolute best—no idea at all.

He decided to start upstairs because it made a kind of sense—top to bottom. The only sense of how he should begin.

A bedroom. *Man!* Drawers had been turned out, clothing left on the floor. If there was any indication that those women had been trying to find something, this was it.

But what?

Closets already ransacked. A desk in the second bedroom with a few bills left behind on the floor. File cabinets open and nearly empty. He searched that room even more thoroughly, finding nothing that might be of interest. After the bathroom, he headed downstairs. More ransacking. Items swept off tables onto floors. Then he spied a small corner of a piece of paper inside a lower kitchen cabinet. A strange place, considering the cupboard was full of pots and pans.

He reached for the paper and tugged it gently out from beneath a cast iron skillet.

Then, shining his flashlight on it, he knew he'd found something that might be important.

A shaky hand had written, *My conscience sorely troubles me, Pastor. I am ashamed of my silence. I will go to hell when.*

Then nothing more. And what the devil was it doing under a pan in a lower kitchen cabinet, easily missed? Or planted?

By Mr. Zeb? Was he trying to hide it? Had he guessed what might happen after he died?

Tucking the paper in a pocket, he decided he'd risked enough for one night. Quietly he walked to the back door. Nothing outside stirred yet.

Then he crept away across nearly bare earth that would leave no trace of his passing. Not even dew had fallen to leave a footprint behind him.

Soon he was back in his own house with Bradley. He spread the sheet of paper on his table and stared at it in the bright light of his kitchen.

What the hell did it mean?

MUCH AS KELL wanted to share his find with Jenna, he hesitated to call her. He'd sure set her off yesterday afternoon. He knew damn well he'd pried when he shouldn't have, but she had grown sharp with him, a warning if ever there was one.

Having stuck his foot in a mire when he should have known better, he figured he might have made himself persona non grata. The thing was, he had no business being a coward about it. He believed Jenna had some big problems and he was concerned. He honestly liked her and wished he could help in some way. Get her to open up and spew the troubles that haunted those arresting green eyes of hers.

He eyed Bradley. "Then there's Misty, buddy," he said to the dog. At the sound of Misty's name, Bradley's ears perked.

"Yeah, I know," he sighed. "But we'll probably get the door slammed in our faces."

WHEN JENNA OPENED the front door and saw Kell and Bradley there, she *did* want to slam the door in his face. Before she could, however, he said, "Bradley's pining for Misty."

A glance down at Misty, who stood eagerly beside her, told her Bradley wasn't the only one pining. "Oh, hell," she groused. "I guess they can play in the yard." She turned to the dog again and said, "Go play."

Misty understood that much English anyway. She was through the door and onto the browned grass in a shot. Having no doubt that Kell would keep an eye on both of them, she started to close the door. She didn't want any more of his prying, but even less did she like the increasing urge she felt to talk to him about the unmentionable.

Before she could close the door more than an inch, however, Kell spoke again. "I found something last night. If you can stand me for a few more minutes, I'd like to show it to you."

Grudgingly, she nodded as curiosity piqued. At least, she could stare at the dogs and not at him, something that had begun to become a dangerous pastime.

"Sure," she said distantly. The sound of her voice nearly made her wince. Did he really deserve that because he'd asked an obvious question?

She stepped out, closing the door behind her, and took up station on the arm of one of the Adirondack chairs, an easy place to escape from. The dogs ran in oblivious joy around the yard.

Kell sank into the other chair, clearly not in any hurry to leave.

"I found something this morning, too," she said reluctantly.

His gaze leaped to her. "You first."

She shrugged her shoulder. "Nothing unexpected, I guess. I went online to the recorder's office and looked up the two properties. Both were turned over to the Church of the Well-Lived about ten years ago. Not uncommon with these types of groups, I hear. Probably meaningless."

"Maybe not so much. Maybe something disturbed them enough to want to live away from the compound."

"The thought crossed my mind."

Kell shoved his hand into his pocket. "I did a bit of illegal searching of the Zeb house last night."

"Why?" Now curiosity was surpassing everything else.

"Because I saw those church women carrying stuff out of the house like they did at Hassen's. Wouldn't even glance at me. Not furniture or anything, just boxes."

"They could have packed anything in them," she said. "Meaningless."

"Perhaps. And since you say the church owns the house, then nothing illegal was going on." He looked at the dogs for a few minutes.

"So why?" Jenna demanded. "Why did you go in there?"

"Because I got an uneasy feeling. As if they were looking for something specific. So I let myself in last night to take a look. They'd ransacked the place."

Jenna drew a quick breath, the last of her irritation subsiding. "Ransacked? How?"

"Since there were no dirty food containers or beverage bottles laying around, it struck me that Zeb couldn't have been living in a mess. But things had been swept off tables; closets and drawers had been emptied out, the contents left on the floor."

"Oh, wow." She bit her lower lip and at last slid into the chair. "Why would they do that? Unless they were searching for something."

"That would be my guess," Kell agreed. "And unless Zeb had a hidden hoard of gold stashed somewhere, there could only be one other reason. They wanted something that was in writing. I mean, even his desk had been completely trashed, just a couple of bills left behind."

"Wow!"

He nodded. "Then I found something in a lower kitchen cabinet, just beneath a cast iron pan. One little corner of paper visible."

"How did they miss that?" Although she had to admit he had a sharp eye.

"Maybe they thought it was an old piece of shelf paper. Or maybe they didn't see it at all. It was just a tiny corner. Anyway…"

He handed her a piece of folded paper. She unfolded it and scanned the shakily written words. "What could that mean?"

"Beats me. But there was a secret of some kind, and it troubled the man's conscience."

Jenna looked at him. "Something that would reflect badly on the church?"

"My thinking exactly. Do you mind if I get a glass of water?"

Jenna forgot all her reservations. "I'll get something cold for us. Plus water for the dogs."

The note had excited her in an indefinable way. It said basically nothing, yet it said something very important. A troubled conscience? About what? And why had it been hidden? Because it must have been hidden. She could think of no other reason for it to have been stashed under a pan.

She returned to the porch with two tall glasses of iced tea, then went to fetch a bowl of water for the pooches, who were beginning to tire.

"He was hiding it," she said as she resumed her seat. "He had to have been. He didn't just put it under a pan. Maybe he had some idea what would happen when he died."

"Maybe. The note's not complete, though."

"Maybe he had every intention of finishing it only he died first." She paused. "I'm just speculating."

"No speculation that I haven't been doing. Something is definitely not right about this. Off. Wrong. Especially when you consider how his house was ransacked. Now I wish I'd checked Hassen's."

She chewed her lower lip. The dogs came to the porch to drink and flop in happy fatigue. Then a thought occurred to her. "This is silly, I guess, but what if he'd told someone that he'd break his silence when he died?"

"I don't think that's silly at all. Right now, I'd say it's a high probability."

She turned that around in her head. "Maybe he intended it to be found, Kell. He had to have known that the church would send people to the house after he passed. Maybe he wanted it to get to them. Anyone who wouldn't have known the secret until he finished the note and died."

"Spilling the beans? Possible. But given the mind control that place appears to exercise, how could he know that anyone wouldn't just turn it over to the pastor?"

This was getting knottier by the minute. "You're right."

"Or maybe not." He rubbed his chin as he thought.

"Maybe he'd told just one person he really trusted to look for it. And *that* person talked about it rather than keeping it secret."

"Which would explain what happened yesterday, the house being ransacked, those women marching out with boxes. Someone talked…"

"But that doesn't really help us, does it? So, he had a secret he wanted to tell, warned a particular person to look for the note, then half the women in the church descend to try to find it, and the note becomes pointless."

"Especially since he never finished it," she agreed.

"Which leaves us right where we were. Except that it makes his death look more suspicious."

"It certainly does." She shook her head slightly. "If I were going into that house to recover things, I wouldn't have left perfectly useful pots and pans behind. That group must have need for a lot of things, including clothing."

"I hadn't thought of that, but you're right. Dishes, pans, flatware, maybe some of his rattier clothing in keeping with their personal sense of style."

In spite of herself, Jenna smiled. Yesterday's unpleasantness and her resulting fear and anger had dissipated. She again felt comfortable with Kell. At least reasonably so. Maybe she was at last taking a baby step forward instead of remaining stuck in sludge.

But talk about it? She didn't even want to *think* about it. Maybe her fury had been a way of diverting herself from the memories?

Not that she could escape them entirely. Hell no, they had a way of rearing up unexpectedly before she could force them back into the cavern they had created in her soul. Which only made her angrier.

During the past year, she'd been an emotional bouncing ball. Shame, anger, regret, sorrow, a loss of trust, hatred, and finally the inescapable realization that there was no justice for her. No, merely more blows from people she *should* have been able to trust.

Feeling her body grow more rigid, she looked at Kell. He appeared to be half asleep, looking nowhere from beneath heavily lidded eyes.

The urge to tell him filled her quite suddenly, but she bit back any words that tried to slip out. How could he possibly understand? He was a man. He was a Marine, the most stalwart and loyal troops on the planet. Sure, some of them failed the high standard the Corps held for them, but most did not. She doubted Kell had failed in any way.

Only look at how he was trying to help Bradley. He could have walked away from the dog, labeling him as being too much trouble. The Corps certainly had. Discharged him for failure to perform.

God, did that sound too familiar.

Her voice sounded rusty as words burst out of her. "I was honorably discharged as unfit for duty."

His head snapped around. He no longer looked sleepy. "Why? What happened?"

"I don't want to talk about it." God, she couldn't believe she had said that much.

"Okay. Whenever you feel like it."

Just like that, he let it go, giving her the space she craved. Muscle by muscle, she relaxed again. But why had she said even that much?

Then she knew why. She had to spew all of this, if for no other reason than to watch him get up and leave, turning his back as so many had. Leaving her in the solitude she evidently needed. A justification for all she had come to feel and believe.

She looked at the dogs, blissfully sleeping now, and

wanted so much to be like them. Whatever it took. Even this, even another rejection.

She felt coiled like a tight spring. Did she dare? But she had to know. Had to know that she was right to stay in this prison.

"Kell?"

"Mm?"

"I was raped."

His head spun toward her, then his entire body turned her way. All he said was, "My God!"

She closed her eyes, squeezing out the words. "Two of the guys I worked with."

"Hell. Double hell. I hope they're rotting in jail."

She shook her head on a stiff neck.

"Why the devil not?"

"Because…because my CO dismissed it when I went to press charges. No witnesses, he said."

"For the love of…" He bit off the words.

"It got worse. The guys heard I tried to charge them. Then the threats began. Subtle, then less subtle. It got to the point where I worried about my safety."

"You complained about that?"

"Believe it. How could I work with those people?"

"Then?"

"No charges. I made a stink, going over the CO's head. I was finally offered an honorable discharge as being unfit for duty. I'd become more trouble than I was worth. I took the discharge because I couldn't see any other way out. I hate myself for that."

Chapter Eleven

Kell's chest tightened until he could barely breathe. He'd known there'd been something else, but he'd never imagined anything like this. Anything so repulsive and unforgivable. He had the strongest urge to find all those who'd treated her this way and wrap his hands around their throats.

His neck muscles tightened to hard steel. His teeth clenched until his jaw hurt.

Realizing his fists had tightened, he forced them to relax. He couldn't do a thing about those men, not now. All he could do was struggle to find a way to help Jenna. But how in the hell did you help someone get over that kind of treatment?

The rape was horrendous all by itself, but to be stonewalled by men who just didn't want the complaints to be sent up the chain of command? Men who should have been helping her? Threatened by the men who had already nearly destroyed her?

The urge to kill grew powerfully, but he pushed it away. Jenna didn't need that from him. Not now. But what *did* she need?

"None of that should have happened," he said presently, trying to keep his voice calm but hearing the rage in it anyway. "None of it."

"It did, though," she whispered. "It did. I'm disgusting. I'm ashamed, I'm guilty, and I'm furious beyond words."

"You're none of those things," he said forcibly. "Nothing about you is disgusting. You shouldn't feel ashamed or guilty for things you weren't responsible for."

"But I feel it. And that makes it *me*."

He couldn't find a way to disagree with that. If she felt it, then it was real. Period. Worse, the longer these feelings persisted, the harder it would be for her to get rid of them.

After a minute or so, she spoke again, her voice ragged. "I wasn't a good soldier."

Oh my God. "What in the hell makes you feel that way?"

"They got rid of me."

He ached so bad right then that he felt as if his heart would break into pieces. "So you feel like a failure, as well?"

"Yes."

He wanted to rend the heavens. He jumped up, filled with fury, and began to pace the porch, heedless of disturbing the dogs.

As his wrath began to ebb to manageable proportions, he found voice to say, "I owe Bradley a debt."

"I'm sure you do," she whispered.

"Not for the rest of it. For bringing us together. I'm very glad that I met you, Jenna Blair. And nothing will ever change that. Nothing."

"Once you start thinking about..."

"Screw that," he said sharply. "Just screw that. What I want is the names and ranks of everyone who betrayed you. *Everyone*. Then they can deal with *me*. I'll go all the way to the Secretary of Defense if I have to."

Her eyes popped open. "No. No! I don't want to go through all of that again."

"You're going through it every damn day. I want some hides nailed to the wall."

"Too late. Too late." She paused. "I'm sorry I told you."

He dropped to his knees in front of her, taking care not to touch her in any way, not even the merest bit. "Why? Tell me why."

"Because all I did was make you angry, too."

He wanted nothing more just then than to wrap his arms around her, to hold her tight and make himself a bulwark between her and the ugly world that had blighted her life.

Aware that he couldn't do anything worse than touch her when she was probably feeling like a raw nerve ending, he kept his hands on his thighs and merely looked at her, waiting for her.

He'd wait for her forever.

JENNA FELT HER pain beginning to seep away. Her anger eased just a bit. Kell hadn't walked away from her as she'd expected. Instead he was kneeling in front of her. Close.

She was letting a man close. Physically. Emotionally.

The risk frightened her, but with Kell, it no longer terrified her. Maybe that was the most frightening part of all.

Or even more frightening that she wanted to reach out to him, to feel his friendly touch. To no longer feel as if the entire world was out to get her. To know there was just one person who listened to her story and grew nearly as angry as she had.

She wasn't being dismissed yet again.

When she met his gaze, she saw only kindness and an

intensity that reached out to her. He never once glanced away. Never evinced discomfort or disgust. Just fury. His fury had been palpable. Someone on her side at last.

The iron bands that had gripped her, that had kept her together through some of the most miserable experiences of her life, started to release her. Just enough that she felt she could breathe more freely.

The day's warmth kissed her skin with a gentle breeze. The dogs lay contentedly at their feet. Kell knelt before her. All of it comforting. All of it welcome.

He cleared his throat. "You okay?"

Her voice still sounded rusty. "Better than I was."

He nodded, then rose, giving her the space to feel she could run if she needed to. But the urge to flight no longer filled her. When he resumed his seat, she wondered if she could trust him as much as she had begun to believe she could.

When would everything turn on her as it had before?

There was no way to know. There was only waiting to see, to learn if he was trustworthy.

If she really wanted to.

Down the street came a young woman with a Yorkie beside her. As she passed, she smiled and waved.

It struck Jenna that there had been other smiles and waves since shortly after she'd come home, but she had pretty much ignored them. Had, in some way, been blind to them.

For the first time she raised her hand and waved back. The smile still wouldn't come, but at least the wave did.

The two dogs on the porch watched the Yorkie pass, expressing interest but no desire to run down and make friends. Did they sense the mood on the porch and decide it wasn't the right time to be playful?

A sigh escaped her as she watched the woman disappear. What was *her* life like? Complicated? Relatively easy? But as Aunt Bernice was fond of saying, you never knew what problems anyone faced unless they told you.

Kell drew her out of her preoccupation. "This church thing is really bugging me."

"Me too." A relief to think about something relatively safe. "If they won't talk to anyone, how could we learn a thing? They've got it all sewn up."

"Seems like it. All I can say is that something terrible must have happened for Zeb to talk about silence that he's ashamed of, that he'll carry the secret to hell. That doesn't sound like drunk driving."

"No, it doesn't." It sounded so bad that her imagination balked.

"I wonder if anyone has left that church. If it's even possible. Maybe I could check around and see if there's someone I can talk to."

She nodded slowly. "I can't think of anything else." She looked at Bradley and said, "I can't ignore your dog's response, though. Yeah, the deaths might have been accidental, but two from the same church in such a short time, especially when you consider that it's such a small group."

"And Zeb was much younger than Miss Hassen," he said, agreeing. "But Zeb's aborted note won't leave me alone. It sounds too important to ignore."

"But why would anyone talk about it? It's a secret, according to Zeb. They wouldn't even know."

"Or they might know something else. Another secret. One that might lead to this one."

They were floundering, he knew. No reasonable way to go at this, no real way to believe the deaths weren't just accidental. Two seriously ill people. Maybe he was falling into a conspiracy theory of his own making.

But Bradley. It all came back to Bradley. He'd trusted that dog through everything, through life and death situations. He couldn't, by any stretch of the imagination, believe that his K-9 hadn't had a good reason for alerting. A reason, perhaps, beyond the bodies smelling unusual.

What if he'd detected another odor around them? The odor of a person? It was possible, though how likely was that with the paramedics already carrying out two bodies in half-zipped bags? Too many new odors.

Or not.

He passed his hand over his face and decided not to make any excuses. This had to be pursued. For his sake. For the dog's sake. For Jenna's sake, as it gave her something else to think about.

Maybe for the sake of two dead people. Maybe for the sake of others in that compound.

He stared out over the sunny street and wondered just what the next step must be. Talking to people, of course. Then he had a thought.

"I live a few doors down from the town's worst gossip. Maybe I'll have a word with her. I swear, that woman knows everything."

Jenna gave a quiet, brief laugh. "It might not all be true."

"Probably not, but she might have a nugget. It's worth trying to find out."

A WHILE LATER, HE ROSE. "I'm going to talk with Barb Traynor. My neighbor. She should be back from her trip by now."

"Nice lady?"

"Couldn't ask for better. How many grandmothers would undertake the care of three young children because her daughter can't right now? Not many. I'm sure you'd like her, though. And she looks like everyone's dream grandma. Plump, gray-haired, pink cheeks..."

"Mrs. Santa Claus?"

He laughed. "Good description."

"Should I come?"

But he could sense the rising tension in her. She didn't really want to, but he had no doubt she would. "Nah," he answered. "Not this time. It'll be easier to get her to talk if it's just me. I'm a frequent visitor to her front porch, and I play with the kids sometimes."

"Trust," she said quietly.

"I guess so. Anyway, I'm taking Bradley with me. Apologies to Misty, but the kids love him, and he can romp a bit with them while I pick Barb's brain."

Barb was at home as he'd hoped, wearing one of her customary brightly flowered house dresses. This time of afternoon, she often enjoyed lemonade on her front porch while the three kids played. Three kids who were over-joyed to see Bradley. The dog appeared almost as happy as they did. Despite his PTSD, Bradley still knew how to take joy when it was offered. A good lesson, maybe.

Barb invited him to join her on her porch and offered him some lemonade.

"Thanks," he said, figuring sharing lemonade with her might smooth the wheels of conversation. It would certainly give him a reason to stay more than a few minutes.

"How was your trip?" he asked as she put a frosty glass in his hand. "Dang, you make the best lemonade."

"The secret is fresh lemons. Oh, and plenty of that nasty stuff called sugar."

He laughed and smiled at her as she sat in the webbed lawn chair beside him. "How's life treating you?"

"Well enough," she answered as she always did. "Unfortunately, my daughter is still refusing to go to rehab. How's Bradley?"

"Seeing some improvement, but he's not quite there yet. Getting better with sudden loud noises, like gunshots. Still bad with thunder. When we get a little further along, I'm thinking heavy equipment."

Barb nodded. "For the rescue work you want to do with him?"

"Exactly. Cleanup from an awful lot of disasters usually involves heavy equipment. We'll get there. That dog loves to work."

She nodded. "I hear that about a lot of dogs. They want jobs."

"Like people."

She laughed. "Some people, anyway. I've told you what a worthless scumbag my daughter's ex is. He was working when they married, but it wasn't long before he seemed to forget how. And helping with the kids? Never. It's a wonder she stayed long enough to have three children with him. And no wonder she became an alcoholic."

"Maybe love makes us blind."

Barb raised an eyebrow at him. "More like love turns us into idiots."

He laughed again and sipped more lemonade. It really *was* delicious. "Hear anything about those two deaths? Miss Hassen and that Zeb guy."

She turned faded blue eyes on him. "What's up, Kell?"

"Just that they both belonged to that sect, and that got me wondering. No big deal, just curious."

She nodded. "Right. And I have horns under this gray hair. You want to pick my brain."

He grinned. "Could be."

At that, she chuckled. "Sometimes you're transparent. But yes, it makes me curious, too. Seems odd, both of them dying so close together and both members of that ridiculous cult. Different ages, too. Anyway, it's natural causes. Somehow."

He ventured a wink. "Right."

She shook her head but was still smiling. "Hard to know about those folks. If any of them ever talked, I haven't heard about it. Seems like they cut their tongues out when they join. Or maybe have them removed at birth. From what I can tell, they're busy breeding. The easy way to get members, right from the cradle."

"Already trained, too."

"My thinking exactly. Well, I'll tell you what I know, which isn't much."

"Probably more than I know."

"Doubtful. Silent as the grave, that lot." Barb resettled in her lawn chair, clearly seeking a more comfortable position. Kell knew she had a bad hip that bothered her from time to time.

"You know," Barb continued after a moment, "I think if those folks ever needed help, they'd have trouble finding it around here, and given the nature of most people in these parts, that's saying something. Even now, when nearly everything else has changed in the world, a helping hand is always here. Even had a barn raising not too long ago, before you got here. General opinion around here is we'll ignore them as much as they ignore us."

She tilted her head to one side, sipped more lemonade. Bradley now lay on the front yard with three young kids climbing all over him. He'd rarely looked happier, except with Misty.

"Anyway," Barb continued, "not to be nasty or anything, but folks don't trust them. Not at all."

"Have they given anyone a reason to?"

Barb's mouth twisted a bit as she shook her head. "You

wouldn't believe the conspiracy theories that have run around about them over the years. Rarely though. They don't draw enough attention as a rule. Live and let live, folks say."

"Too bad all folks don't follow that rule."

"Hah. You got that right, Kell."

"So nobody knows anything about them at all?"

"Not really." Barb fell silent.

Eventually, Kell asked, "Anyone know why Zeb and Hassen didn't live at the compound?"

"They moved into town about ten years ago, as I recall. Never said a word about why they moved here. 'Course they never said a word to anybody. Like the rest of them nuts."

Kell half smiled. "Strong words, Barb."

"Not strong enough, if you ask me. There's something wrong out there. I can't figure it out, though. But people who can't even offer a friendly hello or a smile… Gotta be something wrong with them."

"Some nuns take vows of silence and cloister themselves."

Barb looked at him. "Hardly think it's the same thing. That's no convent, and they don't do any good works, neither. Anyway, cloistered, vows of silence… You know any nuns, Kell?"

He was sitting there, impressed by Barb's openness about her opinion of that cult, but her question took him by surprise. "A few over the years. But none were cloistered."

"Well, I can tell you, they don't mix men, women and kids all together in one house. Most mixing you'll see is nuns running an orphanage or hospital, and that isn't the same. So no, I don't have any reason to think there's anything natural out there."

Kell turned that idea around in his head. "Unnatural."

"The whole thing is unnatural. The way they've cut themselves off. And where do they get the money to come to town to buy things? Not that they buy much, mind you. But they still show up every now and then. How do they pay for it? I don't see any of them with a job."

"That would mean being around people."

Barb nodded her head. "So where do they get money?"

Kell couldn't resist. "Maybe they're growing marijuana out there."

Barb laughed so hard that the kids and dog turned to look at her before returning to their play, which now involved a grungy tennis ball. "Now that's one idea nobody else has come up with yet."

"I can be inventive sometimes. So there's nothing but general knowledge about them?"

"Not that I know…" Barb's voice trailed off. "All this talk put me in mind of something."

Kell reached full alert. "What's that?"

"Well, they say nobody ever leaves that church, even like Miss Hassen and Mr. Zeb—by the way, if they have first names, I've never heard of them—but they didn't really leave, did they?"

"Not from what little I've heard." Kell drained his lemonade and wished he had more. Barb must have read his mind, because she stood and reached for his glass. "You make sure Bradley minds those kids while I get some more. Got a whole pitcher in there and don't want to be giving too much to the grandkids. Sugar rushes may be fun for them, but not so much for me. Getting too damn old."

But there was a twinkle in her eye as she spoke. Two minutes later, she was back with two frosty glasses and handed him one.

"Drink fast," she suggested. "Any time now, those kids are going to realize they're thirsty."

Kell obliged and took a good-sized swallow. "You have to teach me how to make this."

"Like you ever will. I see you're keeping Maude's in business." She settled into her chair again with a sigh and smiled in the direction of her grandchildren. "Having them here makes me feel young again. But I've learned something."

"What's that?"

"Patience comes with age. I wish I'd had this much when my two were their age. Never thought I'd see the day when I'd let a child use a whole roll of tape, sticking it to a box I was trying to unpack. I loved watching it."

Kell smiled. "Nice memory."

"I got more of them now, too. But you don't want to hear all that. You're here about that church. And you want to hear what I just remembered."

Kell had thought she'd forgotten all about it and hadn't wanted to press her to remember. Seemed like it might be a rude thing to do.

"Thing is," she continued, "I recall this one woman and her daughter, maybe ten or eleven, leaving that group maybe a year ago. Just picked up stakes and came here to town with nothing but the clothes on their backs. Good Shepherd Church helped them out, got them on their feet. They still live around here. Never said a word about why they left, but never had another thing to do with that group. You'll see them at Good Shepherd every Sunday morning."

Kell felt his heart skip a beat, and he looked long at Barb. "That's quite a turnaround."

"A complete one. She's got a job, the bakery I think,

but then I never paid much mind to it all except to donate when the church collected money for her and her daughter."

Kell nodded, wondering if he'd just learned the important tidbit that would help find out what was going on. "Nice of Good Shepherd to step up."

"A helping hand," Barb said. "That's as it should be. You'd have to have some kind of shriveled soul not to help that woman and her daughter. Wish I knew what caused them to run. Or maybe I don't want to know."

"Might be for the best," Kell agreed. Although he didn't actually agree with her on that, but he didn't want to take the risk of making Barb feel bad. If something terrible was going on out there, shedding some light on it might be a good thing. Sunlight was a great disinfectant.

Barb spoke again. "Should have tried to find out back then. Or even now. I don't know." She sighed. "But I hate to think what might be going on out there. Can't bear it, honestly." Then she squared her shoulders visibly. "But if folks won't help themselves, who can?"

Good question, Kell thought as he departed a short time later, Bradley at his side. They left three happy and dirty kids behind them.

On his way, he stopped by Maude's again, getting something for him and Jenna to eat. He knew she must be impatiently waiting for him and any news he might have gleaned.

It wasn't exactly news, but it was something.

BRADLEY SHOOK MOST of the dust and dirt from his coat by the time they got back to Jenna's, but as Kell stood at the door holding out the bags from Maude's, he asked, "You want me to take these two dogs out back for baths? Bradley got pretty dirty playing with Barb's kids."

"He's a dog," she smiled. "Let him in."

Bradley drank almost an entire bowl of water while Jenna filled two bowls with Misty's kibble.

"Wow," Jenna said as she looked into the bags. "And here I was just trying to amp myself up into cooking. I think I can remember how to make the meat for nachos."

He smiled. "Tomorrow, if you feel like it, and I'll invite myself."

"I was planning on it. I wouldn't have bought all that hamburger just for myself."

"So, news," she said when the food had been served and they sat at the table together. He noticed, though, that she picked at it.

"Most of it was nothing we don't already know about their insularity. It *does* seem that Zeb and Hassen moved into town about the same time but didn't sever their ties."

"Right. Man, Maude makes a great burger."

"You won't get an argument from me. Let's finish eating before I fill you in, if that's okay?"

"That's fine," she said, agreeing. "I'm famished."

"I'm famished myself."

BUT JENNA WAS feeling impatient as well as hungry and probably ate faster than she should have. The food was good, but she wanted to hear what Kell had learned. It was something he hadn't wanted to discuss over a meal, and that worried her.

At last, they finished, cleaning up quickly, and Kell started the coffee. Jenna's impatience was growing by the minute, and watching coffee brew wasn't helping. Finally, Kell spoke.

"Anyway, Barb remembered a woman and her daughter who left the church. Severed all ties." Kell poured them both coffee from the fresh pot and sat.

Just hearing that little bit filled Jenna with apprehension. "I wouldn't have expected it."

"Me neither. But something *has* to be going on. Barb said that woman and her daughter left the commune with nothing but the clothes on their backs. Good Shepherd Church helped them get on their feet. And as far as Barb knows, those two never had any further contact with Bund's organization."

Jenna looked down at her coffee as her stomach began to churn. "Kell…"

"Sounds like it could be ugly, doesn't it?"

"In the worst way imaginable. Oh, God. How old was the girl at the time?"

"Barb says ten or eleven."

"I think I might throw up." Her stomach felt as if it were rising into her throat, and a warning sheen of perspiration dampened her forehead.

"Not Maude's great meal, please." He succeeded in bringing a faint smile to her face. "Just take a few deep breaths. I thought the same thing you are right now."

Jenna couldn't answer. Desperate, she headed for the kitchen sink and grabbed a paper towel. Wetting it, she pressed it to her forehead, wiped her face with it. Then she repeated the action. Gradually, her nausea eased.

"I don't want to believe it," she said when she thought it was safe to return to her chair.

"Common enough, from what I hear about the world."

"Maybe it was something else?" she added hopefully. But her hope was slim.

"Might could be." He drained his coffee, went to refill his mug. "Topper?" He indicated her cup.

"I'm fine. I don't think I could hold it down right now." She pushed her mug aside and put her face in her hands. "But if someone was molesting that girl, why would *any* woman keep her children there? And why not report it to the police?"

"Hell if I know. I suggested brainwashing once before. You've read about how some cults get a tight grip on members. That it can even require deprogramming to overcome it."

She raised her face and shook her head. "God, I hope our suspicions are wrong. I can't bear the thought."

"Me neither." He sighed and drained his coffee before speaking again. "It could be a lot of other things, I suppose. Maybe the daughter was getting bullied. Maybe the mother had a real problem with someone else in that cult. Maybe some guy wouldn't stop coming on to her."

Jenna snatched at the offered straws. "You're right. Maybe we're making too much about the daughter and forgetting there could be other reasons."

"Maybe."

But as Jenna sat there looking at Kell, she knew he was thinking the same thing about that girl and wasn't willing to dismiss the possibility.

Nor was she, honestly.

Secret. Silence. Bad enough to have a man write he'd carry it to his grave.

"We've got to keep looking," she said. "Even if those two deaths weren't murder. Something's terribly wrong."

"I agree, Jenna, but we've got little enough to go on. And how do we pierce that wall of silence?"

"Find out who the woman is and talk with her?"

"Would you talk about it with a complete stranger?"

Slowly, grimly, she shook her head. She almost hadn't shared her secret with Kell, and he'd no longer been a stranger when she'd blurted out her whole sordid story.

Kell spoke. "She's clearly not talking. If Barb hasn't

heard anything on the grapevine, then I don't think there's anything out there at all."

"But how can we possibly learn anything?" It all kept coming around to the same problem.

"Oh, I don't know," he answered. "Grab those women when they come to town, hog-tie them, kidnap them and demand answers at knife point?"

Despite the ugly feelings roiling inside her, she had to laugh a bit. "Man, you are something else, Kell!"

He smiled. "I hope so." He wiggled his eyebrows. "Can I persuade you keep company with me?"

Jenna drew a sharp breath. He couldn't possibly mean what that sounded like, old-fashioned as it was.

"As in walking two dogs," he said. "I could use the stretch myself."

She relaxed. "Sounds like a good idea."

KELL HADN'T MISSED Jenna's reaction when he asked her to keep company with him. He'd meant to say *keep me company*, but it had come out wrong, the old-fashioned phrase for dating, and he knew it instantly. He'd corrected himself as fast as he could, but he'd already heard her indrawn breath, had seen the way she'd stiffened.

Not good. He kept putting his foot in it with this woman. Ham-handed. He couldn't afford to be careless. He hated the thought that she might pull back, shut him out.

As they walked casually through the darkening streets, he saw Jenna nod and smile as they passed others. Quite a change from their previous walks, he thought, a good one. They paused occasionally to allow Misty and Bradley to meet and greet with other dogs, but interactions were limited to tail wags and sniffs.

Bradley was walking tall this evening, and Kell's heart

gladdened. Soon maybe, he'd be prancing again in that distinctive way he had.

"Does Bradley sleep in your bed?" Jenna asked. "Misty does with me."

"Of course he does."

"That must be a tight squeeze."

"King-sized bed for one thing. It's not bad unless he decides his legs need more room. Or he wants all the covers."

Jenna gave a brief, quiet chuckle.

"He's slept with me for years," Kell said. "He got me a lot of sleep I wouldn't have had otherwise. Long nights, hot days, whatever weather, but it wasn't the weather he protected me from. I could get some real sleep because with him right beside me, I knew he'd keep me safe. He'd alert to any important sound or odor. He'd wake me up in time to save my skin."

"That's a pretty special bond."

"I think so. I imagine most dogs would be that protective, though."

"But they wouldn't necessarily know what the important things were. Or how to let you know."

"It's possible Misty could surprise you. I just hope she never has to."

"Me too," Jenna answered. She glanced at him. "How *is* Bradley doing with his PTSD?"

"I haven't been working with him enough the last few days. I'll get back to it soon enough. Anyway, it won't hurt him to have some downtime from all the stressors I throw at him."

"It must be hard for you to have to do it, though."

His jaw tightened. "Bradley has the hard part. After all he did for me and my unit, nothing's too hard to do for him."

The breeze had cooled as it blew down from the high mountains. Kell saw Jenna shiver just a bit and wondered if they should turn around. She spoke again before he could ask.

"I didn't mean hard for you to do it, Kell. I meant hard on you to have to put him through that immersion."

"I have to focus on the hope I can get him past most of this."

"But not all."

He looked at her. "You ought to know, Jenna. No vet gets past *all* of it."

Misty paused to leave a message at the foot of a tree trunk. Bradley followed suit, aiming higher.

Jenna suddenly giggled. "Was that a dominance thing?"

Kell's spirits lifted at the sound of her laugh, mild though it was. "Ask them. I've never looked into marking behavior, although I probably should some time. Just for informational purposes."

"There's a whole world we don't begin to understand, I guess. I bet you understand Bradley a whole lot better than I understand Misty, though."

"Maybe. I don't know." His thoughts had begun to range back over memories of all the times he and Bradley had shared dangerous situations. "Sometimes I think we share a mind. Then he'll do something that makes me think he reads me better than I'll ever read him. I don't know. All I know is we're joined at the hip, and it's going to stay that way."

Kell realized he was dangerously close to walking some pathways into the past that were better left alone. Then he decided that Jenna's honesty with him earlier deserved his own honesty.

"I haven't left the war behind," he said.

"Who can? In what way?"

"Memories. Waking up in the middle of the night with anxiety, sweating like a pig. Sometimes, even walking down a street, I get a nearly overpowering dread of what might lie right around the corner."

"I can imagine. You went through some pretty traumatizing stuff."

"Most of us did. Like you."

She shook her head. "Not like you. I didn't have to go on patrol or get into a battle with the insurgents."

"No, you just stood there stabilizing a guy who was on the brink of death, maybe assisting surgery, definitely trying to save a life while you were being shelled. Couldn't even hunt for cover." He paused, then said dryly, "Nah. You had it easy."

She stopped walking and looked at him. "Kell, you are one heck of a decent guy."

Decent? He'd take that. "I only said what's true. That makes me decent?"

"In my recent experience, yes."

The dogs were growing impatient at remaining still when they knew perfectly well they were on a walk. Kell resumed his stroll with Jenna.

"I'm going to think overnight about this information problem," he told her. "There's got to be a way to pick the nits out of the cult tangle."

He was delighted to hear her giggle again.

"What a description!" She smiled at him, and this time, there was no stiffness, no reticence. Just a real smile.

He felt pretty good about that, but he'd have felt a whole lot better without the dark cloud that seemed to be hanging over an even darker mess.

"You know what bothers me, Jenna?"

"Hmm?"

"That if our suspicion about that child being molested is true, and I hope to heaven it's not, then why in God's name didn't that cult protect her? Why did the mom feel she had to take her daughter and run?"

"I was trying not to think about that part. Unfortunately, I know how possible that is. Don't rock the boat. Don't get in trouble with the higher-ups. Just sweep it under the rug and pretend it never happened, because it's easier and safer."

"You'd know all about that."

She didn't answer. The twilight continued to deepen, the night air to chill. The earliest kiss of the approaching winter seemed to be carried on its breath.

Chapter Twelve

Jenna woke well before the sun the next morning. The house felt cold, but the heat hadn't been turned on, not in late August. She considered it, then tossed the notion aside. This was the kind of thing sweaters were made for. Or throws. Or…

She nearly laughed at herself, half awake and following a ridiculous line of thought. Wrapping herself in her terry cloth robe and slippers, she headed for the kitchen and a pot of coffee. On the way, she paused to rewind the grandfather clock.

A beautiful relic from an age when time pieces were built to last generations and meant to add beauty to a space. The modern versions just didn't hold the same aesthetic appeal.

The clock's ticking followed her into the kitchen, where she yawned and tried to blink sleep from her eyes as she put water and grounds into the coffee maker. Maybe she ought to get one of those pots with a timer so the coffee would be ready when she woke. But that sure wouldn't have helped this morning when she was up earlier than usual.

She peered past the kitchen café curtains and saw not even the merest hint of dawn's light. Probably just as well that she hadn't looked at the clock when she wound it and discovered the time.

As she turned, however, the digital clock on the microwave betrayed her with blue numbers that said it wasn't quite 4:00 a.m.

"Thanks a lot," she grumbled, stumbling away to the downstairs bathroom to wash her sticky face. She must have wept in her sleep again. At least she didn't remember why.

Finally, she and her yawns were able to sit at the kitchen table with a steaming cup of coffee. She placed her face right over it, eyes closed, inhaling the aroma and grateful for the warmth that reached her face.

Maybe she ought to sit on the porch and watch dawn creep in until the moment when the sun breached the horizon and filled the world with bright light. The idea tempted her even as she reminded herself that it was likely colder out there, especially if the air hadn't grown still.

Misty, who usually ignored Jenna's occasional midnight rambles, padded into the kitchen and sat beside her. Jenna reached to knead the dog's neck. "Too early for breakfast, kiddo." Not that Misty seemed concerned. When she was hungry, she nosed at her empty bowl until it made noise.

Right now, Misty seemed as comfortable as *she* was with just sitting there.

But as Jenna's mind woke up, reaching a nearly normal operating speed, thoughts began to swirl in her head, mostly unpleasant ones.

"Screw the cold," she said to the dog. Finding an insulated mug in the cupboard, she filled it with hot brew and headed for the porch. Misty trotted right beside her.

It *was* colder outside, but that seemed unimportant.

More important was watching the birthing of a new day. Soon a bird or two would trill dawn greetings. Some people would stir to take advantage of the hours before heading to work or sending the kids to school. Lights would come on in houses. Some joggers would run by.

But just then, everything was quiet, even the usual breeze. The air held still, as if waiting expectantly. A gift was on the way.

A gift Jenna hadn't been able to enjoy often in the past years. A field hospital never slept, time turned into unbroken eternity, and a lot of people counted themselves lucky to be able to step outside for a cigarette or find a few minutes to grab food or coffee. Attempts to try to give a steady rhythm to life were too often blasted apart. The sound of incoming trucks. The *whap* of helicopter blades. The sirens.

Trouble was coming. Always just around the next breath. And in between, a lot of time was spent organizing supplies, cleaning treatment tables and gore-covered floors. Everyone pitched in, or they'd never have kept up with the demands. Then, as the war began to wind down, there were fewer field hospitals, but the remaining ones continued to be taxed.

And at last, her own unit pulled out, and she went to work in Germany, where casualties were treated until they could be moved to stateside facilities. Where another kind of tragedy unfolded: her own.

She shook her head, trying to dislodge the memories. She was still touched by Kell's evaluation of her service. There had been a division between medical personnel and combat troops. Not one of dislike, but as if the medical people were somehow unequal. No tension on either side, just a "that's the way it is" feeling.

Jenna had shared the feeling. *She* wasn't the one who

walked out into enemy territory for days on end, a kind
of courage she could hardly imagine. She didn't have
to work out of a forward operating base, just a handful of troops who might have been attacked at any moment while they performed reconnaissance duties over
a large area.

No, she hadn't needed to muster that kind of courage.

Evidently, she'd failed her own test of courage, or she
wouldn't be right here nursing rage and wounds that she
might have fought harder to assuage. *Injustice.* Did anything make a person any angrier than that?

But she had to get herself out of this somehow. She
had a lot of years to look forward to, and she didn't want
to spend them becoming a miserable hermit.

Kell was helping, but he was just one person. A person who hadn't walked away from her in disgust or dis-
belief. A person who had grown furious when he heard
her story.

A decent man, a rarity.

Sighing, she realized she'd finished more of her coffee and went back inside to refresh it. Back out on the
porch, where Misty lay apparently enjoying the chang-
ing scents of night turning into day, she saw the growing gray light. Dawn was about to break over the world.

Seated again, she forced her thoughts away from herself and back to the situation with the cult. There had to
be some way to get past that brick wall, to learn something about what was happening inside that compound.

Except for Bradley, she'd have thought she would have
become part of a pair of wild conspiracy theorists.

And now except for that woman and her daughter.

Putting her chin in her hand, Jenna focused on the
problem.

There had to be a way.

ALMOST AS IF summoned by her thoughts, Kell and Bradley appeared jogging down the street. When he reached her, he stopped.

"You're out early," she remarked. Misty sat up. It clearly wasn't too early for *her*.

"I take Bradley out for a bit of a run just before dawn. He knows it's one of the most dangerous times of day."

"So it's good for him to find it peaceful?"

"Certainly relaxes him. He gets pretty alert at those hours, when us stupid humans are at our lowest ebb."

She nodded. "Good K-9."

"The best."

"There's coffee, and I suppose I can rustle up some kibble if you two are interested."

"Coffee for me," he said as he approached the porch. "Kibble for Bradley. He won't like the coffee and I won't like the kibble."

"God, you are too much," Jenna said, rising. "I'd have thought that was a given."

Kell offered to take Misty on a short walk with him and Bradley. He was back with the dogs in fifteen minutes.

Inside the kitchen, Jenna served up two bowls of kibble and water, then poured coffee.

"Couldn't sleep?" Kell asked.

"It happens. No biggie." Nor was it, really. "I was sitting out there trying to avoid my own thoughts when I got to thinking about that woman and girl who left the compound."

"I can't stop thinking about them, either. But there's no way to get them to talk if they haven't mentioned a word to anyone yet. And like I said, would you want to talk to a total stranger about *your* experience?"

"No. I get that, totally." She put her chin in her hand

and watched him enjoy his coffee. Watched how much time he spent watching Bradley. Joined at the hip, as he'd said.

Then she got his full attention when she said, "I want to try to talk to her regardless." She tensed in expectation of his resistance. She was going to press him anyway.

His head snapped around, his gray eyes intense. "Jenna, it won't work. Besides, we don't know who she is. And she probably doesn't want us to know."

Jenna shook her head. "I think you should introduce me to Barb today."

"She's told me everything she knows."

"I'm not so sure about that, Kell. Can you introduce me? Please?"

One of his shoulders slumped as if he knew there was no way out of this even though he didn't want to do it. "Damn, Jenna. I'm sure Barb will like you, but I wouldn't bet on her telling you more than she told me."

"Maybe not, but it's worth a try." The only chance they had of getting any kind of clue, and she was feeling stubborn. "We try this, or we write those two deaths off as natural."

Kell looked at Bradley again. "I don't want to believe Bradley is *that* broken. Okay. Another stab at this. I sure as hell can't think of anything else."

KELL PHONED BARB later that morning. It was Saturday, and she'd have her hands full with kids and the rounds of shopping that they enjoyed. Which was why Barb didn't do them at a quieter time of week.

"Besides," as she often said, "it gives me a good chance to catch up on the gossip."

Regardless, he didn't want to just drop by and find her gone or find her at a bad time on a busy day.

Barb was only too willing to have them visit midafternoon. "Front porch is always open," she laughed. "Maybe there'll be some lemonade, too."

Kell disconnected and looked at Jenna. "We're on. I hope this works."

Feeling more like he was on a mission than simply making a neighborly visit, Kell set out with Jenna wondering what kind of rumpus the K-9 contingent was going to make with Barb's grandchildren. He bet that it was going to exhaust both the kids and the dogs.

But as they came down the street, he saw that Barb wasn't alone on her front porch. Beside her sat a woman with a snow-white service dog.

"That's Kerri Canady," he told Jenna as they approached. "She's a victim advocate with the sheriff's office, and she's married to one of the deputies, Stu Canady." Stu was a guy Kell had truly come to like over the past year. Well, Kerri, too.

"Service dog?" Jenna asked quietly.

"Shot in the head when she was a uniformed cop. Some kind of epilepsy, I hear."

"That's tough," Jenna murmured.

But now they were too close to talk about Kerri or Barb. Didn't matter, anyway. The dogs tried to take charge. Or at least Misty did. Bradley was too well trained.

As Kell made the introductions, three kids and two dogs began romping in the middle of the yard.

Kerri laughed. "I guess I should let Snowy join in. It must be killing him to have to sit and watch this."

Barb spoke. "He won't be so snowy if he gets out in that dust."

"Which is why I have a walk-in shower." Kerrie

grinned. Bending, she unhooked the service vest. "Okay, Snowy. Off-duty." She straightened. "Not that he wouldn't have known when I removed his vest."

It had been apparent from the instant that vest came off. Snowy shot to the group in the yard, first for a meet and greet with the two other dogs, then a frolic with all of them.

"Dogs got it right," Barb said. "Well, so do little kids. Takes time to warp them out of shape. Most of 'em anyway."

She cocked her eye toward Jenna. "So you're Jenna. I wouldn't have recognized you on the street. You've changed quite a bit since I last saw you when you went off to college. Thinner for sure. Doesn't the Army feed you guys?"

"As much as we want, some of it not so edible."

Barb laughed. "What are you hearing from your aunt Bernice?"

"Not a whole lot. She must be having a wonderful time."

"She would," Barb nodded. "My kind of woman. Or the kind I used to be before three little blessings arrived in my life. She's probably got a half dozen men dangling after her and a whole bunch of women who like to get together for drinks and coffee and all that. She always could get a group going."

Jenna smiled. "Yes, she could."

"A real gift." Barb looked at Kerri. "You wouldn't know, of course, but Bernice raised Jenna from the time she was little."

"I told him. I love Bernice," Kerri said warmly. "She can say the most outrageous things."

"All of 'em true," Barb laughed. "Now, she doesn't

make enemies, mind you, but sometimes she sure makes folks squirm."

"Nothing like the truth to do that," Kell remarked.

Barb eyed Kell. "Okay, what do you want to know this time? I know you like the grandkids—heck, I've seen you roll in the dirt with them and let 'em ride you like a horse—but you didn't just come over on a nice Saturday afternoon for my lemonade."

"Sure I did."

"Didn't make any." Barb's smile widened. "Come on, you've been getting curious about that cult out there. What's going on?"

Jenna looked at Kell. He could tell she didn't want to answer that question, nor did he, come to that. Barb was tuned into all the local gossip, but the only way to do that was to gossip. He didn't want to put something out on the grapevine needlessly.

Kell returned his attention to Barb. "I was wondering about that woman and girl who left the compound."

Barb fell silent. She looked at Kerri.

Kerri quickly shook her head. "I don't know them. I might have heard something about it, but I don't remember."

"Like you'd tell us if you ever saw them professionally," Barb said pleasantly.

Kerri raised her hand. "No, I wouldn't tell if I *had* met them on the job, but I haven't, so I'm not hedging when I say I never met them."

Barb looked wry. "I could drive a truck through that, girl."

"So drive," Kerri answered lightly. "I have to admit, now that they've been brought up, I'm kinda curious, too. They actually *left* that cult? I heard that nobody did that."

"Guess they did," Kell remarked. "Might be the only people who ever *have* gotten away."

"Gotten away," Kerri murmured. "Sheesh, I never thought about it like that. They're sort of background noise. I know they're there, but I don't think about it, if you know what I mean."

Barb answered. "They work real hard at avoiding attention. Most they get around here is a shrug. Might be a smart move." She turned to Kell. "So what's going on?"

Kell didn't have an answer for that. He must have already planted enough red flags in Barb's mind to generate enough speculation for ten coffee klatches.

Jenna surprised him by speaking. Until then she'd been noticeably silent. "I wanted to talk with them. We might have had a similar experience."

"You left a cult?" Barb demanded.

"No, not that."

Jenna might have just dropped a rock in a pond. Silence spread through the group like ripples on the water. Barb leaned back. Kell resisted the urge to put an arm around Jenna, to offer her some support. He could hardly believe she had admitted so much to strangers. Maybe her worry about that girl had driven her a small way past reticence.

She was admirable.

But as he glanced Kerri's way, he saw that she understood all too well what Jenna had meant. Her gaze had softened and she looked as if she wanted to reach out in sympathy.

Okay, part of that cat was out of the bag, he thought. How much more would follow?

Presently, Barb cleared her throat. "Don't know how much good it'll do, but the woman's named Deborah Mixon. Her daughter's in high school, and Deborah works at Melinda's bakery early in the mornings. I *do* mean early. Guess that baking starts in the middle of the night." She shook her head a little ruefully. "Well, of course it does. How else is Melinda going to serve pastries and doughnuts at six in the morning?"

Kell looked at Jenna and saw she was sinking inside herself again, as if she'd exposed herself to pain once more. God, this was awful. He tried to divert her.

"I need to take you by there sometime soon," he said. "You won't find better doughnuts or Danishes anywhere else in the world."

"Her breads are fabulous," Kerri added. "I love to grab a sandwich for lunch when I can."

Kell was glad to see Jenna begin to relax again. They'd all managed to move past the painful moment. As if they all understood. And maybe they did. Good people.

Kerri stood and called Snowy. As predicted, he wasn't quite as white anymore. He sat patiently while she snapped on his vest again. "I promised I'd meet Stu at the office. Hope I see you all again."

Barb spoke as Kerri walked away. "Sorry I didn't get around to making that lemonade, Kell."

"I told you to give me the recipe."

That drew a belly laugh from Barb. "Get on, you two. You got what you were looking for. Next time, for Pete's sake, come back just to be sociable."

JENNA FELT AS if she had just skated over some very thin ice but had escaped without falling through. Not only had everyone appeared to understand, but they'd left the subject alone. Possibly just as important was that she'd been able to refer to her own history, however obliquely. Walking back to the house with the dogs, she began to feel as normal as she could anymore.

"I like Barb a whole lot," she remarked. "Unfortunately, I barely remember her. I guess when I was in school, my life was busy revolving around other things besides my aunt's friends."

"Probably. That would be normal." As they turned onto her street, he said, "You have the information now. What are you going to do about it?"

"I don't know," she admitted. "I want to talk to Deborah Mixon, like I said. See if I can find out if our suspicions are true. I just haven't figured out how to approach her."

"It won't be easy," he remarked. "You don't want to share your secrets. But I wonder, Jenna, just what we'll do about it if we find out that girl was molested out there? Unless she's willing to talk about it with anyone but you, the information might be useless."

"Not useless," Jenna answered firmly. Determination kept growing in her, a kind of determination she hadn't felt in a while. "It'll tell us what Zeb's horrible secret was."

"True."

She felt him looking at her but didn't turn her gaze his way. Her heart had begun to beat more rapidly. What was she getting herself into?

"But it won't prove murder," Kell said.

No, it wouldn't. She eyed Bradley. All this because of one K-9. "I'm sorry, Kell, but I need to know if I can find out. Because if someone out there is molesting children, I'm going to find a way to rain hell on their heads."

"I'll rain it along with you."

"And this," she answered, "is a far better reason to try to investigate than those deaths. Despite your concern for Bradley."

"It was all about Bradley at first," he said. "Now it's something else entirely."

FINDING OUT WHERE Deborah Mixon lived was easy enough. An online phonebook provided the answer. She rented one of those apartments on the edge of town that were now being used mostly by the junior college as dorms.

The place had been built by a long-gone semiconductor plant that had promised to bring some real economic improvement to Conard County. Jenna remembered an influx of workers followed by the plant's shutdown and more economic despair. After only a couple of years, the newly arrived employees had drifted away, leaving the county in its long-term somnolence.

Boom and bust, an ugly cycle. A way of life in some places, like this one. Despite it, though, the town and ranches around survived, and some thrived.

The next afternoon, choosing a time when Deborah Mixon might be at home awaiting her daughter's return from school, Jenna set out in her aunt's car while Kell took the dogs to the agility course.

Feeling like she was about to stage an ambush, Jenna drove along familiar streets to the far reaches of the town where the junior college and apartment complex had brought a huge splash of modernism to the area. All of it built from concrete without even a nod to the area's earlier architecture, it might have been jarring, except that it stood by itself and didn't impinge on hundred-year-old houses.

The mental detour Jenna was taking annoyed her. She was trying not to think about the barriers she needed to pass once she met Deborah Mixon. It would have been nice to be able to phone ahead and set up a meeting, but Jenna figured it would be harder for Deborah to slam the door in her face than it would be for her to disconnect a phone call.

Or maybe not. Jenna sighed, wondering if she'd taken a nosedive off the edge of a cliff that had little to do with reality. But she had to try to find out the story. Had to know with as much certainty as she could that that cult wasn't abusing children behind its silent facade.

The mere idea sickened her, but it also made her angry, angrier than her own experience. She couldn't stand by as others had with *her*.

If that was what was going on at all.

She parked at the building that held Deborah Mixon's second-floor apartment. The entire complex seemed quiet except for music booming from another building. Most of the students must be on campus.

Feeling relieved that she wasn't going to be stared at curiously by a bunch of young people, she climbed the stairs and finally stood in front of Deborah's door. At that instant, she didn't know which she hoped for more: that Deborah and her daughter wouldn't be there or that they were.

At her knock, the door was opened by a woman who appeared to be in her late thirties. She wore jeans and a faded plaid shirt, a far cry from the drab dresses of the women of the cult. Her dark hair was pulled back in a severe ponytail, and her face seemed to be pinched, as if she'd seen too much and carried a huge burden.

"Can I help you?"

"Ms. Mixon? I'm Jenna Blair. I wondered if you could spare me a few minutes of your time."

The door started to edge closed. "I'm not buying anything."

"I'm not selling anything," Jenna said. She hesitated, then decided being straightforward might be the best way to go. "I think you and I, or your daughter, share an experience."

Deborah's thin eyebrows raised. "You left a church, too? So what?"

"That's not the experience I mean."

If it were possible, Deborah's face paled even more. "You… What makes you think you have a right to barge in here and ask about things that ain't none of your business?"

"I don't have the right," Jenna said quickly. "I know that. But if my suspicion is right, I want to find a way to see that it never happens again."

Deborah chewed her lip. "You don't know what you're talking about."

Jenna drew a deep breath and clenched her hands, drawing on what was left of her courage. "I was raped, Ms. Mixon, and nobody listened to me."

As the words left Jenna's mouth, she felt anxiety pour through her. Her legs weakened. God, had she just said that to a perfect stranger? Her deepest, darkest secret? Her biggest failure?

She almost turned away, fearing she had gone too far with this woman, then caught sight of a single tear running down Deborah's face.

After what felt like an age, the woman spoke. "You look ready to collapse. Come in."

Then she was inside, sitting on a battered couch that appeared to have passed through multiple charities. The apartment was tidy and smelled of baked goods.

"You need something to eat or drink?" Deborah asked as she wiped that one tear away with the sleeve of her shirt.

"I'll be okay," Jenna answered quietly, trying to still the hammering of her heart. "I've just… I never said that to a stranger before." Except for the officers who refused to believe her. *That* memory gave her heartburn but brought her strength back with a surge of anger.

She spoke again. "I'm so angry, Ms. Mixon. I'm angry all the time, and not just about being raped."

Deborah sank into a raggedly padded chair. "I...understand."

"Somehow I think you do," Jenna answered. "That's why I'm here. I know what it's like to have everyone turn on you."

Deborah nodded slowly. "Shunned."

"By people you should be able to trust." Heartburn was beginning to turn into nausea. At least part of her suspicion was correct. "Was that what happened to you, too?"

"My—" Deborah broke off sharply. "I can't talk about this."

"You don't have to. I just thought..."

Deborah's entire demeanor changed and her voice tightened. "Thought what? That sticking your nose in our business might make you feel better? Nothing's going to make you feel better, Jenna Blair. Nothing. Take it from me. I won't talk about it. Not about any of it. You should go. I never should have let you past my door."

"I'm sorry," Jenna said, understanding for the first time that she might have hurt this woman by coming here. Not giving her hope that something could be done but taking away a privacy that meant a whole lot to her.

And who should have understood that better? Jenna wondered as she walked away. She felt truly ashamed of herself.

KELL RETURNED WITH two happy and tired dogs shortly after Jenna got home. She sat at the kitchen table staring into space, wrapped in self-loathing. Kell had tried to warn her with his remarks, asking why Deborah Mixon should be any more willing to talk about her experience with a stranger than Jenna was. Kell had been right in more than one way.

She hardly paid attention as he gave the dogs water, started a pot of coffee brewing and came to sit with her.

"I take it you didn't have any luck?"

"Oh, I had luck all right." At last, a tear leaked out of her eye, and she dragged her gaze to his face. "I never should have gone, Kell. You were right."

"That she wouldn't talk to a stranger?"

"No. I'm so freaking ashamed of myself I can't stand it. I should have realized she might feel the same way *I* do. I can't bear to talk about what happened to me. You're the only person I told. I didn't even tell my *friends*, for God's sake. What I just did..." She shook her head and dashed away the tear even as more fell to join it. "I felt like a raw wound. I didn't want anyone to know. I should have guessed she would feel the same!"

He reached across the table and laid his fingers on her hand. "It was that bad?"

"Only in the way she looked at me. Only in the way she told me to keep my nose out of her business. I had no right to do what I did. Who am I to strip the scabs off her wounds? I just got so focused on how awful it might be that I forgot *she* was the one who was living it."

Kell squeezed her hand gently. The gesture felt so comforting that she turned her hand over and squeezed back. At some level, she had just astonished herself. But Kell was different. He was not other men.

"Don't be so hard on yourself, Jenna."

"Maybe I'm not being hard enough. I can't believe how selfish I've become. I was totally insensitive to what that woman might feel. Why? Do I think I can somehow dash in and make it all right? Nobody can do that."

He rose and went to get coffee for them. "I don't think you ever believed you could make it all right for her. But I *do* think we need to know something about what might be going on in that compound."

"That's what I was thinking about, but I failed to think about Deborah Mixon the person. Charging ahead with a single idea stuck in my head, and damn the consequences." She shook her head and wiped her face again, this time with a napkin from a small stack on the table. "You warned me. You asked me if I'd want to talk to a stranger about what happened to me. I didn't hear that question right. I thought I had an entrée with my own experience. That maybe we'd find common ground."

"That's not unreasonable."

She looked at him, her eyes feeling puffy. "Quit trying to make me feel better. I need to own up to this one before I go do it again to someone else. I have become so unbelievably self-centered!"

She turned her head a little and saw both dogs sitting near the table. No grins there, only droopy ears. "Now I've upset them, too."

"A pat will fix them. I wish it could be as easy for you."

"I bet you never did anything this thoughtless."

"I'm sure I have, being human and all that. What's more, the worst thing about thoughtlessness is that you often don't even know you've done it because nobody bothers to tell you."

She held out her hand to the dogs and scratched their ruffs. At once, their ears perked and they started smiling again. One wound patched. Maybe the only one she could.

"Let's go out to dinner," Kell suggested. "A change of scene might do us both some good."

Jenna shook her head. "I don't feel like it. I had my out-and-abouting between visiting Barb and my stupidity today. I want a nice dark hole."

"Okay. I'll run to the market and get us some subs. You might not believe it right now, but you're going to get hungry, and letting me loose in the kitchen might be an awful mistake."

"I've made enough of those for one day." She put her elbows on the table and at last lifted the cup of coffee he'd poured for her. A shaky sigh escaped her.

"Well," she said presently, "my thoughtlessness and meltdown aside, I *did* figure out that Deborah's daughter was the victim and that they were both shunned by that so-called community."

Kell swore. "That does it," he growled. "That bunch needs to be unmasked."

Hopelessness filled her. "But how?"

ACROSS TOWN, Deborah Mixon finally phoned the number she'd been given despite feeling hesitant. The number of a man who helped her and her daughter financially for the last month. The man who had promised to continue helping as long as she let him know if anything surrounding her daughter's experience happened.

"Vince?" she said shakily, still wondering how this man had found out what was behind her snatching her daughter from the Church of the Well-Lived. "A woman was here today asking about…what happened. She seemed kind enough but…"

The voice on the other end of the phone grew gentle. "That won't happen again. Tell me everything you know about her."

Chapter Thirteen

Three days later, during which she, Kell and the dogs had led what seemed like an ordinary life—too ordinary given what they now knew—the mail contained a letter.

That surprised Jenna. Her aunt paid her bills online or had set them up for autopay. The mailbox rarely contained anything except flyers, enough flyers to make her wonder about dead trees.

But this day it was different. She almost left the papers in the mailbox but thought how unkind it would be to the woman who delivered the mail, having to try to stuff the box with another pile of ads.

She had almost tossed the folded flyers and envelopes into the trash when she caught sight of hand-addressed envelope. She pulled it out, then searched the ads more carefully. Real estate agents, grocery stores, life insurance offers—even an ad from a mortuary. Wouldn't Bernice be delighted to see those?

She dumped everything into the trash except that one letter. She studied the envelope, postmarked Charleston, and wondered if her aunt had a friend who had moved out there. But no, it was addressed to Jenna.

Maybe one of her friends from the past? But all of them used email.

Curious, she opened the envelope and saw a folded

letter. Before she could pull it out, one small index card fell out of the envelope. The writing was in block letters and said only one thing:

DON'T INTERFERE.

After that, she forgot about the letter, and just stared at the card. Was it a threat?

At once she called Kell, who had somehow become her rock. He said he'd be right over.

JENNA HAD SOUNDED agitated on the phone, which worried Kell. All this time, she'd seemed to take most things with an air of detachment. That detachment had shattered a few times, but her call was unusual. Something was wrong.

He took Bradley with him, giving himself and the dog a bit of the running they both needed. Bradley was cheerful; Kell was not.

Jenna met him at the door with Misty at her side. Instead of letting the dogs go play, Kell brought Bradley inside with him.

"What's up?" he asked immediately. Jenna looked the same as she always did, except that her face had grown expressionless. The detachment had returned.

"I don't know." She shook her head. "I'm probably overreacting, but come into the kitchen. I have something to show you."

When he got there, he saw the envelope and the card on the table. Neither of them sat down. Jenna handed him the card.

He scanned it quickly. "What the hell?"

She shrugged. "Is it a threat?"

"Who can tell from this? And what are you interfering in?"

"I don't know." Then she held up the envelope and tugged the letter out of it. "I haven't read this yet, but maybe it has an answer."

It had more of an answer than either of them could have imagined.

Dear Vince,
I know it's been over ten years since you saw me, but you kept sending me birthday presents, so I'm sure you give a damn about me. I need to tell you what happened after the last time I saw you.

My stepfather, Aloysius Bund, pastor of the Church of the Well-Lived in Conard City, started abusing me when I was ten years old. I was terrified and ashamed, but I didn't know he was the one who was wrong.

The entire sordid story filled the two pages, written in an almost girlish hand. The two of them leaned over it, reading, then Kell scanned it a second time. "My God." He looked at Jenna and saw she was weeping silently.

"My God," she murmured shakily. "Oh my God. That poor girl…"

At last, her silent tears turned into sobs, and Kell didn't care what kind of risk he was taking. He took Jenna into his arms, hugging her, holding her while she cried her heart out. Holding her until her anguish subsided.

"Somebody needs to die for this," he said, his voice steely.

"Maybe two people already have," she choked out.

"I'm going to kill that bastard."

She eased away from him. "What? And ruin your own

life, too? We've got to take this to the sheriff. Maybe he can do something."

But Kell was having trouble getting a handle on himself. Jenna had cried, thank God, but he had no such relief. Disgust and fury roiled through him equally. He needed an outlet.

"Let's go," he said. "Now. Because if I don't do that I'm going to do something else. I swear, that man isn't fit to walk the face of this planet."

"I know," she said quietly. She grabbed a paper towel and wiped her face. "Okay, I'm ready."

He saw a new determination in her step as they set out without the dogs. Just a few blocks. Maybe just enough time to keep him from erupting. Maybe.

Jenna marched alongside Kell, feeling like part of a unit for the first time since...

She cut that off. She didn't need to be thinking about her past just then. She needed to be thinking about that godforsaken church and little girls. More than one little girl.

Gage was, as always, sitting behind a stack of papers and the computer on his desk.

"I never should have taken this damn job," he said as he waved them to seats.

"Why did you then?" Kell asked.

"Well, you see, there was the former sheriff, Nate Tate. Still known as the 'old sheriff' while I am still known as the 'new sheriff.' Regardless, that man is well loved in this county, and over my objections, he put me up for this job when he retired. I got elected only because of his endorsement, I'm sure. I didn't want to disappoint him, so here I sit pushing paper all day. What's up?"

"Jenna?" Kell said, looking at her.

She shook her head mutely. She couldn't bring herself

to talk about any of it, not her own experience, not the Mixon girl's experience, not about the horrifying letter. She was feeling raw again.

"Okay, I'll do my best," Kell said. "You know we never believed the Zeb and Hassen deaths were natural."

"I'm inclined to agree," Gage nodded. "But there's nothing in the tox results that would warrant an investigation because of their health problems."

"Right. So the two of us wanted to find a way behind the walls of that group. But we were getting nowhere until Jenna heard about the mother and daughter who fled the compound. That set her on fire, and I pretty much agreed with her suspicion."

"I can see why. I never thought about the two of them. Low on my radar. I mean, two people leave that church. Anything's possible and it's certainly not a crime."

Kell agreed. "I didn't much think about it either when Barb Traynor told me about it. I was picking her brain for some information about that group, and the Mixon woman and her child came up. That's when Jenna made up her mind to find out why the two of them had left."

Gage rocked his squeaky chair a couple of times. He looked at Jenna. "It was the daughter part that got your attention?"

"Yes," she answered firmly. "Apparently, they left the group with nothing but the clothes on their backs. I couldn't stop wondering what made them do that."

"Good question, now that you bring it up. So what next?"

Kell looked at Jenna, and she finally took over the discussion. "I visited Deborah Mixon to see if I could learn anything from her."

"Why should you learn any more than anyone else in this county?" Gage asked her.

Here was the moment she'd been dreading. She closed her eyes, wondering if she could spit out the words yet again. Knowing she had to for the sake of some young girls. For the sake of Deborah Mixon's daughter, who could never speak about it. She drew a deep breath, ignoring her hammering heart, and said, "I was raped, too. And nobody believed me. Ms. Mixon said that she and her daughter had been shunned."

"Shunned?" Gage repeated the word, raising the one brow that hadn't been stilled by the fire that had scarred his face. "Shunned?"

"That's the word she used." Jenna fought to calm herself but wasn't succeeding very well. All the feelings she'd just begun to deal with surged to the fore, nearly taking over. Her internal battle had freshened. No time for that now. "She sort of intimated that something had happened to her daughter. I just filled in a blank. I could have been wrong, except…" She couldn't continue. She looked at Kell.

He nodded to her and turned to the sheriff. "Then this, just three days later." He passed the envelope to Gage.

Gage took it and opened it, pulling the letter out and seeing the card flutter to his desktop. He picked up the card first, scanned it, then looked at Jenna. "This looks like a threat."

"Read the copy of the letter," Kell said.

Gage unfolded it, the expression on his face growing darker by the moment. Then he tossed it onto his desk and cursed a few unprintable words. "That poor girl. We were all stunned when she killed herself, but we all thought something had happened to her in the war. Evidently not."

He pulled a yellow tennis ball out of a mug on his desk and hurled it hard against the row of filing cabinets. It bounced off, then rolled across the floor. "That didn't help much," he remarked a minute later. "Nothing's going to help this one."

"Except rooting it out," Kell said.

Gage nodded, then looked at the letter. "Part of the worst of it is that I can't do anything about it."

Jenna stiffened, hearing in his statement something similar to what she had faced. Anger caused words to burst out of her. "Why not? How can you let this go on? How can *anyone* let this go on?"

Gage sighed heavily looking down at his desktop. "There's a difference between knowing something and having useful evidence. Horrible in this case. But what do we have here? A letter making a claim I can't substantiate. A woman and her daughter who should have filed a complaint so that I *could* do something about this. And a veiled threat from a person or persons unknown." He held up the envelope. "Nothing but a postmark. Useless. And even if we could find this guy, all he'd be able to do is repeat what's in this letter."

Gage dropped the envelope and steepled his hands. "I need to talk to the county attorney. See if she can figure a way around this. Something about dying utterances, maybe. But that still assumes Celia wasn't lying, which is what I might hear." He shook his head sharply. "Well, maybe there's one thing I can do right now."

"What's that?" Jenna asked, her hands still clenched until her nails bit into her palms.

"It's not much, but I can sure make these people feel uncomfortable when they show up in town."

"How?" Jenna demanded.

"Cops can stalk, you know." One corner of Gage's mouth lifted, but the expression wasn't humorous. "Perfectly legal for us to keep a close eye on people we believe are suspicious."

"Better than nothing," Kell remarked.

"Oh, much better," Gage said. "We can make them antsy as all hell."

When Jenna and Kell rose to leave, Gage said, "Jenna?"

She turned to look back. "Yes?"

"I'd thank you for your service, but I get the feeling you wouldn't appreciate that."

"You'd be right."

ON THE WALK BACK, Kell could tell that Jenna was fuming. Once inside the door, with the dogs dancing all around them, she asked, "What good is the law?"

"I can understand Gage's position."

"Yeah, no proof, no dice. You have to make a complaint. Well, where does that get you?"

Kell nearly winced. Inevitably, she headed for the kitchen. "I miss Bernice, but I'm glad she's not here. She'd know something was wrong with me, and she wouldn't let it go. I don't want her to be upset, too."

She pawed around in the refrigerator and came up with some sliced cheese and hard salami. She put them on a plate on the table, then sat, picking at them. "Help yourself."

While he liked cheese and salami, he also knew that was far from a balanced diet. But she was the nurse. He took a slice of cheese and wrapped it around a piece of salami.

Mostly he stared at her across the table. She was still angry, absorbed in her own thoughts. Then she looked up.

"I mean it, Kell. What good is the law? You go to someone with a legitimate complaint, and they want to see the evidence. If Deborah Mixon's daughter had complained, where would it have gotten her? Any witnesses are inside that compound and would probably have lied their heads off anyway. All she'd have done was lay herself bare. There'd be no justice. Her mother was right to keep it secret."

He remained silent, knowing she needed to rant. Hell, he wanted to rant, too, just differently. He knew what she was saying, though. Yeah, the law needed evidence, but too many women, even with the evidence, ran into a stone wall. Accusations that *they* must have done something wrong. Sneers and leers and whispers. Jenna must have faced that, too, along with the dismissal of her charges. Something like *her* claims wouldn't remain secret for long.

God Almighty.

She continued speaking, anger contained in every word, not even touching the food she'd put out. "So, now we know what Zeb's secret was. He was one of those who lied and stood aside. The world's full of them. And Celia…my God, Celia. To be betrayed not once but twice. It's no wonder she took her own life. How hopeless do you have to be?"

"That's pretty hopeless," he agreed cautiously. Part of him was glad Jenna was expressing herself so strongly, but the rest of him desperately wanted to pull her out of the pit she'd fallen into. The only thing he could do now, however, was let her blow off that head of steam that had probably been growing inside her for some time.

For a long moment she didn't say anything though. Finally, pushing the plate of cheese and meat to one side, she said, "This is ironic."

"What is?"

"That I came all the way home to nurse my wounds,

and I run into two other cases that aren't so very different. Except the two of them were children."

She looked down at the table, her cheek resting in her hand. "There's the law and then there's justice. Aren't they supposed to be the same thing?"

For that, he had no answer.

LATER, KELL TOOK the matter of dinner into his own hands again. Jenna had never touched that cheese and salami, and he began to wonder if she'd been eating much at all since her visit with Deborah Mixon. He hadn't been hitting Maude's to feed her, hadn't seen her eat anything at all in his presence. Nothing but coffee. She *must* have eaten something, but probably not enough.

She was seated on the front porch in the fading evening light, watching the dogs sniff around the front yard.

"Have you been eating, Jenna?"

"Yeah."

"How much?"

Her green eyes sparked. "Are you my nanny?"

"I'm your friend, and I've been watching your anger and adrenaline bounce up and down. You need some calories to fuel yourself if you're going to keep on doing that."

"Just don't tell me to let go of it."

"No way. You'll let go when *you're* ready and not before. In the meantime…have you heard that combat troops lose weight?"

"Probably from all that lousy food."

He pulled a smile. "That may be part of it. But part of it could be living on adrenaline. Look at you. You're losing weight since I first met you, and that's the last thing you need to do. Regardless, tell me what you'll eat. If it comes out of a freezer case or a can, I'm your man. Otherwise, I'll go visit Maude."

Her gaze lost its edge. "How about that pizza place on the edge of town?"

"We'd be better off doing frozen pizza. Trust me. If that sounds good, I'll go get some. What do you like on it?"

"Everything."

Mindful of the subtle threat that note conveyed, before Kell departed, he left Bradley on guard with the signal to watch the area. The dog's eyes brightened and he stood a little taller, glad of work to do. Amazing pooch.

Running to the store was the easy part. While he was there, he hunted up a few other things that might tempt her, such as fruit. He was sure he'd seen her buy some frozen broccoli but doubted she'd tossed it in the microwave yet.

In fact, he was starting to become genuinely concerned about her health. She clearly was still bathing and wearing clean clothes, but her other self-care also seemed to be diminishing.

But how could he blame her? She'd been slammed into two stories not unlike her own. The universe had an odd sense of humor if it had one at all.

His concern, unfortunately for him, was beginning to exceed simple friendship. As if she'd want anything more.

But he was no less concerned than she about what had happened to those two girls. About the fact that a pedophile had safely ensconced himself behind a wall of true believers.

He just wished he could figure out how to get to that man. There was no telling how much harm he'd already done, but he shouldn't be allowed to do any more.

Kell looked up at the heavens as he reached Jenna's

yard. "I suppose I shouldn't wish for a thunderbolt?" But he'd seen enough death and destruction to feel there was nothing wrong in wishing for one. Even praying for one.

ALLOYSIUS BUND STOOD holding another letter in his hand. The hand shook as he read it.

> *I know Celia wasn't your only victim. Ready to pay the price?*

But how was this possible? He was sure he had silenced Deborah Mixon and her daughter. Not a peep had escaped them since they left his church, and he was certain the other members didn't believe anything they might have heard. Not about *him*.

He'd threatened Mixon with photos he'd taken of that girl naked. Just her. He wasn't in any of them. Anyone could have taken those photos.

Still trembling, he retrieved his cell phone, the only one allowed in his church, and deleted every photo he had of the Mixon girl. No evidence. None.

Still frightened but feeling a little better, he put the phone away. If Mixon decided to start gabbing despite the photos, there'd be no proof of anything. Who'd believe her at this late date anyway?

And Mixon would never know the photos were gone, that he wasn't still hanging them over her daughter's head. No, she hadn't talked and wouldn't talk.

It was an idle threat. It had to be. He burned the note over the sink in his bathroom, watching ashes fall into the running water.

His acolytes—sheep, every one of them—understood that he must be protected at all costs. He was their way to a better eternity. Their *only* way.

Satisfied at last, he left his private rooms to join his flock for their afternoon dose of the truth according to Pastor Bund.

Because if there was one thing he'd figured out about the human race, it was that a large number of people wanted all decisions taken out of their hands. Wanted to lay all those burdens on other shoulders and simply follow. Wanted someone else to do their thinking and show them the way. The easy way.

The way that had made him successful enough to have all this. He just needed to refresh the teaching often.

Chapter Fourteen

The meal of pizza worked well enough. Kell would have liked to see Jenna eat more than two slices, would have preferred to get the feeling that she was enjoying it rather than that she was eating only to satisfy him.

Whatever worked. He was past hoping for more.

Possibly the only thing that would work was a plan to take down that pastor and his group.

One of his purchases had been a couple of pints of ice cream. He didn't wait long to pull one out of the freezer and place it before her with a spoon. Calories if not nutrition.

"If you don't like chocolate, I also bought coffee."

"Chocolate is good. I can't possibly eat all of this, Kell."

"Then eat only as much as you want."

She looked from the ice cream to him and said, "Nanny." But this time, her eyes didn't spark. They even looked faintly amused. "You expect me to eat it out of the carton?"

"I hear that's the best way."

She sighed and scraped some ice cream off the top, pausing with it halfway to her mouth. "I'll get past this, Kell."

"Yes, you will. You're a strong woman. But it might be difficult for a little while."

"But ice cream? Not healthful."

"Feed your face, damn it. You're getting to the point where you'll blow away in the next breeze."

"Not likely." But the ice cream reached her mouth, shortly followed by another spoonful. "I'm having some trouble absorbing all of this. Sitting on my hands isn't helping one little bit."

"I hear you. I feel the same. But we can't do anything without a plan of action."

Which was, right now, the very heart of the problem. Whatever was going on in that church seemed to be silencing people. Assuming they even knew for certain what had happened to the Mixon girl. So how to get to Bund?

Jenna spoke as she finished half the ice cream. "My waistline is going to hate you."

"Your body is going to love me for the extra energy."

That drew a faint smile from her. She rose and put the remaining ice cream away. "I wish I didn't feel so much despair."

"It feels like a despairing situation right now. I've spent days trying to figure out what either of us can do. What we both might do."

"Me too, when I haven't been drowning in shame and self-pity. I shouldn't be feeling self-pity, should I? I loathe that."

"I think you're entitled to some."

"It's useless," she argued. "Feeling sorry for myself isn't going to fix anything, least of all myself. As for those girls…" She trailed off, shaking her head.

Then she shocked him all the way to his toes.

"I need a hug, Kell."

He froze for an instant. "Are you sure?"

She nodded, looking so sad and alone. He rose and approached her carefully. Dangerous territory. He'd been trying not to think about how attractive she was, about what he'd like to do with her if she weren't so damaged. She likely had no idea of how sexy she was, of how much he could want her.

The lens through which she was seeing herself had become all distorted because of all the horror she was dealing with. Her visit to Deborah Mixon hadn't helped her in the least. It had merely freshened her own situation and increased her self-disgust.

He slipped his arms around her slowly, giving her the chance to tell him to go to hell. She didn't. Instead, she melted into him with a sigh.

He just hoped his body would behave. It sure didn't want to, not with her so close.

After a minute or so, he felt her arms rise and wrap around his waist, returning his hug. He closed his eyes against a surge of desire so powerful it almost overcame him. Wrong time. All she sought was comfort. He needed to focus on that, focus on the fact that, perhaps, that was what *he* really needed just then.

There weren't words for this situation, although he and Jenna had tried just about all of them. None were sufficient. Not even close.

Eventually, he cleared his throat and in an act of preservation for them both, he said, "Jenna, unfortunately, this hug is making me aware of just how much I want you." Feeling her soft against him, feeling her breasts press into him, was making him as hot as hell.

He felt her stiffen against him and hoped he hadn't driven her into emotional flight. But she didn't pull away and gradually relaxed.

"It's okay," she murmured presently. "It's okay."

It was okay with her that he was holding her like this? That he wanted her? Another trickle of shock poured through him.

Then he worried where this might take them. If he allowed this to go any further, to head toward full-blown desire, what if she went along and then hated herself all over again?

"Jenna…"

She moved against him, just a little. "Kell, I need to know."

"So you want to use me?" He was suddenly torn between amusement and irritation.

He felt her head move as if she were looking at him now. He was afraid to return her gaze. He might lose it all if he saw real hunger in her face.

"Not *use* you. I need to know if I can still be normal, or if I'm twisted out of all shape. But it's not just that. Much as I've been burying the feeling, I want you, too. And I trust you."

Oh, God, the dam was breaking. He could feel his struggle to protect her losing to his desire for her.

"Jenna…" Another moment without words. She trusted him? Oh, man. Did he deserve that?

"Kell, please."

His jaw tightened. "Promise me."

"What?"

"That you'll stop this at any point you begin to feel uncomfortable. That you won't let me do anything you don't want."

"I can do that."

"And promise me that, no matter what, you won't hate me." Now he was looking straight at her, his heart pounding, his body surging. He saw her desire there, a desire he feared almost as much as he feared himself.

Her green gaze held his. "I promise." Nothing tentative in her voice, in her posture. This woman had made up her mind.

Giving in at last to hammering need, he bent and lifted her into his arms. "If you weighed any more, I wouldn't be able to do this caveman thing."

To his amazement, a tiny laugh escaped her. "Am I allowed to enjoy it?"

"Enjoy it," he told her firmly as he carried her from the kitchen. "As much as you want."

He didn't attempt the stairs. Instead, he carried her into Bernice's ground-floor bedroom and laid her gently on the bed.

"It occurs to me," he said as he began tugging off his shirt, "that once we get going, I might find it extremely difficult to stop. So be very, very sure."

"I'm sure."

Judging by the way she was looking at him, her eyes heavily lidded and her lips parted on rapid breaths, she meant it.

He let his urges take over. In any way humanly possible, he was going to make this a great experience for her.

He never wanted her to stop wanting him. Never.

JENNA FELT HER own desire growing, a hunger she hadn't experienced in so long that she felt almost like a stranger to herself. It was a good feeling, though, one she didn't want to face the future without. She needed this exploration into lost feelings, needed to find a future Jenna. Needed to know that she hadn't been ruined forever.

As she watched Kell remove his clothes, slowly as if giving her time to change her mind, she allowed herself to see how magnificent he was. Took in the scars that riddled his side and one of his legs. Near death once, saved by Bradley. She was so grateful to Bradley.

But scars or not, Kell was a magnificent man. She'd guessed he would be, even fully clothed, but now she saw him without any disguise and admired the breadth of his shoulders, his narrow waist and his finely shaped legs that came from endless miles of walking and running. Perfect.

Exquisite tingles ran through her nerve endings to pool between her thighs. Her skin had grown so sensitive that the merest brush of air felt pleasurable. But she needed more, so much more.

"Kell," she murmured when still he hesitated, standing over her.

"Be sure," he said in a roughened voice. "For God's sake, Jenna, be sure."

In answer, she sat up, although desire weakened her and reached for the hem of her sweatshirt. Kell bent, brushing her hands aside and pulling the shirt over her head. She wore no bra and her nipples hardened in the cool air.

"Damn, you're beautiful," he said. "Perfect."

She doubted it, but the doubt vanished before his heavily lidded gaze. Those gray eyes of his had darkened, grown totally intent on her. He saw only her. More pleasure.

He gently nudged her back and reached for the snap on her jeans. As they slid away along with her undies, a soft moan escaped her. All of a sudden, she didn't want gentleness or slowness.

She needed him. *Now!*

"Kell. Hurry. Please hurry."

He hesitated only a moment, sweeping his gaze over

her naked body, then slowly lowered himself until he covered her with his heat. His warmth. Burying her in his weight, a weight that felt marvelous.

"So good," she whispered, struggling for air.

"I want to take my time," he said roughly.

"Next time. Not now. Please not now."

The only thing that existed for her was his erection, gently throbbing against her own throbbing center. She wanted him inside her. Needed him inside her.

Needed to prove to herself that she could.

KELL WAS AMAZED by Jenna's response, but amazement took a far back seat to the hunger that swamped him. When he tried to raise himself on his elbows to kiss her neck, to fondle her breasts with his tongue, she seized his shoulders and pulled him back onto her.

"Fill me now," she demanded, her voice taut. "Now."

Raising his hips, he obliged, sinking into her silky depths, savoring the welcome he found there.

Then everything vanished except two bodies rising and falling on waves that grew stronger and stronger. Overpowering. Driving. An aching need so strong it almost hurt.

Higher. Higher. He wanted her on that peak with him.

Then he heard her cry, felt her body stiffen, then relax, trembling. Only then did he jet into her, feeling his heat join with her own.

They had arrived together.

ALL TOO SOON, but longer than it seemed, Kell rolled off Jenna. She wanted to cry out at the loss, but he didn't move far. Just far enough to tug an end of the comforter over her. Just far enough that he could draw her into the welcome circle of his arms. She threw her leg over his, opening herself if he wanted to touch her, expressing her trust.

Because she trusted him when she had believed she would never trust again.

Beneath the covers, his warm hand caressed her back.

"You're a firecracker," he said after a bit.

She snorted a laugh. "Who, me? Hardly."

"Let me be the judge of that. You wanted fast. I wanted faster."

That time, a giggle bubbled up in her. "That could be debatable."

"No debate. A waste of time." He paused. "You said *next time*?"

"I did. I meant it." That was true. She wanted a next time with him. Many of them.

"But I didn't even get a chance to amaze you with my foreplay."

This time she laughed out loud, a feeling almost as good as the sex they had just enjoyed.

"God, I love that sound," he said, bringing his hand around to cup her cheek and caress it with his thumb. "Never stop laughing, Jenna."

"I'd almost forgotten how," she admitted. "But it sure feels good." She paused, her cheeks heating. "It was wonderful, Kell. Wonderful."

"I thought so, too." He hugged her tighter, then his stomach growled loudly. "I could stay like this forever. But damn it, Jenna, I'm getting hungry. That measly pizza wasn't enough. I'm going to run out and get us something. I won't be long."

He rose, pulling on his clothes. "Breakfast?"

She glanced at the clock. "Where did the time go? But it's too early for breakfast, isn't it?"

"Well, then, dinner?"

She only had to think for a second or two. "Breakfast," she decided. "But where are you going to find it?"

"Hasty's Diner at the truck stop. When I get back, I'll give the dogs a short walk."

"I can do that," she answered, rising into the cool night air."

"Then I'm off."

The house felt so empty when he left. Jenna sighed, her mind trying to remember every single instant of their hurried lovemaking, to engrave it in the forefront of her mind, a barrier to the past.

Both Bradley and Misty were eager to get out into the yard. Because of Bradley, Jenna let Misty go unleashed. She'd seen Kell tell his K-9 to stay on guard. That was almost as good as having Kell here.

But as she stood in the chilly night air, wrapped in her jacket, she felt the shadows around her darkening. Threats permeated the night, though not threats against her.

Unless you counted that brief note.

Don't interfere.

The accompanying letter from Celia made the reference clear, but what would the writer do if he felt they were interfering?

That alone was cause for worry. Looking around, she felt old fears resurge. The night had always held the worst threats in the war. And later to her rape and the threats made against her after her charge was laid.

She shivered and called the dogs. They came immediately, and she was glad to close the door behind her. To shut out the night.

She gave both dogs some biscuits and watched them gobble the treats down and head for the water bowl. Simple needs. She wished hers were as simple.

Although, she'd just satisfied a simple need that had

become another threat to her. Despite everything, a smile came to her face and lingered. Kell.

She'd been fortunate enough to meet a marvelous man when she hadn't wanted one at all. She ought to be grateful rather than fearful now.

Inevitably, however, her thoughts returned to Celia's letter and to the Mixon question. Ghastly. For some things, there could be no forgiveness.

She didn't doubt that Bund had parlayed his authority as a pastor to carry out his appalling deeds. Did that make it worse? Could anything make pedophilia worse?

In most cases, an authority figure was involved in taking advantage of a child. Maybe it was worse in the case of a religious leader because of where they supposedly stood in the moral hierarchy. Others used other kinds of authority. And then there were threats and terror.

But in the end, weren't they all the same?

She was relieved when she heard Kell return. Her thoughts were spiraling again and getting her nowhere useful. Unless they could find a way to get at Bund, he'd continue. There might even now be another child he was molesting.

Kell came in carrying bags. "Hasty's the fastest short-order cook in this county. Also, about the best. Anyway, we've got scrambled eggs, sausage, home fries, some pancakes and hash browns. Not to mention cinnamon rolls and some Danish."

That list startled her. "Um, wow. That's enough for half the town."

"Just eat what appeals to you. Since I didn't ask, I wanted to make sure I got a variety."

He certainly had. The dogs, who had been watching with interest, now came over to sniff. Kell spread foam containers across the table and opened them. "Should I make coffee?"

"If you expect me to eat anything sweet."

"Consider it done." He went to the counter and started the coffee, then grabbed plates and utensils for them. As he returned to the table, he said, "I've been sharing my grub with Bradley for years. I suppose you don't want me to get Misty into the habit of licking plates or eating tidbits."

"I've been doing it too, even though I doubt Aunt Bernice would appreciate it."

"Those begging eyes have won many a battle."

She smiled. Lord, that man made her want to smile. A pleasant shiver ran through her as she looked at him. Maybe she had some good luck after all.

KELL FELT GOOD watching Jenna eat, this time with evident hunger and enjoyment. One battle won, at least temporarily.

He understood her reaction to learning that Bund was even worse than they had suspected. Bund certainly had a motive for murder.

After finishing a roll, Jenna got herself some fresh coffee. "You?" she asked Kell, holding up the pot in his direction.

"Please."

But then they sat face-to-face again and he watched the change come over her. She was thinking about Celia and the Mixon girl again.

"Kell?"

"Hmm?" He braced himself, afraid he might see her sink into the pit again.

"We've got to get that man as soon as possible. What if he goes after Deborah Mixon and her daughter? What if I'm responsible for them getting murdered?"

Chapter Fifteen

Kell left the food on the table, not caring if the dogs got into it. He picked Jenna up and carried her to bed. She wore flannel pajamas, so it was easy to tuck her under the covers. He took less than a minute to strip and join her.

Then he hugged her tight, having no other answer to her question. God, he had to find a way to put an end to this nightmare. Soon. As fast as possible.

But with Bund behind the walls of his faithful, he couldn't think of a way. Regardless, suspicious as they were, they couldn't be sure Bund was the murderer. It was all circumstantial.

Deborah Mixon and her daughter had remained silent all this time. Why would Bund even suspect they had talked or might talk?

And how could Bund arrange visits to the Mixons now? Unlike Zeb and Hassen, who had remained members of his church, the Mixons had clearly left months ago.

Unless someone had given Bund the idea. But who would be foolhardy enough to plant that kind of seed?

When the morning began to creep into the house, Kell was still holding Jenna as close as he could. At last, she had fallen asleep.

Sleep eluded him but he hardly noticed. He'd gone without sleep on countless occasions. One night would hardly make a difference.

THE PHONE CALL came as the sun was rising. Deborah Mixon answered it. Since Vince had told her he'd take care of the matter, Deborah had been living on tenterhooks, grabbing the phone every time it rang. She knew Bund was still out there. That whole damn cult was still out there. And Bund had the photos. He could ruin her daughter's life forever.

God, she wished she'd never let that woman cross her threshold. Only Jenna Blair's obvious distress, her ashen face, had caused Deborah to act out of sympathy. Even when she said she'd suffered the same experience.

Oh sweet Lord, she hadn't even been able to get counseling for her daughter. Hadn't been able in any way to let the story creep out. Her heart was broken. Each day, in every way, she failed the girl even though she appeared to have mostly recovered.

But Deborah wasn't sure how deep that recovery went, and she knew Bund's actions would plague Leah for the rest of her days. Some scars never went away. They only got easier to live with.

But that now familiar voice greeted her. She didn't know whether to be glad or not. She lived in the constant fear that another bad thing was about to happen.

"Vince," she replied, now wide awake, sitting on the edge of her bed.

"I want you and your daughter to leave town for a while."

Deborah's heart nearly stopped. "Why?" she whispered.

"Two people are poking the hornet's nest. I can't stop

them. I'm not even sure anymore that I want to. So pack your bags and take a trip. Anywhere. Don't tell anyone; just go. I'll wire extra money to cover it."

When she didn't answer, he said, sounding like steel, "Promise me, Deborah. One way or another, matters are coming to a head, and I want you and Leah out of the way. Promise."

"I promise."

"Get going."

Click.

Deborah stared at her phone as it beeped, the red sign telling her the call had been disconnected. She rose and got started.

AT THE CHURCH of the Well-Lived, one woman stood staring out a window at the brightening day. She lived in constant anxiety now. It was wearing her down.

But she'd done it. Although she'd been forbidden to do it, a few months ago she'd answered the phone at the Hassen house because it rang so persistently. When that voice over the phone had promised money for information, she hadn't been able to resist. She wanted to flee, but the voice had told her not to, or all that money would disappear. Her escape money, the only money she had in the whole world. Sitting in an account she couldn't access unless he told her how.

She'd been at Lydia Hassen's house, doing her frequent task of caring for the woman, increasingly hoping that she wouldn't spend her last days the way Miss Hassen was. Cared for, to be sure, but otherwise friendless except for the visits by Pastor Bund.

Pastor Satan.

And then the voice, the promise.

She'd guessed why the Mixons had fled in the dark

of night. She suspected many had guessed, but none had spoken. Spoken of what? None knew for sure, and only Eliza had believed it was possible. For that reason she had stayed silent.

But the man who had phoned had only wanted to know about the Mixons. He'd heard they left the church and wanted her to tell him why.

She'd voiced her suspicion then. Desperate to get it off her chest, where it weighed as heavily as a boulder, she was relieved when she did.

But now she had to wonder what would happen if Bund found out. The possibilities that began to fill her mind were scary. The man had total control of the lives here.

Only when the Mixons fled with nothing did she begin to doubt her devotion. Those doubts had grown like a seed taking root, wrapping tightly around her heart until it fractured.

She began to see herself as a woman who'd been terribly deluded. She vowed to never again be deluded in this way.

But vows weren't getting her out of this mess.

GAGE DALTON WASN'T sleeping well. Since Celia's letter. Since the information about the Mixons. His hands were tied by the law, but for once, he hated the law.

Emma, his wife, had begun to fuss over him.

"It's the pain," he'd said. "It'll go away. It always gets better." Pain, the signature note of his life, brought on by a car bomb that had killed his first wife and his small children, a bomb intended for him while he'd been undercover for the DEA.

The loss had torn him up. The pain of the burns and

injuries seemed like a small price to pay for what he had brought on his family.

But then he'd met Emma, and rays of happiness had broken through the cold, dark hell he had lived in. She brought him back to life.

And now she was worried. He hated that.

"The doctor should be able to give you something," she had argued more than once.

And more than once, he'd answered, "Not these days. Anyway, I couldn't work if I was drowsy."

"Then retire, damn it!"

His burn-scarred face had quirked into his half smile. "She still won't be able to prescribe anything. Relax, darlin'. I always get better."

He was sure she hadn't relaxed, but she didn't keep pressing him.

So he stood staring out at the brightening day after another restless night. Maybe he should try to sleep in Justin's old room so he wouldn't disturb Emma. Their son had long since moved on to a life elsewhere. They'd kept the bedroom for when he and his wife visited, but it could double as a bolt-hole. Or as could any of the rooms in this big old house. Emma had once rented out those rooms. Rented one to him.

He sighed. God, there had to be a way.

ON THE EAST COAST SOMEWHERE, Vince stared at the phone. He'd gotten the Mixons out of the way of whatever might be coming. That was one good thing.

The only good thing. That woman, Jenna Blair, and her friend, Kell McLaren, were still nosing around. Nothing overt, but he still had a few tentacles in that damn county. Blair and McLaren had taken the letter and his warning to the sheriff. He had gotten the measure of those two then. They wouldn't let go. Another warning would be useless.

He'd already warned Bund, though. Twice. The guy had to be sweating bullets. He wanted the man to sweat. Rattle his comfortable cage. And that was only the beginning.

He'd planned to sweat the guy a while, then have him taken to pieces. Those two busybodies might beat him to the punch.

Maybe he'd just let them run a while. Why not? They were bound by the law, but Vince wasn't. He'd been on the wrong side of that particular street for a dozen years now.

So he could let Bund keep sweating while he kept an eye on it.

For now.

The landline phone rang and he answered it. A familiar voice said, "Amigo."

"Carlos. How goes it?"

"Muy bueno."

The shipment was on its way to its destination. *Muy bueno* indeed. The two of them chatted for a while about families and kids neither of them had, then disconnected.

But then he stared at the phone again and thought about Celia. About how much he wanted payback.

IT WAS POSSIBLE, it was always possible, to find a way around obstacles, Kell thought as he and Jenna walked the dogs. "You know," he said after a bit, "maybe we need to keep an eye out for Bund."

"How? He only ever came out of that compound to visit Zeb or Hassen."

"They've been emptying out Zeb's house bit by bit. If

they don't find what they're looking for, the man himself might show up."

"Then we attack him on the street?"

Kell chuckled a bit. "No. But you remember what Gage said about making them antsy? Bradley could do a good job of that."

"To what end? Bund just goes back behind his walls."

"With something to worry about."

"And then?"

"I'll get to that. Soon, I hope."

Jenna sighed. "It's an impossible situation."

"Nothing's impossible. The only thing lacking is imagination. Cut your brain loose, Jenna. You've got a good one. Stop looking at the obstacles as insurmountable. We've both been guilty of that."

"Reluctantly, I admit you're right."

"Only reluctantly?"

She gave a quiet laugh. "I hate to be wrong."

"We're not going to be wrong about this one. When we move, we'll do it right."

BY LATE THAT DAY, word had gotten around town that the Mixons had left early that morning. Chins wagged as people wondered if they'd taken advantage of Good Shepherd. But no. The people who'd seen them leaving said they only packed a couple of suitcases in the trunk. Must just be a trip, and didn't they deserve to have a good time?

Kell and Jenna heard about it from Barb as they were walking the dogs one final time for the day. When Barb waved them up to her porch, they joined her and the kids for some of her patented lemonade. Both dogs and kids were happy to romp on what the summer had left of the lawn.

"You were curious about the Mixons," Barb said while they sat on the webbed lawn chairs. "They left early this morning. Two suitcases, so folks figure they went on a vacation."

Kell and Jenna's eyes met.

"A few not-so-nice people think they just took advantage of Good Shepherd Church and moved on, like they did from that crazy compound." She eyed them both. "I don't think that's true at all. If they're running, and I'm not saying they are, they're scared."

Without saying anything about the Mixons, Jenna and Kell carried on with casual chat about kids, dogs and Bernice. They stayed a while, then returned to the dog walk.

"God, they must be afraid." Jenna's shoulders sagged. "I did that to them."

"You didn't give them the reason they're afraid in the first place."

"I didn't need to go over there. I didn't need to *know*."

"You needed to find out if our speculation was right. To know the magnitude of that man's crimes. It was a real propellant, wasn't it? It kicked us into high gear."

"I don't see any high gear right now."

Neither did he, but he was damn well going to find one. Or she was. He was sure she was more inventive than she realized. All those times in a field hospital, she must have been inventive in her attempts to save lives. Some of the best advances in emergency medicine had come out of those hospitals.

"You know," he said presently, "if Bradley alerts to Bund…"

"We'll know he murdered Zeb?"

"That's my thought. One question answered."

"Then let's start our search."

"I don't want you there, Jenna. Because I don't want him to recognize you if we need you to do something later."

He saw her jaw set stubbornly and waited for an argument. It never came. After a bit, she squared her shoulders. "You're probably right."

THEY MADE LOVE again that night. This time was slower, at first, a languorous, gentle pas de deux. He worshipped every bit of her with his hands, mouth and tongue, and she reciprocated with an abandon that delighted him.

But then the tenor changed, becoming almost ferocious when they could dally no longer. It was a night Kell would never forget.

But later, as they lay hugging, his mind returned to working the problem.

All well and good to want to keep Jenna out of sight so Bund wouldn't recognize her if… If what?

He wished he had an answer to that, because there was a truly troubling problem staring him in the face.

Don't interfere.

What exactly did that mean? Was it a threat to do harm? Was Jenna at risk?

If he followed through on his plan to keep her out of his and Bradley's little expedition, he'd have to leave her alone and unprotected. He didn't doubt for a minute that Misty would protect Jenna with every cell in her loving, loyal body, but would that be enough?

What if this guy was violent? What if Jenna's visit to the Mixons had alerted him that she wasn't backing away? What if he decided that her interference was a threat of some kind to him?

They were hunting an enemy, but how many? Did this guy even qualify as an enemy? And how the hell had he known that Kell and Jenna were poking their noses into the two deaths?

That letter from Celia, though, seemed to indicate they were all on the same path. So why that talk of not interfering? Did this guy have some kind of plan already in place, one that he didn't want blown up?

Possible. But impossible to know the extent of the threat he might be.

Ah, hell.

Staring into the dark, his mind spiraling uselessly around the same problems, he wondered if he should just let the unknown correspondent take care of the matter.

But he knew he couldn't. What might be happening over in that compound since the Mixons had fled it? They had to find a way to stop it, to prevent it happening in the future. Some way to expose Bund for the creep he was.

Once again the urge to kill rose like bile in his throat. He was capable of it. War had taught him that. He knew a dozen ways to do it. Training and experience had taught him that.

He could just march out there, knock aside all those namby-pamby followers and grab Bund by the throat. That would be satisfying.

But it would solve nothing. He'd become the criminal, and Bund would never be proved to be the murderous, thuggish pedophile he was.

Chapter Sixteen

In the morning, Kell had reached a few conclusions, which he discussed with Jenna over a breakfast of oatmeal and orange juice.

"I hate oatmeal," he remarked.

She looked up. "Why didn't you say so?"

"Why should I? I've eaten a lot of things I hate over my years with Uncle Sam's Misguided Children."

"I never heard that one before." A smile leavened her face.

"Plenty of wags in a barracks. USMC was too good to leave alone, I guess. Everyone in the Corps has heard it."

"Any others?"

"None that are repeatable in polite company." He ate another few spoonfuls of oatmeal, hoping he didn't gag on the gelatinous consistency. Then it was time to dive in.

"I've been thinking."

She shook her head a little. "Who hasn't?"

"Thanks. And here I thought I was doing something remarkable."

Another small laugh escaped her. He wished he could pull a full-throated belly laugh out of her. Someday he would. He made himself that promise.

"Anyway..." he continued, dragging out the word in a long-suffering tone, bringing another smile to her face.

"Anyway," he continued more briskly, "we need Bradley to tell us if Bund was the scent that disturbed him about those two bodies. And not only to justify our suspicions."

She nodded, pushing aside her oatmeal bowl. "We need to know what he's capable of."

"Exactly. Just how much of a threat is he to the Mixons?"

"They left," she reminded him.

"I'm not just talking about them. There are others in his congregation. Is he willing to murder them, too? Regardless, we've got to find a way to cut him out of his herd before he can kill again. Or pull a Jonestown."

"I agree. But since we haven't found a way to get to him yet, I'm not sure that's a primary consideration. At least not now." She lifted her coffee mug.

"No, but we're going to formulate a plan. You know it and I know it. Neither of us is going to let this continue. But first we need to know the dimensions of the threat Bund poses so we can plan accordingly. Minimal casualties."

"Zero casualties," she corrected.

"Couldn't agree more." He looked at Bradley, who was curled up with his snout between his paws, watching them. Misty was sound asleep. "You know, buddy, you'd better live up to your reputation because I am trusting you to smell the truth."

"And if he does but we don't like it?"

Kell looked at Jenna. "Then we'll probably keep on wondering if those two deaths were murders, suspicious or not."

She poured them both more coffee and sat again. "So how are we going to do this?"

"I'm going to take Bradley with me and we're going to park on my front porch until that son of a gun shows up."

"But?" she asked. "I hear a *but* in there."

He knew he was about to irritate her, but there was no way to avoid it. "I'm thinking that I don't like leaving you here alone."

"Because of that note?"

"Because of that note."

She just shook her head. "If it was a threat, someone would have acted on it by now. Anyway, are you telling me you don't think I can take care of myself?"

There it was, the green fire sparking in her gaze. Yeah, he'd annoyed her. "I'm not saying that at all." Although he guessed he was.

"Then just what the hell *are* you saying, Kell? You know where I've been. I resent the hell out of the implication that I'm just some dame who needs protecting."

"Dame? Did you just use that word? You've been reading too many hard-boiled mysteries."

"I'm past the damsel in distress age." But one corner of her mouth lifted.

Skated past that one, Kell. Mostly. "Look, I'm a Marine. We don't leave our buddies hanging out there all alone. This has nothing to do with your capabilities. It has everything to do with my feelings about right and wrong." That was definitely true.

The fire in her eyes faded, becoming gentler. "Okay, I can accept that. But I'll be fine on my own. I'm sure Misty is a good security alarm. If anything's up, I'll get plenty of warning."

"Okay, then. I'm going back to my place for a stakeout. You know how to reach me if you find out anything."

She nodded. "Now get going. I want us to take this bastard down."

BACK AT HIS own place, Kell watched from the front porch until a car pulled up across the street in front of the Zeb house. And who should emerge but the man himself. Portly, looking entirely too successful compared to his followers. Wearing a knee-length black coat like a message.

"It's time, pal," Kell said to Bradley. "Hang on just a minute."

Inside, he opened the hall closet and took out Bradley's K-9 vest. The dog hadn't worn it since his discharge, wasn't entitled to wear it now. Kell held it for a few moments, hoping like hell it wouldn't awaken bad memories in Bradley.

But it was a damn good intimidation factor. The door was open, Bradley still obediently waiting outside. Kell gave a quiet whistle and Bradley trotted in to sit before him.

Those damn brown eyes were so trusting. Kell came close to hating himself as he held out the vest.

Bradley shoved his nose forward, sniffing at it. But he didn't run. He didn't express any kind of fear. He rose to his feet and stood waiting for the vest.

"Time to mount up, big guy."

And Bradley wagged his tail.

A FEW BLOCKS AWAY, Jenna paced the house. Misty gave up following her and laid down, snout between her paws, watching Jenna's show of agitation.

Call him if she found out anything? How the hell was she going to find out anything cooped up in this house? She'd so studiously avoided talking to people that she couldn't go out there and try to start any kind of useful conversation. It would look too weird.

God, she hoped Kell found out something soon. She had no idea how this might help them plan a takedown, but as they'd agreed, it was important to know the dimensions of the threat Bund posed. Although, if those people wanted to drink the Kool-Aid…

No, there were children out there. They had to know the dimensions of the threat before they did anything, because they had to minimize the repercussions. For the sake of those children.

But several days of this waiting was going to drive her nuts thinking about what that man might be doing even now.

"I'm going to go bonkers," she told Misty.

Misty wisely yawned at her.

Smart dog.

AN HOUR OR so later, Bund emerged from the Zeb house, a box in his hands. While he paused to lock up, Kell crossed the street with Bradley at his side. The dog knew he was working and seemed happy about it.

He reached the sidewalk near Bund's gray car just as Bund was crossing the last few steps.

Kell spoke, stopping the man in his tracks. "I hear Zeb left you his house. No family?"

Bund paused, then smiled. "Mr. Zeb was devoted to our church. He gave his life to it, so why not his house?"

"Gave his life to it, huh?"

Bund seemed to stiffen. "I'm sure you know about giving your life over to a cause."

"That I do." Kell glanced to his side and saw Bradley at full alert. One question answered. He returned his attention to Bund. "The difference is that we didn't kill each other."

Ahh. There it was. Bradley's alert was confirmed as Bund's face paled.

"What do you mean by that?" Bund demanded.

"What should I mean?" He signaled Bradley, and the

two of them marched back across the street leaving Bund to stew behind them.

"Good job, Bradley."

The dog's tail wagged again.

A SHORT TIME LATER, Kell and his K-9 headed over to Jenna's. Bradley still wore his vest, because every time Kell moved to take it off, Bradley pulled away. He wanted to wear it. So be it.

"My, how impressive we look," Jenna said, bending to greet Bradley as he and Kell came into the living room.

"Bradley. At ease."

Jenna, still half bent, twisted her head to look over at Kell. "Why did you say that?"

"Because while he's wearing that vest, he knows he's on duty. And right now he's not letting me remove it, so I had to let him know it was okay to relax."

"Wow." Jenna sat on the floor, crossed her legs and stared at Bradley. "You amazing dog." She reached out to scratch Bradley under his chin. "You don't want to give up your vest, huh?"

Kell sat beside her, and Misty half crawled into his lap. "Share the love time, I guess."

Continuing to pet Bradley, Jenna asked, "I'm on tenterhooks, you know. So give."

"Well, a certain K-9 alerted to Bund."

Jenna turned her head toward Kell. "I gather he came to the Zeb house."

"He sure did. I only had to wait a few hours."

"And?"

"We marched across the street, met Bund at his car. Long and short of it, Bund made some reference to how I know what it means to serve a cause, and since Bradley had already alerted, I said something about how we don't kill each other. The guy turned gray. He got the reference."

"Double wow," Jenna breathed.

"I wish I could read that dog's olfactory nerves the way he does. What did he smell when those two people were being carted out dead? How did he link it to Bund? But he sure did."

Jenna regarded Bradley. "Your nose is amazing. Wish I could share it."

Kell snorted. "Fat chance."

"Maybe we should ask *him* to come up with a plan for us."

"I wish. I have no doubt he'd be willing to attack Bund if I asked him to, but what good would that be? He'd be labeled a dangerous animal. Same if I attack the slimeball. I'd be guilty of a crime, and that guy probably has thirty people to back up his innocence."

Jenna tilted her head to one side, forgetting to keep scratching Bradley. "You said we had to cut him away from his herd. To protect them."

"The sooner the better. I may have lit the wrong fire under him."

A COUPLE OF hours later, Bradley parted with his vest while Jenna ransacked the fridge for cheese and meats, and pulled down some wheat crackers from a cupboard. The service was anything but impeccable: a paper plate and fingers for utensils.

Jenna's mind wouldn't stop trying to work the problem. Kell might have scared Bund from coming to town again for a while, not that they could confront him there. No, it had to be some place more private. No witnesses who could get involved.

But what good would it do to glean no useful evidence.

Eventually, she spoke as her heart sped up. She had an idea. "I could deliver a note out there, one warning him to meet us at some place private we can think of. Telling him we'll expose him about Celia. I don't want to mention the Mixons though."

"Agreed."

"But evidence? If we're going to do anything at all useful, short of murder or mayhem, we've got to have more evidence than Celia's letter. Gage made that clear."

Kell grew silent and still. Jenna watched him as his gaze grew distant, then harder.

"Jenna? Pull out Bernice's computer and find out what Wyoming law says about recording a conversation."

KELL WATCHED OVER her shoulder. It took a few minutes for Bernice's old laptop to boot, but only fifteen seconds to find the law and an interpretation of it. There it was.

"One-party recording of a conversation is legal without consent as long as the recording party is participating in the conversation."

He and Jenna exchanged looks.

"I'll go out right now and get a digital recorder to back up our cell phones," Kell announced. "Then we'll figure out how to move ahead with this."

He left Bradley behind. The K-9 still looked proud.

That did Kell's heart good.

"TOMORROW," KELL SAID, "you can deliver a note to that damn place in a sealed envelope. I'm willing to bet that nobody out there is allowed to open any mail except Bund. Another lever of control. He'd want to know everything that might be going on with the outside world."

Jenna nodded. "And the note will be easy enough. Just

tell him to meet me in a certain place at a certain time if he doesn't want Celia's letter to be made public."

"I agree. Except we need to add that she wrote a letter all about it and that we have it."

Jenna chewed her lower lip. "Right. But there's Celia's mother. What part did she have in all this? Why didn't Celia tell *her*? Why isn't she mentioned?"

"I hate to think. Regardless, once we have Bund, the law can deal with his coconspirators."

"I suppose so." Jenna shook her head as if trying to dislodge an unpleasant memory. "And I thought I knew ugliness."

"There's sure enough to go around. Too much."

KELL AND JENNA slept wrapped around each other that night, the closeness satisfying *him* at any rate. Maybe her, too. She'd been alone against the world for so long. Finding no comfort anywhere. If that was all she'd accept from him, he'd gladly give it. But he wanted to give her so much more.

Sighing, he once again stared into the night, hoping they weren't too late. Hoping this wouldn't turn into a Waco situation.

But they had to tell Gage what they were going to do. They had to make sure he didn't have any solid objections to their plan. Make sure he supported it.

Kell was sure Gage would. The man was probably furious that his hands were tied.

Well, he and Jenna were going to untie them, and Gage had to be ready to arrest Bund. The rest of that den would have to wait.

Chapter Seventeen

After a quick breakfast of oatmeal, coffee and orange juice, Kell and Jenna set out for the sheriff's office, leaving the dogs behind. They marched the few blocks, enjoying the cool morning as much as they could under the circumstances.

"Man," Jenna said, "I hope he doesn't nix this."

"I don't see why he should, but I could be wrong. I bet he's sitting on a mountain of rage, though, just like we are."

"He probably is. He's always been a decent man."

Decent. Not good but decent. Kell supposed that was the highest praise Jenna was willing to give a male just yet. Or maybe it *was* the highest praise in any context for anyone.

He just hoped she was beginning to reassemble the shattered pieces of her identity. She was sure mission-focused right now.

Gage didn't keep them waiting. He waved them into his office and told them to close the door. They sat facing him across his cluttered desk.

"I hear," the sheriff said without preamble, "that you and a certain K-9 confronted Bund yesterday on the street."

"Not a confrontation," Kell said. "Just a little conversation with a suggestion attached. Sure as I'm sitting here, that man murdered Hassen and Zeb."

"But no proof?"

"Not unless an ashen face and a K-9 alert will stand up in court."

"Hell. Well, you didn't come here to tell me that."

Kell looked at Jenna. "Jenna has a plan."

She spoke. "We need to know if it'll work. Well, it'll have an effect, but can it be used in court?"

"What's that?"

"We're going to get him to admit what he did. And we're going to record him doing it."

Gage gave a low whistle. "Recordings work. How are you going to achieve that?"

Jenna answered. "I'm going to leave a note, telling him we have Celia's letter and to meet me at a certain place and time if he doesn't want it made public."

Gage winced. "Extortion. Don't tell me that. I just went deaf."

Jenna glanced at Kell, whose jaw was working. "Okay, we didn't mean that part. Call it an enticement."

"I can live with that. Try rewording it. Simply say you'll turn the letter over to him or something like that. An inducement, no threats, okay? Because neither of you wants to have to lie under oath. Clear?"

Jenna and Kell both nodded.

Kell spoke again. "Just one thing, Sheriff. You'll need to be ready to arrest him."

"Nothing will give me greater pleasure."

JENNA AND KELL spent the day trying to word a note that would work without turning into extortion. It proved surprisingly difficult. Each word had to be selected with care, chosen to make Bund come to a meeting without containing even a veiled threat.

"Whoever thought this would be so difficult?" Jenna wondered out loud.

"It's difficult only because we want to put an 'or else' in here to make sure he shows."

She sighed. "You're right. We don't want it to be ignored."

Kell finally went out to get some grub from Maude's diner. *Screw the balanced diet,* he thought. They needed energy right now, as much as possible. Their cortisol levels must be through the roof.

He also stopped at the feed store to pick up more dog food. Bradley had been eating a lot of Misty's lately, and the bag was getting low. He added a bag of crunchy treats and one of soft treats. The dogs, at least, were going to be happy.

When he arrived back at the house with his burdens, he found Jenna at the kitchen table, an empty pot of coffee in front of her. She was staring at a piece of paper.

She looked up with a smile. "I think I've got it."

He dropped his load and bent over her to look.

I HAVE INFORMATION ABOUT CELIA THAT YOU MIGHT WANT TO KNOW. DO YOU WANT TO HEAR IT?

Then he raised his head to smile into her green eyes. "I think you have."

"When do I go deliver it?"

He thought for a minute. "First, we have to decide on a meeting place and time."

Jenna immediately went to work, pulling up the property plat from the tax assessor's office. "It's a big place, and I don't see many buildings on it."

"You know how often a tax assessor comes out to check such things? Very rarely."

She smiled faintly. "Probably."

After a quick meal, they set out in Kell's crew cab truck, the dogs tucked in safely behind them. The evening air was only starting to chill, so they rode along with open windows.

Kell spoke. "Best if we find a spot that's still just inside his property. He might never set foot off it."

"If the inducement is right, he will."

"Well, then, not far off it. He'd feel more exposed."

"If he comes alone, he'll be exposed anyway."

Kell's jaw tightened. "If he doesn't come alone, I am going to find the biggest newspaper I can to publish that poor girl's letter. It might not do anything to him legally, but it would still ruin him."

"Only if his followers find out, and I don't imagine they read the paper."

"Hell."

"Kell? I want more than to ruin him in public. I want vengeance."

He could tell by a subtle note in her voice that she meant it but that she didn't like feeling that way. A good soul, Jenna Blair. "I'd like vengeance, too. But the law is going to have to provide that."

"Yeah. And maybe it finally can."

"Justice might be just around the corner." For Celia. For the Mixons. But not for Jenna. It was too late for justice for her. That maddened him, but he understood why she didn't want to fight it all out again, didn't want to expose herself again. The first time had been enough of a horror.

Then he saw it. "There, Jenna. That stock grate. It crosses their damn fence. Of course it does. If they raise goats, they might be selling some of them for income. Gotta get that stock in and out somehow. I sure don't see a field of cannabis."

"But there's a gate across the grate."

"It's good enough and I can unlock it somehow. enough open land to see if anyone else is there. Which I honestly don't expect. The guy wants to keep his secrets without having to explain why he suddenly needs a bodyguard. Or asking one of his fools to bring a gun to a parlay." He paused, scanning the area. "See that barn over there?"

"It looks like it might be falling down."

"Still good enough. Bradley and I will hide just inside, a couple of hours before the meeting time. We'll be ready. I don't want to spook Bund. Little does he know just what he'll be risking if he tries any funny stuff with you."

"Bradley?" she asked.

"Bradley. Not to mention me."

WITH THE APPOINTED time and place added to the printed-out note, Jenna wrote Bund's name clearly across the front of the envelope. "I hope no one else opens it."

"How likely do you think that is? This creep's security depends on keeping his secrets. All of them. I bet he doesn't even let that crew see junk mail."

"I hope you're right."

"If I'm not right, Bradley and I can still deal with a bunch of them if they show up. But that won't happen. The man simply doesn't want his flock to know what's going on. Any lie he gives them about being threatened is going to bring about questions, if not to his face, then among his cult. He can't afford that."

"Maybe not." She closed her eyes briefly, thinking about it. "Zeb and Hassen knew his secret. Something made him wary enough about that to kill them."

Kell's voice grew icy. "Celia killed herself. That must have made him edgy about those other two speaking out after that. They might have an attack of conscience."

"Or maybe this Vince guy who sent us her letter sent him something, too."

Kell remained silent for a minute. "That might be it. The guy sure seems bent on getting to Bund."

Jenna couldn't argue with that. From the inclusion of the warning with Celia's letter, she could easily imagine someone else with a bigger need for retribution than either she or Kell.

"Okay, how do you want to do this?" she asked.

"I'll drive out, and Bradley and I will get into the barn before you deliver the note. You'll be away in Bernice's car before Bund has a chance to read it. Then get through the gate and wait at the barn. He'll show up."

WITH HER CELL phone and the digital recorder in a deep pocket of her jacket, Jenna set out for the compound a couple of hours after Kell departed with Bradley.

Talk about minutes creeping by like hours! At last, the appointed time had arrived. She gave Misty a hug and left her behind with a bowl of fresh water and a couple of biscuits.

Driving out of town and entering the browning wide-open spaces beyond its edges only enhanced her concerns. But why? None of them would dare kidnap her or harm her. The group had spent years keeping the lowest of profiles.

Firm in her determination, however, she quashed her misgivings and decided to trust the plan. What was the worst that could happen? Bund showing up with some of his men? She hadn't the least doubt that Kell and Bradley could deal with that.

Or she just wouldn't speak to him but would walk away. Those people couldn't stop her. Not unless they wanted the law breathing down their necks.

KELL AND BRADLEY had no trouble reaching the barn unseen. Nobody was out on that range, and whatever goats or animals they kept must be penned elsewhere. He paused just long enough to make sure Jenna could open the gate.

Bradley wore his vest, once again appearing to take pride in it. Fantastic buddy. The best K-9 ever.

The wait was long, just as he'd planned. Bradley lay on the ground beside him, clearly ready for action. The barn itself was musty, full of old scents of horses and even goats. Hay up in the hay lofts. An empty rusting water trough. He judged no animals had been kept in here for a while.

As the breeze outside picked up some force, he heard the structure creak around him. Hearing that, he decided *he* wouldn't stable anything in this barn, not even a barn cat.

Just as he had the thought, one showed up, regarding him steadily from green eyes, perched atop a rafter. Well fed enough, beautifully gray in color.

The eyes were hypnotic, though. Almost seeming to speak to him.

"I'd adopt you cat, but you're probably feral and wouldn't like it. Come to think of it, you might not like Bradley, either."

Bradley spared the cat a look or two, then ignored

it. The cat, for its part, blinked slowly, then resumed its watchful pose.

"Just don't jump us at the wrong time," Kell muttered to the cat. Mayhem with a screaming cat could cause all kinds of trouble.

NEARLY A MILE AWAY, Jenna pulled up at the compound's gated entry. A man stood there, appearing ready to drive away outsiders. He gestured her to keep going.

Instead, heart beating a little faster, she climbed out of the car, envelope in hand. She walked up to the man and reached across the low gate. He gave her an angry stare as she held out the envelope.

"For Pastor Bund," she said as pleasantly as she could manage. "He'll want to see this right away."

The man took the note from her, waited until she was back in the car, then trotted up toward the house.

Jenna pulled away at a slow pace, but once the man stepped inside, she pulled a fast U-turn and headed rapidly for the barn.

AT LAST KELL saw Bernice's car pull up just outside the gate. He watched as Jenna climbed out, then opened the fence and walked over to the barn. With her back to the building, she waited.

"I haven't seen anyone," she said quietly.

"He's got some time to get here," Kell said, although he wasn't feeling very patient. He wanted this confrontation done and over with.

"There he is," Jenna said suddenly.

Kell made sure he and the dog were in deep shadow. He saw the big black car pull up just outside the gate behind Bernice's car. "We're on," he told Bradley.

The dog immediately rose to the sitting position. The

cat decided it might be a good time to disappear. And Alloysius Bund came striding across the open ground, the tails of his knee-length black coat flapping in the wind. Dang, that man wanted to look like an old-time pastor. All he lacked was a wide-brimmed hat.

Kell saw Jenna's hand slide into her pocket. Bund froze. She pulled out her empty hand and held it up. "It's getting chilly out here." She had turned on her phone and the recorder. Kell followed suit.

Bradley sat in utter silence, awaiting his moment.

"What's this about Celia?" Bund asked as he got within a few paces of Jenna. "The poor girl hanged herself. We all grieve her."

"Bull," Jenna answered succinctly. "You have a reason to be glad she's dead."

Bund suddenly became the picture of sorrow. "You don't know what you're talking about."

What an actor, Kell thought.

"But *you* do. She wrote a letter right before she took her own life. Zeb and Hassen knew the reason, didn't they? Is that why you killed them?"

Bund stiffened. "I would never do such a thing. They were both old and ill."

"Maybe so. But maybe they worried you even after all this time."

Bund shifted uneasily. "What is all this about?"

"It's all about you and your depraved mind. Your black soul. The least you can do is admit what you are."

"I'm an upstanding man, a man of great rectitude."

"Right," said Jenna. "So maybe you want to tell me about what really happened with Celia."

"Lies. All lies."

"I don't know about that. How would you know what's in her letter?"

Go, Jenna, go, Kell thought. He and Bradley edged toward the door, getting ready.

"I'm guessing! She lied about me all those years ago. Why wouldn't she repeat those lies?"

Bund was growing visibly agitated.

"So just tell me the truth. That's all I want."

"She was a temptress! She was evil. She kept flouncing around in front of me. She wanted it!"

"Ah. So you, a grown man, were unable to resist a ten-year-old girl? Is that what you're telling me?"

"In some ways, I'm only a man." Then Bund stepped toward Jenna. "Give me that letter now." He lifted a hand as if he were going to strike.

That was it. Kell and Bradley emerged from the barn. Kell gave Bradley a small signal. The dog took up station behind Bund, at the ready.

"I don't think that would be a good idea, Bund," Kell said. "You're outnumbered. So you raped Celia?"

"I didn't rape that girl!" Bund was sweating now. "She begged for it! She wanted it!"

"You're a lousy excuse for a man," Kell told him, steel reinforcing every word. "I suppose the Mixon girl tempted you, too. And how did she do that?"

"She exposed herself to me! I have pictures of her doing it!"

"Really?" Jenna asked sarcastically. "And you just stood there taking pictures of the ten-year-old temptress?"

"It was proof of what she did."

"Who were you going to show them to?" Kell demanded. "Your followers? Or did you threaten Deborah Mixon with them? Was that why she and her daughter fled with nothing but the rags on their backs?"

Bund's face twisted into a look of terror. He turned to

flee to his car, but Bradley got in his way, clearly ready for action. He growled and bared his teeth.

"Don't move, Bund," Kell said. "My K-9 has a taste for biting arms and legs. One word from me, and he'll make you sorry you were ever born."

Bund froze, Bradley right in front of him, Kell and Jenna behind.

Then Kell pulled out his phone and called the sheriff.

THREE SHERIFF'S CARS arrived fifteen minutes later, lights flashing, sirens screaming. Six men came racing across the field, Gage Dalton limping behind them.

When Gage reached Kell and Jenna, he asked, "You recorded it?"

"You bet," Kell answered.

Gage turned to look at his men. "Arrest Alloysius Bund for rape and murder."

It was done. Jenna sagged into Kell, and he wrapped his arms around her.

"You did it," Kell said quietly to her. "You got him good. I told you that you were a hero."

She shook her head slightly against his shoulder. "You were part of it, too."

"I didn't do a damn thing. *You* were the one who pulled the confession out of him."

VINCE ABERNATHY GOT all the information before the day was over from that old friend who owed him a few favors from their school days.

A friend to whom *he* now owed a huge debt of gratitude. They might be on opposite sides of the law, but Vince knew he'd find a way to repay the man.

But part of Vince was disappointed. He had seriously

wanted to send a man, one who enjoyed such things, to literally take Bund apart slowly, piece by piece.

Deborah Mixon and her daughter were now safe. That was good any way he looked at it. He hadn't gotten to Bund himself right away only because he'd wanted Bund to suffer some of the fear he'd inflicted on little girls. On Celia.

So Vince had waited, but Blair and McLaren beat him to the punch.

As for prison—well it wasn't as satisfying to him— but from what he knew of prisons, Bund would suffer for the rest of his life. Prisoners, as a rule, hated pedophiles.

Content with that, at least for now, he folded Celia's letter and placed it in his safe. He could always get to Bund inside prison walls if he wanted to.

But not yet. Instead, he allowed himself to enjoy the images of Bund's suffering inside those walls.

Yeah, that would do for now.

He could have sworn that he felt Celia in the room with him. His poor little cousin. He just wished she'd told him before Zeb and Hassen. He never would have doubted her.

He spoke to the empty room. "I hope you can rest, Celia. The man's getting his payback."

THE NEXT DAY, in a considerably lightened atmosphere, Kell and Jenna sat on her front porch while the dogs romped in the afternoon light.

Jenna spoke. "Bradley did seem proud of his vest."

"I can't tell you how happy that makes me. He's come further than I thought."

"Isn't that wonderful?"

He thought so, but he also thought the woman sitting beside him was wonderful, too.

"I can only imagine how much you must hate men,"

he remarked. He felt her gaze turn to him but was almost afraid to look at her.

"Not all men," she answered. "You have definitely become an exception to my rule."

"I was hoping." Now he rotated to return her gaze. "There's something else."

Her eyes dimmed a bit.

Oh, God, he was going at this all wrong. But considering he'd never done this before, he didn't know a right way.

"What else, Kell?"

Maybe this was the most courageous thing he'd ever done. "I told you I believe you're a hero. I meant it, you know."

She waved a hand. "Maybe when the chips were really down for me, I was a coward."

"Never. Not once. You're too hard on yourself. Anyway…"

She nodded encouragingly.

"I admire you. I respect you. Not only that; you're beautiful. But even that isn't all of it." He drew a deep breath.

"Out with it, Kell." Now she looked almost amused.

"Hell. I know you're not ready to hear this, but Bradley and Misty made me fall in love with you."

She actually laughed, the sweetest sound he'd ever heard. "So it wasn't my charms?"

"Oh, woman, you've got plenty of those. Anyway, there you have it. If you ever come to feel the same way about me, let me know."

"Kell?"

"Yeah?" He expected resistance. He expected a letdown. Instead, he could hardly believe his ears.

"You made me trust you. Maybe Bradley had something to do with that. But mostly it was you." Now she drew a deep breath. "I not only trust you, Kell. I love you, too."

He felt his heart soar.

"Anyway, you're also gorgeous," she said. "Did I tell you that?"

Now *he* laughed. "Can I sweep you off to bed?"

"I thought you'd never ask."

Hours later, he dared to say, "Will you marry me?"

"I naturally expected you to make an honest woman of me."

They both laughed then, truly the sweetest sound on earth.

* * * * *

ONE NIGHT STANDOFF

NICOLE HELM

To the old men who study history and spill soup on
their keyboards.

Chapter One

It couldn't be happening again.

Hazeleigh Hart stood in the doorway to her boss's office and was sure she was in the midst of a nightmare.

There was blood. So much—too much—blood.

Mr. Field was most decidedly dead.

There was grief and denial. Emotions battered Hazeleigh, but the one that finally made her move was fear.

This was not the first dead body she'd uncovered in the past year. The last time it happened, the police had been sure she'd had something to do with the murder, before her sister had helped clear her.

Murder. Who would want to kill poor old Mr. Field, an eccentric man who paid for her to do research, and to organize his own, about a supposed bank robbery in Wilde back in the 1800s?

But it didn't matter who. It didn't matter how or when. It only mattered that she was alive, and the only one standing here looking at his dead body. He had to have been murdered. There was no other explanation for all that blood.

She hadn't had a bad feeling this time—like last year, when her sister Zara had accidentally dug up their other sister's body. No, Mr. Field's lifeless body—slumped over his work in his office—was a complete and utter surprise.

Would anyone believe it?

No.

Her whole life she'd been plagued by bad premonitions, so to speak, but they were neither consistent nor always correct, which meant no one ever believed her. They didn't believe her if she said something bad was going to happen before it did, and they didn't believe her when she said she hadn't felt anything before something bad *had* happened either.

Except Zara. Sometimes. Her living sister was the only person who ever believed her, but Hazeleigh knew even if Zara trusted her innocence—and she would, because Zara always believed her to be innocent—she wouldn't be able to do anything about how bad it looked.

No one would.

Slowly, Hazeleigh backed out of the office. Her stomach was queasy, and her eyes burned with tears. Mr. Field was a sweet old man. He wouldn't hurt anyone. The harshest thing she'd ever heard him say was "fiddlesticks" when he spilled soup on his keyboard.

She'd had to type all his emails for him while he waited for it to be fixed—he hadn't wanted the expense of buying a new one, though he could have afforded it easily.

A sob rose in her throat, and she managed to turn away from the body.

She would have to go away. Away from here. The death. The blood. Away from poor Mr. Field and all his research. Away from Wilde, Wyoming—the only place she'd ever really been.

She would have to disappear.

She had been to jail. Well, a holding cell. It wasn't the end of the world, but… She felt something *wrong* deep inside of her. Consistent or not, *right* or not, she just *knew* letting the police investigate her would end badly for her.

She had to disappear. She walked out of the fort—the

historic building where Mr. Field had his office—to her car in the parking lot. She began to drive to the Hart Ranch, eyes always in the rearview mirror, certain sirens and lights would appear behind her at any moment.

She would go to her cabin, pack up her things and start driving. It didn't matter where she ended up. She just had to escape.

Dimly, in the back of her mind, Hazeleigh understood this was blind panic. She couldn't really disappear. She needed time to think. To settle and *think*.

She parked in front of her cabin. It wasn't safe here. They'd come for her here. She couldn't go to Zara. Zara would call Thomas, their cousin, who was a police officer. Zara would think he could help.

But Hazeleigh wouldn't get her sister and cousin wrapped up in this. Or Jake, one of the Thompson brothers who'd been shot trying to unravel the whole mystery revolving around her other sister's murder.

Jake, who she'd just gone to the jewelry store with yesterday to help pick out a ring for Zara.

It had taken some time, but Hazeleigh had finally felt comfortable around him. He'd won her over with patience and kindness and space.

She didn't feel comfortable around men as a rule. Her father had blamed her for Amberleigh's disappearance long before the murder, and he sometimes got violent when he could hide it from Zara.

The two men she'd trusted enough to date had both turned violent in the end—Douglas had even murdered Amberleigh, thinking it was Hazeleigh.

Hazeleigh shuddered. No, she didn't trust men—at least ones who showed any interest in her.

But Mr. Field and Jake were fine. Even the Thompson

brothers had gotten easier to be around. They ran the Hart Ranch now, after all. She had to be around them.

And they would all want to help. Hazeleigh knew every last one of them would try to help her. But no one would be able to prove she hadn't done it. She would end up in jail.

She couldn't. She couldn't.

Panic was its own beat inside of her now. No amount of reason could penetrate. She packed a bag.

Where are you going? Where can you go?

She surveyed the ranch outside her cabin. She wasn't safe on the ranch, but there was an awful lot of land to cover, and would they think to cover it? If she wasn't in her cabin, if she cleared everything out, wouldn't the police expect her to get as far away as possible?

She blinked at the horizon. No, she wouldn't run away. She'd hunker down right here.

And no one would ever know.

LANDON DAVIS-THOMPSON, these days, let the horse beneath him *run*.

When it came to the six men who'd come to run the Hart Ranch, Brody was more than proficient on a horse. Jake and Dunne were sidelined by injuries, but both could ride in a pinch. Henry and Cal were both too stiff and too bitter not to struggle, but they did what had to be done.

Landon, though… Landon *loved* it. He'd always loved horses. Growing up dirt-poor on a farm that barely fed its tenants, let alone its animals, he'd never dreamed this would be his life.

Even when he'd dreamed of escape, it had been to join the military. To strive for excellence there and make something out of his life—anything other than ending up like his family. His abusive father drinking himself to death, his mom grieving herself to death and all his brothers winding up in jail or six feet under.

So when Landon had been recruited by Team Breaker, a secret, elite military group meant to bring down various terrorist rings in the Middle East, he figured he'd succeeded. He'd peaked.

Then hell had broken loose, and military mistakes had turned Landon and his military brothers into direct targets. So they'd been erased. Sent to Wyoming to disappear. New identities. A new life.

Landon Davis was dead, but Landon Thompson had a future. Even if it was ranching this big spread in the middle of nowhere, Wyoming.

Landon figured he'd hate the cold northern winters, figured ranch work would be too similar to that farm life he'd grown up on, drowning in everyone else's rage and bitterness.

But as it turned out, he was happy here.

Horses. Ranching. His military brothers, this small-town life. It suited him, surprisingly enough.

Then there was Hazeleigh Hart, the pretty and far-too-skittish woman who lived in a cabin on the property the "Thompson brothers" now owned. Something about the woman had tied him up in an uncharacteristic number of knots.

Strange, considering he'd never once had a problem attracting female attention.

Except when it came to Hazeleigh. She'd never looked at him twice. Didn't even notice that he sometimes looked for too long, paid too much attention, tried a little too hard to get her to smile and stop being so nervous around him.

Which was why when he saw the telltale tangle of dark hair trailing behind a running form, pink scarf fluttering behind her, he thought maybe he'd conjured up the image in his imagination.

Because what would Hazeleigh be doing running around the far edge of the property line? Landon had spent many an afternoon running the horses out this way and never saw anyone that wasn't bovine this far back.

But it *was* someone, not a figment of his imagination, and he honestly couldn't fathom it being anyone else. "Hazeleigh?" he called out.

She looked over her shoulder, but she didn't stop running. There was terror in her eyes, which had his instincts kicking in.

He urged the horse into a run until he caught up with her, stopping the horse and swinging off in one fluid movement. He didn't grab her, like he might have with just about anyone else who appeared to be running for their life in the middle of nowhere.

He'd learned to give Hazeleigh space, so he merely placed himself in her path and held out his hands in a *stop* gesture.

She slowed, but she didn't stop, passing him on the side as she shook her head. "Please don't, Landon. Go back to the house and pretend you never saw me. You can't tell anyone you saw me."

She was breathing hard, clearly struggling. But she just kept moving, the backpack she was wearing slapping against her back. He fell into an easy jog beside her.

"Hazeleigh, I think you need to stop and take a breath and tell me what's going on."

She kept shaking her head. She was obviously running out of steam, but she kept propelling herself forward.

"I can't. I can't. You just have to go. Don't tell Zara. Don't tell anyone. Please."

When he didn't do as she asked, she finally stopped

and pinned those big, brown eyes on him. "You don't understand." Her eyes filled with tears. "Mr. Field is dead."

"What?" he said, brain kicking into gear. Was this grief? *Should* he leave her alone to deal with it?

"Someone killed him." Her voice broke. "His blood…" She shook her head like she couldn't bear to say the words. "They're going to think it was me."

"I don't…" He trailed off, because her hand gripped his. Hazeleigh, who usually did everything she could to put distance between her body and his, reached out and grabbed him like he was a lifeline.

And then he heard the same thing she did.

Sirens.

Chapter Two

Already? Could it be already? It had to be. The sirens were far off, but the highway was just a few miles north. The only reason sirens would be this close, getting closer and closer, would be to make their way from town to the Hart Ranch.

"You can't tell anyone you saw me." She squeezed his hand, so big and strong even as it hung loosely in her death grip. Usually the Thompson brothers made her nervous—so big and male and…they had a kind of predatory stillness about them.

She didn't think they were bad men. Certainly not Jake, who loved her sister so much, or Brody, who'd fallen for her childhood friend, Kate. She understood they weren't mean or bad.

But there was something about their physical presence that set off that *flight* response in her, which stemmed from her own bad choices, she knew.

She was too afraid of what waited for her to be afraid of Landon and his all-encompassing *maleness* in this moment.

His left hand came up and covered her hand, which was clutching his right. He pinned her with his dark blue gaze. "Let's figure this all out. You take a deep breath and let it out," Landon instructed. He seemed so certain and so sure that she followed his orders without even thinking about it.

"Now, you found Mr. Field dead? Where? The fort?"

She nodded emphatically. "His office." His messy little office at the old historic fort he loved so much. She couldn't squeeze her eyes shut because she'd see his poor body, bloody and lifeless. So she squeezed Landon's hand. "He left me a message in the middle of the night that he'd found something, and he wanted me to come in first thing." Hazeleigh tried to blink back tears. If she'd answered, if she'd gotten there earlier, would she have been able to stop what happened?

"Now, that's evidence enough you didn't hurt him, Hazeleigh," Landon said. "Why would you think they'd try to blame you?"

She tried to pull her hand away, but Landon held firm. In the moment, she didn't fully realize that it didn't cause the panic it should have. Instead, he was something like an anchor, tethering her to reality instead of panic.

She sucked in a breath and slowly let it out again. He was right. She needed to breathe. The sirens were coming and if she was going to survive, she had to *think*.

Landon was a complication, though. She somehow needed to convince him to let her go. He couldn't get involved in this—he'd involve Zara, and Zara would want to fight for her and...

The last time that had happened, Jake had ended up shot.

Wasn't it better to take Amberleigh's original way out? Run away?

Amberleigh wound up murdered herself.

"Hazeleigh."

She blinked up at Landon. "I just...know they will." She hadn't had a feeling something was wrong, but she knew— she just *knew*—she would somehow be on the hook for this.

The sirens were closer now, likely at the front gate of the ranch. They'd go to her cabin first, or maybe the main house. Not all the way out here. She still had time.

"Please, can't you just go and pretend you never saw me?"

He frowned, which was rare. Landon was easygoing, always ready with a joke. He was the only one of the brothers who seemed genuinely cheerful. She would have called him charming, if she didn't second-guess herself when it came to charming.

"This is what we're going to do," he said, with a take-charge air that usually came from his brother Cal. His eyes scanned the horizon. He squinted and she knew he was looking at the building she'd been heading to.

"That little building out there—anyone ever use that?"

Hazeleigh shook her head. "Technically, it's on Peterson land, and mostly the last generation of Petersons left Wilde but kept the land, and let all their buildings go to rot. It was once a schoolhouse, but it's just a shack at this point." She didn't mention it had been her plan to hide there.

He nodded. "All right, let's go."

He didn't let her go, just started pulling her along. He grabbed his horse's reins and walked her alongside them.

Hazeleigh gave the horse a side-eye. Buttercup had once been hers. She'd never loved the ranch like Zara. She'd been far more interested in books and history and homemaking pursuits over cattle and crops and chores.

But Buttercup had been *hers*, and then Dad sold Hart Ranch and everything on it to the Thompson brothers, because they'd been willing to pay over market price.

It had been Zara's fast talking last fall that had convinced the Thompsons to let Zara and Hazeleigh rent their own family's cabin, and Zara stay on as a ranch hand.

Landon looked down at her, caught her staring at the horse. Hazeleigh blinked and looked straight ahead.

So her father had sold off her beloved horse. Hazeleigh got to go down to the stables and feed the mare some apple slices, her favorite, when she wanted. It wasn't as though she'd been cut off, thanks to Zara.

But Buttercup wasn't hers to ride anymore. The wildflowers that dotted the landscape weren't Hazeleigh's to pick. It seemed everywhere she turned, things were being taken away from her.

"Zara said she was yours."

Hazeleigh shrugged, trying not to be frustrated with how easily he saw through her. "More or less, but I never spent much time doing ranch work like you all. She's a ranch horse. She should be used as one."

He tied the reins to a tree at the fence line and then studied the barbed wire. "You're going to have to let me give you a hand." He found a spot where the wire was a little loose, then put his booted foot on it and used his weight to push it down. He held out his hand.

It was different this time, to take it. Because he'd offered it. Because she'd stopped panicking. She knew that this was a man who would help. The problem was she didn't want it. He was a complication she didn't have the time or wherewithal to figure out.

But he'd seen her, so she didn't have a choice. She flicked a glance at the horse. She never would have guessed Landon for the riding-by-himself type.

That was the problem. She did not trust her instincts when it came to new people, particularly men. She'd learned a very hard lesson there.

But she had to deal with the reality of the situation. He'd seen her. He would help. She had to figure out a way to use his assistance to suit her purposes.

So she had to go along with him for the moment. Until she could figure out what to do next. Until she had time to think without needing to run.

Though she was hesitating, Landon just stood there patiently. Hand outstretched, boot on the barbed wire.

Hazeleigh forced herself to move forward, to put her hand in his. He gripped it and waited for her to put her own booted foot on the wire. She lifted her skirt off the barbs with her free hand as she hopped over.

Then immediately dropped his hand.

"There we are," he said, and she knew he was trying to encourage her to keep taking the next step. Like he might encourage a horse. A skittish one at that.

He hopped over the fence in an easy movement she found oddly mesmerizing. He had a grace about him, from the horse riding to the fence hopping.

"We'll just get you hunkered down in there and then I'll get it all sorted out," he said, smiling at her reassuringly as he moved toward the old school.

"How come your brothers don't sound like you?" she asked. It was a question she'd pondered for *months*, but never felt comfortable asking. Panic had dulled her senses, or put all her anxiety somewhere else, so the question just fell out.

"I grew up in Mississippi. They didn't. Surely Zara's told you we aren't all full brothers."

Hazeleigh nodded, but something about the way he said it gave her that odd feeling she sometimes got. That something bad was coming. Something wrong.

She shook her head and looked at the little school in front of them. Mr. Field had studied this school as part of his bank-robbery research, and though it had historical importance, being on private land meant it hadn't been well cared for like the fort.

Still, did that research mean someone might look for her here? Would every place she went to hide connect to Mr. Field?

Dead Mr. Field.

She didn't have time to worry about that as Landon pushed open the door. He stepped into the musty, dim room. The desks were gone, but there was still a chalkboard on the front wall—it was cracked and probably impossible to use.

The lone window was cracked as well but not broken out, which made the interior less stuffy than it might have been.

"You weren't wrong about the shack part." He shook his head and turned to her, looking pained. "Hazeleigh, let's go on up to the house. I'm sure no one really thinks you killed Mr. Field."

"I know they do," Hazeleigh replied flatly. She just *knew*.

He studied her, then nodded. "Okay. You stay put right here, all right? I'm going to see what's what. You don't take off on me—you got that? I'll be back as soon as I know what's going on."

She chewed on her bottom lip. She wasn't sure she should trust him. "But…"

"Let's just make sure this is what you think it is. You stay put, and I won't tell the police or Zara a thing. Promise." He held out his hand again.

He said it so fiercely, so sincerely, she thought she had to believe him. And she had to promise. She reached out and shook his hand. "All right."

She'd stay put…for now.

LANDON WASN'T CONVINCED Hazeleigh would stay, but he knew he needed to prove to her that she wasn't and wouldn't be a suspect, which meant he had to get back to the main house and determine what those sirens had been about.

He didn't know who in their right mind would think Hazeleigh was guilty of *murder*, but he understood why she thought they might, since she'd been held in connection to her own sister's murder not all that long ago.

Anyone who spent more than five minutes with her would have known better, but he supposed it wasn't the job of the police to know Hazeleigh. It was to follow evidence. Hazeleigh did work closely with Mr. Field, but who would want to kill an old, eccentric man in the middle of Wyoming, anyway?

Landon rode back to the house at a gallop, only slowing Buttercup once he could view the house. No matter how much he wanted to rush, he took his time. Even if he thought Hazeleigh was overreacting, he'd promised her that he'd see what was what without giving her away. He'd keep his promise.

He stabled the horse, then forced himself to whistle as he walked toward the house.

The scene had his instincts humming and the hope he'd had that this might blow over evaporating. Zara was standing there talking to two deputies. Her hands were on her hips and she looked furious. Kate was on the porch, and she was talking to someone on the phone.

Henry was outside the little outbuilding he'd converted into his living quarters, arms crossed. "What's going on?" Landon asked as he approached.

Henry shrugged. "Not sure."

"So you're just going to stand here?"

Henry didn't respond with more than a shrug. Landon rolled his eyes and walked over to where Zara was facing off with the officers. "What's the problem?" he asked with a pleasant smile and his best casual stance.

"Mr. Field's been murdered," Zara said, and by the way she was glaring daggers at the cops, Landon had the sinking suspicion Hazeleigh was right.

Landon had to work very hard not to match Zara's antagonistic approach, but he managed to keep calm.

"We had a call," one police officer said calmly. "A car

matching Hazeleigh's was seen leaving the fort this morning. We just want to talk to Hazeleigh. That's all. I don't want to cause a scene, Zara, but I will if I have to."

"She isn't home. I already told you. And you came up here sirens blazing, so don't give me that BS about you just wanting to talk."

"Sure looks like her car sitting there, matching the description we were given," the cop said, ignoring her complaint about his sirens.

"Let's just go on over and see then," Landon suggested, pointing the two deputies toward Hazeleigh's cabin. "No harm in knocking on the door, is there?" he said to Zara, trying to remain cool under the circumstances.

He was practiced at pretend genial Southern charm.

He started leading the cops over to the cabin despite Zara's spluttering objections. He wished he could assure Zara he knew where Hazeleigh was and that this was some very strange misunderstanding, but for now he had to put himself between Zara and the officers and let them knock on Hazeleigh's door. As he did, Brody pulled up in his truck, and Jake and Cal appeared over the rise on their horses.

Making it clear Kate had been calling in reinforcements.

Brody came over to stand with Landon and Zara, while Cal and Jake disappeared into the stables, but they would no doubt be up here once they secured their horses.

When there was no answer from inside the cabin, one of the deputies turned to Zara.

"Why don't you let us in, Zara?"

"Why don't you—"

"You'd need a search warrant for that, wouldn't you?" Landon interrupted, trying to keep his voice casual—friendly, even. "Just to make sure it's all on the up-and-up?"

The cop was very quiet for a moment. "I hope you all know this doesn't look good for her."

"It doesn't look good for you harassing innocent people," Zara returned.

"If any of you see Hazeleigh, I'm going to need a phone call. She has to come in. Just for some questions."

"Does Thomas know about you dropping by?" Zara demanded, mentioning her cousin, who was also a Bent County deputy.

"Thomas isn't my boss, Zara."

"Neither is your mom, but I don't see that stopping you from—"

Jake easily stepped in between Zara and the deputy, but he didn't address the lawman—he spoke to Zara. "Come on now," he said quietly. "We don't need to make this a scene."

"Maybe I want to," Zara said, glaring at the cop over Jake's shoulder.

"I know you do, but let's think about Hazeleigh," Jake said quietly. "We've got to find her."

Landon kept his mouth shut, but he was very much on Zara's side for this one.

With Jake's interference taking Zara's attention off him, the cop stepped away.

"I'm calling Thomas," Zara said. "I'm going to get to the bottom of this." She looked at the cabin and where Landon was still standing near the door. "Where could she be? What if she's in danger, too?"

Landon felt badly for keeping his mouth shut, but Hazeleigh had been right. Those cops might just want to ask questions at the moment, but if someone had called in that Hazeleigh's car had been leaving the scene...things would get complicated. Delicate.

It was best if he was the only one who knew where Hazeleigh was until they got to the bottom of what was going on.

Chapter Three

Being alone in the old, dilapidated schoolhouse did not do much for Hazeleigh's peace of mind. It simply gave time for panic to multiply. Minutes felt like hours. Hours felt like minutes.

She was no good at subterfuge. At lying. She did not charge through with a plan—that was Zara's department. Hazeleigh knew herself *very* well, and none of her talents were ones that would allow her to handle this with aplomb.

It was why escape and running away was the only answer. It was why, back when she'd been held for Amberleigh's murder, she'd preferred jail over telling Zara everything she knew.

At her core, Hazeleigh knew she was a coward. Her two older sisters—even if only by minutes—had gotten all the bravery and verve, the strength and hardheadedness.

Before Mom had died, she'd always said Hazeleigh was as soft as dandelion fluff. It had been a good thing when Mom said it. But it hadn't felt good since, and that had been over fifteen years ago now.

"This is such a mess," she muttered aloud, because it felt good to fill the air with something other than dust motes.

Although… She frowned as she looked around. The floors were oddly…not clean, exactly, but free of the debris that should have built up over the years. That window should have been grimier—especially with the crack in it.

Maybe someone had been taking care of it? Maybe even Mr. Field. Or maybe there was a Peterson hiding about?

If someone had been here, though, and recently, she wasn't safe. They could come back at any moment, assuming it wasn't Mr. Field. But someone could come. They'd call the police, and she wouldn't have time to run.

She had to get out. Now. She could not wait for Landon, promises or not. She grabbed her backpack, but before she could get both arms through the straps the door was creaking open.

She nearly screamed, searching the area for a weapon to ward off whoever was coming to find her. But she found nothing that could cause blunt-force trauma—something she probably wouldn't have been able to go through with, anyway.

But it was Landon, of course, easily and almost soundlessly sliding inside the building. Nothing to scream about.

But his face told her everything she needed to know about what had gone on with the cops.

"They came to arrest me."

"Question you," he corrected.

But she knew too well where questions led. Especially questions with no good answers. And she had *no* good answers.

"I want you to tell me everything that happened. Starting with when you got the message from Mr. Field."

While his authoritative voice was something of a comfort—it was nice *someone* thought they knew what to do— she knew he was wrong. She shook her head. "It doesn't matter. I have been *through* this. I know how it goes. I can't answer the questions the way they want me to, and I am dead meat."

"Hazeleigh, someone made a call to the police."

"What do you mean?"

"The deputy said someone called about seeing your car leave the fort." He frowned at the cracked chalkboard. "But that'd be normal, wouldn't it? You leave in your car? Why would someone call the cops about that?"

"I don't know. I don't keep normal hours. It wouldn't be of note, unless the police were asking around."

But Landon shook his head. "The cop said someone *called*. That doesn't sound right. It doesn't add up."

"You think…someone is trying to make it look like I did it?"

"Wouldn't be the first time, would it?"

"I was complicit in being framed last time. I let the police arrest me because I knew I'd be safer." She clasped her hands together to keep herself from screaming or running or both. "I can't do it again. It won't work like last time, and Jake ended up shot anyway. I have to leave."

"Let's take it one step at a time. Right now, they want to question you because of a phone call."

"I won't. I can't."

Landon nodded, and she knew he was purposefully keeping space between them. Purposefully holding up his hands. She understood the Thompson brothers had all very consciously decided to give her a wide berth.

Because she was *skittish*.

That old feeling of jealousy welled up inside her. That she couldn't be more like brazen Amberleigh or certain Zara.

But Amberleigh was dead, wasn't she? That's what being brazen had gotten her. Zara had turned out all right, she supposed, but Hazeleigh knew that wishing she was more like her sister was pointless. They were just different…and she loved Zara. She wanted her to be happy after all she'd done to try to protect Hazeleigh over the years.

"I want to know more before we do anything," Landon said. And Hazeleigh didn't miss the *we*, which made no sense to her. "About this call. About the murder. But I don't think you should run away. Keep a low profile here, sure, but you could be in danger."

"Why would…" She swallowed at the lump in her throat. It was silly to ask him why he'd help her.

She had spent her childhood dreaming of knights in shining armor. Men who swooped in to help, like a cowboy in the old west. She loved a noble, good-hearted hero.

She'd stopped believing in them at some point, put away fictional ideas of good men, but then the Thompson brothers had shown up last year. Jake had stepped in to help Zara, before he'd meant anything to her. They'd all rallied around Kate to help her. The Thompson brothers were just the kind of men who felt they should help.

Hazeleigh was still having a hard time going back to believing in good guys, but still she knew Landon was one of them.

"Why would I help?" Landon smiled at her. It was a kind smile. A handsome smile. Still, he kept his distance. "Your sister is marrying my brother. That makes us family, more or less. She is going to say yes, isn't she?"

Hazeleigh knew he was trying to draw her into a conversation about something else. Distract her from all the problems at hand. Still, he was so kind about it, she could only let him. "She better."

Landon chuckled. "Yeah? Why do you say that?"

"I love Zara with everything I am. I'd be lost without her. But she is *not* an easy woman. I can't imagine anyone but Jake putting up with her."

Landon grinned. "Jake's had lots of experience with difficult. He's dealt with Cal all these years without punching him."

Hazeleigh smiled in return. "Cal is definitely…" She struggled to come up with the words for Landon's taciturn brother.

"A SOB?"

She laughed. She couldn't help it, even though it was mean. And not altogether true. She thought of Cal as more… troubled than mean. A control freak, but she'd watched Zara try to control things in a similar fashion. That sort of behavior was often born out of…well, desperation more than anything else.

But his brothers and her sister aside, there was really only one solution to her problem.

"I appreciate you trying to distract me, Landon, and wanting to help, but the best thing for me to do is run. Really. I've had time to think, to calm myself. It might not be safe to stay here. This is all a part of Mr. Field's research, and I just… I don't know why anyone would kill him, but when the police look into what he's working on, someone might come looking here."

"You can't run, Hazeleigh," Landon said, gently enough, but she didn't particularly like him telling her what to do. "They'll only follow." He looked around the schoolhouse. "We'll figure this out. Together."

We. Together.

Hazeleigh didn't have the faintest idea what to say to that.

HAZELEIGH GAPED AT him in a weighted silence that Landon let go on for as long as he could, which wasn't long. "I can hardly leave you to fend for yourself. Running is no joke, Hazeleigh, trust me. What's more, I know you don't want to do that to Zara."

Her frown deepened. "You don't understand."

She had no idea how much he understood. Maybe he hadn't had to run in the traditional sense, but this wasn't his life. He was living a fake life because a terrorist organization would want him dead otherwise.

Maybe he was making the best of this life, but he was still…a runaway. A hideaway.

"Give me a few days, okay? Just to get to the bottom of what the police think; who made that call. Give me a few days." He kept his steady gaze on hers. Calm. But he wasn't feeling much of that underneath the veneer. He felt a little desperate. A lot angry.

Here was a sweet woman, who helped an old man do silly research, mostly kept to herself and never hurt anyone, he'd be willing to wager. And she kept getting dragged into other people's drama, likely because she was sweet and kept herself a bit apart.

"I'll stay close," he continued when she said nothing. He kept his shoulders loose and his mouth curved in an encouraging smile. But he couldn't quite get the message to his hand to unclench from its fist.

"You can't stay out here with me. People would notice you missing. I don't want anyone else to know, to lie for me. I don't… I should do this on my own."

He wanted to scowl. It felt an ugly kind of familiar. All the ways he'd tried to help every single member of his family to get out from his father's thumb, or escape all the trouble they'd gotten themselves into.

Not one person had accepted his help. And look where they'd all ended up? "You're innocent. You should have help. I'm not going to tell anyone else. Not yet. I won't be here with you 24/7, no, but I'm going to keep tabs and make sure you're safe and hidden here. Any poking around I do people will chalk up to you being Zara's sister, or me being a little sweet on you."

"Sweet on me," she echoed, her cheeks turning a pretty shade of pink.

He shouldn't have said that. Now was not the time for the truth, no matter how it was wrapped up in a joke. He shrugged easily, keeping his tone light. "Sure. You're pretty. I'm a man. That's what some people will assume. No harm in it."

"But… I have terrible taste in men," she blurted.

Since he knew one of those men, he could hardly argue with her. That doctor she'd dated hadn't just been an absolute jerk, he'd been a murderer. And since he felt bad about her thinking about *that*, he grinned. "Maybe I don't have terrible taste in women."

Her mouth dropped open a little, and a little sound came out, but otherwise she said nothing, which was probably for the best. For both of them.

"Let's focus on the task at hand. Tell me exactly what happened."

Chapter Four

Hazeleigh was so rattled by this whole conversation that she went ahead and told him everything. From waking up to Mr. Field's message, to finding him dead.

A little sweet on you. She kept hearing him say it, in that faint Southern drawl, and she didn't know what to do with it.

Surely, he was joking. Trying to lighten the mood. If he was *sweet* on her…

Well, he wasn't. So she needed to focus.

"Was anyone ever overly interested in Mr. Field's research?" Landon asked. He still kept his distance, but he wasn't still. He walked around the schoolhouse, studying the window, the screw holes where desks used to be drilled into the floors, the cracks in the plaster walls.

"What would constitute 'overly interested'?"

"Lots of questions from someone. Strange attention to something seemingly minor. Meetups. Et cetera."

Hazeleigh shook her head. "I don't think you understand how history buffs work. Mr. Field was always exchanging emails—asking questions, answering questions. He wrote and argued on message boards. He was involved in a few Facebook groups—though I had to do most of that for him as he claimed it was too complicated for him to learn."

Landon nodded, though his expression reflected puzzlement. "Okay. We'll have to make a list." He continued to move about the room, talking about next steps and prioritizing, and all Hazeleigh could do was watch.

He was taking over, and there was a part of her—that forever-a-coward part—that wanted to relax into it. Thank God someone else wanted to take over.

But part of her knew it was wrong. She had to handle this herself. No matter how nice or noble Landon might be, he shouldn't get mixed up in her running away.

"Landon, I don't want you…"

He turned to face her and she…lost all the words. The denials. Because she very much wanted him to… Well, she didn't know quite yet. Just that she wanted him here because the thought of being alone right now terrified her.

He waited for her to finish her sentence. And waited. She struggled to find the words, especially when he was watching her intently, as if her answer was important. Like the wrong one might disappoint him.

"I should do this alone," she said, trying to be firm and as certain as he was. "You don't want to entangle yourself in it."

Landon shrugged. "Too late. Now, let's talk about this phone call."

"Landon."

"We can bicker about it later when time isn't of the essence. Now, does anyone live close enough to the fort to have seen you go to or leave the parking lot?"

"No."

"Not even if they had binoculars or a telescope or something?"

She shook her head. "Nothing. Someone would have had to have been on the road. Or in the fort itself." Someone had called the police about seeing her car. She still couldn't process that information. The fort was isolated. It was rare to get visitors without a big advertised event—and even when they did get the random visitor, it wouldn't have been so early in the morning, a good two hours before the fort opened to the public.

She'd gone in and found Mr. Field dead, and someone had seen her. Seen her leave. Upset and in a hurry. That *would* look bad.

But why would someone be looking? Who had alerted the police that Mr. Field was dead in the first place?

"We need to know who alerted the police," Landon said. "It doesn't add up that someone found him *and* saw you leave."

"You think…it could be whoever killed Mr. Field?"

"We just don't know until we know who called and where they called from. I'll need my computer."

She knew Landon was some kind of computer whiz. He'd helped Kate get to the bottom of her family troubles, but… "Landon—"

He held up a hand. "No more arguments, Hazeleigh. This is where we are. We can either work together, which will yield much faster results, or I can tell Zara where you are."

She frowned. It was like some kind of ultimatum, when she had repeatedly told him she didn't want his help. "That isn't a fair either-or."

He smiled gently. "I never said I was fair."

"You can't just—"

He pulled his cell phone out of his back pocket. "Okay. Zara it is."

She practically leaped forward in an attempt to grab the phone out of his hand. Of course, he held firm, and she ended up in a pointless tug-of-war she wasn't going to win.

She huffed out a breath and glared at him.

His mouth quirked. Clearly he was not intimidated by

her. Clearly she *amused* him. She wanted to be mad about it, but it was hard to blame him. She was the opposite of intimidating.

But she could do other things…even if she couldn't physically intimidate.

"It isn't right to bring Zara into this. You know that. She'll worry. She'll fume. She'll probably get *herself* tossed in jail trying to prove I didn't do it."

Landon's mouth firmed and Hazeleigh knew she'd scored a point.

"In fact, if she was with the police, I'm willing to bet she was yelling at them and someone—likely Jake—had to step in and stop her from doing something rash."

He said nothing. Hazeleigh nodded her head as if he'd confirmed her suspicions. "I know my sister. She can't handle this with an even temper or a cool head. I think you understand—I *hope* you understand—that it's a situation that needs both. I panicked a little bit in the beginning."

"You found your boss, your *friend*, murdered. Of course you did."

She didn't *need* him to make her feel better about that, but it did ease some stress inside of her. That she hadn't reacted completely wrongly. Or maybe it just made her sad all over again so she didn't feel the stress.

"If you promise to sit tight," Landon said, "I'll see what I can do about finding some answers, okay?"

"I can't promise… You need to understand. I don't regret running, even if it *was* panic. I knew I'd be blamed for it, whether that's my weird intuition or just having the sense God gave me, I don't know. But I *knew* I'd be blamed. And I refuse to sit around in a cell while everyone else tries to save me again."

Landon shook his head. "That doesn't mean running is the answer, Hazeleigh."

"What other answer is there?"

"Fighting for the truth. Why can't we all help you fight for the truth?"

"We have to keep everyone out of this. If I can't keep you out, that's... Well, it's already happened. But I can't drag Zara into it. I can't."

"She'd support you."

"She'd *fight* for me, Landon. And I know I'm lucky to have a sister who would, but I don't need a fight. I just need...to disappear."

"No, Hazeleigh, you need the truth. I'm damn good at finding it. Stay put. Let me get to the bottom of this for you."

"How is that different than jail, Landon? Hiding here while you do all the work?"

"Because you're going to help me do the work. You're going to do some of that fighting yourself."

That sounded...better than the other options she'd thought of, but... "How?"

"Just stay put, and I'll show you." Then he was gone.

Leaving her alone. And conflicted.

LANDON'S BIGGEST CHALLENGE was going to be explaining his absences. He could look into Mr. Field's murder easily enough. Like he'd told Hazeleigh, everyone would think he was helping out because their families had connections. His brothers would likely give him that look that told him they knew—even if Hazeleigh didn't—that he paid a little too close attention there.

Neither reason bothered him.

He stabled his horse. He'd disappeared again after the cops had left by giving the excuse he'd ride the property and see if he could find any trace of Hazeleigh. He knew he'd have to lie to Zara, and he had no trouble lying to people. But when he knew someone was worried, and he could ease that worry with the truth, that made the lying harder.

Before he even was up the porch steps, Zara had the door open. She stood there at the threshold of the old ranch house. "Any sign of her?" she demanded.

Since he'd already been preparing himself, he managed an apologetic smile. "Sorry." Zara frowned, but she held open the door for him and he stepped into the living room. Almost everyone was situated around the room. Cal stood in the threshold between kitchen and living room. Kate and Brody sat next to each other on a couch, Jake on an armchair. Zara paced. The only two people missing were Henry and Dunne.

"Did you guys find anything here?" Landon asked, hoping to take the focus off himself.

"Zara went through the cabin," Jake offered. "Hazeleigh had taken some things. Not just her everyday work things, but personal belongings and cash savings. It's likely she was spooked, but she wasn't taken or harmed," Jake said, watching Zara the whole time.

"I don't know where she could have gone—would have gone." Zara wrung her hands as she paced. Landon could tell she was trying to keep a strong facade, but worry had dug lines into her forehead, and her eyes were sad. The angry warrior of earlier had softened into a sister worried for her sister's safety. "There's no family or friends to go to. Unless she went to Thomas, and he's not telling me."

"We could always make an impromptu stop by his place in Bent," Brody suggested. "Maybe she's with him and didn't want…" He trailed off, pulling a slight face.

Kate rolled her eyes. "You stopped about three words too late," she muttered.

"Didn't want *what*?" Zara demanded.

Brody raised an eyebrow, causing Zara to scowl.

"Let's try to be methodical about this," Cal said. As the former commander of Team Breaker, he was used to taking charge. No amount of time being here, being equals and out of the military, could get him out of the habit of trying to take control of a situation.

"Hazeleigh is *missing*," Zara retorted. "I don't need methodical. I don't need patience. I need to know my sister is safe."

It was a difficult thing for Landon not to say anything or give anything away. He wanted to offer Zara *some* reassurance, but he couldn't. Not yet. He'd find a way.

"I'm going to do some digging into what the cops know but aren't telling us," Landon said. Maybe he sounded a bit like Cal, trying to take over, but so be it. "If you could get any information out of your cousin that would be great, but the bottom line is someone called the cops saying they saw Hazeleigh leaving the fort. Why would anyone call about that? It's not out of the ordinary, and they'd have to have known there was something bad inside to call the police. It doesn't add up."

"Someone's framing her?" Kate asked.

"We don't know until we figure out who called. That's step one." Landon held up a hand before Zara could start in. "I know you want to find her, and you want to make sure she's safe. I get that. But she took things from her cabin, right? And she's been in this position before. She knows they could take her in, right? Why wouldn't she run away to avoid that?"

"Without telling me?" Zara demanded.

"Maybe she's protecting you," Jake said softly. Zara whirled on him, but she didn't say anything when he got up and put his hands on her shoulders. "Just like you'd protect her."

Zara huffed out a breath and leaned into Jake. "You

all know Hazeleigh. She's too sweet, too soft and a damn sight too skittish to be off running away when there's no one for her to run to."

Landon didn't have a clue why that estimation of Hazeleigh bothered him. It wasn't far off the mark, but he couldn't keep his mouth shut all the same. "Maybe you need to give her some credit, Zara."

"I'm not *not* giving her credit," Zara replied, but not with her usual anger. There was a softness to the denial, like she was afraid that's exactly what she was doing.

"I think it's clear she was scared, and why wouldn't she be? She's been through this before. So we do what we can to give her a reason not to be scared."

"I'm not going to quit looking for her."

Landon nodded, wondering how he'd keep Zara from searching the ranch. "No, we don't have to do that. But we should be careful we aren't leading the cops to her."

"She didn't do it," Kate said firmly from her seat on the couch. "Even if she was capable of murder, she never would have shot a gun. She hates guns. And she loves..." Kate swallowed, tears filling her eyes, though they didn't fall. "Mr. Field," she finally said.

Kate worked at the fort, so she also worked closely with Mr. Field.

"When was the last time you heard from Mr. Field?" Landon asked. What he really wanted to ask was if she'd also received a middle-of-the-night message from Mr. Field, but he couldn't ask without outing himself.

"Yesterday at work. He was closeted in his office, so I didn't pop in to say goodbye because he was deep in research mode." Brody slid his arm around Kate and she leaned into him. "It doesn't make any sense. He was an old man. Why would someone murder him like that?"

"We're going to figure it out," Landon assured her. He

looked at Cal, who was staring at him with some suspicion. But Landon wouldn't let that get to him.

He was going to get to the bottom of it all, one way or another.

Chapter Five

Hazeleigh spent the next few hours talking herself in and out of leaving. The thing that kept her in the old schoolhouse was the fact she couldn't think of a reliable way of getting away. They'd be looking for her car if she took it—and any of the Thompsons' vehicles if she got the guts to steal one of their ranch trucks. A horse wouldn't take her far enough, and she wouldn't be able to feed it long enough or be assured the horse would be cared for if she needed to leave it behind.

Cabs and ride shares were few and far between out here in the middle of nowhere, so she'd be noticed. Someone could call the cops.

Staying and accepting Landon's help seemed to be her only sensible option.

At least for now. Running was always a possibility if things went badly. Even if she had to do it on foot.

She spent some time sitting down and breathing, meditating over the situation before her. She let herself imagine what it might be like to go to the police. Express her innocence and hope for the best.

But thinking it—imagining it—left her with the same blind panic she'd first felt. Deep in her bones, whatever it was that told her bad things were coming was warning against letting the law handle it.

She thought about what Landon had said. That she'd be doing some of the fighting herself.

She'd never fought a day in her life. She hated confrontation. Avoided it. Ignored it. Ran away from it.

Wasn't right now an excellent example?

But Landon had made it sound so possible. He'd *show* her. The idea left her feeling…strange. It was a new feeling, amid all this old hat fear and running. Unsettled, but not the kind that made her want to retreat. This was something more she wanted to lean into.

It wasn't that she *liked* being a coward, it was just…it had often been the best way to handle her father growing up. Or even the best way to handle poor Amberleigh's temper. And the few times she'd been brave enough to stand up for herself, Zara had swooped in and taken the brunt of the reaction. Hazeleigh had never learned how to be the one who fought.

You're going to do some of that fighting yourself. Maybe she didn't know how, but Landon *had* said he'd show her how. The idea of that did not give her a bad feeling, did not send her into a panic.

But how did someone fight a lie? Or public opinion? Or whatever it was against her? She sat in the now dark schoolhouse and mulled things over.

Information. Facts. She was good at all those things. Organizing. Analyzing. Drawing conclusions. She just needed…

The door squeaked, moved. She had only a second of fear before she heard Landon's voice whispering assurances as a dark shadow slid into the room.

And then light.

The small camping lantern didn't offer enough light to see the whole room, but enough to make out Landon. He had a laptop under his arm, and a small backpack.

"You're probably starving," he offered, setting the pack between them.

She hadn't thought about food. Or sleep. She'd been too tied in knots to feel anything but the stress of the day.

"I had to be careful about what I took so no one notices and asks why I'm taking more food than usual." He pulled out a plastic snack bag full of nuts. An apple. A water bottle and a can of Zara's favorite pop.

Something about the whole thing made her want to cry. Because even though Landon was insisting on helping her, until this very moment she'd still felt very much alone. Separated.

But Landon hadn't just brought his laptop and the idea they were going to get to the bottom of Mr. Field's murder, he'd brought her food.

"Go on now and eat something," he insisted, pushing the supplies at her. "And I'll catch you up to speed."

Hazeleigh followed his instructions. Another one of her strengths. As she munched on the apple and sipped some water, she *did* begin to feel less shaky and untethered— even if she still didn't feel hungry through the knots in her stomach.

"Poked around a bit in the police database, and Zara talked to Thomas and he told her a few basic things, but nothing much. Still, that phone call was an anonymous tip that something bad had happened at the fort, and your car had been seen driving away. The cops are looking into it, as they aren't totally sold on an anonymous tip when it comes to murder. I know you've already made up your mind, but right now the police view you as a person of interest, not a suspect."

He was looking at her carefully in the dim light of the lantern. He wanted her to turn herself in. The apple turned to a lump in her throat, and she had a difficult time swallowing it down. When she spoke, her voice was shaky at best. "I can't turn myself in now." There was no sensible way to explain it to him. "I just…can't."

Landon nodded, and she was surprised that he didn't argue with her. He pointed to the nuts. "Eat those, too," he said instead, before continuing his explanation of what he'd found out.

"There weren't signs of a struggle according to the report I managed to get my eyes on. But the office was a mess. So not necessarily a defending-himself struggle. But a mess. Did Mr. Field keep anything valuable in his office someone might have been after?"

Hazeleigh sipped her water and sighed. "Unfortunately the only answer I have is maybe. He was a disorganized soul—that's why he paid me to keep track of things, organize them. His office was often full of random things. Sometimes he'd stuff cash in his desk. Sometimes he'd leave it in his car. But nothing specific. Nothing… I'd think if someone really wanted money, they would have gone to his house. He didn't trust banks."

"Is there anything other than cash someone might want their hands on?"

Hazeleigh tried to think. Mr. Field collected historical artifacts—some were rare and valuable. Occasionally people contacted him wanting to buy them from him, but Mr. Field never sold. He couldn't part with anything—from scraps of paper to sentimental matchsticks. "It's possible? But it also seems far-fetched."

Landon nodded thoughtfully, then pointed at the bag of nuts again. "All of it," he instructed.

Hazeleigh wasn't the biggest fan of pistachios, but she knew this wasn't about what she liked to eat. It was about keeping her strength up. If he had to be careful about the food he brought, she had to be smart and eat whatever he brought.

"So the police think someone was after something?"

"I don't know what the police think. That's my interpretation. Based on what little information was in the report, and what even less information Thomas gave Zara. A mess that wasn't about a self-defense fight has to be someone looking for *something*."

Hazeleigh's stomach sank. "That just makes me an even bigger suspect. I'm the one person in the world who knows what he has."

"But wouldn't you know *where*?"

"It just depends, but I'm willing to bet those are the exact questions the police would ask me. Do I keep track? Does he hide things? Are any valuable? And it would all come back on me. No matter what."

Landon's mouth firmed, but he didn't argue with her. "That's why we need to know if anything was taken. Or even what the focus of the search was. If we know what, we can prove that you wouldn't want or need whatever it is."

Hazeleigh wasn't convinced that would prove her innocence, but it seemed like a step in the right direction. "How are we going to do that?"

"Well, we're going to break into a crime scene. If you're up to it."

HAZELEIGH SPLUTTERED ON the sip of water she'd just taken. Landon winced. Perhaps he should have timed that statement a little better. "I'd say you don't have to go with me, but I need your eyes."

Once she was done coughing, she shook her head. "I don't understand."

"If we can get into Mr. Field's office, which presumably you had a hand in organizing, you could see what is missing, or messed with. You're the only one who might be able to figure out what the murderer was after."

Hazeleigh chewed on her bottom lip for a moment, and Landon had to busy himself with zipping up the backpack rather than allowing himself to be distracted by her mouth.

"What if I can't? What if it's just a mess and I don't know anything?"

Landon shrugged, risking a look back at her. She wasn't chewing on her lip anymore, but her eyebrows were furrowed and her dark eyes were lost.

It made his heart twist in his chest. "Look, to get to the bottom of something you sometimes take a few steps that don't get you anywhere. That's okay."

"What if we get caught?"

He offered her his most reassuring smile. "We won't."

"You can't guarantee that," she said with an expression that reminded him of a scolding schoolteacher. Why he found *that* attractive was beyond him, and he couldn't quite keep the charm out of his drawl.

"Trust me."

She didn't smile back, or even blush and look away like she might have a few weeks ago. She held his gaze, her eyes heartbreakingly serious.

"I do trust you."

Her answer hit him too hard, but he was also good at hiding his emotions when something hit far too hard. "Good," he replied.

She sighed, looking down at the last handful of nuts. "I don't want these."

He held out his hand and she transferred them into his palm, their fingers brushing briefly. If she felt any of that buzz of electricity he did, she hid it well.

Which shouldn't irritate him as much as it did. He tossed the nuts into his mouth and crunched hard enough to keep his mind on the important task at hand. "They'll have the office taped off, but I'm willing to bet they don't have someone stationed out there overnight. We'll head over now."

"How?"

"I've got the horses waiting. I've never seen you ride, but Zara always says you're capable."

"Yes, I can ride," she said, a thread of insult running through her tone. "I *did* grow up on a ranch."

"You're not exactly dressed for it."

She looked down at her skirt and frothy, vintage sweater in the dim light. Then she looked up at him, angling her chin slightly so that she reminded him of Zara—a rare feat, no matter how much the sisters looked alike. "A true rider doesn't need *pants*, Landon."

There was really something wrong with him that the primness in her tone affected him the way it did.

He could not focus on that right now. "So we'll ride over. I'll scope out the area, and then we'll see what we can do to get inside. If we've got the opportunity, we'll do it tonight. If not, we'll make a plan to go back."

"How long do you honestly think I can hide out here?"

He didn't touch her as a rule, but this seemed like the kind of thing that needed a connection. Even if it was just his hands on her shoulders.

Of course, that reminded him that Jake had done the same to Zara, and they were in a committed romantic relationship. He was just a friend, at best, offering a helping hand.

They started that way.

He pushed away the thought, gave her shoulder one squeeze then let go. "As long as it takes," he said firmly. A promise. Maybe something closer to a vow.

Her expression was pained. Worried. "Do you really think—"

Frustrated he couldn't seem to get through to her, he cut her off. "Hazeleigh, I wouldn't be doing any of it if I didn't think it was worth a shot. Look, I know how to..." He wasn't sure what the right words were. There was an entire decade of experience he couldn't tell her about. "It's not going out on a limb. I know how to assess a situation, and I'm not about to put you in the middle of anything dangerous or that might get you caught before we have enough information to make sure you're not the suspect."

"I'm not worried about...danger," she said, clearly picking that word very carefully.

"Then what are you worried about?"

She shook her head. "I don't...know. It just doesn't feel right. None of it feels right. Except..." This time when she trailed off, he didn't think it was because she didn't have the words, but because she was stopping herself from saying them.

"Except what?"

She wasn't looking at him anymore. She had her gaze down on her fingers, all twisted together in anxiety. "I trust you, Landon," was all she said. Quietly. Almost...shyly, as if trusting him was some great admission, even though she'd mentioned it once before.

But, he supposed, if he put it all together, she was saying the only thing that felt right was that she trusted him. And that meant far more than it should.

"You don't think your brothers will notice you missing?" she asked.

"If they do, I'll just tell them the truth. Without you in it. I went to the fort. *I* looked around."

"So we're going to ride our horses over to the fort in the middle of the night. We're going to break into a crime scene. I'm going to somehow figure out what the murderer might have been after. Then we're going to prove to the police that I'm innocent by…"

Tracking down the murderer, Landon thought to himself. But he wasn't about to say that out loud. Not yet. Besides, she wouldn't necessarily be involved in that part. If he could help it.

"Let's take everything one step at a time. The first step is to ride over to the fort and see what's what. You're a local girl. Surely you know a shortcut."

She bristled again, like when he'd mentioned her outfit for riding. "Of course I know a shortcut."

He didn't smile, though he wanted to. He liked those little flashes of pride and temper. She should let them out more often.

"So that's the first step. Ready?"

Some of the worry crept in around the pride, but Landon watched carefully as she steeled herself. She clenched her fingers and let them go, straightened her shoulders, then gave a firm nod.

Because underneath all that…skittishness she wore like a shield, she was a fighter. She just didn't give herself enough credit for that yet.

Maybe at the end of this, when they'd proven she was innocent, she would.

Chapter Six

Hazeleigh could admit here, in the middle of the night, on the back of her horse, that she'd missed riding Buttercup. She'd missed feeling like the ranch was part of her. She didn't want to be a rancher, never had, but she'd grown up in the pastures and fields. She'd loved and lost horses and dogs and cats. She liked ranch *life*, even if she wasn't cut out for the work.

When the Thompson brothers bought the ranch last year, she'd felt like she couldn't enjoy the ranch anymore. Even the cabin that she'd shared with Zara before Zara moved into the main house with Jake was just a rental.

She should be over it, let it go, but it still irked. Dad had sold it all out from under them without even a second thought or apology. He'd considered it his right. His *due*. His wife had died, and he'd had to raise his triplet daughters alone, only to have his favorite kid run away at sixteen. Why shouldn't he take a bigger payoff than the ranch deserved and leave?

Hazeleigh inhaled sharply. It wasn't any good getting angry with her father all over again. What was done was done. She couldn't change it and being angry didn't help. It only made her feel...well, angry. And anger was never a thing she knew what to do with. It sat there in her stomach, churning like acid.

The night whirred and chirped with nocturnal life. The stars above shone like a quilt of glitter, so big and vast. All those things settled in her bones like they always did. Contentment. Hope. Belonging.

She'd never understood why Amberleigh had such a driving need to leave when they were young. This was home. Built on generations of hard work and tragedy and all that hope.

No, Hazeleigh didn't really want to run away from her problems. Not when Wilde and the ranch were home, ownership or not. It simply felt like it might be the only option. The best option for both her and Zara.

But if Landon really could prove she wasn't the murderer...

She breathed out a sigh. That was a big *if.* "The highway is coming up," she said softly to Landon. "We'll have to cross it to get to the fort."

"All right. Let's get off the horses and lead them."

They both dismounted and Landon came to stand next to Hazeleigh, horses bracketing them in the moonlight. They walked the next few yards, leading their horses by the reins.

When they reached the ditch before the highway, Landon paused. "I'll cross first," he said. "Then I'll give a whistle when it's your turn."

"You don't think we should cross together?"

"I know it's a pretty low-trafficked highway, but we can't be too careful. Someone comes by and sees me cross, you'll have time to get away."

"And leave you here?" What kind of coward did he take her for? She was at least a *loyal* coward.

"I'm not a person of interest in a murder case, far as I know, so I should make out okay even if I get caught."

Hazeleigh didn't correct him out loud. Just in her head.

She wasn't a *person of interest*, no matter what the cops said. She was a *suspect*.

Still, she didn't think she could just…ditch Landon, even if he could talk his way out of trouble. He probably could. Flash a grin, really amp up the Southern drawl and anyone would fall under his spell. But she wouldn't want to leave him to deal with it. She couldn't.

Hopefully it wouldn't come to that.

The highway was dark, quiet. Hazeleigh didn't expect to see anyone except maybe a random semitruck, but even that was unlikely as this was a two-lane road that ran parallel to the bigger interstate closer to town.

Landon crossed first. She listened as his horse's hooves clip-clopped against the hard surface of the road. She petted Buttercup as she waited for Landon's whistle. When it sounded, she took a deep breath. She looked up and down the highway and saw no sign of any lights or vehicles.

She crossed, *knowing* no one was going to pop up, and yet she held her breath, her heart pounding in her chest louder than Buttercup's horseshoes hitting the pavement.

She made it to the other side. No one appeared. Nothing happened.

"How much farther you think?" Landon asked.

"Not much. Maybe a quarter of a mile. We'll come up on the back of the cabin side of the fort."

"All right. Lead the way."

He held Buttercup's reins as she mounted her horse, then got up on his in an easy, fluid moment.

"You're good with horses."

He smiled, his large, scarred hand moving across his horse's flank in all that silvery moonlight. "Yeah, we get along all right." He urged his horse into a forward walk and Hazeleigh did the same.

"Zara said you guys didn't know much about ranching when you got here."

"I suppose we didn't. She was a great help."

No further explanation. Hazeleigh knew she could press, but she held herself back. There were more important things to accomplish tonight.

She urged Buttercup forward. Toward the fort. Toward... Her stomach churned, a mixture of anxiety and fear. An image of Mr. Field, slumped over his desk and bloody, flashed through her mind—unbidden—over and over again.

The fort and its buildings looked like they always did in the moonlight—stark and lonely against all the surrounding nothingness, with only the far-off shadow of mountains hinting at any Western roots.

"Let's tie the horses here, and then walk across the yard," Landon suggested. "Just to make sure the cops don't have anyone posted."

"Okay." Hazeleigh couldn't make out all the shapes in the dark, but it didn't look like there was anyone for miles around. They dismounted their horses and Landon tied both their reins to a post near the historic cabin.

There was a beat of hesitation and then Landon held out his hand. "Just in case, we want to be absolutely silent. Hold my hand. Squeeze if you need anything."

She stood stock-still for a moment. She'd touched him or been touched by him more today than she'd been touched by *anyone* in the last few months. A purposeful choice on her part after everything with Douglas.

But this wasn't about her bad choices. This was about finding out the truth. She slid her hand into Landon's and felt a kind of...comfort or protection. Maybe her instincts were all wrong when it came to people, but Zara's weren't.

And Zara trusted all of Jake's brothers, even uptight Cal, irritable Henry and taciturn Dunne.

Landon was the nicest out of all of them, except maybe Jake, and even then, it might be a tie. So... So this was fine. She could hold his hand and trust him to get her out of this mess.

She could always run away if it didn't go well. She had to keep that reminder in her back pocket. It was always important to have a Plan B.

They walked hand in hand across the yard between the cabin and main fort building. A surreal experience in the cold evening, pretty and magical even though danger seemed to lurk in every shadow.

"I don't see signs of anyone. We'll clear the tape and get in if we can, okay?" Landon whispered.

Hazeleigh could only nod as they inched closer and closer. She could see—and hear—the crime-scene tape now. It flapped in the breeze, a wiggling phantom in the light of the moon. Behind it was the fort.

Hazeleigh had loved this place. It was like a second home. An homage to a past that might have been tough and lonely and sad, but it couldn't change. It was what it was. Solid. Sturdy.

Now it was the place Mr. Field had been murdered. In his cluttered office, with his favorite possessions—documents and photographs from the past, some over a century old.

"I don't want to go in there." The words fell out. It wasn't a thought so much as a feeling—sudden and real and backed by panic. The panic didn't get a foothold though, because Landon kept her hand squeezed in his, and it felt like an anchor again.

"I know, but sometimes it's best to face the things we don't want to do. Especially if it helps us figure out what happened. Mr. Field seems like the kind of guy who'd want everyone to know what really happened."

He was. Absolutely. His entire life was studying an old bank-robbery story about gold that had mysteriously disappeared. He wanted answers.

And never found them.

"Just keep your hand in mine," Landon said reassuringly.

She did, and it made this whole horrible situation feel a little bit more survivable.

LANDON COULD FEEL the resistance in the way Hazeleigh held his hand. She was gripping it tight—something that surprised him even as they ducked under the crime-scene tape—but without much warning, she'd suddenly pull. Not against his hold, but against their forward progress.

He knew no one was here. Unfortunately, that didn't bode well for the police having another suspect aside from Hazeleigh. Hazeleigh wasn't the kind of suspect who went back to the scene of the crime. She was the kind of suspect who ran.

They reached the door of the fort.

"I have my key," Hazeleigh whispered beside him as he used his free hand to test the knob. He knew it would be locked, but he wanted to get a feel for what he was working with.

"I'd rather the cops think someone broke in if they figure out anyone was here at all. Using your key only keeps pointing the finger at you." Reluctantly, he dropped her hand. The knob was old. It bothered him the cops hadn't put up more security around the murder scene, but maybe they'd scrubbed it already. Gotten everything they needed.

He pulled his pocketknife out of his pocket and got to work on jimmying the lock. Once it clicked, he slowly pushed open the heavy door, trying to avoid any creaking sound.

"Should I ask where you learned to do that?" Hazeleigh asked, close at his back as he got the door open enough for them to slide in.

"A story for another time." They stepped inside the fort. The air was stale and smelled of commercial-grade cleaning products. The murder room had likely been scrubbed, but would they have taken everything in the office, making this entire trip a worthless enterprise?

Only one way to find out.

He pulled the small penlight out of his other cargo pocket and flashed it on. It offered a very narrow, dim line of light.

"Can you show me the way to his office?"

Hazeleigh audibly swallowed and didn't move.

"He's not in there. They likely cleaned everything up, too. That's what that smell is. Cleaner and bleach."

She nodded, but she still didn't move. He slid his arm around her shoulders. She seemed to be getting used to him taking her hand, letting him touch her shoulder. She didn't flinch or run away.

She trusted him. If he spent too much time thinking about that, he might be downright humbled.

But they didn't have time for that. He propelled her forward, getting her to take those first few steps, and then she led him toward the back. She paused at a door.

"Don't touch it," he instructed.

"If you're worried about fingerprints, mine are already here. Everywhere. Yours aren't."

"I can wipe mine. I did it out there."

"You did?"

He reached out and turned the knob. It wasn't locked either. This time, he slowed down his movements so she could see him wipe his prints.

She frowned as she watched, deep in thoughts she didn't verbalize. He pointed his light inside the office, making sure his body blocked her view until he was sure things were clean.

It was a tiny, windowless room. Though it was clear the office had been cleaned and things had been moved around, there were still a lot of things jammed into corners and drawers. He drew Hazeleigh inside.

Since there were no windows, he shut the door behind them and flipped on the light, making sure to wipe his prints again.

Hazeleigh stood with her back to the door, her face as white as a sheet as she looked at the empty spot in front of the desk, where Mr. Field and the chair he was sitting on would have been this morning.

Landon weighed his options, and in the end he decided the quickest way to get through this was to push forward. It made his gut twist into knots, but the sooner they were finished, the sooner he could get her out of here.

"We have to keep in mind the police would have taken anything contaminated along with anything they thought was evidence."

"Contaminated," Hazeleigh echoed.

Landon worried she might throw up, her pallor turning a little green around the edges. But she breathed out as she took in the scene.

"Almost everything is here," Hazeleigh said, her voice thready. "Just the way it was. Except for what was on his desk, where…"

Landon nodded. That was strange. If Mr. Field had been shot in the office, if there had been as much blood as Hazeleigh had said, many more items should have been cleared out of this room.

"Any research that's a primary source, or historical

document in any way, would have been kept in archival boxes or protectors. Since it's a historic site, the county likely would have sent someone over to make sure artifacts weren't cleaned or destroyed without inspection first."

She swallowed and then finally stepped forward, her gaze sweeping over the desk. "His computer is gone, obviously. He was slumped over it." She took a shuddering breath. "I don't know if he had anything on his desk in front of him. I didn't see. I didn't…"

Landon stepped forward and rested his hand on her shoulder. "It's okay. Whatever you saw or didn't. We're just getting an idea. If you don't remember, don't notice anything, that's all right."

She nodded. "I do all the organizing. Usually at the end of the day he leaves his desk a mess, and I come in and clean and file. Going by how I left things the night before, there's an entire box missing from right here," she said, pointing to a corner on the desk. "It held any photographs of the bank. Mr. Field's area of interest was the supposed bank robbery here back in 1892. He kept any and all real and photocopied pictures of the bank—past and present— in this box. There was also another photo album with pictures of sites people thought the stolen gold was hidden."

"Were the albums here when you came in this morning?"

"I don't…know."

"Okay, that's okay." He squeezed her shoulder in reassurance. He'd be able to hack into the photos the police took of the scene once they uploaded them to their system. He wouldn't put her through looking at the crime scene the way it had been found—with a bloody Mr. Field—but if he knew what to look for, that was a step.

"If he had things on his desk, it would have been…file folders from the cabinet over there. There was blood all over the desk, so the police would have… It would be ruined."

"Was there blood anywhere else?"

"I don't…" She swallowed and closed her eyes. "It's a blur. I can't…"

"Okay, let's focus on the here and now. Can you look through the filing cabinets and maybe see if anything's missing?"

She took another tentative step. With shaking hands, she touched the filing cabinet next to the desk. "We keep any newspaper or magazine articles, printouts of anything we've found online in the top drawer. Biographies of all involved in the second. The third door is random things Mr. Field thought might be related."

"Go ahead. Take a look."

She wiped her hands on the front of her jeans and then nodded. She pulled open the first one carefully and frowned. "There's a lot missing here."

"Could you make a list?"

The task seemed to steady her. She found a piece of paper and a pen and began to mutter to herself as she wrote. Landon watched the clock as she went through each drawer, her list growing and growing.

"I don't think it would make sense for the police to have taken all these, and Mr. Field wouldn't have had them *all* out on his desk."

"Then that's where we'll start."

She nodded, holding the list to her chest. "I don't know what we'll find."

"I don't either. But we'll go through, see if you can come up with some connections, and…" Landon paused. Something…wasn't right. "Don't say a word," he ordered, and flipped off the light, plunging them into darkness.

Chapter Seven

Hazeleigh wanted to scream. She bit her lip instead and was surprised to find herself reaching out for Landon's hand. But she needed that connection. That tether to reality and the reminder she couldn't just…crumble to the floor and wail at her bad luck.

She didn't know why he'd turned off the light suddenly, but she knew it couldn't be good.

So she stood completely still, holding on to Landon for dear life. He didn't move. He was as still as a statue himself.

Then she heard it—a creak, followed by a very faint shuffle.

A footstep.

She gripped Landon's hand harder. Bit her tongue harder. Everything inside of her screamed to react in some way, but she couldn't.

After another few moments passed and she heard nothing because her heart echoed so loudly in her ears. Landon pulled her from where she'd been standing by the filing cabinet. Gently, he moved her to the little corner on the same wall as the door. He kept maneuvering her until her back was pressed against the wall.

She realized that if someone opened the door, she would be effectively hidden by it. Landon leaned in, his mouth just about brushing her ear.

She narrowly swallowed down a squeak.

"Don't move," Landon said, his whisper barely audible even as she felt his breath against her cheek.

But then he tried to let go of her hand, and she didn't know what he planned to do, but she just knew… She just knew it was wrong. She *felt* it, the way she did sometimes. Whether it was a true feeling or not, she didn't know, but even after so many different ways she'd been burned, she still couldn't let people go out there into something that was *wrong*. So she held on to his hand for dear life rather than let it go.

She spoke once she trusted herself to keep her voice as quiet as his. "You stay right here."

"Haze—"

She pulled him closer, so that they were effectively chest to…well, he was quite a bit taller than her so it was more like her chest to his midsection. He didn't say anything, but Hazeleigh felt as though he was…fighting with himself. Deciding whether to stay close to her and the door that would hide both of them, or to find his own hiding spot. Or maybe he'd planned to go out there and face whatever they'd heard.

She didn't like any option that wasn't him, right here, with her. So she kept his hand in hers and used her free arm to curl around him. To hold him closer. To keep him exactly in place, where they could both hide. Together.

As long as no one turned on the light.

It was sort of like a hug, no matter how she told herself silently, over and over, that it was *not* a hug. It was a hold. It was for their safety and their protection that she had her arm snug around his waist.

If they were somewhere else—just about anywhere—it might look like they were dancing. Slow dancing.

She wanted to laugh at the absurdity of it all, so she

forced herself to swallow. To focus on the danger lurking outside that door. Not how tall and sturdy he seemed, like she could lean her cheek against his chest and be perfectly safe.

She knew better than that. No one could keep her safe, not even herself.

In the quiet of only their careful breathing and beating hearts, she heard the slight jiggle of the doorknob. As if someone had tried it and, finding it locked, given up.

Please give up and go away. Please. Please. Please.

She didn't say anything and neither did Landon. He kept his free hand straight at his side, didn't make any attempt to touch her the way she was touching him. Almost like he was keeping that hand free to be ready to fight.

But the door never opened. Time stretched on and on and on and nothing happened. Except she could hear the easy, steady beat of Landon's heart as he stood perfectly still with her.

Landon began easing away, and gave her hand one last squeeze before he disentangled himself. "Stay right here. I'm just going to make sure they're gone."

"But—"

She hadn't even gotten the full word out before he'd slid out of the office, leaving her in the dark, completely unsure what to do. Follow him? Follow his instructions and stay put? She didn't fully understand what had just happened.

Clearly someone had been in the fort with them, but they hadn't tried to get past the locked door to Mr. Field's office. Would it have been a police officer checking up on the crime scene? Were they about to be caught and arrested?

Hazeleigh closed her eyes and took a careful breath. She'd have to find a way to get Landon out of it. Claim that she'd…forced him to help her.

Like anyone is going to believe you forced him to do anything.

Still, she'd try. She couldn't stand the idea of him getting into trouble for her. She hadn't wanted him to help her in the first place. She should be halfway to Nebraska by now, but instead he'd stopped her. Tried to help.

Why couldn't he have just listened and let her handle this? Why couldn't he have just…?

Oh, she didn't know. She only knew the idea of him being in trouble because of her made her sick to her stomach. She didn't want to be anyone's burden, anyone's blame. Ever since Amberleigh had disappeared ten years ago, Dad had blamed her. Before that, he'd never come out and said it, but she'd always thought he'd somehow blamed her for Mom's death, too.

Hazeleigh shook her head. This had nothing to do with Dad. Or even blame and bad feelings. It had to do with… Mr. Field. He was dead. For some random missing files?

None of it added up.

Landon returned and she figured his flashlight being on was a good sign they were alone again.

"Whoever it was is gone. And we need to get gone, too."

"You don't think it was the police?"

"No."

Hazeleigh's anxiety changed—from worry over Landon getting into trouble, to worry over who on earth was also sneaking around the fort in the middle of the night. "Then who?"

"I don't know, but we're going to find out." He grabbed her hand—no gentle offering this time. He began to pull her out of the office, then hurriedly locked it from the inside and shut the door.

"How are we going to find out?" Hazeleigh asked as he all but dragged her through the front room and toward the door through which they'd entered. It was open, but she was almost certain they'd closed it behind them.

But Landon didn't seem to care about that. He slid out the door, pulling her behind them. He left it open as he led her back toward the horses.

"You know the way back to the schoolhouse," he said sternly. "Go there and—"

"What are you going to do?"

"I'm going to track whoever was in here. We have to know who if we're going to figure out why."

Hazeleigh pulled her hand out of his, though it was a bit of a struggle to get her hand free. But no, that wasn't how this was going to go. She stopped in her tracks. "No. Not without me, you aren't."

THERE WAS NO time to waste. Landon had already given the intruder too much of a head start for his liking, but for Hazeleigh's sake he'd had to wait and really make sure the intruder was gone.

Who would it have been? Certainly not a cop. A cop would have unlocked the door. And wouldn't have been sneaking around in the dark, even if he'd suspected someone had broken in.

Who else would be sneaking around in the middle of the night, trying to get into the office? To Landon, the only sensible answer was the actual murderer.

He couldn't just let him get away.

"No?" he said carefully to Hazeleigh. Maybe she'd hear how ridiculous that *no* was if he said it back to her.

"You can't just…send me away. I have to go with you."

"I know how to track someone, Hazeleigh. And what to do if I'm caught. We don't even know who we're dealing with."

"You said I was a part of this."

"You're the center of this." He had to fight the frustration rising inside of him. He didn't want to snap at her. She'd likely flinch and do that thing that was far too close to a cower for his tastes, which would make him feel like he'd kicked a puppy when all he was trying to do was *help*. "But I'm the one who knows how to handle things like this."

"How would you know that?"

"Why are you so full of questions now? Why can't you listen so I can get you out of this mess?" He regretted the words, and the snap in his voice, almost instantaneously.

But she didn't flinch or cower. She stood very still. When she spoke, her words were steady. And accusatory. "You said I was going to fight for myself, Landon. You said that. Because I wanted to do this on my own, and—"

"You wanted to run away," he corrected, as softly as possible.

"I still do. I don't want to worry the police will connect you to this. I don't want to worry that I'll be the reason you—"

"Stop," he said, and he did his best to keep his emotions tethered, but it was a tough thing to do, and his words came out clipped. "Let's be clear. This is my choice. My choice to get involved, to help, to break into the fort. More than yours, in fact. You're not the *reason* I'll get in trouble. I am. And whoever started this whole thing by killing an innocent man."

She remained very still, and he couldn't read the exact change of her expression with only the light from the moon and stars to illuminate her. "But..." She couldn't seem to come up with anything to refute his statements.

"No *buts*. Now, time is wasting. I know what I'm doing. I can do this. But I need to know you'll go back to the schoolhouse and hide while I do it." He'd need daylight now. At least a little of it.

"You're going to track him. And then what?"

"See who he is."

"And then what?"

"It'll depend on a lot of factors. Identifying him is the first and most important step. I'll wait right here while you get across the highway. Then I'll follow the tracks once I get some daylight."

"How do you know there are tracks?"

"I saw a few. Heading south behind the fort."

She seemed to mull over his plan, then shook her head. She untangled Buttercup's reins and began to mount her horse. "We don't need to wait for daylight," she said, swinging into the saddle.

Landon could only stare up at her. "Huh?"

"I have an idea where he's going."

"How?"

"Pretty much the only reason to go that way is to get to Mr. Field's house."

Landon didn't have a clue where Mr. Field lived. He was reasonably sure with some daylight he could track the intruder. Even more certain that if Hazeleigh gave him directions right now, he'd be able to find it in the dark.

But she wasn't taking no for an answer. And she knew the way, so there'd be no mistakes. She wanted to fight, and in the strangest way it was progress for her. Good for her.

Why did it have to be now, when he wanted to pack her off and hide her away, and handle the situation without putting her in danger?

Landon sighed and got up on his horse. "All right. We'll do this together, but I'm in charge."

She stared at him for a moment or two, solemn and serious. "Of course you are."

And though she said it as though she meant it, Landon had the sneaking suspicion they were both very, very wrong.

Chapter Eight

Hazeleigh urged Buttercup forward. She had no idea why. The sensible thing would be to go hide in the schoolhouse and let Landon handle this. He knew what he was doing. He'd said so himself.

She didn't quite know what that meant, but she believed him. Landon seemed endlessly capable of just about anything.

But she knew how to find Mr. Field's house in the dark. She knew what to look for…sort of. Maybe.

It just felt like a thing she needed to do. If she wasn't going to run, how could she just sit around and wait for someone else to clean up the mess? Someone who might get in trouble on her behalf.

She just…couldn't.

"Not too fast," Landon cautioned. "Whoever it was had a head start, and even if the only sensible location they're headed to is Mr. Field's house, we still don't know who or why."

"What *do* we know, Landon?" she asked, slowing Buttercup's pace. It felt like a crawl. She knew it wasn't fair to be grumpy with him, and he was probably right about the don't-go-galloping-into-danger thing. But she was tired, and she wanted this whole mystery *over*.

"We know someone—who wasn't the cops—came lurking about the fort tonight."

"And gave up when the door was locked. Some crazed murderer."

Landon was quiet for a long time before he spoke, and when he did, it was in a grave tone. "It doesn't take a crazed, unpredictable person to kill, Hazeleigh. That's the problem. Someone called the police when you left the fort. There's premeditation written all over this. From Mr. Field's death, to you finding him, to someone calling the police on *you*." He was quiet for a few moments. "It has to connect to the work. If there are files missing, and he was killed in his office… Tell me more about Mr. Field's research and what files were missing from his office."

"He wanted to find the gold that disappeared in this supposed bank robbery. But that's the problem—most historians agree the bank robbery never took place, that it was just a myth. A lot of locals believe it was all a ruse to keep the railroad and the land speculators out—make them think it was too dangerous. That's also why they named the town Wilde."

"Didn't most towns back then want railroads and land speculators?"

"Towns, yes. Ranchers, no. Bent was close enough for railroads, without being close enough for people to start encroaching on pasture."

"If there's no evidence it happened, why was Mr. Field dedicating his life to studying it?"

"He believed. I love history as much as the next person. No, that isn't true. I love history *more* than the next person. And there have been times I got caught up in Mr. Field's enthusiasm and thought he might be right, but at the end of the day, it's…lore, and he *wanted* to believe more than he had evidence to believe."

Historical research was supposed to be about facts, not feelings. Not hopes and maybes. Dates, artifacts, first-hand accounts. Not fanciful dreams of bank robbers and *gold* that might still be around today. But more often that not, she'd *wanted* Mr. Field to be right, more than she'd ever actually believed he was. "He's been doing the same research for decades. He's never found anything that'd be enough to kill over."

Landon sighed, and the sound was sad. Sad enough that she looked over at him, and though she could just make out his profile in the moonlight, she had the aching wish she could comfort him somehow.

"You'd be surprised what people are willing to kill over, Hazeleigh."

"That sounds like you have personal experience."

He shook his head in the dim light but didn't refute her statement. He didn't explain his experience either. Hazeleigh found it odd that she wanted to press, because she wanted to *know*, when usually she much preferred keeping to herself.

But Mr. Field's cabin was just up ahead. "Not much farther now. If this person was heading there, should we stop now and walk, like we did at the fort?"

"Yes," Landon said. "Is there any cover around the house?"

Cover. Such a strange word for places to hide. It made her wonder what Landon's life was like before he and his brothers moved here. But now was not the time for wondering or questions. "Not really in the front. It's just a little cabin in the middle of a stretch of land. There's a creek that runs through his backyard and there are a few heritage birches."

"Heritage birches?"

"Trees."

"You know the types of trees?"

He sounded a little *too* amused for her tastes. "I know lots of things, Landon."

He chuckled. "I know you do."

She wanted to take offense, to feel like he was laughing at her. He had to be, didn't he? But it didn't *sound* mean. It didn't *feel* mean, the way so many men in her life had been.

She let out a long breath. Landon wasn't her father, or Douglas, or even Kenny, her high-school boyfriend. But the fact of the matter was, she did like Landon, so surely *something* about him had to be suspect. Right?

None of that mattered now though. She thought about the layout of Mr. Field's land and cabin. "Follow me."

He did without question, or trying to make her feel like she didn't know what she was doing. She kept waiting for a complaint or one of those snide questions disguised as concern that she was so used to from the men she'd let into her life.

He simply followed.

It was such a confusing feeling Hazeleigh *had* to focus only on where they were going, or she might second-guess herself and even she knew in this moment there was no time for that.

She gave the cabin a wide berth and led them around to the back of the Field property. They couldn't get too far from the cabin in the back without crossing the creek. The horses would probably be fine, but Hazeleigh would want more daylight for the horses to make the crossing.

"Here," she said. It was far enough away from the cabin that even if it was daylight, the horses wouldn't be visible in this cluster of trees, which also gave them a place to tie the horses.

Landon would have to take them back to the ranch soon. Not only did they need to be fed and watered, but also if daylight dawned and two horses were missing, his brothers and Zara were bound to know he was out helping her.

"We can't take too much time," she said.

"Yeah, but we can't let this opportunity pass."

Hazeleigh wasn't so sure about that, but she got off Buttercup and tied the reins to the tree while Landon did the same with his horse.

"Okay, they're good. Lead the way."

It was even stranger having someone tell her to *lead*, but she was the expert here. She had to remember that. They also needed to stick close to one another, and until the cabin came into view and Landon knew the target, they needed to…

Well, like they'd done back at the fort. She held out her hand. She couldn't read Landon's expression in the dark, but it felt like there was a slight hesitation…just like her own not so long ago.

But before she had time to process it, to try and understand his hesitation, his big hand gripped hers.

The touch affected her. She couldn't deny that. His hand was warm and calloused and *big*, and it felt safe. She should know better than to feel safe, but she couldn't fight the warmth that moved through her.

She could ignore it though. She could move forward without *dwelling* on it. She led him over the soft swells of land. The moon was beginning to fade, the stars giving way to a lighter sky. This was taking too long, but…

The cabin was right there. It was still shrouded in darkness, and she couldn't make out anything that might give away someone sneaking around.

"Let's stay in the trees as we get closer," Landon said quietly.

The brush wasn't exactly full cover. There were spaces to walk through between some of the trees, but she hoped the dark hid their moving shadows. She held Landon's hand and drew him closer and closer to the cabin.

"There," Landon said, pulling her to a stop and pointing at…something.

Hazeleigh didn't see anything. It all looked dark to her, but she believed he'd seen something. She had no doubt that Landon knew what he was doing.

"What do we do now?" she asked in a whisper.

"You'll wait here."

"Landon."

"Behind a tree. Out of sight." He dropped her hand and began to step away from the trees. "Stay—" With no warning, Landon lunged, grabbed her hard and jerked her behind the narrow bark of one of the trees.

Almost at the exact same time, a gunshot rang out in the dark.

IT WAS CLOSE. Too close. Landon figured the only thing that saved them was the dark. The sting on his shoulder was little more than a graze, and he was damn lucky for that.

He knew Hazeleigh wouldn't see it that way. But that wasn't important now. What was important was finding cover.

"We have to get you out of here."

"Me?" she all but shrieked. "Us," she hissed.

Another shot. Hazeleigh winced and grabbed on to him. Landon tried to survey where the shot was coming from. He'd seen a silhouette *inside* the house, but it couldn't be whoever was shooting at them…unless the shooter had a window open.

Possible. Far too many possibilities.

Landon stilled, pushed Hazeleigh out of his mind and listened. He'd been here too many times to count. Shot at.

Waiting. Planning. He knew how to do this. He knew how to protect his team.

But Hazeleigh wasn't part of an elite military team. She was a civilian. This wasn't the Middle East and he wasn't in tactical gear and...

He blew out a slow breath, finding that old center of calm. He pushed away all the worries, concerns and possibilities, and focused on the *now*.

A cold ball of fear pitted in his stomach. Footsteps. Coming for them. He grabbed Hazeleigh's hand again and began to lead her away. He had to get her somewhere safe.

They couldn't run for the horses when he didn't know how many people were here. What kind of guns they had. But if they took a roundabout run back to the horses, maybe they could lose whoever was after them.

The biggest problem was that the shooter seemed to have something that allowed him to see in the dark.

So Landon stuck to the trees. He didn't exactly know where he was going. Cover was more important than where they ended up for right now. Moving quickly and as soundlessly as possible—something Hazeleigh was surprisingly good at—was all that mattered.

He thought they were making headway. There hadn't been any more gunshots, and when they paused to take a breath, there were no more footsteps.

"If we cross the creek here, we can get more tree cover and then double back to the horses," Hazeleigh said. "I don't know if that's a good idea, I just—"

"It's perfect." Another shot rang out and Hazeleigh jolted, but Landon held her hand tightly. "Farther away. Wrong direction. Whatever our shooter is following, he lost us. So let's get even more lost."

"It'll be slick. Especially in the dark. Rocks can seem

sturdy and then move on you. It'll be shockingly cold. So brace yourself."

He wanted to laugh. It was downright sweet of her, trying to warn him. She had no idea what he'd done, seen, endured. And it felt…a little too nice for someone to worry over him like he was just your average civilian.

"Yes, ma'am," he murmured, trying to make sure neither his amusement nor the way her concern touched him came through in his voice.

Hazeleigh pulled him a few more steps. He could hear the gurgling, the rush of water over rocks. Some worry slid under all that good feeling. "That sounds like something a hell of a lot bigger than a creek."

"It isn't deep, but it'll be icy. It'd be tough to cross in the daylight. In the dark, it's downright dangerous. But…"

Yeah, *but*. He looked around. The dark was getting lighter all the time, even if the sun hadn't fully risen yet. Still, his flashlight would give them away. Hopefully the roar of the rushing creek would hide the sound of them trying to cross it.

He squeezed Hazeleigh's hand. "Well, hold on." He inched forward, toward the creek. The bank was steep and that made things difficult. When his boot touched water, he had to fight the urge to pull back. March in Wyoming wasn't exactly *spring* and getting wet didn't hold any appeal.

But they had to get out of here. Resolutely, he stepped into the water. He bit back a string of curses. Holy *hell* it was cold. But the icy bite of the water only came up to about mid-calf. Once his feet were steady, grounded on two solid rocks, he looked back at Hazeleigh.

"Get on my back."

"What?"

"You're going to put your arms on my shoulders, your legs around my waist, and we'll get across that way."

"Don't be—"

"We don't have time to argue. Just do it."

The stern tone must have caught her off guard enough that she didn't argue and followed his order. From the taller part of the bank, she braced her hands on his shoulders, wrapped one leg around his left side. He gripped it. She gave a little hop and he managed to grab her other leg.

Then he began to walk. It was much harder with the added weight, but he'd endured worse. Heavier loads. More difficult challenges. And he thought about all of those challenges, rather than her pressed up against his back, or his arms hooked under her knees. He thought about the desert in the midafternoon rather than the stabbing frigid ice swirling around his legs.

He got about halfway across before another gunshot sounded. Much closer now, as if the gunman had figured out where they were. Hazeleigh jerked, but he managed to keep his balance. But the gunshot was too close.

There was only one option, no matter how much Landon hated it. "You're going to have to get down." He crouched and lowered her into the icy water, holding her and giving her as much of a steady hand as he could so she didn't fall.

She hissed out a breath as her feet came down, but she didn't complain. Water splashed around their legs, no doubt soaking her skirt. They had to get out of the water.

"I'm going to let go of your hand," he said as quietly as he could over the rush of the water. "When I do, go. Crawl out. Run. Just run. Zigzag pattern, just in case. Head for whatever cover you can find."

"But—"

"No *buts*. I'll be right behind you." He gave her hand one last reassuring squeeze, then let go. "Now!"

She scrambled away, a little more noisily than he'd have liked. But she followed his instructions, and he hadn't lied—he was right behind her. He gave her a boost out of the water on the other side of the creek.

"Go," he hissed when she hesitated. Then she did. He could see her move in a zigzag pattern, no doubt slowed down by her sodden skirt. He hefted himself out of the creek with one arm, dragging a decent-size rock out of the water with the other. He heaved it as far down the creek in the opposite direction as he could.

When another gunshot rang out, he hit the deck, but he was pretty sure it had been aimed in the direction of the big splash he'd made with the rock. He kept moving, crawling forward on the ground, until he caught up with Hazeleigh.

She was also on her hands and knees. He grabbed her hand. "Come on. Fast as you can."

They got to their feet and ran. He hoped to God they were going in the direction of the horses.

When Hazeleigh gave his hand a little yank, he changed course, trusting her to know where to take them.

When they reached the horses, he nearly shouted out a hallelujah. The sun was beginning to peek over the swell of land to the east. "No time to waste."

She nodded and they both got into their saddles.

"I'll follow you."

She nodded again. It concerned him that she wasn't saying anything, but then she was off, and he could only urge his horse to follow.

Chapter Nine

Hazeleigh thought she might pass out. Her body was shivering so hard it was almost impossible to hold on to the reins. But she had to get Landon back to the schoolhouse.

With the sun rising, she knew they had to get far away from Mr. Field's, but it also freed her to urge her horse into a run rather than the careful pace of a night ride.

She didn't hear another gunshot. She knew that didn't mean they were out of danger, but it allowed her to *think* a little.

Back to the schoolhouse. Then what? She didn't know. What had they figured out? As far as she could tell, a fat lot of nothing. And she might have gotten herself hypothermia for the trouble.

They rode and rode for what seemed like forever. She nearly sobbed in relief when she saw the schoolhouse come into view. The sun was fully rising now, a pretty pale orange and pink. Landon had to get back to the house. Someone would know he was gone, that he'd taken two horses. She glanced at him, riding right next to her. Wet and bedraggled.

No, he couldn't exactly go straight to the house either.

She urged Buttercup to go faster, and they made it to the schoolhouse quickly. They dismounted and her legs almost gave out she was shaking so hard, but she managed to grab onto the stirrup and hold herself up.

Landon cursed, his hands immediately going to her arms and beginning to rub up and down. "We've got to get you some dry clothes."

"I'm o-k-k-ay," she said, her teeth chattering in direct contrast to her words. "The sun will d-d-dry me r-r-right up. Wh-what about you?"

"I'm fine." He sounded very firm and sure, but she didn't believe him. He looked around, then shook his head. "Take off what you can."

She blinked at him. Surely he didn't mean...

"I know we don't have anything dry to change into, but if we can get some of the excess water off our clothes, it'll help."

He wanted her to take her clothes off. In front of him. She could only gape.

Something in his expression changed. She didn't know what, but it got a little harder. Then he pulled off his sweatshirt. Underneath, the T-shirt he wore was wet and plastered to his skin, outlining every ridge and every muscle. She made an involuntary noise that she hoped he didn't hear.

He wrung out his sweatshirt and an entire stream of water dripped onto the ground. "See? Just wring the water out. Damp isn't great, but it's better than soaking."

She swallowed. Her mouth felt like dust. *You are an imbecile*, she told herself harshly.

He shook his head when she still didn't move. "Tell you what," he said gently. "You step inside. Take things off, one at a time, hand them to me, I'll wring them out, then hand them back to you. I'm not looking to be a peeping Tom, Hazeleigh."

"Of course not," she said. What little heat she had left in her body seemed to rush for her cheeks. She hadn't even considered he might want to *see* something. She remembered him smiling when he'd made that comment about being *sweet on you* and honestly, the cold had gone to her brain.

"Y-you need to get b-b-back."

"I'll handle it." He kept rubbing his big hands up and down her arms, but they were covered in the thick, wet sweater and even the friction didn't do much. "I promise. If I have to lie through my teeth, no one's going to know I know where you are, okay? I promise."

And she wasn't sure she'd ever believed anyone's promise as wholeheartedly as she believed his. Which she knew was a problem, but she was shivering too hard to care.

"Go on now," he said firmly with a last squeeze of her arms. "Or I'm going to end up having to take you to the hospital, because I will hide you through a lot of things, Hazeleigh, but I'm not about to let you freeze to death just to avoid a false accusation against you."

She swallowed and then managed to move away. She opened the door and stepped into the dark of the schoolhouse. It was *almost* warmer inside. She sucked in a breath and peeled off the heavy, dripping sweater. Even the wind of the horse ride hadn't done much to get rid of the water.

She looked at the gap in the door. Landon's hand was just...there, patiently waiting for her shirt so he could wring the water onto the ground outside.

She handed him her sweater through the gap in the door. "Do the outer layer first," he instructed. "Then switch, all right? So get the skirt and whatever was under the sweater off. I'll try to get the sun to warm them up a little, then we'll switch."

Switch. Like her *underwear*. In his *hands*. She didn't know what to do with that, but when his hand reappeared in the gap, she knew she had to take off her skirt and hand it to him.

His hand disappeared for a few minutes and Hazeleigh pulled the camisole off so that she was only in her bra and the slip shorts she wore under her skirts. She looked at the quickly dawning day through the crack in the door.

She was cold and miserable and on the run, but her heart felt…oddly bruised by Landon making promises to her when he didn't have to. He'd been shot at because of *her* and he just kept moving forward like it was all par for the course.

Like it didn't bother him at all that they'd gone to the fort, and to Mr. Field's house, and found more questions than answers.

The door moved, the gap getting a little bigger as he shoved his hand in again. But she was looking, and she could see him now.

He was standing there in his boxers, not looking at all as if he was shivering like she was. But that wasn't what caught her attention, or not only that. "Landon…" And she forgot she was in just her bra and the shorts. She stepped through the crack and reached out to touch the long, deep scar that went from shoulder to hip. It was a jagged line, and though it had clearly been there for a very long time, the mark was so clear against the marble of his skin, it nearly took her breath away.

She didn't know *why* she felt compelled to touch it, or why her heart ached when she did. It was just…instinct. Coming from that same place inside of her that her bad feelings usually came from.

But reality eventually crashed in, reminding her she was touching his abs. And they were *abs*. All of him was pure muscle, and while she'd always figured he was well built under layers of winter clothes, she hadn't had a *clue* he might look like a movie superhero underneath all that.

Or that it might jangle around inside of her, making her forget everything including propriety. And some kind of *consent.*

She jerked back like she'd been scalded. And maybe she had. Or maybe she had hypothermia of the *brain.* "I'm sorry."

He shrugged easily. "It's a shocking scar."

"How…? No, I'm sorry, it's none of my business."

"Doesn't mean you can't ask."

She finally looked up from the scar. His mouth was curved in a kind of amused line, but it wasn't a smile. And his eyes were sad. She wanted to step forward and hug him. He looked like he needed a hug.

He also looked like he'd be warm.

The weak morning sunlight was shining on them now, but it didn't really offer any warmth. She was pretty sure any warmth she felt was a figment of her imagination, or maybe embarrassment powering her from the inside out.

Then she noticed the little trail of red on his arm. An arm he was angling away from her. Quite purposefully, now that she was paying attention.

"You're bleeding."

"It's nothing," he said, even offering a smile. "The important thing is—"

He was angling it even more away from her, which made her reach out and grab him to keep him in place. She moved around him. The bleeding was hardly *nothing.*

"How did that happen?"

He tried to pull away, but she held firm. She tried to think of anything she might have in the schoolhouse to patch him up. "You need it cleaned out. You need a bandage."

"We have a lot bigger problems than a scratch. You need to focus."

"I am focusing! You're *hurt*." And it was because of her. "A scratch," she scoffed. "What macho nonsense is that? The only way you could have gotten that deep of a cut is if…" She stopped, felt the heat rush out of her and the chilled shaking start again. He'd been *shot*.

"I'm *fine*." He pointed to his scar. "I've been seriously injured before, Hazeleigh. I know what it's like. This? It's nothing."

"It's something to me."

His sharp inhale kept her from saying anything else or moving forward to see what she could do about the cut— which made her feel a little woozy if she looked too closely at it. But Landon looked at her like she'd impaled him because she cared that he was hurt *because of her*.

"Lan—"

She couldn't complete his name, which was fine enough, because she didn't have an earthly clue what she was going to say, only that the moment seemed to call for *something*.

But he put his hand on her face. It was gentle and it was sweet, and she might not understand the emotion moving through him, but she saw it on his face.

And she wanted to lean into it. No matter how cold or scared or mixed up she was. *This* was warm and real and good. And there wasn't one bad feeling or red flag here.

"That's very sweet," he said, his voice soft. His hand was still on her face and his gaze was…everywhere. Like he was memorizing her face.

She found herself returning the favor, or maybe she was just looking for a road map. A way forward.

"But I've laid my life on the line for a lot less. This is just a scratch." With his free hand, he pointed to the scar across his chest. "My father did this to me in a drunken rage. He wasn't sorry. He didn't feel any kind of responsibility. It was the whiskey's fault, in his mind. So I appreciate that you're trying to take some kind of blame here, but it isn't yours. I understand blame. I understand the weight of injuries you go into with your eyes wide open. I know what I'm risking here, Hazeleigh, and I don't mind risking it for you. So I need you to stop blaming yourself for anything that happens in the course of trying to prove you're innocent. Helping you is an honorable task that I'm taking with my eyes wide open."

The lump in her throat grew with intensity. She knew—just knew—he didn't want her tears for *him*, but she knew...

His father's *physical* abuse was not the same as her father's emotional abuse. A clear fact with all these marks on. It wasn't the same, but she understood. The difference in choosing something and having it happen to you. When you chose things that might end in being hurt, it didn't feel so bad because at least it wasn't your parent inflicting the harm.

"We've got a long way to go on this," he continued in that same soft, earnest voice that she'd never once heard come out of him. There was no smile, no joke. Just honesty. "So let's agree on this right here, right now. Everything from this point on? A choice. Eyes wide open. No guilt."

"But I'm so good at guilt."

He laughed and flashed that lightning-quick grin that made her knees weak. Or maybe it was the cold and the shivering. "Yeah, you are," he agreed. "But you're going to have to let that go." His smile faded, the blue of his eyes seeming to deepen. "For me."

HAZELEIGH WAS LOOKING at him, eyes so wide she might as well be a Disney princess. Her hand had drifted back down to his scar, and he didn't know how it could feel like some kind of healing. She could hardly make it go away, hardly make him forgive his father for those hellish years.

But she'd taken…the weight of it, somehow. He'd been injured before. He'd carried his brothers on his back and known they'd do the same—that was a kind of care deeper than any blood tie because they'd been through hell together, trusted each other through hell.

But it wasn't the same as Hazeleigh… He didn't even know how to explain it. Only that her compassion or empathy undid him.

Not the time or place. And Hazeleigh was stronger than she gave herself credit for, but he should be more careful with her. She'd been through a lot, and this was far from over.

He cleared his throat and took a step back. "You're going to get hypothermia." The words came out clipped, and both confusion and hurt registered on her face before she smoothed it out. "Your clothes won't be dry, but if you take off the—" he had to clear his throat again "—wet underthings and put the sweater and skirt back on until they dry a little, you should be okay until I can come back with some dry things for you."

She nodded carefully. Then squinted at the horses. "How are you going to explain two horses missing?"

"I'm not. I'm leaving Buttercup with you." He had to get away. He had to…act. He moved to the clothes he'd spread outside and began to pull them back on. He hadn't had a chance to ring out his boxers, and the sun had done very little to dry his socks or jeans, but he'd be back to the ranch soon enough.

She was the one to be worried about. He got dressed, then gathered her things and handed them to her. "You switch out those clothes. I'll be back with food and dry clothes soon as I can." He didn't make eye contact.

Not because he was embarrassed. It wasn't even self-preservation. If he looked at her, he wouldn't go. And if he didn't go...

Well, he had to get moving. The end.

He stalked toward the horse, trying to untangle his brain. He had Hazeleigh's list in his pocket, waterlogged maybe, but hopefully intact. Either way, he'd hack into the police server and find some new information. Maybe figure out a way to make an anonymous tip about someone shooting near Mr. Field's house. Maybe the police would be smart enough to realize Hazeleigh didn't have a gun, so it couldn't have been her.

Before he could fully untether his horse from where he'd been tied, Hazeleigh stopped him with her hands, taking his in hers. He knew he shouldn't, but he couldn't stop himself. He looked down at her.

She looked pretty and he kept his eyes on hers, because if he looked lower and took in that expanse of pale, freckled skin...

"Get your arm looked at," she said. Insisted, maybe. "Please. If you have to out me, that's fine. The most important thing is that you're okay."

He looked into her dark eyes and he could barely think through the driving desire to kiss her. Just once. Just to get a taste.

"I'm not going to out you," he finally said, hoping it didn't sound as strangled as he felt. "But I promise, I'll get it patched up before I come back."

She squeezed his hands and smiled up at him. "Thank you."

He gave her a stiff nod and got up on the horse, having to shift and adjust a few times to find a comfortable sitting position. "For the love of God, get yourself dressed, Hazeleigh. A man can only take so much," he muttered, and then urged his horse into a run.

Away from her. Away from desire. And toward responsibility. He wondered when he'd gotten so damn straight and narrow.

Chapter Ten

A man can only take so much.

Hazeleigh had stood there for probably too long looking down at herself. The bra was a serviceable cotton one. The shorts were functional. She couldn't really imagine she looked *alluring* even in her underwear. Her hair had to be a mess and her makeup from *yesterday* was long gone. She was a shivering mess.

Douglas had once refused to take her to a concert they'd bought tickets to because she'd been too *shabby*-looking, and that had been right after she'd spent almost an hour getting ready. Kenny had often complained bitterly about everything to do with her appearance, after he'd gotten what he wanted from her.

It had been a whole thing, and once she'd gotten herself out of it, she'd seen it for what it was. A kind of…self-punishment. Because while she resolutely told herself Amberleigh's disappearance hadn't been her fault, sometimes she'd agreed with her father.

Why hadn't she had any of her bad feelings that might have predicted Amberleigh's runaway attempt? Amberleigh wasn't just her sister, they were *triplets*. Hazeleigh should have felt it, she should have known.

Hazeleigh blew out a breath and did what Landon had instructed. *Focus.* Her misguided assessment of male partners and self-punishment was not on the table. She had to avoid hypothermia at this point. She had to figure out who…

Someone had *shot* at them. One of the bullets had grazed Landon's arm. It made her stomach churn even now.

He'd told her to stop blaming herself and as much as she wanted to take offense, how could she? It was the truth. She did, in fact, do that, and it made things harder.

Still, it wasn't easy to just *accept* he might get hurt or be in trouble on account of her. When she was…

She closed her eyes and walked into the schoolhouse. She would change out of her underwear, into the damp but not sopping-wet outer clothes, and she would deal with what she could.

She'd spent too long letting herself feel like her father wanted her to feel. A failure. Worthless. It had taken some hard times, and eventually talking to a counselor, to start climbing out of that self-destructive behavior.

She had every right to fight for her innocence here, and if Landon chose to fight alongside her—as he was insistent on doing—then it wasn't about what she deserved or not.

Sometimes, people wanted to help. Zara had always been there. Of course, that was about love and family, and Landon wasn't family.

Hazeleigh paused for a moment, completely naked and frozen to the bone in the old, crumbling schoolhouse, and heard Landon's voice in her head. *A man can only take so much.* What would it have been like to tell him he didn't have to *take* it? What would it be like to…believe someone could love and be there for her by *choice*? Not because of family ties.

Love. She had a long way to go before she could worry about being in love with *anyone*, and it seemed wholly inconceivable to imagine a man like Landon ever being in love with her. So it was quite foolish to stand here and daydream. She pulled on the sweater, shivering anew because though it might not be *as* wet, the sun hadn't been enough to really warm the material.

She'd hang her underwear somewhere out in the sun. See what she could do to feed and water Buttercup. Maybe brush her down. And she would think about the files missing from Mr. Field's filing cabinet and try to find some kind of clue. Pattern. *Something* that might hint at who had killed him.

She would be productive. Proactive. For Mr. Field. For herself. And she wouldn't let herself think about *love* or scars or the way Landon's hand had fitted against her cheek at *all*.

But as she turned for the bag she'd packed and the bag Landon had left last night, she frowned. Something…wasn't right.

Hadn't she very carefully put her bag up on the little shelf in what had once been a closet that no longer had a door? And Landon had hung his up on the hook in the back, rusted and ancient but still there screwed into the plaster.

Now, both sat by the door, open.

Hazeleigh hesitated then reached out for hers. She wanted it to be an animal. Bear. Giant raccoon. Something that had grabbed their bags and moved them in search of food. It *could* be.

But she didn't know any wild animal that would take the bags to the same spot and leave them leaning against each other by the door.

Anxiety arced through her, but she opened her bag as far as it would go. Everything appeared to still be in there, but it was… She was almost certain it had been upended and then repacked.

She hesitated in touching anything, but there was no bad

feeling. No inner signal of danger. It wasn't a foolproof system, but she couldn't just…ignore the bag.

She pulled out the scarf she'd forgotten she'd packed and wrapped it around her neck, willing herself to think clearly. Someone had been in here and gone through her things. She pulled out every item carefully. The only thing missing was the cash she'd had in the front pocket, but the other stack of bills she kept hidden in her planner was still there.

It could have just been a random passerby who had glanced through, seen some cash and taken it. She *hoped* for that.

She grabbed Landon's bag next. She didn't know everything he'd packed, but it seemed lighter than it should have. It had seemed pretty stuffed when he'd put it down yesterday. Someone had taken something he'd brought, she was almost sure of it, and it wouldn't have been cash.

She stood, looked around the room. Someone had been in here. Long gone before she and Landon arrived? Or had they seen them coming and bolted?

But who else would be using this as a hiding spot? Who else would be sneaking around and running away? And if someone was following her, why not approach her?

Or would they have seen her coming and left to call the cops and turn her in?

The cops.

She sucked in a breath. If someone knew she was here, the police might know, too. And all this running away would make her seem so much more guilty than she was.

No. It wasn't going to go down like that. And she was hardly going to sit here, waiting to get caught. She couldn't.

She grabbed both bags, stuffed her wet underwear into one of them and then went back outside. She looked around her, heart beating too hard. People could be watching. The cops could be coming.

She had to find somewhere to hide. She'd…run. Like she'd always planned. Landon might be a little put off, but—

Buttercup whinnied.

Hazeleigh stopped. Landon's voice repeated in her head. *Focus.*

Not panic. Focus.

She couldn't abandon her horse, and maybe that was a good reminder that she could hardly abandon the man who'd been *shot* because of her.

She had to swallow at the bubbling fear that Landon would suffer so much more before this was all done. But it wasn't the real kind of fear, the bone-deep bad feeling. It was panic, plain and simple.

Focus.

She looked at the vast countryside around her. The sunrise had blossomed into a sunny morning with nothing but blue sky. There weren't a lot of places to hide, and she could hardly fight the cops. She wouldn't abandon Landon, but she had to find a way to protect herself.

"All right, Buttercup," she murmured, approaching the horse, letting the steady rise and fall of her body calm her. "Let's figure something out." Something smart. Something right.

LANDON THOUGHT UP a million excuses on his way back to the house. He thought about forgoing stabling his horse and just sneaking somewhere to pretend like he'd been around all night and up early this morning. Holed up with his computer, hacking into things.

It wouldn't explain the damp state of his clothes. Or the gunshot wound on his arm.

So he'd have to do what he'd told Hazeleigh he would. Tell as much of the truth as he could without admitting he knew anything about where Hazeleigh was or that she'd been involved.

It would still be tricky. Landon might be able to lie, but his brothers were pretty good BS detectors. In a different circumstance, he would have told them. Even in this circumstance it was hard not to, because he didn't think they'd be exactly…disapproving of his actions.

It was the Hazeleigh factor that complicated things. That Jake was in love with her sister, and if Jake knew Landon knew where Hazeleigh was, Zara would know. And Zara just…wasn't one for subtlety or sitting back and letting anyone take care of things.

Maybe that wouldn't be so bad, but Landon knew Hazeleigh wanted to keep Zara out of the investigation. Hell, she wanted to keep *him* out of this, and he wasn't close to her at all.

It's something to me, she'd said, so seriously, those brown eyes on his so wide and earnest. The way she'd touched his scar. It would be safer to convince himself he didn't matter to her, but she made it hard. Maybe she didn't care about him the way he was finding himself caring about her, but that didn't mean she didn't care at all.

If he was the reason Zara got mixed up in this, Hazeleigh would blame him. She might even hate him, and he couldn't stand the thought.

He stabled his horse, did his best to clean up in the rough-in bathroom in the stable. But no amount of barn cleaning could make him look like he hadn't been traipsing about the Wyoming wilderness hiding in creeks and getting shot at.

He'd have to show Dunne his arm. While it was nothing compared to a lot of the injuries he'd suffered—at home and in the army—if he went back to Hazeleigh with a little bandage slapped on it, she was going to be mad.

It's something to me.

He came out of the stable bathroom to find Cal standing at the entrance, arms folded, as if waiting.

Of course he was waiting.

"Morning, Cal," Landon offered cheerfully. With Cal, the best bet was always to proceed as if everything was just fine.

"I don't suppose you're going to explain where you were all night? With two of our horses."

Landon did his best to look suitably confused. "Only had my horse, Cal."

Cal's mouth firmed, a clear sign he didn't believe Landon. "That doesn't explain where you were."

"Nope, sure doesn't." Landon stepped forward, smile firmly in place, but Cal blocked his exit from the stable.

Landon struggled to wrestle his temper. Temper was never the answer—especially with Cal. So he raised an eyebrow. "Do you really want to have a fight, Cal?"

"Do you?"

"I could take you, old man." He'd always loved to tease Cal about their five-year difference in age, but today it didn't come out as teasingly humorous as it should have. He needed some sleep.

And Cal was in his way. Saying nothing. Just *looking* at him with that disapproving, I-am-your-superior-officer expression.

"I don't have to answer to you anymore. That's the beauty of Team Breaker no longer existing." Landon kept his hands at his sides, though the desire to shove his way out the exit was screaming through him.

"Are you not a part of the team anymore?" Cal asked with that same maddening calm that had always made him a great leader.

But they weren't in the military anymore. They weren't

Team Breaker anymore. They were brothers. Ranchers. Business partners in a way.

But they weren't a team—because there was no team. "The team doesn't exist."

"Doesn't it?"

Guilt, yeah, Cal knew how to use that, too. Landon could shove his way free. He could even have a fistfight with Cal. It'd be a toss-up who'd come out on top, and it might even feel good—pounding *or* getting pounded. A concrete thing instead of all these what-ifs in his head.

But he didn't want to fight with Cal. Fighting the people he loved only ever made him feel like his father.

So he told Cal the story. Sort of. He left out every mention of Hazeleigh. He was the one who'd gone to the fort, alone, to see if he could figure anything out. He'd noticed someone else, followed them to Mr. Field's and then been shot at and had to escape.

"And what possessed you to do all that?" Cal's voice was deceptively mild, which was the worst. Because Landon wanted to defend himself, when that would only dig him into a hole.

He needed to play it cool. "We all know Hazeleigh isn't a killer. I don't know why you'd be surprised I might try and figure out a way to prove it to the cops."

"Alone?"

"We're supposed to keep a low profile. You're always telling me that." Not that they'd done a very good job of it in the beginning. Jake and Brody had both gotten tangled in messes that had led to them getting town attention.

But nothing had come of it. Team Breaker was still in hiding. No one suspected the Thompson brothers were terrorist targets.

"You got yourself shot."

Landon scoffed and held up his arm. "We both know this is nothing."

"But the danger isn't nothing. You shouldn't be handling this alone. I get you want to help—we all want to help—but not alone. We all know teams work better."

"Sometimes you have to work alone," Landon insisted, because as much as he appreciated Cal wanting to work as a team, it was best for everyone if he was the only one who knew where Hazeleigh was.

Cal didn't respond, so Landon took the opportunity to leave. Or try to. Cal stopped him again, this time with a hand to the shoulder. Before Landon could get irritated, he said something that made no sense.

"Keep your distance from Jake best you can."

"Huh?"

"You're a horrible liar. If he suspects you know where Hazeleigh is, like *I* suspect you do considering it's her horse missing, he and Zara will be on your butt and you won't have a prayer. You want to keep this a secret? Avoid Jake."

Landon had to take a second to get his bearings. He was that transparent? Or Cal just knew him that well? Neither revelation sat particularly well with him, but he figured Cal was right.

Cal patted his shoulder then turned and walked away from the stables.

"Cal?"

Cal stopped and looked over his shoulder, and Landon grinned—not because he felt particularly *amused*, but because it was… Cal could be a cold jerk, but Landon had always known deep down it covered up the depth of what he felt. And if Landon poked at that depth, Cal really would leave him alone. "You old softy you."

Cal grunted and stormed away.

Because they weren't a *team* anymore.

They were family.

Chapter Eleven

Hazeleigh had found a place to lie in the sunshine not too far away from the schoolhouse. There was a little rock cropping, and it hid her on two sides and gave her something to lean against as she soaked in the sun.

It was still cold, so dang cold, but it was better than the dark, dank building.

Buttercup was tied to a tree, and if someone came sniffing around, she'd likely react in some way. This area was flat enough that she should be able to hear someone coming, and the area was isolated enough she doubted anyone would stumble upon her.

If someone found her, they'd really have to want to.

Her stomach trembled a little at that thought, because it was certainly possible, but this was a sensible, calm course of action. Isolated spot. Warming up and drying out her clothes. Not so far she wouldn't be able to see Landon return to the schoolhouse.

She hadn't panicked. She'd thought through her actions. Of course, she'd fallen asleep there for a little while, which wasn't smart, but here she was. Just fine.

Maybe she was still cold, and maybe she was starving and really thirsty—what little water she'd been able to collect she'd given to Buttercup—but she was okay. Everything was going to be fine.

Then she heard rustling.

Heart in her throat, she looked at Buttercup, who was happily grazing on the pasture grass—definitely not making rustling noises. Carefully, Hazeleigh got to her feet. She turned in a slow circle but saw no one.

Hazeleigh didn't have anything that could be used as a weapon. She grabbed a rock from where she'd been sitting. It was small and likely wouldn't do any damage, but it was the best she could find.

Swallowing against fear, Hazeleigh began to tiptoe toward the noise. It was probably just a squirrel. A raccoon. Maybe even a bear.

But one never knew.

She inched forward, peering through the tree branches. She thought she saw a little flash of…blue. She kept the branches between her and it, creeping around the tree. Maybe she should be running in the opposite direction. Would someone pull out a gun and kill her?

Someone had tried last night, hadn't they? Of course, that had been in the dark with her and Landon following someone.

Hazeleigh finally caught a glimpse of the blue flash for what it was.

It was…a little girl. Hazeleigh looked all around for an adult, for someone to jump out and grab her after using the girl as some kind of diversion, but there was only the little girl. Maybe about ten years old. Reddish brown hair in a flyaway-laden braid, dressed in flannel pajamas and cowboy boots.

She turned and froze when she saw Hazeleigh.

"Hello," Hazeleigh finally said, without sounding too strangled. Her heartbeat hadn't returned to normal yet, but this little girl shouldn't be out here alone. Was she lost?

The little girl just stared at her with wide hazel eyes. Some mix of fear and guilt was evident on her face.

Hazeleigh searched the area. "Are you out here alone?" she asked carefully. Maybe it was still a trap. It certainly didn't feel...right.

The girl didn't stop staring, and she didn't answer Hazeleigh's question.

"What's your name, sweetheart?"

She shook her head. "What's yours?"

Hazeleigh also wanted to shake her head, but that would be suspicious. She was certainly suspicious of this little girl. But Hazeleigh had something few people had.

A nearly identical sister. "I'm... Zara. Zara Hart." Hazeleigh forced herself to smile. "I live right over there on the Hart...well, Thompson Ranch."

"What are you doing here then?"

Now that was a question. Still, Hazeleigh kept the smile on her face. She liked kids. She'd worked at an after-school day care in high school and she knew how to deal with children. She crouched down so she was at eye level with the girl even though there was still a distance between them.

"Can I tell you a secret?"

The girl looked around, so Hazeleigh did, too. Was a parent going to come crashing through looking for their lost daughter?

But the girl's gaze came back to Hazeleigh and she shrugged. Nonchalantly, even if her eyes gleamed with interest. "Okay," the girl said.

"I like this side of the fence better. It feels...enchanted."

The little girl's eyebrows drew together. "It's just grass." She eyed Buttercup. "But I like your horse."

"Me, too. Her name's Buttercup." *And she isn't mine any longer.* "Do you want to pet her?"

There was a longing so deep in those hazel eyes that

Hazeleigh wanted to step forward and give the girl a hug, but the girl shook her head. "Can't. I'm not supposed to be here."

Me either. "You don't seem lost."

"I'm not." She sighed heavily. "Is that your stuff in that old house?" the girl asked, pointing to the schoolhouse in the distance.

Hazeleigh considered. Should she admit those bags were hers? She still wasn't sure what this girl was about or where she'd come from. She hedged. "I'm not sure. What stuff are you talking about?"

The girl started walking away. Hazeleigh didn't know whether to follow or demand more answers or just let her go. It didn't make any sense.

Maybe she was delirious, and this was a hallucination. But she didn't like the idea of this girl alone in the wild, particularly with a murderer and people shooting on the loose. There weren't any livable houses on the property, and if she wasn't a local, she shouldn't be wandering around on her own. It was easy to get lost. Even being born here, Hazeleigh had always been cautioned not to go too far alone as a girl.

She followed. The girl kept walking deeper into Peterson land. Hazeleigh hesitated, but… This girl could hardly be *luring* her into something bad. If she was, she was in something bad herself and maybe Hazeleigh could help.

So she kept following.

Eventually the girl stopped, as if she knew just where she was going. She scrambled up a little pile of rocks and then disappeared behind them. Hazeleigh was mired in indecision. None of this felt particularly right, but she couldn't bring herself to leave the girl alone.

When the girl climbed back over the rocks, she had two things in her hands. Hazeleigh didn't remember packing her pink mittens in her backpack, but they were hers. Likely they'd been put in the pack sometime back in the middle of winter and Hazeleigh had just forgotten to take them out.

The flashlight had probably been in Landon's bag, as it wasn't Hazeleigh's and it looked suitably heavy and military-grade. Something Landon would definitely have.

The girl held them out. Her gaze was on the items, like she was loathe to give them up. But she knew it was the right thing to do and she was doing it.

Hazeleigh knew she could use both items. A flashlight and mittens. They would definitely come in handy, but the girl…

Hazeleigh waved a hand. "Keep them."

The girl looked at Hazeleigh in confusion. "Why?"

"If you took them, you must really need them. Besides, I have more."

The girl chewed on her bottom lip. "But…they're yours."

"Do you need them?"

The girl nodded slowly. "It'd help my mom to have them."

"So take them. I'll be okay without them." Hazeleigh offered a reassuring smile.

"Okay, well, thanks." The girl hesitated. "I have to get back to my mom."

Hazeleigh had to stop herself from reaching forward, out to the girl. "Do you know how to get there?"

The girl nodded. She even began to walk away, then she stopped and turned. "Please don't follow me. I know where I'm going."

Since following was exactly what she'd been planning to do, Hazeleigh was surprised the little girl was astute enough to realize that. "It's easy to get lost out here."

"I know. They won't let me get lost."

Hazeleigh thought it should be comforting, but there

was something sad about the way the girl said *let*. "What's your name?"

The girl shook her head. And then she ran.

LANDON WAS BEYOND irritated it took him hours to return to Hazeleigh. But he'd needed to eat, to get more computer elements together, then collect things on the down low. Dry clothes that would fit Hazeleigh, more food and water, a blanket, a heavy jacket. Plus a few things for Buttercup, so Hazeleigh could have her out there for the next few days.

The sun was already setting when he finally got to his horse. Everyone else was inside, eating dinner, trying to talk Zara out of going down to the police station to yell at…well, everyone.

Landon was still amazed by Zara's loyalty. He knew that Zara's personality was just…like a bulldozer, but it was more than that. She loved her sister wholly and unconditionally and was going to stand up for her no matter what.

Landon had found that in his military brothers later in life, with other men who'd had no unconditional familial love to speak of, so it still baffled him when it came from blood. Particularly when he knew, from town gossip, that Hazeleigh and Zara's father had left them high and dry when it came to selling the ranch.

Maybe it was the triplet thing, particularly since Amberleigh had been murdered. Hazeleigh and Zara had to stick together extra now. Their love for one another was born of experience as much as genetics.

Not that anything he'd dealt with as a child had brought him closer to his biological brothers. The family he'd been born into wanted to make anyone else hurt the way they did, and though Landon had dealt with some dark times, he'd never had that mean streak.

He rode his horse a little faster than necessary, trying

to leave the past and thoughts about love and protection far behind him.

He had a mystery to solve.

When he arrived at the schoolhouse, Buttercup was nowhere to be seen. His instincts began to hum. Something was wrong.

He could deal with wrong, though. He was a soldier. He would handle whatever this was. The important thing was to focus. He got off his horse and searched the schoolhouse, but didn't find any sign of Hazeleigh. Even the bags were gone.

Had she...taken off on him?

Shock and anger and fear all mixed together, because he didn't know what conclusion to jump to. Had the person who'd shot at them taken her? Had something spooked her, and she'd run? Or had she just...run, like she'd been planning to do in the beginning?

He swung back on his horse. She wouldn't, which meant someone was after her.

He looked around the grass for prints. He took his horse over to where Buttercup had been tied and saw the telltale sign of horse tracks, moving away from the schoolhouse.

It hadn't been at a run. Landon tried to let that deduction settle him. He followed. It only took a short trot to see what made his blood run cold.

Buttercup, tied to another tree not far away. The bags next to some rocks. No sign of Hazeleigh *anywhere*.

Focus. Calm. He repeated the words over and over, trying to will his military training to take over, but a cold, overwhelming fear had gotten into his bones. He swung off the horse, tied him to where Buttercup was tethered and touched the horse.

"What went on here?"

Of course, the horse didn't answer or seem perturbed

at all. This should have calmed Landon, but it didn't. He found some tracks in the grass—hard to pick up, but enough of a depression to see two sets of prints. But one was so... small. It didn't make any sense. The less sense it made, the more panic took over.

He followed the tracks, trying to will his heartbeat to slow enough so he could hear. Listen. Figure this out. But his breathing came in little pants as a million terrible bloody scenarios worked through his mind.

He kept walking, kept panicking, and by the time he saw a flash of pink scarf, like yesterday, when he'd seen her running, all rational thought fled his mind.

She was running. If he could think straight, he'd realize it was not the same breakneck speed, but something more like a jog. But he'd lost hold of rationality a while back.

He scanned the area, looking for a threat, his hand on the gun he'd holstered under his shirt. He pulled it out, ready for anything.

She finally looked up. "Landon." She stopped on a dime, like she thought he was going to shoot her. Like she was *surprised* to see him.

He wanted to shake her. He wanted to hold her to him until his heart stopped skipping every other beat in utter terror.

"Get behind me," he ordered.

She blinked and rushed behind him. "What are you looking for?" she asked in a whisper.

"What am I...?" He looked over his shoulder at her. "What happened? Where did you go?"

"I..." She looked at the gun, then at him. "You could probably put that away if this is just about me."

He turned slowly, holstering the gun with more care than was necessary as it began to dawn on him. "You weren't running from anything?"

"No, I was running back. I didn't want you to worry, so I was trying to hurry and—"

"What the hell were you thinking?" he demanded, and he couldn't keep his hands off her shoulders. He didn't shake her, though he wanted to. He just…had to make sure she was really here and whole and *fine*.

Then, as if she'd heard his thoughts, she reiterated them. She patted his chest gently while he gripped her shoulders. "I'm fine, Landon. It's all right."

And she was. Perfectly fine. Standing here, not bloody and not dead, not even pale or scared. Just here and trying not to worry him and… The dam just broke—all the things he'd kept such a tight lid on since the first time she'd smiled at him, and it had felt like a damn *thunder strike*.

He kissed her. Because it felt right and solid and reassuring.

Fine. All right. That's what she'd said.

None of this was any of those things.

But her mouth was. The way she melted against him was just right. She tasted like the promise of spring and felt like salvation, and everything disappeared except the feel of her mouth under his. Like everything might be okay from this moment on.

But nothing was okay because they were in the middle of nowhere, hiding from her family and the police, with the threat of someone who wanted her to take the fall for a murder.

He pulled back, shocked to his core that he'd gotten so…out of control. Not just the kiss, but the last twenty minutes he'd…come unglued. That was unacceptable. "I am…so sorry."

"You're…sorry," she repeated, her tone devoid of emotion. Or maybe he was so lost in his own lack of control he couldn't think about anyone else's emotions.

"I… You weren't there and I…" He raked his fingers through his hair, trying to find a center he was usually so good at finding. "I panicked. It's no excuse, but I was just…" He didn't know. He was at a complete and utter loss. Everything from the point of her not being at the schoolhouse to here was *madness*. And his fault. His utterly idiotic, uncontrolled fault.

"Does your cure for panic often involve kissing women?"

He blew out a breath. Her amusement mixed with a kind of haughty cool disdain brought him down. She was fine. He was being irrational, sure, but she was fine. And just a little irritated with him—and he didn't think it was about the kiss so much as his reaction to it.

"No." He paused and took a bolstering breath before he said, "You know, I'm usually charming and smooth. But with you… Why the hell do I fumble?"

Her mouth curved. "I don't know, but it's kind of cute."

"Cute?" He groaned. "Put me out of my misery while I've still got time."

She laughed, and he thought maybe they could find some even, sane ground *somewhere*.

"You don't have to apologize for kissing me. I didn't exactly push you away."

"You didn't."

She stared up at him and this time *she* was the one who fumbled. She stepped back a little bit, broke eye contact. "There was a girl," she blurted. "A little girl. Maybe ten years old? She'd gone through our bags, stolen a few things."

"I'm sorry, I don't follow. What?"

She explained. A little girl. Stolen items. Wanting to help, but the girl telling her not to. "Then she just took off on me. I… Something wasn't right there." Hazeleigh looked back to where she'd been coming from. "I feel like

I should *do* something. She wasn't old enough to be tramping around by herself."

"You'd be surprised what kids are capable of."

She looked back at him, her gaze drifting down to his chest. Though it was covered by his coat and sweatshirt, he knew she was thinking about his scar.

Something he wasn't ready to talk about right now. Bad enough he'd told her this morning. Now with that kiss ricocheting through him, he just…

They needed to move beyond the kiss. Maybe she'd kissed him back, but she'd also put distance between them. Because the moment wasn't right. They had a lot of things to figure out before anything about that could be…made right.

"It'll work in our favor," he said instead, keeping himself stiff. "I go back to the ranch in the morning, say I had your encounter with the little girl and I spent the evening trying to find her. Then one of my brothers can look into it and find her, make sure everything's okay."

"If they find her and she says she spoke to a woman who claimed to be Zara Hart, they'll know it was me out here. They'll know you're with me."

"You pretended to be Zara?" He didn't know why that pleased him, only that he would have liked to have seen it. Hazeleigh purposefully engaging in some subterfuge would be entertaining.

"I didn't know what else to do. And Amberleigh and I used to practice being each other all the time. Triplets prerogative."

"But not Zara?"

Hazeleigh huffed out a laugh. "She always refused to dress like us, and said she was quite happy being herself. But we'd pretend to be her, each other, to see what we could get away with."

"Are you telling me underneath all that good-girl exterior there's a secret bad girl lurking?"

She laughed. "Not exactly, but Amberleigh could bring it out in me." Her smile was warm and fond and sad, and he wanted to hold her again, so he cleared his throat and shoved his hands into his pockets.

"Let's get back to the schoolhouse before dark. I've got some things for us to go over on my computer." He resisted the urge to slide his arm around her shoulders or reach for her hand. Best to keep all those physical responses to a necessary basis and this was definitely not necessary.

No matter how much he wanted it to be.

"What kind of things?" she asked, falling into step next to him but keeping a good distance between their bodies as they walked back to Buttercup.

"I'm going to hack into the police server and try to get photos of the crime scene. I've been working on tracing the call that implicated you. We'll see what they've got."

"Photos of the crime scene would include…"

"You don't have to look at Mr. Field, Hazeleigh. We can figure this out without you going through that again."

"But do you think it would help if I did?"

Landon sighed. He could lie, but… "I don't really know. You might see something no one else would notice, but there might not be anything there. I can describe what I see to you and—"

"I can do it." She nodded, as if convincing herself. "I can do it. If it gives us answers, I can look at it. Mr. Field deserves answers, and so do I."

Chapter Twelve

Landon didn't say anything to her after that. They walked in silence back to Buttercup, then they walked with her to the schoolhouse. Settled the horses, fed and watered them with the supplies Landon had brought.

He insisted she change her clothes even though hers had mostly dried out. He'd brought her one of his own sweatshirts and a pair of Zara's jeans he'd snagged from the wash. Her underwear and bra were still a damp clump in the bag. The bra was no problem, but she was hardly going to put on jeans without underwear. So she switched out her shirt for Landon's, but kept her skirt on and tried to find a somewhat secluded area to smooth out her underthings so they'd eventually dry.

Once she let Landon in, he turned on a battery-powered camping lantern. He pulled a blanket out of the duffel he'd brought and settled it on her lap.

Hazeleigh found herself speechless at the small, sweet act.

He said nothing and went through setting up his computer equipment. All sorts of things she didn't understand—especially considering there was no power source out here. But *he* clearly knew what he was doing.

"How do you...know how to do all of this?"

He looked up briefly, but he was distracted, clearly uninterested in her presence at the moment. That shouldn't have bothered her. So he'd kissed her like she was oxygen? Clearly, he could turn passion on and off and that was *fine*.

She scowled.

He turned his gaze back to his machines, shrugging. "Training."

"What kind of training?" she persisted.

"Computer training."

That was *not* an answer. In fact, it was a very purposeful *non*answer, but he was so focused it seemed pointless to push him on it. They had more important things to focus on.

Crime scene photos.

She swallowed at her queasy stomach. She didn't want to relive it, at all, but if she saw something no one else would notice, how could she avoid it?

She had to be brave and do what she could, because Mr. Field was dead. As much as her brain couldn't let go of her worry over the little girl, Landon was right. Kids could take care of themselves when they had the tools, and that girl had seemed to have all the tools she needed.

As for the kiss… She glanced at Landon out of her peripheral vision. He had a serious expression as he studied the computer screen.

She'd never been kissed like that. With urgency, but… gently. There had been desire, but it hadn't been *about* sex.

He'd kissed her as if it had soothed something inside of him. He had *kissed her*, and she had backed off when he looked like he might do it again. An inner-flight response she wasn't particularly thrilled with right now because it had been a *great* kiss. All-encompassing and real, and she hadn't thought about her nerves.

She'd simply enjoyed. Her brain kept insisting something had to be wrong with it—him, her, it. But her heart was telling her other things. She had no idea which one to trust.

"It occurred to me last night there might be something to go on if we can see what Mr. Field was researching and connect it to the missing files," Landon said, fiddling with wires and tapping at his keyboard. "He was murdered at work, when it would have been easier and more isolated to murder him at home. I'm still working on the phone call, but it's a lot of dead ends. Whoever made that call made sure to hide themselves."

Hazeleigh's stomach churned. She'd been here before. Framed for something she didn't do. She didn't understand it—she was hardly *murderer* material—but it was clear someone wanted her to take the fall.

And the thing that connected her and Mr. Field was his research. Very little else.

"But we know something about Mr. Field caused him to be a target. This was not a random homicide. Or the person who shot at us wouldn't have gone to his house."

Hazeleigh sucked in a breath. She didn't want to see Mr. Field there again. It was vivid enough in her memories, but if it would help, if it would offer a clue... "I can do it."

He looked up at her, his blue eyes direct and compassionate. "I know you can. Doesn't mean you have to. I blocked out the body. You'll still see some of the blood, but you won't have to see him. Okay?"

"Okay, but... I have to do whatever I can to figure out who did this to him. I *have* to."

He gave her shoulder a quick squeeze. "Okay." He turned the screen toward her. He had blocked out Mr. Field's body, but she could still see it in her mind. She could still smell it. Feel the shock and terror and grief welling up inside of her.

Until a steady pressure broke through the fog of panic. "Breathe, Hazeleigh," Landon instructed, his hand still on her shoulder. Always offering that anchor she needed.

She wished she could be strong enough to be her own

anchor, but she thought about Zara. Stronger than anyone Hazeleigh knew. So certain, so determined. She fought for anything and everything.

And she'd learned to lean on Jake. She *loved* Jake. In a way, it had made Zara stronger. Because she didn't have to take everything on her own shoulders. Maybe leaning had some strength in it, if Hazeleigh ever learned to lean on the right people.

She sucked in a breath, let it out slowly when Landon told her to. She knew he was about to tell her she didn't have to do this, again, so she really focused on that breathing. On the facts, not her feelings.

"What am I looking for?"

"What was he looking at? It looks like some kind of photo album," Landon said, pointing to the desk. Most of it was blacked out to hide Mr. Field's head, which was slumped over the pages.

"Yes, it's the album that's usually kept in that box I told you about." She pointed to it in the frame of the picture. It was open and splattered with blood in the background. "It would have been in there. So Mr. Field must have been studying the photographs when he was shot."

She didn't want to say the rest, but knew she had to. She looked back at Landon, meeting his steady blue gaze. "You need to let me see the whole picture."

"Haze—"

She shook her head and cut off his objection. "I already saw it. I can't erase it. If I can help, I need to see. Your blackout blocks are hiding most of the album. I know his head is hiding some of it, too." Hazeleigh swallowed. "But if I can make out the pictures and the page he's on, maybe we have a clue."

Landon looked pained, but he nodded and then clicked a

few keys on his keyboard. Mr. Field's slumped form, bloody and dead, appeared.

Hazeleigh swallowed down her body's revolt. The photo album might be a clue. She studied the pictures, trying to pretend Mr. Field wasn't in the photo. "This is the page with pictures of..." She trailed off. Was it just a coincidence?

"What?"

"It's the album of places they thought the gold might be. This page is photos of Peterson land." She cleared her dry throat. "Where this schoolhouse is. Where the girl was." Surely a little girl didn't connect to Mr. Field's murder.

"Why?" Landon asked. "Why would he be looking at pictures of Peterson land in his photo album?"

"One of the theories is the robber was a local, someone everyone knew, who just hid the gold on his land. Johannes Peterson was one of the suspects. These are pictures of his house, and... One's missing."

"One what? Picture?"

Hazeleigh nodded, squinting as she leaned closer to the screen. She couldn't make out the page number on the album, due to blood and poor Mr. Field's hair, but she'd organized that album. She could figure it out. She pointed at the space where a picture should have been. "Right here. The murderer must have taken it."

"Mr. Field wouldn't have taken the pictures out himself to look at?"

"No. They were delicate enough as it was. That album is archival grade, and it protects the historical artifacts from further damage," she explained to Landon. "He wouldn't have removed the photo without gloves." Or without a threat leveled at him.

"So whoever killed him took that one picture," Landon said. "Do you know what it was of?"

"I can figure it out." The grain of this picture was too

fuzzy, and she couldn't read the page numbers, but it wasn't impossible. "Probably."

"Did Mr. Field have digital copies of these pictures? The album?"

"He didn't," Hazeleigh said, and there was hope struggling to sprout for the first time in days. "But I did." She pushed out a shaky breath. "The thing is, Mr. Field had found them…somewhat illegally in the attic before they condemned the Peterson house. No one would know he had those aside from me."

As IT WAS the first lead they'd had, they both jumped into action. Landon didn't have time to think about anything else. Hazeleigh had copies on her work laptop, which she'd left back in her cabin. Easy enough for him to grab, especially at night.

She was confident—or at least tried to act confident—that she could figure out the missing picture. Something about Peterson land. Which was where they were.

Landon didn't believe in coincidences when it came to murder and framing innocent people. It all had to connect.

But right now he had a lot of pieces he *knew* connected, but didn't have a clue as to *how.*

"It has to be a Peterson, doesn't it?" Landon went through the rest of the pictures he'd hacked, to make sure the photo album wasn't clearer on any of them. Then he went through the list of the items the police had collected from the office.

"Johannes had twelve sons. Only three of them stayed here in Wyoming. Two died young and without children, although there was always a rumor that Lars was *really* the father of Mrs. Minnie Harper's youngest. If I ignore that rumor, Oscar had six kids." She continued naming people, as if he had any idea who she was talking about.

"I'm sorry. You lost me somewhere around Oscar."

She smiled indulgently. "Yeah, I get that a lot. The bottom line is there aren't any Petersons in Wilde anymore. So if it does connect to the Petersons and that long-ago theory, it's not someone local." She frowned, clearly thinking about something else as she said it.

"What?"

"It just seems to me... Whoever this person is, if it has to do with those pictures and the bank robbery, knew an awful lot. I suppose it could have been someone Mr. Field was communicating with online, but he usually had me do his typing for him, and he hasn't had anyone interested in the Peterson theory communicate with him in years. Far more people are interested in the prostitute theory."

"There's a prostitute theory?"

She rolled her eyes. "Why does everyone always get excited about the prostitute theory?"

"Well, it's all very *Tombstone*, isn't it? Bank robberies and ladies of the night and dashing cowboys." He tipped his own hat, making her laugh as he'd hoped.

He knew she was sad about Mr. Field, hurt and worried about everything going on. If he could get her to laugh every once in a while, it would do them both some good.

"I suppose it is."

"Is it possible Mr. Field had emails or communication he didn't tell you about?"

Hazeleigh frowned. "Well, I suppose anything's possible. I suppose he had to have, because I'm the only one I know of who knew he had these." She chewed on her lip for a moment, distracting him into thinking about when he'd kissed her earlier.

He blinked and looked back down at his computer screen.

"The thing is, I have access to his emails. So if he had a secret, I doubt it would have been hidden there."

"Maybe I can check phone records." He added that to his mental list of things to research. "When I get you your computer, could you access his emails?"

"If I had an internet connection."

Landon nodded. Thanks to his *training,* he could handle that. Even out here with no electricity and service. The beauty of military-grade technology. "I'll go. Get your computer. It might be a while since I might have to stop into the ranch to keep anyone from getting suspicious. I want you to get some rest. I'll set up a lock and alarm on the door, so you'll be safe."

She didn't agree, just stared at him for a long while, expression grave. When she spoke, her voice was firm. "I want to go with you to get my computer."

He shook his head. "It's an unnecessary risk and you have to be exhausted."

"If I'm exhausted, you're just as exhausted."

He opened his mouth, *this close* to making a quip about military training and lack of sleep, but she wasn't supposed to *know* that. He needed to get a handle on wanting to tell her things.

"It's a half-hour ride," she said, and clearly she'd been thinking this through. "That gives us plenty of nightfall to make sure we don't get caught. I know just where the laptop is without you fumbling around my cabin or leaving prints. It's just like the fort. Best to take me."

He didn't agree with her in this case, but he also suspected her insistence on going had something to do with looking at Mr. Field's murdered body for far longer than he'd wanted her to and being left here in the dark alone.

"I'm not worried about the cops. We can handle avoiding

them. I can't promise you we can get through your cabin without one of my brothers getting wise and stopping us."

"So you'll go into the ranch house and make sure they don't."

"Hazeleigh."

"I can get through my cabin and grab the computer in ten minutes flat. It will take you much longer, at least twenty minutes, which gives your brothers far more time to *get wise*."

"It would hardly take me twenty," he muttered irritably. Mostly because she wasn't wrong. But that didn't make *him* wrong. "You're the one on the run. And I know you want to keep Zara out of this. I can convince her I'm working on my own if you're not there. If she sees you? All bets are off."

Hazeleigh shook her head, unmoved. "I won't sleep. I won't rest. I'll worry. I'll obsess. I need to be a part of this. When I was accused of murder last year, I sat in a holding cell and just answered all these questions. While Zara and Jake, and then you and your brothers, all risked your lives for *me*. I can't do that again."

"I'm not risking my life."

She stepped forward and put her hand on his arm—where his bandage was underneath the sleeve. "Someone shot you. This is *all* a risk."

Her brown eyes held his. And she was just… He didn't have the words.

He wanted to protect her, but it was bigger than that. He wanted to find her a life where she wouldn't need protecting. Where maybe it could just be them. He could make her laugh and she could worry over him and they could… just be.

All his years in the military, all the pain and loss and stress of coming to Wyoming and building a new life had made the simple act of *being* his biggest goal. She made it sweeter.

And now was not the time. But she moved closer, her one hand staying on his arm, and the other one coming up to his chest. And she didn't look down, like she was remembering the scar underneath. She held his gaze instead.

And angled her mouth to his…

Chapter Thirteen

Hazeleigh didn't know what she was doing. There were far more important things going on, and besides, she was probably reading things all wrong. Somehow.

But she wanted…that feeling from before. All-encompassing heat and a giddy kind of settling. Like *finally* something would be okay. She knew it wouldn't be, but she wanted to chase the feeling anyway.

This isn't the answer, that nasty little voice in her head said. *It's a distraction. For him. For you. There's nothing here.*

Usually when her brain and heart were at odds, she didn't have the faintest clue what to listen to, but there was something else here today. Zara would probably call it her *gut*, and it wanted to kiss him, just as much as her always too-soft heart wanted her to as well.

So she did. She rose to her tiptoes and pressed her mouth to his, still holding on to his arm. His hands came up to frame her face, angling her just so as he kissed her. It wasn't *just* like outside when he'd found her. This was calmer, more gentle.

And yet the kiss spread through her like a warm fire on a cold night. Something inside of her clicked. A lock being opened. Or closed maybe. She didn't know, only that something inside of her eased. Settled. *Yes.*

She clutched him as he led her to everywhere she wanted to go in the short space of a kiss. And there was nothing but this, him. She could forget it all, just exist in this space where their mouths touched.

For eternity. For far too short a time.

Landon eased away, but held her still, his fingers all tangled in her hair, his eyes only half-open. "You don't know how long I've wanted to do that," he murmured, still just a whisper from her mouth.

"Long?" His hands were still in her hair and her heart was still pounding so hard she wasn't sure she'd made out the words correctly. He kissed her cheek, her jaw. She wanted to melt into the floor, but... "You've wanted to kiss me for...a long time?"

"Ages," he said, his mouth pressing against her neck and making her shiver. He held her like she was precious, and there was no nasty sharp possessiveness to it. It was just sweetness. She knew he had edges—she'd seen them. But when it came to her...

You're fooling yourself again, Hazeleigh.

But it wasn't *hard* to fool herself. She used to have to really work at it to convince herself a man cared. She didn't have to try at all to believe Landon did. She was trying to convince herself that he didn't.

And isn't that far more dangerous?

But she couldn't quite believe the voice in her head. Not when he was saying he'd wanted to kiss her for *ages.* "Since when?"

He didn't release her, but he did stop kissing her. He looked down at her. "Well. When we first got here, you were so skittish."

She frowned, hating that the descriptor was correct. *Skittish.* Landon had arrived right after she'd broken up with Douglas, and she *had* been skittish. As she tried to figure out why she always picked the wrong guy, what kind of danger she might be in, she'd wanted a lot of distance from *all* men.

"And I'd try to get a smile out of you. Make a joke. Show off. Whatever I thought might get a smile, but you never did. You were always so serious. Then I was in the stables singing some dumb song to the horses and I looked over and there you were. Just smiling at me."

She remembered. It had been a few months ago. Kate had settled into the ranch and Hazeleigh had started to believe something...nice might have happened out of the Thompsons moving onto the ranch. Zara and Jake. Kate and Brody.

But she'd felt lonely, and a little outnumbered by all the *men* around. She'd come out to the stables to give Buttercup a treat, a rare occurrence since the Thompson brothers' arrival. It had taken screwing up some courage, and believing the Thompsons were elsewhere.

Most of them had been on that occasion. Except Landon. He'd been in the stables, singing to the horses. A song she hadn't recognized, and half suspected he'd made up himself. She'd watched him for a moment or two, perfectly in tune with the horses while he crooned to them.

It had warmed her to him considerably—the singing, the way the horses reacted to him. The moment had broken down some of her defenses. Or maybe she'd just finally been ready to *let* them down and his way with the horses reminded her that she could.

"You have a nice voice."

His mouth quirked up. "That's what you said then. With a smile. And it just...hit me. Harder than it should have. I don't know what that was. I've tried to figure it out, but it's... I don't have the words for it. Only that it made me crave your smiles. It made me want…to find a way to be around you without making you nervous."

It was hard to believe Landon had been standing around…craving *anything* from her. But she'd been wrapped up in her own stuff, and if she looked back, well… He had always gone out of his way to make her smile.

But she was still *her* and that was still a bit of a mess. She felt the driving need to be up front about that. "I have…"

He raised an eyebrow. Like he remembered her blurting out yesterday she had terrible taste in men.

It didn't feel fair right now because he wasn't terrible taste at all. But she was still…her. "I have issues," she admitted lamely.

He chuckled, but it wasn't his normal, happy chuckle. "Don't we all?"

She could leave it at that. She could do a lot of things in this moment, but she swallowed and told him a truth she hadn't even told her sister. "I don't really know how to trust myself."

He studied her, as if that wasn't a terrible thing to be. So unsure, so lacking confidence and strength of purpose.

But he still didn't let her go. "You said you trusted me."

She nodded. "I do."

"We can start there." He sighed, like he gravely regretted what he had to say next. "But for tonight, we've got about six hours of dark, and we'll need them all to get your laptop."

LANDON ALMOST LAUGHED at the way her mouth turned into something very close to a pout. Laughed because he wanted to pout a bit himself. Or maybe punch a few holes in the wall. He wanted to say screw the laptop and murder cases and spend the rest of the night learning each other.

But it wasn't an answer, and he didn't want to be…a distraction. Something she could excuse away later. If he had a chance with Hazeleigh, he wanted a real one.

Which meant proving, once and for all, that she was no killer. And hopefully, somewhere in all that, she could learn to trust herself the way she so clearly wanted to.

"You said we. I hope that means you agree with me about me going with."

He wanted to scowl, but he managed to keep his mouth impassive. With a mountain of regret, he pulled his hands away from her face and took a step back. "It's not that I don't think you're right about being quicker—"

"Excellent. It's settled, then." She strode for the door like she could steamroll him into bringing her. And there was something about her trying to steamroll him that made him want to let her.

It was dangerous, but so was leaving her here…even if he set up an alarm for her. And maybe if she could do this, be involved, she could trust herself.

Or maybe he'd lost all his good sense and was putting her in danger just because he wanted to be with her. And that was the kind of split focus Cal had forever been warning them about back in their military days.

This *was* like those days. It was about finding the truth, protecting the innocent. It required focus and strength of purpose and not letting anything compromise clearheaded decisions.

But that kiss still lingered, and the way she'd held onto him, sighed against him. Been wide-eyed asking him how long he'd wanted to kiss her, as if she couldn't imagine such a thing. And he wasn't in the military any longer. People had shot at them, a man was dead, but it still wasn't the same.

He was a person. Not a soldier.

He wasn't sure he knew what to do with that, but Hazeleigh was already outside the schoolhouse, getting Buttercup ready in the silvery moonlight.

He walked to his horse, hating the uncertainty that swirled within him. "Hazeleigh…"

"I'm doing this," she said simply. "I don't need your permission any more than you needed my permission to help me against my will."

He supposed she had a point there. "Can you at least do it my way?"

"And what is your way?" she asked, primly enough to make him smile.

"We'll ride the horses to the stables. You give me time to do a perimeter check, see where everyone is, and then we devise a plan from there. *Maybe* it's you going into your cabin and getting your laptop, but maybe it's something else." He couldn't make out her expression in the dark, so he simply had to wait for her response.

"Perimeter check," she echoed.

"Yes, it's when I—"

"I think I can figure out what a perimeter check is. What I can't figure out is why you talk like that, talk like you know how to handle *murderers* and gunshot wounds, and have all that fancy computer equipment I've never seen outside a movie."

Landon didn't have the faintest idea how to respond. The truth wanted to tumble out. He wanted to lay it all at her feet.

But that wasn't allowed.

You're a person now, not a soldier.

But he was still a member of Team Breaker. Whether they were a team or a family, he'd made an oath.

Do you think Jake and Brody have kept that oath?

"Landon?"

He swallowed at all this *feeling*—which was bad to have.

He had so much to accomplish without emotion getting in the way.

"I just need you to agree to follow instructions."

It was her turn to be quiet for a shade too long. "I'll be honest—I'm a little tired of following everyone else's instructions."

"I'm only trying to keep you safe."

"Especially when they're meant to keep me safe. Does it occur to anyone I might want to stay safe myself? Kind of why I ran away."

"And does it occur to you that people want to keep you safe because they care?" He managed to keep his voice as even as possible, though all this conflicting sentiment was still coursing through him.

She inhaled sharply, and there was a poignant silence where he thought she might ask just what he meant by *care*. But she didn't.

She let out the breath. "Yes, I know. All right. I promise to follow instructions with one caveat. You won't take any unnecessary risks for me."

"Define unnecessary."

She sighed heavily. "You always have a comeback."

"That I do. Now, time is wasting. Let's get going." He made sure she was on Buttercup before he mounted his own horse. They both knew the way back to the ranch and Hazeleigh's cabin, so she didn't lead him or vice versa. They kept their horses abreast of each other and began an easy trot in the direction of the cabin.

"Landon, I keep thinking about…"

Landon braced himself for a mention of the kiss, a conversation about what it all meant, but apparently *she'd* forgotten all about it.

"The little girl."

Landon shifted, trying to ignore the disappointment

coursing through him. He should be *relieved* she wanted to talk about mysteries, not kisses and feelings. "I know you're worried that she's on her own, but if she seemed okay…"

"No, it isn't that. Or it isn't only that she was alone. It's just… That first day I went into the schoolhouse I thought it looked off. It wasn't as dusty as it should have been. Like someone had been in there, sweeping up."

"You think it was her?"

"I don't know what to think. But if Mr. Field's murder really does connect with this silly old bank robbery, and that bank robbery really did connect to the Petersons back in the day, isn't it odd that there are people hiding and sneaking about on Peterson land?"

"People or a child?"

"She mentioned her mother. That the flashlight and mittens would help her mother."

"Well, then, she isn't alone."

"I suppose not." Landon didn't have to see her to know she was frowning. She remained quiet for the next few moments, but he knew she hadn't stopped thinking about the girl.

"I guess the important question is, regardless of the girl, why are people hiding on Peterson land? *Any* people."

Landon had wondered that himself, but he didn't know enough of the town or family dynamics to determine if that was strange or not. "Did Mr. Field have any connection to any Petersons? Any emails he might have sent about the theory?"

"Not to my knowledge. And I'm not saying Mr. Field told me everything, but I did organize his life. It seems…unlikely there was something going on I didn't know about."

Landon considered that. He wished he could believe it. But there had to be *something* Hazeleigh didn't know or she'd have some theories about why someone might kill Mr. Field.

"It wouldn't be out of the realm of possibility that it's a bit of a random thing. There are those treasure-hunter-type people, always on the lookout for old gold or what have you. Sometimes obsessed people get desperate and sometimes desperate people murder."

Hazeleigh considered it. "A desperate treasure hunter would be…desperate, right? It would be about the obsession or frustration, but we know this had to be a little premeditated or how would they know to frame me for it?"

Landon wished he knew.

Chapter Fourteen

They didn't speak much after that. Every question Hazeleigh had just took them in circles and she was tired of the circles. She was tired of not knowing what to fight against.

She knew part of why she was tired was because Landon had kissed her. Suddenly she had something...to look forward to. She didn't want to run. She wanted this to be over so she could...figure out what life might look like with Landon in it.

A *good* man. Who liked *her*.

She rolled her eyes at herself. Timing was everything, and hers continued to be terrible. What did she even have after this? Mr. Field was dead, which meant she was *jobless*, and... He was gone.

The waves of grief came at odd points, washing over her. It still didn't feel real.

But they rode through a beautiful starry Wyoming night and Hazeleigh had some...hope maybe, that they could figure out this mystery. The album was a clue. Maybe if she got into Mr. Field's emails, they'd find another. Maybe, just maybe, she could help solve this and feel like she'd done something for Mr. Field, since she couldn't go back in time and save him.

Since her bad feeling hadn't saved him.

She resolutely pushed away the thoughts that wanted

to follow, most in her father's voice about what good she was if she couldn't use that bad feeling to help the people she loved.

She couldn't go back in time. So she could only move forward. She stroked Buttercup's mane and allowed herself to relax into the saddle. She was exhausted. Wrung out and a little jumpy, but there was this driving need inside of her to keep going.

She needed an answer. *Some* kind of explanation.

The ranch came into view in the moonlight. Just shadows, but the shadows of her childhood and adolescence. Amberleigh had loved to sneak out of the house at this time of night and sometimes Hazeleigh had been brave enough to go with her—never off the ranch, like Amberleigh often did, but to sneak around the stables or their grandparents' cabin, giggling and feeling like cat burglars.

Hazeleigh sighed at the pain in her chest. Amberleigh hadn't been perfect, but she'd been…vivacious. Hazeleigh had always felt alive around her. She'd been brave with Amberleigh.

Now Amberleigh was dead and Hazeleigh was here. Still right here. For years she'd been hiding away in plain sight, and it suddenly struck her as very, very wrong.

"We'll stop here," Landon said while they were still a little way from the cabin. But they were behind the stables, which would hide them from just about any view from the house.

"You stay right here while I put the horses up. They'll water, feed, rest. If someone comes, you stay right here, hidden as best you can."

"Why would anyone come out here in the middle of the night?"

Landon was quiet for a moment, and she heard his quiet footfalls as he got off his horse. She waited for him to come to her. He took her hand and helped her off the horse. She didn't need the help to get off so much as she did for the landing, since she couldn't see the ground beneath her— the stable blocked most of the bright moonlight.

He held her steady when she stepped a little wrong and stumbled. Part of her wanted to lean into him. Give up. Go inside. Let everyone in that house take care of everything while she slept.

But she was done being a coward. So she found her own two feet, gave his arm a grateful squeeze and then stepped out of his grasp.

"Just stay right here, okay?"

And she didn't realize until he'd gone, that he hadn't explained to her why one of his brothers might come outside in the middle of the night.

She scowled at the stable wall. But she waited, because she understood that even if she chafed at instruction, Landon really did want to keep her safe. And he wanted to solve this for her. Or maybe even with her. Still, she cheated a *little*.

She moved as quietly as she could to the edge of the stable so she could see around the building. In the distance, just a smudge of dark in the faded starlight, was her cabin. It was dark, as it should be. There was almost no movement. No breeze to flutter the grass or new leaves. The occasional whir of an insect or flapping sound of what was probably a bat could be heard, occasionally interrupted by the huff of a horse from inside the stables.

She nearly jumped a foot when she heard the rumble of voices. Coming from inside the stables. She strained to hear, but the words were muffled by the walls of the stables.

It had to be Landon talking to someone. Hopefully one of his brothers. But what if it wasn't? What if he was being confronted by the shooter from Mr. Field's house? What if they'd been followed and—

Hazeleigh sucked in a breath to calm herself. Landon knew how to handle things, and likely how to defend himself. Besides, the murmurs sounded calm. Still, she inched her way closer to the doors so she could make sure.

She *had* to make sure it was a Thompson. That Landon was safe. She knew he'd do the same in her position.

She kept moving as quietly as she could toward the open door, only stopping when she could finally make out the words.

"I'm not going to pretend like I didn't see you with Hazeleigh's horse that's been missing," someone said. Dunne, she thought. The low rasp. That emotionless way of speaking that he had. Still, it seemed odd he'd be out here. Because of a leg injury, he didn't ride horses unless he had to, and it *was* the middle of the night.

"I don't see why you couldn't," Landon replied, and his tone was genial enough. That teasing lilt he used when he was trying to get someone to his way of thinking without having an argument about it.

She wondered if it ever worked on his brothers. She'd certainly never seen any of them fall for it.

"Do you enjoy putting Zara through hell?"

Landon was very quiet for a *very* long moment that stretched out and made her own guilt settle heavy on her heart. She knew Zara would be worried about her, but... she just didn't see any other way.

"Didn't know you cared," Landon said at last, but there was no teasing lilt. His voice was almost as flat as Dunne's.

"What are you doing, Landon?"

Hazeleigh held her breath and waited for his answer. Because there had to be more to it than just *helping* her, didn't there?

But she didn't hear any answer, because an arm came around her from behind, pinning her arms to her side and propelling her forward.

LANDON HAD KNOWN this would be a mistake. Why had he come? Why had he let Hazeleigh come? He couldn't afford mistakes now, because Hazeleigh was the one who was going to pay for them.

But he stared at Dunne, trying not to let the pulsing anger out in his tone as he answered Dunne's question. "What I have to."

Before Dunne could argue with him, or express more disappointment, Landon heard a noise. The *snick* of a footfall, and a squeak that could only be Hazeleigh.

He pushed past Dunne and out into the cool night air, hand on his gun as his heartbeat raced.

Then he sighed, irritably. Because it wasn't some nameless face holding Hazeleigh against her will.

It was his brother.

"It's her, Henry," Landon said, trying to keep the growl out of his tone. "Let her go."

It was dark, but he knew his brothers. How they moved. How they thought. He could recognize their shadows as well as he could recognize the back of his hand.

Hazeleigh wriggled, still in Henry's grasp, and Landon had to clench his hands into fists to keep himself from moving forward and lunging at his *brother*. "I said let her go."

"You're not in charge of me, Landon," Henry replied, his voice dark. But he was always dark. Henry had never fully learned to moderate the on-guard soldier in him.

Hazeleigh wriggled again. "This is ridiculous," she hissed. "Let me go right now."

Landon had to breathe very carefully. He'd learned to

deal with his emotions, control them. Unlike Henry, he'd honed his military training and used it very rarely.

But few things tested that leash on his temper as the way Henry was holding onto Hazeleigh like she was some kind of common criminal. There was nothing he could say. If he moved…hell, if he *breathed* at this point, he was going to go after Henry.

As if sensing that, Henry let her go—slower than necessary—and dropped his arms. Still, he didn't step away. And Landon knew Dunne was standing behind him. Like they were at odds. Two against two.

"We'll go inside and talk this out," Dunne said, his voice devoid of anything except a flat kind of certainty. Two sides of a coin, really. The one with too much tension, the one with not enough.

And Landon, somewhere in the middle.

"I am *not* going inside," Hazeleigh said firmly. And she didn't stutter or hesitate like she might have a month or two ago if she'd been in a room alone with three of them.

It helped ease the apprehension inside of him. *Look at her. Coming into her own.*

He had to get her out of this confrontation with his brothers. "Hazeleigh needs to get a few things from her cabin."

"Hazeleigh needs to go inside and tell Zara she's all right. And then perhaps go to the cops and—"

"Zara knows I'm all right," Hazeleigh retorted. "She might be worried about me, but she knows I'm okay."

"Does she?" Dunne countered. "Because I'm pretty sure I'm the one who has been listening to her yell at everyone in her vicinity for the last two days."

"You wouldn't know how to read an emotion if it hit you over the head and said, 'Hi, I'm an emotion.'"

Landon and his brothers were struck dumb for a moment. Hazeleigh had just…been snotty and rude without even a fumble.

"Well," Henry said, the first one to break the last silence. "Who knew Hazeleigh had some fight in her."

"I do. And I'm doing this my way. I'm not putting you all in the middle of it. So you're going to go back inside and let me do what I need to do without telling *anyone*."

"You put Landon in the middle of it," Dunne said darkly.

"He put himself in the middle of it," she returned.

Landon didn't interject. It was…amazing, watching her spar with Henry and Dunne. It was a shame that it was murder and false accusations that had gotten her to this point, but it was still a sight to behold.

But his brothers turned to him in the inky dark, clearly wanting his verdict.

"I think we all know the cops can't help. Not until we have some better proof that Hazeleigh wasn't involved. And I think we all know that as much as Zara would feel some relief knowing Hazeleigh is safe and sound, she would not handle the information in a way that would allow us to be *subtle*."

Henry snorted a little. "All the subtlety of a freight train."

"Exactly. Hazeleigh needs to get into her cabin and grab a few things. Then she'll go back into hiding."

"With you?"

"Not *with* me," Landon replied. "I'm helping her with access to a few things. Information."

"Someone shot at you," Dunne pointed out. "That scratch wasn't an accident. So why not go to the cops and—"

"No," Hazeleigh said firmly. "I know you all don't trust me, or think I'm just some—" she was clearly struggling to find the words "—weak-willed, scaredy-cat, foolish… whatever. You aren't the first, likely won't be the last, but I know one thing. I cannot go to the cops."

"I've never thought you were *foolish*," Henry muttered in return.

Landon barely resisted the urge to punch him in the nose. But Hazeleigh kept talking.

"It's important that I clear my name before we go to them. It's important to figure out who's trying to frame me. I might be the *only* one who can determine who killed Mr. Field—particularly if the police think I did it and won't listen to me about what I know about Mr. Field's life. I can't quite do it on my own, and Landon has inserted himself in the whole thing to help. And I appreciate that help. Now, I'm going to ask for yours. Pretend you never saw me. Please."

Landon didn't know how anyone could ever say no to that request, and both Dunne and Henry shifted uncomfortably—very rare indeed.

"All right," Dunne agreed after a long silence. "But not forever. You've got a leash, Landon. Three more days. Tops."

Henry huffed out an irritated breath. "Forty-eight hours, then we barge in. Take it or leave it."

"I preferred Dunne's deal," Hazeleigh replied.

"Tough."

Hazeleigh sighed and though it was dark, he got the feeling she was studying him. Considering…everything. "Fine," she said after a moment or two. "Forty-eight hours."

"You better come inside with us," Dunne said to Landon. "Jake's going to notice something's off, and even if he *would* keep something from Zara, I think we all know he can't. So you'll need to come in and pretend to go to bed."

"I'm not leaving Hazeleigh out here alone."

"It's okay," Hazeleigh said. "You go inside. I'll go to my cabin and get what I need."

Landon took her arm in the dark, pulled her away from

Henry and Dunne, but before he could say anything, she was already pleading her case.

"I can do it myself, Landon. I'll get the laptop and meet you back behind the stables. I promise, I won't go anywhere without you."

"Hazeleigh…"

"I can do it, Landon." She grabbed his hands. Squeezed. "I have to do it."

It went against every instinct he had. But he couldn't refuse her. "All right," he muttered. "Fifteen minutes, then I come after you."

"It won't take me more than ten," she assured him. Then she dropped his hands, and began to walk through the dark, toward her cabin.

Landon watched her go—just a shadow—and still it felt wrong. Bone-deep wrong.

Henry clapped him on the shoulder, hard, and didn't let go as he practically pushed Landon toward the house. "We've got a *lot* to discuss, brother."

"Don't have time for discussions." He'd go inside, make a joke, then go straight to bed. Then out the window and over to the cabin. He looked over his shoulder as Henry pushed him to the porch.

She shouldn't be out there alone in the dark.

"Shocks the hell out of me, but seems like maybe Hazeleigh can handle herself," Dunne said.

Maybe. No—no maybes. Landon knew she could.

But that didn't make the clutching terror of worry loosen in his gut.

Chapter Fifteen

Hazeleigh walked confidently across the front yard she'd spent her entire life walking across. During the day. At night. Barefoot. Bundled up for a blizzard. Every Hart going back one hundred and fifty years had done the same. Tragedy. Triumph.

Now her.

She would be brave. She would be strong. She'd held her own—not just with Landon, but with Henry *and* Dunne. Truth be told, they were the two Thompson brothers she found the most intimidating.

Funny, because she knew they *all* looked to Cal as kind of a de facto leader. She supposed it was some oldest-brother thing, but still, for all Cal's scowls and dour proclamations, he didn't have the same edge Henry and Dunne did.

Henry in particular.

No, she'd never felt comfortable around Henry, but back there she hadn't *shown* it. She'd hidden her nerves away behind bravado and the driving need to do just this.

She walked around to the back of her cabin, weaved through the gardens she loved to tend in the summer.

"I'll be home soon," she whispered. A promise to her plants *and* herself.

She paused at the door and looked out over the yard to

the big house. There was a light on in the kitchen window. She didn't see anyone lurking around the house, so assumed Landon and his brothers had already gone inside.

There was the familiar pang for all that had been lost. Her mother. Amberleigh. Her childhood. Mr. Field and the job she'd loved.

Hazeleigh swallowed at the lump in her throat. Mr. Field was the only one who'd ever *needed* her. Now he was gone.

She closed her eyes and breathed deeply. In the dark she made a promise to him, too. *I'll find out who did this. No matter what it takes.*

The nonexistent breeze picked up for a moment, and for a fleeting, crazy second she thought she smelled peppermints—the kind Mr. Field always had on hand.

Silly.

She pulled her keys out of her pocket and unlocked the back door, stepping immediately into her kitchen. Everything was still and quiet. It smelled…stale. Like old coffee and…other people.

The cops had no doubt searched it. Gone through her things and… She couldn't think about it. It wasn't the first time.

The first time they had found something much worse: evidence against her.

She was pretty sure they hadn't found anything this time because Dunne or Henry surely would have said something. Or Landon would have found out and said something.

So if someone was trying to frame her, at least they hadn't planted evidence in her cabin. *That* was something. Something she'd hold on to.

She closed the door behind her very carefully, making every effort to make no noise—not even a squeak. She didn't flip on the lights. She stood, trying to remember where she would have left her laptop.

She took it everywhere—worked from bed, from the couch in the living room, from the kitchen table. When she was deep in research or organization mode, she thought of little else. But the last time she'd been home...

It had been the morning of Mr. Field's murder. She'd woken up, checked her phone, seen his message. Which meant her laptop was probably still in her bedroom, as she'd been working from bed the night before.

She took a deep breath to settle her nerves, and then carefully began to move. The cabin was dark, but she knew where everything was, and her eyes had adjusted. It wasn't the first time she'd tiptoed through the cabin in the pitch-black. At times, Hazeleigh woke in the middle of the night, parched from some terrible nightmare and needing a drink of water or some fresh night air. When Zara had still been her roommate, Hazeleigh had always kept the lights off as she made her way through the cabin.

So this was old hat. Everything was fine and safe, and she would get the laptop and meet Landon at the stables.

She'd figure this out. And she'd do it in *thirty-six* darn hours. Just to prove Henry—Mr. Forty-eight Hours—and his bad attitude wrong.

She liked that. Having a sense of purpose. Having an enemy with a face, even if it was Landon's brother and he wasn't really her enemy. Just kind of a meanie. Maybe not even that. Maybe he was simply mad that Landon was wrapped up in something that might get him in trouble, and was blaming her.

Could she blame Henry for that?

She puffed out a breath. She had to focus on finding the laptop. Leave everything else behind. She moved through the kitchen in the dark, easily avoiding the small kitchen table and feeling her way down the hall until she reached her bedroom.

She considered turning on the light, since the only window in her room faced away from the main house, but that would be an unnecessary risk. She'd just have to sit down on the bed and paw around for the laptop where she usually set it on the ground, between her bed and her nightstand.

And she'd need her cord, which she usually kept out in the living room. She muttered a curse under her breath. She'd told Landon she'd be ten minutes, and so far she was moving about as quickly as molasses.

She sat on the bed, reached down to where she usually kept her laptop. Her hand clasped over the cool metal. *Success.* She picked it up and clutched it to her chest. Now she just needed the cord.

She moved to the living room, felt around on the ground until she touched the cord. She unplugged it and then…

She straightened, then stilled. Had she…heard something? A creak? A rustle? Her heart leaped into her throat.

It might just be Landon. Maybe her time was up, and he'd gotten worried, but one of her old bad feelings overwhelmed her.

She lurched forward, suddenly sure she had to get out of there. But her shin banged against her coffee table and she narrowly swallowed down a yelp of pain as she hopped on one leg.

She stilled, tried to get her breathing under control, and *listened.* She waited and waited and waited and waited.

Nothing happened. There was no sound. No one jumping out—friend or foe. There was nothing.

Silly, Hazeleigh. Your feelings are wrong and pointless and you should stop thinking there could ever actually be something inside of you that might actually have any sense of what's going on around you.

She swallowed down her emotional response to the nasty

voice in her head. It wasn't true. As unreliable as her feelings could be, they did occasionally help.

Just sometimes, they were very far off the mark. Or maybe… Maybe someone else was in danger. Usually she had a sense of who. She'd saved Zara more than once from a bad accident, though maybe twice in a lifetime wasn't enough to really count on.

But she *had* been right. She'd known about Amberleigh—had a sick, horrible feeling just like now, before Zara had accidentally dug up their sister's body.

Maybe Zara was in trouble. Maybe Landon was…

No, he was with his brothers, and so was Zara. Maybe they were simply arguing or something else had given her a bad feeling. Hardly as serious as the end of anyone's life.

She blew out a breath and moved forward. Everything was fine, or as fine as it could be, and if someone out there was having something terrible happen to them, well, that was a shame, but there wasn't much she could do about it unless her "feeling" decided to give her more information.

She moved to the kitchen, pausing once more to listen for noises, but she heard nothing out of the ordinary. The bad feeling was still churning around in her chest, but she didn't know what to do with it. No one was in here with her, and she'd gotten what she'd come for.

She licked her lips, swallowed at her dry throat, then opened the kitchen door. She stepped back into the night air, her garden. Down the stairs, a few steps across the pathway and into the yard. Landon was likely already waiting for her behind the stables.

God, she hoped so.

But before she made it, arms came around her from behind, a too-tight hold that had the laptop and cord clattering into the grass.

"Let me go, Henry." But she knew, even as she said

it, that it wasn't Henry. Or Landon. Or Dunne. It was a stranger.

"We knew you'd come," the voice said, and she struggled to recognize it, but there was absolutely nothing familiar about it.

LANDON BIT BACK impatience with himself. He hated leaving Hazeleigh alone, but he knew his brothers. He had to do this or they wouldn't even give him the allotted forty-eight hours.

Forty-eight hours wasn't enough, even with the leads they'd gotten today. He needed more time. Hazeleigh needed more time.

Landon took a seat at the kitchen table and smiled blandly at Cal.

Everything would be fine. Hazeleigh knew her way around her cabin. It was the middle of the night and there were no cops hanging around.

Everything was fine.

He closed his hand into a fist under the table. Nothing felt fine.

Dunne also sat at the kitchen table. Henry paced. Cal stood stock-still.

"Going to call in the rest of the cavalry or can we let this slide, fellas?"

Dunne sighed. Henry all but growled.

"I don't think we need to include anyone else," Cal said evenly, after a time. "But you should know better than to sneak around here with *her* when Jake could have easily been the one to find you."

They all looked at the kitchen entrance like just mentioning Jake might make him appear. He didn't, but the thought that he would made Landon feel guilty. Although, he wouldn't be sitting here worrying about guilt if Henry and Dunne had minded their own damn business.

"So what can we do?" Cal said.

Henry and Dunne both shot Cal surprised glances, immediately hidden away. Then they turned to Landon. Because the three of them preferred pretending like they were still in the military. Like Cal was the leader and they were on some kind of mission.

Landon had understood at first, but the more Jake and Brody settled into *real* actual lives, the more he wanted that. Not just because being a soldier had been taken away from him, but because they seemed…happy.

These three? Not so much.

But they wanted to help, and Landon wished he knew how he could use their skills to figure this out.

"We're following some leads. I'm not sure there's anything you can do." Landon remembered Hazeleigh's story about the little girl. He related it to the men. "I don't think it can connect. What would a little girl wandering around on her own have to do with Mr. Field's murder?"

"Nothing, on the surface," Henry said.

"But we all know better than to believe the surface," Dunne added.

"We'll see what we can figure out about the girl." Cal's frown deepened. "A kid shouldn't be running around on her own out here. Especially on land that's supposed to be deserted."

"Hazeleigh had the same concerns. But she said she seemed…okay. Capable. Hazeleigh told her she was Zara, so another thing to keep Jake out of."

"They keep adding up," Cal muttered.

"I don't like it either," Landon said. "But it has to be done."

"For now," Cal replied. "I'm with you on this, but I'm

with Henry, too. If you can't get it done in forty-eight hours, we've got to pull the plug. Before someone gets hurt."

"Hazeleigh being arrested is someone getting hurt."

Cal held his gaze. "Maybe she thinks that, but it's hardly the end of the world. And it's happened to her before and she survived."

"Yeah, because we got her out of it. Jake and the rest of us. So how about instead of expecting a woman who has never had anything to do with murder or war to suck it up and deal with jail, we get this done."

"You're emotionally involved," Cal said, sounding shocked. Disappointment was threaded through the three simple words.

It took way too much effort to keep his voice low, but he wasn't going to deny it. No matter how little Cal approved of him being *emotionally involved.* "You're damn right I am."

"What is it with you three?" Henry muttered disgustedly. "You can't help someone without falling in love?"

Love felt…heavy. A bit much, a bridge too far. But he wasn't about to argue semantics for being emotionally involved at the moment. "The bottom line is she *needs* help, and I can give it. Take emotions out of it. It needs to be done."

"But you can't take emotions out of it. You have them."

"So what? Who said being detached and unemotional was the be-all end-all? Here we are, washed-up soldiers who had to be wiped off the grid not because we got too emotional or invested, but because some computer tech pushed the wrong damn button."

No one moved. No one said anything. Because it was true, but maybe not a truth any of them had really considered. Had maybe even *avoided* considering.

Landon stood. "I don't want her out there alone longer

than she has to be," he said quietly, but with enough venom to keep anyone else from arguing. "We'll do our best to figure this out in forty-eight hours. We have a lead. We have something to go on. But I need you to remember she isn't *us*. She isn't a soldier. She has a family and a life that was already upended—by her dad selling this place to us, by her sister being dead and buried on our land and her getting blamed for it for a time. Now her boss is dead, and she found the body. She might be stronger and braver than we've given her credit for, but she's not an automaton like we were. She's a person."

"Quite a speech."

Landon didn't turn around, but he did close his eyes and let out a long sigh. "How much of that did you hear?"

"More than I wanted to," Jake replied. "Landon, I can't—"

"Then don't," Landon said, cutting him off. He moved for the exit. He wasn't going to sit around and talk about this anymore. "Do whatever you guys need to do. Me? I'm done talking about what I'm *going* to do. I'm going to go do it."

He pushed passed Jake. Luckily none of his brothers tried to stop him. Maybe they'd come after him. Maybe they'd let him handle this. He genuinely didn't care at this moment, because he couldn't take another second of Hazeleigh being out there alone. She was likely waiting for him.

But when he got to the stables, Hazeleigh wasn't there.

And the terrible feeling he hadn't been able to shake intensified.

Chapter Sixteen

Hazeleigh wanted to fall apart, but she knew everyone around her was in danger if she did. Her sister was in the house, just a short distance away. Kate. Landon and all his brothers. If the man had a gun, and someone came running…

The thought swept through her in a shudder. So she stood very still while this man held on to her…too tightly.

She swallowed down the revulsion of being pressed to some stranger's fleshy body.

"Who are you?" she asked, though her voice wavered. Not quite the show of strength she'd wanted.

"You don't know?" He laughed in her ear, his hot breath fluttering her hair. She wanted to wretch.

Instead, she kept holding herself still. Landon would come and get her. He would know something was wrong. He'd known when Henry had grabbed her. Certainly he'd know things were amiss and he'd…fix them. He wouldn't barge in. He'd sneak in. He wouldn't get shot.

Not again.

In the meantime, she'd do everything she could to remain unhurt and right here.

"Pick up the computer," the man said. "You try to run, the whole house goes up in flames."

Hazeleigh remained absolutely still. The statement had

cold shock moving through her. The house. Did he mean her cabin, or...?

"And not just fire. I mean the whole thing explodes. Won't be too many survivors. How many people in there, you think? Seven? Or is it eight now?"

He meant the big house. "How would you do that?"

He laughed again. His hot breath close to her ear. "You think any of this was spur-of-the-moment? We've been planning it all. Bit by bit. Now, you're coming with me."

"This doesn't make any sense," she muttered. And who was *we*?

"Of course it doesn't. To someone as stupid as *you*."

Without thinking, she jerked her arm. An instinctual retaliation. He held firm, jerked her back just as hard, if not harder. It sent a shock of pain down her arm, and she made a noise of distress.

He jerked her again, even harder. "Shut up or I'll have to kill all of you."

"You're *hurting* me."

"I haven't even started hurting you. Pick up the computer. Shut the hell up and let's go."

"If you take me, they'll know," Hazeleigh said desperately. "And the police will know I didn't kill Mr. Field, because I've been kidnapped. If you shoot me, you don't have a scapegoat for Mr. Field's murder."

He was quiet for a moment, studying her. "Who would know I took you? You ran away on your own. Pretty dumb if you ask me."

She didn't want to give up Landon's identity since this man didn't seem to know about his involvement. So this man hadn't been following her. Had just been sitting at her cabin, waiting. She had to use what he didn't know against him. "You think I've been avoiding the cops on my own? You think I came here in the middle of the night *alone*?"

She thought about mentioning Mr. Field's house, but she didn't know enough. Was this man working alone? Was he the same man who'd shot at them?

He knew enough to know where she lived. He knew enough about her to wait and—

"Pick up the computer and give it to me. Or they explode." He loosened his grip a little, so she could crouch and reach for it with one arm.

Hazeleigh let out a shaky breath. She would try to bide her time and keep the man right here, where Landon would find them. She kneeled. Took a breath. Picked up the laptop.

"Come *on*."

She slowly stood, and he pulled on her arm again. A hard, bruising grasp.

She had to think. He was big. The top of her head just barely came up to his chin. His hand on her arm was meaty.

He ripped the laptop out of her grasp.

"You won't be able to get what you're looking for without my passwords." She had no idea what he was after—but if he was after what *she* was after…

The guy snorted. "That's why you're coming with me." He started dragging her, and she realized if he held her *and* the computer, there was no hand free for him to somehow set off the explosives.

So she fought. She kicked. She wrenched her arm from every angle she could think of as he tried to pull her. The man grunted and fought right back, holding her firm.

But the house didn't explode, so that was something.

Then she heard her name shouted from a distance.

Landon.

She didn't have time to think—she could only act. With one well-placed kick, she managed to free herself from the would-be kidnapper's tight grasp as he let out a gasp of pain.

She managed one step toward Landon's voice before the man grabbed her by the hair. He ripped her backward. Pain exploded all over her scalp and she stopped fighting as a protective measure.

"Tell him to back off, or everyone inside dies," he hissed into her ear.

Hazeleigh had to marshal all her emotions, all her thoughts. She knew she was taking too long when the man yanked her hair again. She gasped in pain.

"Hazeleigh." It was Landon's voice. Too far away. But calm. Deadly calm. In the darkness. "Don't move."

"Tell him," the man said. Odd that he wouldn't call out to Landon himself.

Hazeleigh managed to clear her throat. "He—he says he has explosives in the basement."

Landon laughed. Actually laughed. "My ass."

"That house isn't watched twenty-four-seven," the man whispered again.

Hazeleigh reiterated his words to Landon. She couldn't see anyone, but she assumed some of the brothers were out there as well. *Please.*

"No, but it's full of six men who'd know if it was broken into. Why are you lying? And so badly?"

All of a sudden, the man dropped her. She kneeled in the grass, utterly confused, pain radiating over her scalp. But she could hear his retreating footsteps, and then footsteps approaching her.

There were hands on her. All over her. But it was Landon. Maybe Dunne. Checking her to make sure she was okay.

"He has my computer."

"Not important," Landon said sharply.

"It *is* important. All the information we—"

Landon spoke, like he wasn't even listening to her.

"Dunne, sweep the basement. He claimed he put explosives there."

"My ass," Dunne muttered, but he hurried away to check.

"Cal, Henry, Jake, go after him. Don't lose him."

"Landon—"

But Cal spoke over her trying to speak. "Brody and Jake are already on it, Henry not far behind. We'll spread out, make a circle. You should stay here."

"Don't lose him," Landon said, and then Cal was gone, too.

Landon scooped her up like she couldn't walk herself. She pushed at his chest. "I'm fine. I'm okay."

"We're getting you inside," he said grimly. Sternly. "And you're not leaving my sight."

LANDON CARRIED HAZELEIGH the whole way inside. So much for keeping everyone out of this. So much for—

The terror he'd felt raged so high it had turned to a frigid cold, and as he didn't trust that feeling, he said nothing. Did nothing. He called on that old robotic-soldier facade to make it inside with her. He carried her to the couch and carefully deposited her.

What Landon really wanted to do was take after the man who'd had his hands on Hazeleigh, but he knew he couldn't. Not because Hazeleigh needed him, but because it wouldn't end well for the man. And while that didn't matter in the least to him, they needed information. They did not need Landon to exact revenge.

Landon took a step back from the couch, looking down at Hazeleigh critically. She was a little pale, but otherwise not too worse for wear.

The man had touched her. Tried to kidnap her. And a few more minutes…

He swallowed against his anger over the situation clogging his throat. "Are you hurt?" he asked.

She blinked, eyebrows drawing together as if she was confused by the question. "No, not—"

"What is going—" Zara appeared from the kitchen. Apparently she hadn't known about what had gone on outside, and that it involved Hazeleigh, because her eyes widened, she dropped the dish towel she'd been strangling and rushed over to Hazeleigh, then threw her arms around her sister.

Hazeleigh put an arm around Zara, but her eyes remained on his. That same confusion in the brown depths.

Zara looked up at him next, and while Hazeleigh's gaze was soft, if confused, Zara's was squinted and angry. "What the hell is going on?" she demanded of him.

But Hazeleigh put a hand on one of Zara's. "Where's Kate?"

"She wasn't feeling well. Probably sleeping through it all. I'll catch her up in the morning, or Brody will. Now, if you avoid my question one more time…"

Hazeleigh sighed, looking down at her hand over her sister's. Landon looked at their hands, too. He shouldn't be here. He didn't *belong* here. Why'd he think he was the one to step in and fix things?

"I snuck back to my cabin," Hazeleigh explained, clearly leaving out his involvement in the situation. "I wanted my computer. I thought maybe I could figure out some things if I had my computer. I could read Mr. Field's emails and such. But someone was at the cabin waiting for me." Her gaze returned to Landon. "Whoever it was had been waiting for me for a long time."

She was trying to absolve him. That he couldn't have known simply because the man had been waiting. Which

made the cold inside of him branch out. Douse more mol-
ten-hot fury. He had to freeze it out. If he didn't…

Because he'd known something was wrong, and he'd
ignored it. He'd known leaving her alone was wrong, but
he'd done it.

There was no absolution to be had. Every choice from
the beginning had been wrong. Because he'd let emotion
and his own ego sway him. Just like Cal had always warned
them.

"Why?" Zara asked, still clutching on to Hazeleigh as
if her sister might disappear again.

"Whoever it was wanted information. I think… Zara,
I know this sounds crazy, but I think this all ties to Mr.
Field's research. This man who'd been waiting wanted my
computer. The only thing he could want is access to Mr.
Field's research on the bank robbery."

"Fake bank robbery, Haze. Who cares about some old
myth?"

"Someone, I think. Maybe I'm wrong, but…" She snuck
another glance at Landon. But he could neither move nor
speak. Not without shattering.

"Okay, so you have a lead. Take it to the police and—"

Hazeleigh withdrew herself from Zara's grasp. "No."

"Haze—"

"I won't. I can't. Not until we can prove someone else
did it. We need evidence. I just… I had this feeling, Zara.
Bone-deep. I can't go back to jail. Or even a holding cell or
whatever. I just know the police can't help me. I *know* it."

Zara sighed, but she didn't argue with Hazeleigh.

"Dunne's checking the house," Landon said, but his
voice sounded like little more than a rasp. "The rest of
them are on the guy's tail. If they catch him, we'll call the
police. Go from there."

Hazeleigh frowned. "He didn't kill Mr. Field. Whoever it is, he's involved, but he didn't kill Mr. Field."

"How do you know that?" Zara asked before Landon could.

"He's not working alone. He said *we*, and he talked about planning. And he just… He didn't strike me as very smart. Or at least, he thought I was…" She trailed off, looked at Zara, then at him.

Landon didn't know what she was about to say, what she wanted to hide, but he had the sneaking suspicion she was trying to save him from Zara's wrath. Or maybe Jake's.

At the moment, he wanted everyone's wrath. He wanted nothing but anger and blame and guilt and anything dark. Because that's what he deserved for these missteps and failures.

"Tell her the whole truth," Landon said flatly.

She closed her eyes as if in pain. "Landon."

"What's the whole truth?" Zara demanded.

Hazeleigh plastered a smile on her face and took Zara's hand in hers. "Landon's been helping me."

Zara shot to her feet, but Hazeleigh held firm. Landon supposed it kept him from getting a punch in the nose, but he wouldn't have minded that right now.

"You've been *lying* to me? To Jake?"

"I begged him to," Hazeleigh said before Landon could say something that might make Zara angrier. "And you'll be relieved to know Landon was the one who convinced me not to run away completely. He thought we could figure out who did this, clear my name. And we're making progress."

"Progress," Landon scoffed. "You were almost kidnapped."

"But I wasn't," she returned firmly. She was far more calm than he was, which was wrong. She should be shaken up. Afraid. As damn terrified as he was underneath it all.

Instead, she seemed to have it all figured out and he wanted to *shake* her. The man inside her cabin could have shot her dead. Done. The end. Because Landon had let her go alone.

"And that's why I think this guy wasn't very smart," Hazeleigh continued, maddeningly casual. "I kept slowing things down. Talking to him. Taking my time. Because I knew you'd come, and…"

The rest of her words were lost to the buzzing in his head. *I knew you'd come.* But he hadn't come soon enough. He should have. The minute he'd felt something was wrong. Instead he'd sat in the kitchen *chatting* with his brothers. As if talking ever got the job done. As if their approval or support mattered when Hazeleigh had been in trouble.

Knowing he'd come.

"Landon." She stood and reached for him, but he stepped away before her hand could take his. Something once so rare that had now become almost a habit.

He'd crumble if she touched him now. Into dust. "Zara, keep an eye on her. I'm—"

The screen door behind him squeaked open and Jake popped his head in.

"We've got him," Jake said. He eyed Hazeleigh and Zara. "Brought him into Henry's shed. We thought you'd want to question him yourself."

"Yes, I do," Landon said. "I'll be there in a minute."

Whether Jake sensed the tension in the room or just didn't want to face Zara's inevitable wrath quite yet, he nodded and disappeared back into the night.

Landon turned to the sisters. He held his hands behind his back, spread his feet. *At ease, soldier.* Sometimes a man needed to be a soldier and nothing else.

"This is what's going to happen," Landon said, and he knew how stiff he sounded. How stiff he must look considering how frozen he felt. And it might have amused him any other time, as he realized how much he sounded and probably looked like Cal.

Maybe after all this was over, he'd understand Cal better. But for now, he could only focus on himself. On surviving. On making this as right as he could for Hazeleigh, even though he'd failed miserably tonight. "You will stay right here. We will question this guy. If it's enough to call in the cops, we will."

"If it's not?" Hazeleigh demanded, sparks of temper in her eyes. The sisters looked especially alike in the moment. Hazeleigh in his sweatshirt, even if she was wearing her skirt. Zara rumpled in sweats and a T-shirt.

"We'll decide what's next," Landon said in a tone that brooked no argument.

Somehow, Hazeleigh found one. "By *we* you mean you and me?"

"No, I mean my brothers and I." He turned toward the door.

"Landon." Her voice was very direct. Very serious. And he had no choice but to stop, turn and meet her gaze. "You will not bulldoze me," she said. "None of you. You may have crashed in, you may have helped, but at the end of the day it's *my* life on the line."

There was such a complicated tangle of emotions inside of him that he simply didn't trust himself to speak. Her life on the line—which might have been over. So easily.

And it would have been his fault.

So he said nothing and left her with her sister.

Chapter Seventeen

Hazeleigh stood and watched him not respond, just... leave. She didn't understand what had happened, what had changed. Why had he gotten so cold? She'd never seen him like that.

It made her want to cry, and she wasn't even sure why. But crying and wringing her hands had gotten her nowhere.

Instead, she focused on all the frustration she felt inside. Better than sadness. Better than all the fear she'd felt when that man had grabbed her.

"Can you believe him? *We'll* question him. *We'll* call the police." She fumed. "*I'm* the one wanted for murder. And he's just sweeping in. Taking over. *Telling* me what to do." Hazeleigh began to pace. She wanted to break something. She wanted to...

She caught Zara staring at her with a slightly open-mouthed expression. "What?"

"I've never seen you like this," Zara said softly. "Never."

Hazeleigh stopped pacing. "Well, no one's ever tried to kidnap me before."

"Maybe not, but you've been suspected of murder before. You've been manhandled before. Dad was always a high-handed jerk to you. And you always..."

Hazeleigh looked down at her hands. She knew what she always did. Cowered. Hid. Heaped a bunch of self-blame on herself. She sucked in a breath and met Zara's gaze. "I don't want to be that person anymore."

Zara finally stood from the couch. She stood in front of Hazeleigh, looking strangely…moved. She even reached out and took Hazeleigh's hands in hers. "Good." But Zara studied her face, as if still looking for that old cowardly behavior.

"Zara…" She didn't know what she wanted to say. Or she didn't have the words. Things had changed. And it wasn't just all of a sudden. It was like…all paths she'd been on the last few months had led her here. To a place where she could finally grab on to a…new self.

No, not new. Someone who'd grown out of bad things and bad habits and was determined to find something stronger within herself. Something braver. So she could face… well, everything she was up against now.

She had to face it. Whatever was going on with Landon couldn't influence *her*. This was *her* life, and she appreciated his help—she didn't want him to stop *helping*. She just couldn't stand the thought of him sweeping in and taking over, leaving her here to wring her hands.

She looked down at her hands, caught in Zara's, who was not the touchy sort. But she held on.

There was no ring where there should have been though. Hazeleigh frowned. "Don't tell me you said no."

Zara's expression scrunched into confusion as she looked down at their hands. "No to what?"

Hazeleigh realized her mistake. Because, of *course*, Jake wasn't going to propose while Zara was worried over her sister being on the run. "Erm…"

Zara tugged her hands away. She laughed, but there was a little hint of panic behind it. "You don't mean…" She shook her head. "You're being ridiculous."

But she wasn't. And… Well, it was kind of nice to watch

someone else freak out about something in the midst of her own problems. "I helped him pick out the ring. I told him I thought you were ready. I hope I wasn't wrong."

"A ring," Zara echoed, as if Hazeleigh had said something like *poison*.

"I suppose I ruined the timing of things when I ran away," Hazeleigh said. "I am sorry for that. Although I guess it's more Mr. Field's murderer's fault." Because not everything was her fault. She didn't need to blame herself for everything that happened, just like Landon had told her.

"I..." Zara blinked, completely speechless.

A feat indeed.

"I hope you'll pretend to be surprised when this is all over and he does ask." Hazeleigh had to bite back a grin. It was so rare to see Zara off the mark that even with everything going on around them, Hazeleigh enjoyed it. "I'd hate to be the reason the moment was ruined."

"Ruined?" Zara seemed to get a hold of herself, though she had her fist pressed to her heart like she was trying to keep it from exploding through her chest. "No, I think... I think I'm glad I had some forewarning."

"You think?"

Zara looked up at Hazeleigh. "He really wants to *marry* me?" she whispered. Even though they *lived* together. And Zara still seemed uncertain. Not about Jake's feelings so much as...the future.

It was like something clicking into place for Hazeleigh. She'd always fancied Zara the strong one, and her the weak one. But...people—all people—were far more complicated than that.

No matter how strong. How weak. Life was a series of challenges, and sometimes you met them with mistakes. But sometimes...wonderful things happened. She was ready for some wonderful things.

"Of course he does. He loves you. You make each other happy." Hazeleigh smiled at her sister. "Zara, you've never been so happy. Don't overthink it."

Zara swallowed. "But…"

"No *buts.*"

"This is ridiculous," Zara said, shaking her head vigorously. "Why are we talking about this in the middle of the night while those six imbeciles take care of everything?"

"I don't know. They really are imbeciles, aren't they?"

"Honorable, wonderful imbeciles, but imbeciles nonetheless," Zara said with a sharp nod. She opened her mouth, and Hazeleigh knew she was about to outline a plan. Take over. Be in charge.

But Hazeleigh realized for the first time that it was her job to do that. "I need to talk to that man who tried to kidnap me. I need to get to the bottom of it, so we can all get on with our lives."

"So we'll go barge in there and demand to ask your questions."

Hazeleigh blinked. "What?"

"You don't have to sit here. You don't have to wait around, and you don't have to run. You can fight. You can do what *you* think is right. The Thompson brothers might be a muscly, loudmouthed group of bossy imbeciles, but they're going to have to bodily remove us if they don't like your plan."

Your plan. Why did that feel so good? But she thought about Landon carrying her all the way from the cabin to the house no matter how she'd protested. "I think Landon might bodily remove me right now."

Zara studied her carefully. "Yeah, he just might." And Hazeleigh got the distinct feeling Zara understood that maybe something was happening there. But then she shrugged it all away easily enough. "I'll fight him, you ask your questions. Teamwork."

It was ridiculous. The idea of Zara going in there, fighting Landon, while Hazeleigh faced her attempted kidnapper and asked questions. It wouldn't go down that way. But Zara was right.

The brothers might be bossy and controlling when they thought they were doing the right thing, but they weren't going to…just toss her out.

They'd try. They'd argue, but if she pleaded her case, especially to Landon, he'd cave. When it came to her, he seemed to always cave. "I can do it. I can fight him," she decided. Maybe not with fists. But with reason. And emotion.

"I'm still coming with."

"Shouldn't I do it on my own? I can do it on my own. It's time I… Well, stand on my own two feet, I guess."

"You can be strong and stand on your own two feet *and* have support, Haze. It isn't all one or the other."

"Since when do you think that, Miss Independent?" Hazeleigh asked with a smile, though she knew the answer before Zara even said it.

Zara wrinkled her nose. "I guess since Jake," she said, sounding embarrassed. But Hazeleigh didn't think it was anything to be embarrassed about.

It was beautiful.

Jake and Zara deserved more of their happily-ever-after. And Hazeleigh deserved a little of her own. Which meant, they had to end this. "Let's go."

IT IRRITATED LANDON that Hazeleigh's estimation was right. The man who'd tried to kidnap her wasn't smart. He was capable of killing, maybe, but not of killing a man and framing someone else, all the while having some deeper plan clearly in place.

Not that the would-be kidnapper knew the plan. Oh, he thought he did, but the more questions he was asked, the more he seemed to realize how little he really did know.

Which made him mad. He fought against where he was tied to the chair. Seemingly not thinking through that even if he did get free—which he wouldn't—he'd have to get through *six* trained ex-military men.

"What's with the explosives talk?" Dunne asked when it was clear they weren't getting anywhere with a name for the alleged murderer. "I went through the whole house and there wasn't anything."

"Had to get her to come with me without screaming, didn't I?"

Landon's hands curled into fists. He took a step toward the man without even realizing it.

"Why not knock her out? Drug her? A million ways to take her." Henry said it flippantly, but Landon could picture those possibilities all too clearly. As if that's what had actually happened.

"You're right about that." The guy grinned, licked his lips. "A million ways to take her!" Then he laughed, like he expected them all to join in the joke.

Landon's fist unclenched, but only enough to land on the gun still on his hip. He could end it right here. No questions asked.

Cal stepped between him and the man. For a second, Cal's face was unfocused and Landon had to blink to see. Past the need for revenge and payback for hurting Hazeleigh. Past the thudding violence inside of him.

Like father, like son.

"Stand down, Landon."

"You're not my commanding officer anymore." Because maybe this was just who he was and trying to be someone else all these years was pointless.

"No," Cal said evenly. Then he reached out and put his hand on Landon's shoulder. Squeezed. "I'm your brother. Step outside."

Landon didn't know what it was, but whatever was locked tight eased, and though he didn't step outside himself, he did let Cal lead him outside. Henry and Jake followed.

"What do we do with this bozo?" Henry asked.

"We can't let him go. Dumb or not, he's a danger," Jake replied. "And not just to Hazeleigh."

No, they were all involved now. What a mess.

"Speak of the devil," Henry muttered.

Landon looked up to see Hazeleigh and Zara step out onto the porch. It was still dark, but someone had flipped on the porch light, and they were two dimly lit shadows as they marched across the yard.

She *was* a devil. His own personal Satan. Because he hadn't made mistakes until she'd come around. Even now he simply wanted to bundle her up and hold her and make this bad stuff all go away.

She stopped in front of him, and even though he had the impression she was trying to pose her demand to all of them, she held his gaze and his alone.

"I need to talk to that man."

"No." Landon was gratified that Henry and Cal's *no's* echoed with his even if his was overloud in his ears.

Jake's *no* was missing, but Landon could only assume that Jake would play traitor and be on Zara's side for this.

"I did not request permission," she said firmly. "Move." She raised an eyebrow. First at Landon. Then at Jake.

None of his brothers moved.

"What's the harm of her asking some questions?" Zara

demanded. "She might think to ask something your brain trust doesn't."

"Did it ever occur to you to ask nicely, Zara?" Jake muttered.

"Why don't you tell us your questions and we'll ask him," Cal suggested. It was reasonable enough.

Hazeleigh's mouth firmed. "Open the door, Landon."

"I'm not your lapdog, Hazeleigh."

For a second, hurt flashed through her expression. But all that emotion had gotten them nothing but trouble. He couldn't give in to it.

She turned to Cal. "You seem to be the de facto leader around here, and I appreciate all that you and your brothers have done or tried to do for me, but the fact of the matter is I am the one being framed for murder. *I* am the one who almost got kidnapped. I feel like I'm owed a little face time with the man who wanted to take me and my laptop against my will."

Landon watched Cal's face remain impassive, but there was a little flash of something at the end. And he turned to Landon apologetically. "Let's just open the door."

Landon said nothing. And he didn't move. It wasn't so off-base. Her argument was good. But he didn't trust…anything. So why not let Cal lead, just like old times?

He said nothing to Hazeleigh, didn't even look at her, just opened the door. She lifted her chin and sailed into the outbuilding Henry had converted into a little detached bedroom and office.

They all filed in behind her. Jake and Zara, Henry, Cal. Landon hesitated. He thought about leaving. Just…leaving. Completely. Maybe he'd go back to Mississippi. Maybe he'd just start hiking to Alaska. Maybe…

But Hazeleigh's voice was strong and demanding as she faced the man who'd attacked her.

"Why did you try to kidnap me?"

Landon had to...see this through. He just had to. He turned in time to see the would-be kidnapper shrug his shoulders, looking totally unconcerned that he was tied up and being questioned by eight strangers. That didn't sit right. It *wasn't* right.

"Who sent you here?"

"We already asked that one," Henry muttered.

"A little birdie," the man said, then chuckled at his own joke.

"Where's my computer?"

The man smiled slyly. "What computer?"

She whipped her head around to look at him and his brothers. "Where's my computer?"

"He didn't have it when I tackled him," Jake said. "But I didn't know I was looking for a computer."

"We need it," Hazeleigh said firmly.

"Once it's daylight—"

"No, we need it now," she said, cutting off Cal. She gave the tied-up man one last haughty look. "You said you know me, but I don't know you."

"Oh, you know me."

Hazeleigh was clearly frustrated by that—clearly did not know the man—but she didn't argue. She looked at Zara, who nodded almost imperceptibly, and then they both left the building.

Landon followed. "That was it? Those were the oh-so-important questions we couldn't ask for you?"

She ignored him and looked at Zara. "You recognized him?"

"I think. He looks a lot different, but I'm pretty sure that's Hamilton Chinelly."

Hazeleigh frowned. "Who?"

"Don't you remember? He was one of Dad's ranch hands when Mom was sick."

"That was almost twenty years ago. Chinelly... Chinelly..." Hazeleigh was tapping her fingers together and Landon was about ready to come unwound, but Jake had a hand on his shoulder...like Cal had done before. Keeping him steady.

"Let them work it out," Jake said quietly.

Zara paced. Hazeleigh tapped. Landon wanted to howl in protest.

"Don't they have a connection to the Petersons?" Hazeleigh asked, pointing dramatically at Zara.

Zara stopped pacing. "Why's that matter?"

"Just...what was it? Do you remember?"

"I think a Chinelly married a Peterson. I remember thinking anyone related to Ham getting married was quite the accomplishment. He's never been the brightest or nicest man."

"Okay, town gossip. Blah, blah, blah. What does it *mean*?" Landon demanded.

"I think it means we need to go search the Peterson place. But first, I need my computer." And then she just took off. She strode across the yard, away from the glow of the porch light and toward the cabin where she'd nearly been kidnapped.

Landon made a strangled noise, but Jake's hand on his shoulder kept him from moving. But then Zara was there.

"Let him go," Zara said to Jake quietly. "They need to work some things out, and I need to talk to you."

Landon barely heard what Jake said in return, just felt the hand on his shoulder loosen, then he took off after Hazeleigh's quickly retreating form.

Was she insane? Was *everyone* insane? She could hardly

just go off on her own. "Where are you going?" he demanded once he was close enough not to yell.

Once he was calm enough to trust himself not to rage.

The sun was beginning to rise. They'd barely slept in something like two days. This was all spiraling out of his control.

"I am going to find my computer. My computer has the answers." She stopped briefly in the backyard of her cabin, searching the grass with the toe of her foot. Then she set out again. Off in the direction the kidnapper had run.

"Do you want to get caught? The cops? More kidnappers? They're all out there ready to take *you*, Hazeleigh."

She whirled to face him and flung her hands wide. "I want to live my damn life." The pink pearly light of dawn glinted so she appeared showered in something like gold. Fire. Everything. She'd been *everything* ever since she'd first smiled at him—that thunderclap. "For once I am going to do everything I can to make that happen instead of stand around waiting for someone else to make things right for me."

He wanted that for her. He wanted *everything* for her. To make it right, to help her make it right. Anything. Whatever it took. These emotions all whirled inside of him, with the exhaustion, with the failure, with the fear, and with this much bigger thing he didn't know what to do with. He'd never known what to do with.

She looked at him like all those emotions had shown up on his face. She even stepped toward him. "What's wrong?" she asked, like she cared. Like it mattered. She reached up and touched his cheek. "Landon. What on earth is the matter?"

"I love you."

He'd never said those words. Not once.

Because no one, not once, had ever said them to him.

Chapter Eighteen

It might have been comical. Maybe it should have been.
Landon had just said the three sweetest words he could
possibly utter, and then looked so horrified by them, it was
hard to be warmed.

But he had said them. And Hazeleigh didn't think it was
a lie. What would be the point of a lie? He wasn't trying to
get her to do something or believe something. He wasn't
using love as a weapon. It was more like love had overwhelmed him and he didn't have the foggiest idea what to
do with it.

She wanted to step closer, lean into him, but he seemed
so frozen in shock by what he'd said, she held herself as
still as he was holding himself.

"Is that the matter?" she asked quietly.

"I can't help you if I'm…compromised."

His eyes looked so anguished. She stroked his cheek.
"Compromised. Now, you're being silly. You're exhausted."

"I knew something was wrong and I left you to the
wolves!" he exploded. But he didn't move away, didn't pull
away from her hand on his stubbled cheek.

She took that to heart. And she understood the meaning
beneath the words. "Landon, I know that guilt. I live that
guilt. I felt something wrong myself going in there, but I
talked myself out of it. Do you know how many times I've

fought my gut, for worse or for better? Do you know how long I spent listening to my father tell me if those feelings I had were worth anything, I could have stopped Amberleigh from running away? How awful I've felt wondering why I couldn't have had a bad feeling that would have saved her from being murdered?"

He started to say her name, but she shook her head. "I know what guilt is, Landon, and it's misplaced here. You told me not to blame myself for everything that happens, so you can't blame yourself for not listening to your gut. We both ignored our feelings because feelings *aren't* facts. They're right sometimes, wrong other times. You can only do your best in the moment, and in the moment...we're both alive and well."

His hand closed over her wrist. "I could not live with myself if something happened to you. I cannot bear the thought of..." He licked his lips, clearly trying to clarify his thoughts before he spoke. "You can't be alone. You need to take one of my brothers and—"

"One of your brothers? Why on earth would I do that?"

"They have the necessary emotional distance. Nothing will cloud their decision-making. It's better, safer—"

"I don't care about the necessary emotional distance. I care about *you*, Landon..." Did she love him? The words had bubbled up, unbidden, in response, but maybe that was just a reflex. She'd convinced herself she was in love before.

This was more—deeper...stronger. She just *felt* it. And she couldn't explain it exactly or rationalize her way through it.

It simply was.

That was the difference, wasn't it? That it just was. That it felt right, without any need for convincing or reasons. He was good, and he cared. He kissed her and the world fell away. He wanted her to be safe, without a worry for himself.

She trusted him. And now she needed to trust herself. "I love you, too."

He inhaled sharply. "Don't…say that."

"Why wouldn't I say that? I mean it."

"But—"

"No *buts*. You won't argue my feelings, Landon. I won't listen to it. Not anymore." Too many people had tried to tell her what to feel or what she should be, and she'd listened for far too long. That would be over now.

Landon swallowed. "No one's ever said that to me."

"No one? Surely your mother…" But she trailed off at his bleak expression. No one had ever… Her heart broke. She'd had a rough relationship with her father, but her mother had been love itself. Her sisters, for all their arguments and complications, had always expressed love to each other.

To grow up without that. She put her other hand on his other cheek, rose to her toes and pressed her mouth to his. "Well, now I have, and you'll have to get used to hearing it."

"Hazeleigh…" He sounded so strangled. "There are things you don't know about me."

"I'm sure there are things you don't know about me. Does that change anything for you?"

"Of course not, but—"

"Then it doesn't change anything for me. I don't believe love is some magical, easy feeling and we'll skip happily into the sunset, Landon. I don't say 'I love you' because I think everything's *fine* now. Maybe we find something about each other we can't get over. Maybe we don't."

"Doesn't this right here just prove my point? The sun is rising and we're standing in broad daylight arguing about *love*. We need to be focused on the man who tried to kidnap you."

"Yes, I suppose that's a good focus."

"You suppose," he scoffed. "You can't be out here in

broad daylight. You don't know when the cops might come. You don't know who else is out there. Whoever this Hamilton Chinelly is working for. They're all out there and you're a target to them all."

"Maybe," she replied. Something about his lack of calm had her feeling the opposite. The panic had been in the not knowing of it all, but now they had clues. There were steps to follow.

"Hazeleigh."

He sounded so...broken. She wished she could ease that brokenness in him, but if love couldn't, then nothing could at the moment. So she'd go for the facts. "There's something bigger here. I'm a pawn, yes. A scapegoat. But doesn't this feel..." She trailed off. She couldn't put her finger on it. "The man—this Hamilton, who I don't really remember though I never enjoyed ranch work the way Zara did—waited in my cabin for me to appear. Waited. Then he botched the kidnapping attempt."

"He doesn't know anything," Landon said, finally sounding more like himself. "You could see it on his face. He *thought* he knew things, but the more I asked, the more confused he got."

"If you were trying to...hide something, or find something, would you send that guy to do your dirty work?"

"It's a distraction." Landon blinked, then focused on her. "Why would it be a distraction?"

"I don't know, but I don't want to be distracted." She squinted into the rising sun. "Maybe this all works in our favor. We're not on our own anymore. It's the nine of us against whoever is out there."

"Whoever is out there plus the cops."

She supposed that was true, and she had no desire to deal with the cops until she'd found more. But she felt...hopeful.

She looked up at Landon. There were shadows underneath his eyes, lines dug around his mouth.

He loved her.

And she loved him.

"Why don't you help me find my computer? And then we'll both get some rest." She took his hand, because Zara had said it herself. Just because you were strong didn't mean you couldn't use support. "We're going to need it."

THEY DIDN'T FIND the computer, despite looking for an hour. They retraced the kidnapper's footsteps along with those of his brothers' who'd gone after Hamilton. No laptop.

Eventually Landon convinced Hazeleigh to go back to the ranch house. Of course, in order to convince her he had to agree to go himself. They'd both been awake too long. Too strung out on stress and...

Love.

She'd said she loved him.

It made everything weigh a little heavier, even as it lightened something inside of him that had been weighed down so long he'd stopped noticing it. He didn't know what to do with that—heavy and light, confusing and...right. Somehow.

"Either he hid the computer, or someone was waiting to take it," Landon said as they walked back to the ranch.

Hazeleigh held his hand and frowned. She had dark circles under her eyes, and her shoulders were slumped. Exhaustion clung to her like a physical entity. He let go of her hand and slid his arm around her shoulders. She leaned in as they walked.

"Why hide it? Did he think he'd get back to it? What does he think he can get off of it without me?"

"The way you explained it he only let you go because

we came. So maybe he thought he'd come back and get you at another time."

She chewed on her lip. "Maybe. Can't say as I like *that* thought."

"Yeah, me neither." He held her a little closer. "But I still don't know what they thought they'd find on your computer."

Hazeleigh sighed as they reached the house. She paused, looking up at the house with a frown. "Landon, I didn't want to involve anyone in this and now everyone's involved."

He didn't know what to say to that because everyone was involved. There was no going back now. He could maybe secret her away somewhere again, but it would have to be farther and—

"I think I'm actually...relieved," she said, interrupting his thoughts on how to fix things for her. "It feels more like... It's just..." She looked up at him, studying his face, as if she didn't know what she was looking for. "I know Zara's my only real family here, but she's marrying Jake. And he's a Thompson brother. And then Kate has been one of my friends since forever, and she's involved with one of your brothers and maybe this is what... Well, maybe it's what family is like when your own wasn't very much to speak of. One you cobble together yourself."

Family. Cal had mentioned that, too. He'd always assumed it would just be the six of them. They were all so alone, so...well, screwed up, he hadn't pictured picket fences and Wyoming ranches and marriages.

But it was nice. It was *good*.

"Maybe it is," he agreed.

"Family should stick together. They should help each other." She kept looking at him, like she was waiting for him to have some kind of answer.

"I…guess." He didn't really know what family *should* do. He only knew he had his brothers' backs and they had his.

"So it's good. We'll work together, figure this out and we won't let anyone get in trouble because of me."

"It isn't because of *you*, Hazeleigh. You didn't ask to be framed for your boss's murder."

"Okay, but…"

"No *buts*. We're not being martyrs, remember?"

She wrinkled her nose. "I guess. Hard habit to break."

"That it is," he agreed.

Then she smiled up at him. "I guess we can learn to break it together."

He tucked a strand of hair behind her ear, enjoying the feel of her skin under his fingertips. She was safe, and now there were eight of them to keep her safe. She wouldn't like it phrased like that, so he didn't say it out loud. But it settled him nonetheless.

Everything would be okay. They'd fight like hell to make it okay.

He lowered his mouth to hers, half convinced all that love talk in her backyard had been a sleepless delusion, but she leaned into him, kissing him back, and he knew… Whatever they'd found here, just the two of them, it wasn't going anywhere.

Someone was clearing their throat. Landon struggled to come up for air, and when he did Zara was standing on the porch. Scowling.

"Why don't you just *call* the cops and ask them to come arrest you?" Zara said irritably. "Standing in the front yard making out, for heaven's sake."

Hazeleigh smiled a little and disentangled herself from him. But she still held his hand as they walked into the house, and that felt like…something. Family cobbled together. Love and connection.

Zara led them to the basement, where she'd set up cots. If the cops came, Hazeleigh would be out of sight and Landon could help take her somewhere if they got another warrant to search the house—always a possibility.

Zara gave Landon a disapproving look, but left them alone in the basement without saying anything.

Then finally, they had a chance to sleep. Landon thought he should say something—about love or families or keeping her safe—but she was asleep the minute she was horizontal. So he crawled into his own cot and did the same.

When he woke up, she was gone.

Panic blinded him, and he couldn't think past it. He jumped out of his cot and rushed upstairs, only to find her sitting at the kitchen table, a plate of crumbs at her elbow and Kate standing in the kitchen area eyeing him suspiciously.

"You're up," Hazeleigh said casually. "Kate set me up with her computer from the fort. It doesn't have access to Mr. Field's emails like mine did, but it does let me see some things he saved to the historical server, including the photograph that was missing from that album."

"How long did you sleep?" he demanded, ignoring Kate's considering gaze.

She turned to him and smiled. "I woke up just about fifteen minutes ago, so not much longer than you. It's hard to sleep when all this is going on."

"Sit," Kate instructed him. "Eat."

He obeyed, if only because he didn't have the foggiest idea what else to do.

Hazeleigh turned the computer monitor toward him. "Here," she said, pointing to a picture on the screen. "This is the picture whoever killed Mr. Field took."

Landon frowned at the screen, squinting. "It just looks like an old shack."

"It is an old shack." She pointed to the corner of the picture where there was the fuzzy edge of another building. "But this is the corner of the schoolhouse—I'm almost certain."

"There weren't any other buildings out there around the schoolhouse."

"No, this is a picture from 1897. The shack either fell down or was torn down long before the schoolhouse was abandoned, but what if there was some kind of cellar or something? In the ground?"

"You don't honestly think the mythical gold is in some hole in the ground on Peterson land?" Kate said, sliding a plate next to Landon.

He murmured his thanks and they all peered at the screen.

"It doesn't have to be there," Hazeleigh said. "Someone only has to think it is."

The side door opened. Zara, Jake and Cal entered, probably after having done ranch work all afternoon.

"You should have slept longer," Zara chided.

"Slept as long as I could," Hazeleigh replied with a smile. "Where's everyone else?"

"They're coming," Cal said. "They were taking care of our friend Hamilton."

"Taking care?"

"Just drove him out a way. Dropped him off in the middle of nowhere with some supplies so he won't die. But far enough away he can't be a problem until we've solved our own."

Landon supposed it was the best option, though he would have liked to have left him in the middle of nowhere with *no* supplies and left him to rot.

Dunne, Henry and Brody returned not long after, saying they'd been successful. If Hamilton went to the cops, it'd be his word against theirs, and he'd have to explain why he was at the ranch in the first place, so it wasn't likely he'd go after them.

They positioned themselves around the table after getting snacks and drinks, settling in to see what was next.

It was exactly what Hazeleigh had said. A family. Cobbled together between a lot of people who hadn't been blessed with the best genetic relatives.

Landon took Hazeleigh's hand under the table and she smiled at him. But then she released it and stood. "Now that everyone's here, I have the beginnings of a plan."

"You do?" he and Zara said at the same time.

"I do," she said firmly. "I think we need to search the Peterson land. Something is going on there or centered there. The little girl I saw? She mentioned her mother. I don't know how a little girl could connect, but it points to the fact there are people there, one way or another."

She looked so…in charge. So sure of herself. It made him oddly proud.

"It's a big spread," Zara said, but she was clearly considering it. "Lots of buildings. All in bad condition."

"Which means there's a lot of places for people to hide, undetected," Cal said. "If a killer is really hiding out there, it's a dangerous proposition. One maybe better left for the—"

"Don't say police, Cal. You know that isn't true," Henry muttered irritably.

"They're law enforcement."

"And we're trained, better than small county law enforcement, to deal with an enemy hiding in a broad, unknown terrain," Jake returned.

"Trained?" Hazeleigh said, and Landon didn't have to look at her to know she was staring at *him* in confusion.

Everyone around them got a little still, a *lot* uncomfortable. Jake cleared his throat. "Sorry, I thought Zara would have said."

"I can keep a secret," Zara muttered, but she gave Landon an accusatory look, as if it was *his* fault Hazeleigh didn't know.

"I'm sorry. There's some kind of...secret?" Hazeleigh asked, in that careful, prim voice she only used when she was hurt.

Landon sighed and stared at his hands. Here it was. He'd been fooling himself to think anything could be different. "I was in the military. We were...all in the military."

"Oh."

"I told you there were things you didn't know about me."

"So you did." She blew out a breath. "I wish I'd known. Then I might not have been so insistent on running away. But, now that I do, I agree with Jake. You all are far more equipped to help."

"Help? Uh, no." Landon shook his head. "We'll handle it."

"No," Hazeleigh returned evenly, holding his gaze. "Zara and I are going, too."

Chapter Nineteen

Hazeleigh didn't quite know how to feel about this military thing. Not so much that Landon had been in the military and hadn't told her, but that it was supposed to be some kind of secret. That seemed odd and strange. Why would it be a secret?

But she couldn't deal with that right now. There was a murderer to find. "It's a big spread, like Zara said. Zara and I have a much better idea of the lay of the land than you six do."

"We also know what to do when someone shoots at us."

She raised an eyebrow at Landon. "Get shot in the arm?" she replied sweetly.

"Better than the head," Henry replied with his usual lack of tact. Because she could clearly see poor Mr. Field's body, with exactly that. A shot to the head.

She stiffened and Landon's hand came over hers. She had a feeling he was about to stand up and defend her, but that wasn't necessary. She opened her mouth to keep speaking, but Henry spoke first.

"Sorry," Henry grumbled.

It felt a bit like a coup to earn an apology from him without any prompting. She'd take it as a good sign. She forced herself to smile even though she figured she'd probably gone a little pale there.

"If you all want to draw up some kind of military plan, that's fine. Maybe even smart. But you need someone— or in this case some*ones*—who know the land. Where the buildings are. What to look for."

Jake shook his head. "I don't like it."

"No one asked you to like it," Zara replied. "It's the smart thing to do. Isn't it, Cal?"

All eyes turned to Cal, and for the first time since she'd known him, Hazeleigh thought he looked a little uncomfortable.

"In your unbiased, military opinion," Zara continued. "Do we go, or do we stay?"

Cal sighed. "Since I know Zara knows how to handle a rifle, I'd say she could go." He frowned at Hazeleigh. "Can you handle a gun?"

Hazeleigh had always hated guns, but Dad had insisted she know how to use one. "I don't like to, but I can."

"Cal's not in charge," Jake said stubbornly.

"No. I am," Hazeleigh said. "And I say we go."

"That'a girl," Zara said. She turned to Jake. "Look, we'll play it your way. Draw up your tactical plans. We'll follow them. But we go. You need us."

"And then what?" Cal asked. "Let's say we find the murderer, maybe even proof. What then?"

"Then we call the cops."

"And if they don't listen?" Henry asked.

"Thomas will," Zara said loyally.

"He's your cousin. The cops might not listen to *him*, even if he's one of them," Dunne pointed out.

"He'll find a way," Jake said, not sounding all that happy about it. "He found a way to help when Zara was in trouble. And look, I don't think anyone *wants* to believe Hazeleigh did it. We just have to prove she didn't. Whatever way we can."

"Together," Hazeleigh said, feeling the truth of that deep in her bones. "If we work together, we'll be all right. And we'll figure out who killed Mr. Field. He didn't deserve to die, especially if it's about this silly bank robbery." She looked back down at the picture. Something about it... bothered her. "I want to look at this picture, in person. This picture means something to someone, and we need to get to the bottom of it."

"Landon, you haven't said anything," Cal pointed out.

Hazeleigh looked down at him—he was still sitting at the table with an unreadable expression. But slowly, he stood.

"Here's how it will go. I'll take Hazeleigh to the spot with the picture. The rest of you will fan out on the edges of the property in teams of two and slowly close the circle, doing a sweep. We'll take walkies. Keep in constant contact. If one group comes into contact with someone, we try to avoid it. If we find evidence of people, we investigate. We'll go at night."

"Tonight," Hazeleigh said. "The longer this goes on, the more chance whatever is going on just disappears." Especially if they found the gold.

She'd never believed in this bank-robbery gold. It was too far-fetched. She'd spent years following Mr. Field down every avenue of research and there'd never even been a glimmer of reality in all the stories passed down.

She still wasn't sure she believed the mythology, but what she *did* believe was that someone out there thought it was true. And was going to kill to find this supposed gold.

Something in that picture was a clue. She just didn't know what it was yet.

She looked around the kitchen—six cowboys, who'd apparently all been in the military, and her fearless sister.

Along with her childhood friend, who'd hold down the fort, so to speak.

She never would have believed this for herself. Confidence. Bravery. A strong, sweet man who loved her. A family they'd made themselves out of a lot of happenstance.

Maybe unbelievable things could be true. Maybe there *was* old bank-robbery gold out there. She didn't dare say it. She knew how people rolled their eyes when Mr. Field had said it. It wasn't what was important anyway. What was important was finding out who'd killed Mr. Field. Who wanted her to take the fall for it.

"I don't want anyone to take chances for me—" Hazeleigh began.

"Oh, stuff it," Zara said firmly. "Family takes chances for each other. And *this* family takes chances to do what's right. Everyone got it?"

Everyone agreed, in words or nods. Everyone.

Except Landon.

LANDON HAD OUTLINED the plan to everyone. He'd listened as his brothers argued details, pros and cons, what weapons to use, what time to leave. They honed the plan with what little time they had.

Landon didn't know what he was feeling. It was different from a military mission, because Hazeleigh was involved. Because *lives* were involved—not just the idea of being alive, but actually leaving something behind.

Perhaps it was the first time in his life he didn't feel particularly fatalistic about an outcome. He wanted everyone—including himself—to make it. To the other side, not the next mission.

There was no room for all that want, that worry, that fear. There was only moving forward with the plan.

At nightfall, they all assembled, going over the plan one last time.

Dunne and Cal were going to be in the truck, just in case. Zara and Jake were a pair, Landon and Hazeleigh, then Henry and Brody, all on horseback.

Flashlight in hand, Cal pointed at a map Landon had printed out and went over the plan one last time. "We spread out. Wait for the signal before we all start pulling in. Except for Hazeleigh and Landon, who will go straight for the schoolhouse. Any sign of *anything*, you walkie and everyone stops. We do this together or not at all."

Landon looked down at Hazeleigh in the quickly fading light. She was the only one who didn't nod or look to be in agreement, but she didn't say anything. Dunne and Cal went for the truck, and everyone else got on their horses. Jake and Zara had the farthest to go to get to their checkpoint, so they set off first, Henry and Brody not far behind.

Hazeleigh was hesitating, but eventually she got up in her saddle, so he did, too.

"You'll let me know if you get one of those bad feelings, huh?"

She looked over at him and smiled. "Only if you promise to do the same."

He could tell she was nervous, simply by the way she held Buttercup's reins.

"I'm not going to let anything happen to you," he said. A promise. A vow.

"What about yourself?"

"Hazeleigh."

"No, I know… I just keep thinking about how Jake took that bullet meant for Cal last year. That's what family does, I suppose. That's what love does. And I guess I ran because…well, mostly because of panic, but a lot because I didn't want anyone taking any bullets for me."

They both urged their horses into a trot as they made their way back toward the schoolhouse.

"But in the last…day, I guess, I started to think maybe that's because I didn't think I was *worth* it. That's sort of been the thing I had to pull myself out of since last year. That I might be worth something."

Landon wanted to assure her she was worth *everything*, but his throat was closed tight. Because he'd been there. The only thing that had given him any worth had been the military, Team Breaker, and he supposed that, in the worst of circumstances, he and his brothers had banded together. *Together.*

So he said nothing at all, and Hazeleigh continued.

"I don't want anyone to be hurt because of me. I don't. But I would want to stop someone else from getting hurt. I'd want to step in front of that bullet like Jake did. Because that's love. I want to give that to other people—so I guess that means I might need to let other people give it to me."

She looked over at him, though he couldn't see her face in the darkening night. Just the impression of her head moving toward him.

"So maybe you're not about to let anything happen to me, but the same goes. I think it goes across the board. Because this isn't just about you rushing in to save the day. It's us all working together to right a wrong."

Which was everything he'd been through with his brothers. For years now. But they'd begun to let other people in. Let love in. And it made everything more…dangerous. Heavy and scary and stressful.

But a real life, with a richness that the military, and righting wrongs, hadn't given them. A future to look forward to—to build toward.

"Then let's right this one."

Chapter Twenty

Once they reached the schoolhouse, the time for introspection and thoughts on love and family were gone. Hazeleigh had to figure out what was going on. She had to get to the bottom of things. If nothing else so she could have her *life* back. A better life than she'd been living for a long time.

Something in that picture showing the space between the schoolhouse and the old shed that no longer existed had to give them some clue. Some next step.

Someone had to be here. Someone had to be on this property. Maybe it all connected. Maybe it didn't.

But they'd find the answers. They had to.

Darkness had engulfed everything, and if there were people on the Peterson property, they were very well hidden. Hazeleigh didn't let that depress her. For now, her focus was on the picture and the reality.

Every so often Landon pulled out a flashlight to make sure they were on the right track. When they got to the schoolhouse, he helped her off her horse, clearly reluctant to turn on the light.

"We're awfully exposed," he said, sounding uncertain and not letting go of her waist even now that she was steady on the ground.

"No bad feelings yet."

He huffed out a laugh. "Yeah, that makes me feel better

after all our talk about feelings not mattering as much as we think." But he released her, and the very narrow beam of a light flipped on.

She made out the schoolhouse and the patch of grass around them. She pulled out her phone and brought up the picture that she'd saved on it.

She oriented herself and then tried to find what would have been the remains of the shack. Landon followed behind her, keeping the flashlight pointed on the ground in front of Hazeleigh.

They worked as a team, without even having to discuss it. She knew without looking that he was on high alert for anyone around them, and it allowed her to focus. She looked from the picture to the ground, walked in circles. "A few spots have been…" She poked her toe against the odd unearthed bumps. "It's like someone's been digging out here."

"Looking for the gold?"

"I suppose, though they tried to cover their tracks by putting the dirt back." Hazeleigh looked on her phone at the picture—it was over one hundred years old. Obviously things had changed, and the land had been worked at least a while after this had been taken. Whenever the shed had been removed or fallen down, surely whatever had been hidden in it would have been found then. "Why doesn't this add up?"

"There's something we're missing," Landon agreed. "Maybe we're looking at all the pieces too closely. Too… separately."

"Maybe, but I don't know what else…" Hazeleigh trailed off. There was something different about the picture besides the shed. The corner of the schoolhouse was…brick. Not the wood it should have been. "Point your light at the schoolhouse."

Landon did as he was told. The narrow beam illuminated the schoolhouse corner enough to see the wood was old and worn and splintering. Why would anyone have covered up brick with wood? Particularly a schoolhouse that hadn't been in use in some time. When had it happened? Why had it happened?

Did it mean anything or was she driving herself insane?

She moved for the corner, Landon right behind her shining the light at the building. "This is different than the picture," she explained. "In the picture it's brick. But here it's wood." She trailed her fingers along the wood, following Landon's beam of light.

"Someone's already been here," Landon said flatly. "Look." He pointed the beam of light at the other side of the corner, where the wood had been ripped away. "I don't think it was like that before."

"No, it wasn't." Hazeleigh was struck completely dumb for a moment. "Was Mr. Field right? Was there really bank gold here?"

"Something was here." Landon flashed the light into the hole in the wood. "Something was hidden between the wood and the brick."

"But if they sent someone to kidnap me, aren't they still looking for something? They had the picture since the murder, and this just happened."

"So the picture didn't give them the information they needed. But something had to have."

"My computer." It only dawned on her because Landon had all that crazy computer equipment that could do who knew what. "My computer would have had a map of pictures connecting to the land. I'm not sure how they would have logged on and found it, but I did have a document on there placing the pictures on the map." Hazeleigh blew out a breath, because the puzzle just kept getting more confusing. "But you guys stopped Hamilton. We didn't find my computer, but…"

"Maybe Hamilton handed off your computer, or hid it somewhere for someone else to find. Then allowed himself to be caught as a distraction."

"A distraction from *what*?" Irritation simmered through her. All these questions. No real answers. Worst of all... "If there was really gold from some old bank robbery, why would anyone need to go through all this trouble to kill? Why not just find it and go from there?"

"People will do a lot of things for money. I assume old, mythical gold might be worth a pretty penny."

"It still doesn't add up."

"No, it doesn't. Maybe we should join the search crew. See who we can round up out here. If nothing else, we know that little girl has a mother around here somewhere."

Hazeleigh knew he was probably right. There were no answers to be found here. No gold, either. Or maybe the gold had been found and was long gone now. But then wouldn't they leave? The girl? Whoever was involved? And why keep Hazeleigh's computer? Why distract with Hamilton Chinelly?

"Sometimes you just have to keep gathering clues until they start adding up," Landon said, placing a hand on her back and giving her a little pat. "We don't know whether they found something here or not, but we know they looked. That's...something."

Hazeleigh wanted to pout. It didn't feel like something. It felt like a whole lot of *nothing*. And nothing was starting to feel worse than danger or kidnapping attempts because *nothing* was starting to feel like it might be *forever* that the police thought she'd killed Mr. Field.

She leaned forward to look a little deeper into the space between the wood and the brick, but Landon clicked off his light. "Hazeleigh, don't move. Not an inch. Not an inch, okay?"

"Bu—"

She didn't even get the word out before Landon jumped forward and knocked her to the ground.

THE EXPLOSION SOUNDED, a terrifying *boom*, and heat engulfed his entire body. He covered Hazeleigh in every way he could. Something rained down on them. Shrapnel? An old memory tried to take over, but he pushed it away.

Not war. Just Wyoming. The objects raining down on them didn't exactly hurt. Because they were just clumps of dirt. Whatever had caused the explosion had been underground. In the holes. Someone hadn't been digging up supposed gold, they'd been setting explosives.

Landon's ears rang, his skin burned, but he could feel Hazeleigh's scrambled heartbeat beneath him and the heavy rise and fall of her breathing. Okay. She was okay.

But someone wanted them dead.

Them…or someone else? If Hamilton was a distraction, how would anyone predict they'd come here?

When a problem was more complicated than an answer, maybe that was the answer in and of itself. His problem wasn't their problem.

Maybe the problem, the confusion, came because they were in the *middle* of something.

But he couldn't think that thought through. They had to get out of here in case there were more explosives. Landon blinked open his eyes, tried to survey the damage. Smoke burned in his lungs, and the schoolhouse was on fire. Enough fire to see by.

"Are you okay?" Hazeleigh asked, her voice a rasp beneath him. "Landon, are you all right?"

"I'm fine. I'm okay." He probably had some burns, but nothing too bad. She'd likely have some bruises from him knocking her to the ground, so maybe it evened out. "Don't move just yet, okay?"

He surveyed the night around them. The explosion had to have been loud enough to be heard for miles around, which meant his brothers would be worried about them. He shifted ever so carefully so he could pull his walkie out of his pocket.

"All good here. Stay where you are for now."

There was the quiet chorus of affirmatives in response. There could be more explosives out there, so they had to be careful. Especially with the horses. They didn't appear to be serious bombs, causing a significant amount of damage, but they'd definitely ripped up the ground they'd been buried in.

Why? Why? Why?

He had to trust the answers would come, because right now he had to get Hazeleigh away from potential danger. They'd figured out the reasoning for the photograph, sort of, and now they knew someone was out there.

Maybe a retreat was in order.

"When I get up, you're going to run for Buttercup. Get on her and go." His mind scrambled for the best, safest place for her to go. "Toward where Cal and Dunne are in the truck. Walkie them so they can meet you."

"Landon, what about you?"

He opened his mouth to say he'd be right behind, but...

Someone was coming or watching. He could feel it. He knew it the way he'd known to dive and cover her. A tenseness in the air. A quiet ticking of something he'd honed in the military. His gut told him something was coming, and he wanted Hazeleigh far away from it.

"I'll be behind you."

"Landon, we should stick together."

"We will. But first, I need you to get to Cal and Dunne. Okay? When I say to, get up and run and don't stop. Get on Buttercup and don't stop. Walkie as you ride. I will be right behind you, on your six. I promise." He wouldn't stay here to fight off whatever was coming, but he'd protect her, no matter what it took.

She let out a shuddery breath. "If you break that promise, I'm going to be really mad."

"Understood. Now, I'm going to count to three. Pop up. You run. Do not worry about me. I will be behind you. There might be some distance, but I *will* be behind you."

"All right. All right."

Landon gave them both a moment to breathe, to ready themselves. Then he began the countdown quietly in her ear. *"Go!"*

She popped up in time with him and took off running for Buttercup. Landon pulled his gun out of its holster and followed her slowly, watching the world around them. When Hazeleigh stopped at Buttercup and didn't get on, he had to tamp down his impatience to speak quietly.

"Go, Hazeleigh," he said as quietly as he could over the crackling blaze around them so she could hear.

"I can't." Hazeleigh angled her body slightly, and in the flickering flames he made out a little girl. It must be the little girl Hazeleigh had talked to the other day. Obviously they couldn't leave her behind. They'd have to take her with them.

But as Landon moved forward, he realized why Hazeleigh had said she couldn't move.

The little girl's face was streaked with dirt or grease or smoke. Her hair was half falling out of a band. She wore dirty jeans and an even dirtier sweatshirt. Her eyes were flat as she stared right at him.

In each hand, she held a very large gun—one was pointed at Hazeleigh.

And now, one was pointed at him.

Chapter Twenty-One

"Drop the gun," the little girl said. Her voice, high-pitched and lilting, sounded like she belonged on a children's show. But Hazeleigh had no doubt she was serious. She had her fingers wrapped around the triggers. "The walkies, too."

Hazeleigh didn't know whether to be more terrified that the girl was a good shot and knew what she was doing, or that she might accidentally shoot them.

Hazeleigh glanced back at Landon. He looked positively thunderstruck. Though he held his gun, he didn't aim it at the girl. It was pointed at the ground, even though she had two guns fixed on them.

This was not good.

"Do I need to count to three?" the little girl asked, and there was no hesitation, no quiver in her voice. She was in control and knew just what she was after.

Landon looked at Hazeleigh, and she…didn't know what to do. He could hardly shoot a little girl…even if the girl was armed. She gave him a slight nod and he nodded back. He crouched to the ground and placed his gun on the over-turned earth.

"The walkies," the girl said, gesturing with both guns.

The move made Hazeleigh nervous enough to fumble with hers. It clattered to the ground while Landon calmly placed his next to his gun.

"Did you plant those explosives yourself?" he asked, taking a careful step toward Hazeleigh.

"Don't come closer," the girl said.

Landon held up his hands a little, like a gesture of surrender. The poor schoolhouse crackled and creaked as the fire licked up the boards.

"Now, I don't know what's going on or who you are, but my brothers are on their way. I don't want you to get hurt, sweetheart, so why don't you put the guns down and—"

The little girl snorted and even Hazeleigh sighed. The Southern drawl could be charming, but what little girl holding guns aimed at adults wanted to be called *sweetheart*?

"Doubt it. I heard you telling them to stand down on your walkie. Besides, they probably didn't get far. No one gets far here."

Those words sent a cold chill up Hazeleigh's spine, but she tried not to let it show. The girl wasn't paying attention to her, even though one gun was pointed in her direction. She'd correctly guessed Landon was the bigger threat and focused more on him.

But… "I helped you," Hazeleigh said softly. "I let you have that flashlight and my gloves."

There was the flicker of something in the little girl's expression, but she didn't drop the guns. "I don't know you," she said with a jerk of her shoulders. "I stole those things fair and square. You didn't *let* me have them."

But she had. She'd tried to give them back. She hadn't been threatening or cold. She'd been skittish, and alone, but not…angry.

"Where's your mother?" Hazeleigh asked gently.

The little girl's mouth firmed, and she adjusted the guns, like they were getting too heavy. But she wasn't about to drop them, that was for sure.

"If I bring you to him, he'll let her go. So you have to come with me."

"Who's him?" Landon asked, clearly trying to match Hazeleigh's quiet, calm tone. Not entreating, not condescending. Just like they were having a normal conversation.

With no guns pointed at anyone.

The girl said nothing, and that quiet refusal to answer made the chill in Hazeleigh's spine spread to her gut.

"We'll go. Won't we, Landon?" she said, not looking at Landon. She kept her gaze on the little girl. On the guns.

Landon hesitated. Hazeleigh knew he wanted to press more, ask more questions and demand some answers.

But he didn't. "Sure, we'll go. I guess you'll lead the way?"

Again, something flickered in her expression, but Hazeleigh didn't know what it was this time. Uncertainty of some kind.

"What's your name?"

"None of your business," the little girl muttered. She frowned at both of them. "You," she said, pointing to Landon. "Take five steps—no less, no more."

Landon nodded, his hands still slightly up in the surrender position. Then he took five careful steps—long strides—that put him almost next to Hazeleigh. He began to take another one.

"I said five," the girl snapped, positioning both guns to aim at him.

Without thinking it through, Hazeleigh stepped in front of him. Gently, Landon moved her aside. He was calm and collected.

"I miscounted," he said, attempting a smile at the girl.

She didn't smile or soften in return. "I didn't."

They all stood there, Landon next to her, the girl with the guns in front of them still pointed, while the fire crackled.

She said nothing. They said nothing.

Hazeleigh had the strangest urge to start *laughing*.

"Okay," Landon said gently, whether at his wit's end or sensing Hazeleigh was at hers. "You're trying to figure out a way to get us to go where you want without one of us overpowering you."

"You try to overpower me, I shoot you."

"I don't think you want to shoot us," Landon replied gently. Then he considered the look on her face in the firelight. "Or at least not Hazeleigh."

"Thought your name was Zara."

"Zara is my twin sister."

"So you're a liar. I don't care about shooting liars."

Hazeleigh swallowed. She agreed with Landon—the little girl didn't *want* to shoot anyone. But that didn't mean she wouldn't. There was a desperation in her that made Hazeleigh very nervous. Still, she smiled as best she could while the schoolhouse burned down. "Won't you tell me your name?"

"Bigfoot," the little girl replied.

"All right, Bigfoot," Landon replied easily enough. "How about this. You tell us where you want us to go. We'll go, you follow, guns pointed. That'll work, won't it?"

"Like I'm gonna take *your* advice when *you're* my prisoner," she scoffed, sounding every inch a little girl.

Hazeleigh couldn't help but feel sorry for her. Something was very wrong if a ten-year-old was wandering around *alone* with two big guns trying to... Her mother. She was trying to get someone to let her mother go.

"We can help," Hazeleigh said. "We can help you, if you let us."

"Why would you help me?"

"Because it's the right thing to do," Landon said firmly.

He took a step toward the girl, then another. "Go ahead and hand over the guns and you have my word that I'll help—"

One of the guns went off. On purpose, or by accident, Hazeleigh didn't have a clue, but it caused a loud, shocking slam of sound against the night around them.

Hazeleigh screamed in surprise, Landon hit the deck and the girl fell backward, probably from the harsh recoil of the gun that was far too big for her frame. Landon was back on his feet in seconds, clearly unhurt. Wherever she'd been shooting, she hadn't hit anybody, thank God.

Without thinking, Hazeleigh moved forward to help the little girl get up, but she scrambled back, angling the guns in Hazeleigh's direction again. "No. Don't come any closer. I'll shoot you. I will."

"I want to help."

"I don't care. Step back. Now."

Hazeleigh did as she was told. She looked over at Landon. He shrugged his shoulders, clearly as much at a loss as she was. The girl was dangerous, but neither of them were willing to hurt her to disarm her.

"If someone has your mother nearby, won't they be coming here to see what the commotion is?" Landon asked gently.

"They'll round up all your people first. I've got time. I've got time." She repeated it like she was convincing herself. "They aren't stupid. I have to do this my way. *My* way. I'm not going to fail."

Hazeleigh's heart just about broke. No matter how dangerous this girl was, she was trying so hard to save her mother. She clearly believed she was doing something right. She kept one gun pointed at them and looked wildly around, then her hand shot out and grabbed a bag that had been on the ground behind her. She pulled something out of it and threw it at Landon.

"Tie your hands together. And make it good. I really only need one of you. You make me mad, I'll hit you this time."

Landon sighed and looked at Hazeleigh. "I guess we'll have to do what she says," he said to her. Very seriously. And she realized what he was trying to tell her.

They'd go with the girl, because that was the only way to help her. Because he wanted to help this little girl who'd shot at him, just like Hazeleigh wanted to.

So Hazeleigh nodded and held out her hands.

LANDON KEPT ONE eye on the little girl while he carefully tied the wire around Hazeleigh's wrists. Then he tied what little was left of the wire around his own. He didn't tighten the knots and kept a little room in the bonds so there'd be an easy enough escape, but didn't make it too obvious that was what he was doing.

"It's not really long enough, and I can only do one of my hands."

"I could just shoot you and leave you here. I think they only want her."

"Trust me, they'll want me, too."

Whoever *they* were had clearly terrorized this little girl. He cared less about avoiding getting shot—been there, done that—and more about finding out who was behind this whole mess. Not just because they'd hurt Hazeleigh, but because they'd driven this little girl to…this.

He recognized that desperation, that hopeless panic. He'd seen it in his biological brothers' eyes. He'd never been able to stop them from ruining their own lives. He'd never been able to save them.

He was going to find a way to save this little girl.

"Here," Hazeleigh said softly. She tried to arrange her hands to help him tie off his second wrist. It was a struggle, and he could tell the little girl had grown impatient, but they did the best they could.

"She needs help," Hazeleigh whispered.

"I know. We'll give it to her. Let's just try to keep her talking."

"Shut up," the little girl said. She stalked over to them. She'd left one gun behind in the dark, but still held the other. It was far too big and powerful for her. Landon thought he could reach out and rip it from her hands.

As if she'd read his mind, she angled her body so her gun hand was out of his reach. She reached forward with her other hand and clipped a bright pink dog leash, of all things, to one of the loops around his and Hazeleigh's wrists.

She pulled. "Follow me," she said.

He shared a glance with Hazeleigh. They seemed to be on the same page. Worried about the girl, but well aware she was dangerous if they weren't careful with how they dealt with her. So they fell into step, wrists tied together so they had to do an awkward sideways shuffle step to keep up with the girl's purposeful strides into the night.

Landon looked at the leash. One clean jerk and he could overpower her. She'd likely drop the gun, though it wasn't a done deal, and it was clear she was volatile enough, desperate enough, to shoot them.

He kept his voice low, inclined his head as much toward Hazeleigh as he could. "Let's do our best to keep her talking. Calmly."

Hazeleigh nodded.

"Where do they have your mother?" he asked.

The little girl just grunted, gave the leash a tug that had them both stumbling a little. "You'll see."

"Why do they want me?" Hazeleigh asked.

She looked back at Hazeleigh. Now they were far enough

away from the fire that it was impossible to make out her expression in the dark.

"You're the only one who knows."

"Knows what?"

"Everything the old man knew. My grandpa, I guess."

Grandpa. She had to mean Mr. Field.

"Who's your grandpa?" Hazeleigh asked, clearly confused.

Another hard tug, and this time Hazeleigh stumbled enough that it was only his quick thinking to redistribute their weight together that kept her from falling flat on her face.

"Doesn't matter," the girl said, and there was a hint of sadness in her detached, resigned acceptance. "All that matters is Mom."

"Can you tell me about your mom?" Landon asked.

"Stop talking!" the little girl shrieked, sounding as close to tears as she had this whole time.

Landon scrambled for a plan, but the little girl was… nothing he'd expected. All his normal reactions went out the window. He still needed to protect Hazeleigh, his brothers and her sister, who were out there somewhere along with this mysterious *they*.

But figuring out a way to stop this girl while still helping her felt like an impossible task.

So they walked in silence. Deeper and deeper into Peterson land. Based on the map in his head, he felt as though she was leading them to the very center of the property.

Where the old house was supposed to be.

The night drew darker around them, and it didn't take long for the fire to be completely out of sight behind swells of land and bunches of trees. The smell of smoke still hung in the air, but maybe no one would necessarily be able to see how to get to the mysterious fire.

Maybe. Far too many maybes.

"You know, we do really want to help you. This 'they' sounds pretty bad if they've got your mom. What can we do to help?"

"Nothing. No one can help us."

Landon felt that fatalism, deep in those old childhood hurts. "I know how that feels." His father's temper. The violence of it all. How it seemed so impossible to find someone to help. And then, as he'd gotten older, the failure of never being enough to help his brothers or his mother.

"You don't know anything."

"My dad liked to beat up on my brothers and me. It felt like a prison. When I was probably around your age, I thought I could escape. But I never could because no one would help me. I'd help you."

"I would, too," Hazeleigh said. "I gave you my flashlight, my gloves. I'd help."

"You're only saying that because I'm a little girl, but I can help myself." She grumbled something, then said very clearly, "You can only trust yourself."

"I used to believe that, too," Landon said softly. It wasn't comfortable, but he let those old emotions into his voice as he spoke. "I believed it for a very long time. And it never helped. Never got me out of anything bad. If anything, it sunk me deeper. Until I found people to trust and realized that...not everyone is out for themselves. There are good people out there. Who want to do right. Who want to help."

"Needing help or support doesn't make you weak," Hazeleigh added softly. "We want to—"

The little girl groaned in disgusted dissatisfaction. "You two are the most annoying people in the entire world. You don't know me. You don't know anything about me. All you really want is for me to let you go." She gave a jerk and again Landon narrowly saved Hazeleigh from a tumble.

But she didn't keep walking and tugging them along. She stopped. A little beam of light clicked on. Landon could make out a tree and the shadow of the little girl.

She tied the leash around the tree. "I'll be back."

Landon didn't say anything, but he listened to the direction her footsteps went. In the distance, he could see the hint of a light.

With speed and ease, he loosened the knots on the wire around his wrists. It was time to do his best to save everyone.

Chapter Twenty-Two

Hazeleigh huffed out a breath. What *now*?

But after only a second of the little girl being gone, Landon's hands came to her shoulders.

"How did you get free?" she demanded.

"I want you to stay here," he said urgently, ignoring her question.

"Landon—"

"No, listen to me. I want to tell you to run, but I know you won't. You want to help her. I want to help her. But we still need answers, and we still need to stop whoever this is. So you'll stay here and if 'they' come and get you, at least I'll be around to save you. And her. And the mom. If we both disappear, I worry she'll get hurt. She wanted you more than me. If she comes back, you need to be here."

Hazeleigh's heart warmed. He wanted to help the little girl as much as she did. He was willing to risk *her*, and that was something. "So I stay here, and what will you do?"

"I'm going to see if I can find the others, or if the little girl was right and they've been rounded up. Then I'm going to see what's going on in that house."

"Okay."

"Hazeleigh…"

"No, it's okay. It's good."

"I don't want to leave you here."

"But you know you have to. It's okay. I'll be okay. They want me for something, so that means I'm not in any danger."

"That's hardly what that means," he said darkly. He sighed. "Hazeleigh, is it possible Mr. Field was this girl's grandpa? She said you're the only one who knows what the old man knew. Her grandpa."

"I know, but it doesn't make sense. He didn't have any kids as far as I know. Never married. Never with anyone. But as for possible?" Hazeleigh blew out a breath. "If that gold was real? Anything is possible."

"Yeah. Yeah." He gave her shoulders a squeeze. "Okay. Just…be careful. Okay?"

"Same goes." She hated the thought of separating, but it was the only way to try to protect themselves and the little girl.

He pressed a kiss to her mouth. "I'll be back. I promise."

"I love you."

There was a pause, and she knew he was absorbing those words no one else had ever given him. "I love you, too." And then he was gone.

She was in the dark alone, tied to a tree. It wasn't the most comfortable position, but the bonds on her wrists were loose enough that it wasn't so bad. She could even get out if she wanted to.

But she kept thinking about that poor little girl. She wanted to help her—needed to help her. So she'd wait. And hope.

Hazeleigh had no idea how much time had passed when she heard the distant rumble of an engine. She didn't think it was big enough to be a truck, which was too bad because that would have meant Cal and Dunne were here to save her and tell her everything was fine.

Instead, this sounded more like some kind of four-wheeler or small utility vehicle. It got closer and closer, and then came to a stop not far from her. A light clicked on and Hazeleigh had to flinch against the sudden brightness against her eyes—headlights from the small vehicle.

"Well, well, well, you don't disappoint," a man's voice said.

Hazeleigh managed to blink her eyes open. The light was still too bright and shining directly at her so she couldn't see him, but she could make out the little girl to the side.

"But where's…?" The girl frowned in confusion, but the man didn't express any dismay at there only being one person tied to a tree.

So Hazeleigh maintained eye contact with the little girl. "Thank God you're back. I hate being left all alone in the dark."

The girl frowned but said nothing else. The man finally stepped out from the bright light so she could see him. Tall, broad. Older than her, definitely, but the heavy beard made it hard to discern a real age even with the flecks of gray. Dark eyes, thick eyebrows, and all together it made Hazeleigh realize something that made her stomach sink.

He looked like Mr. Field. There were differences, and maybe she was looking so hard for *some* understanding that she was making things up. But she'd spent the last seven years spending a lot of time with the man, and they looked very similar.

"Who are you?" Hazeleigh asked.

"You don't recognize me? That hurts my feelings." He did not in any way sound like his feelings were hurt. "Of course, you and your obnoxious sister were always too good to pay much attention to the help, weren't you?"

The acidic words didn't make sense to Hazeleigh. Dad had never hired on much help. Except… "The only *help* we had was when my mother was *dying*."

"Oh, boo-hoo. Zara was out working while you and the other one were living the high life."

The high life? Watching her mother wither away at *nine*. But if he was working at the ranch, surely… "So…you're a Chinelly." Not a Field?

"Don't put that on me. Hamilton might be my mother's brother, but that doesn't make me a Chinelly. Good blood blots out the bad. Right, Sarabeth?" He gave the girl's hair a rough tousle and she winced. "Maybe my blood will win inside you yet."

Sarabeth didn't respond. She looked at the ground.

Hazeleigh's heart ached for her.

"Are you going to let my mother go now?" she asked him. But she already sounded defeated, like she wasn't sure he would.

The man laughed, the sound dark and mean. "Sure. We'll just let you both run off. I was wrong—you are as dumb as your mother." He gave her a rough shove, knocking her down.

Hazeleigh made a move to step forward and help the girl, but the ties on her wrists and the leash stopped her.

"All right. Let's get you somewhere we can really talk." He moved to the tree and untied the leash but didn't untie the wire around her hands. "God, Sarabeth. Learn how to tie a damn knot, huh?" He tightened them with one rough jerk then dragged Hazeleigh to the utility vehicle. He shoved her into the passenger seat and then hopped into the driver's seat…leaving Sarabeth sitting in the grass.

"What about your daughter?"

The man threw back his head and laughed.

Hazeleigh could only watch over her shoulder as the man drove them away, the girl disappearing into the dark.

LANDON FOUND ZARA and Jake first, though he was out of breath with a cramp in his side that felt like fire. His skin burned everywhere the fire of the explosion had hit, but he did his best to hide that. Ignore it. He explained everything that had happened, and they relayed their end of things. They'd been closing the circle, but no one had been found out yet. No signs of life. So none of the mysterious "they" had rounded them up.

"This just gets weirder and weirder," Landon muttered. "Look, if you guys haven't found signs of anything, they have to be at the house in the center. Let's walkie everyone. Meet at that spot on the map Cal and Dunne were supposed to stop at with the truck."

The walkies crackled in the quiet dark, but everyone agreed to meet. Jake got off his horse and gave it to Landon, and then got on the back of Zara's with her. With no words spoken, they took off—closer to the supposed house, closer to the center of everything.

It had to be the center of everything, because if it wasn't…

Landon didn't let himself think of the bad possibilities. He could only think of finding answers. Only the mission.

He was a soldier now. Nothing else.

He wasn't sure how long it took them to all convene at the spot behind a swell of land. They were still quite a way from the house, but there was a little light visible now. Someone was definitely down there in the valley.

"Well, this is a mess, isn't it?" Henry muttered.

"Always so positive," Zara replied.

Landon ignored them both. He had a plan. It wasn't perfect, but it was fast, and with Hazeleigh tied up alone somewhere out there, he figured it had to be.

"We stick in teams of two, except Cal will go with me and Dunne will stay with the truck. Things get bad, he can call the cops and we'll deal with that fallout later. The rest of us will circle, moving forward until we have a better idea of what's going on in there. They have someone, this little girl's mother. They're after Hazeleigh for information. They've killed before."

Landon waited for someone to argue with his plan, but no one did. The silence of the night settled around them. Agreement.

He blew out a breath, ready to give the order to move forward. But the echo of running horse hooves had them all turning. His brothers had their guns drawn. Landon hoped against hope it was Hazeleigh.

He flipped on his flashlight, trusting his brothers to know what to do if it was someone here to hurt them.

He recognized Buttercup first, but it wasn't Hazeleigh on her. "Stand down," he said in a low voice to his brothers, still holding their guns. "It's the little girl."

"You mean the one who shot at you?" Henry replied dryly.

"Hell, Landon, you're burned," Jake rasped now that he could see in the light.

"Nothing serious."

"Nothing serious? You have to—"

"End this. First and foremost. We have to end this."

The girl pulled the horse to a halt in front of them. "He has your friend. I know where she is. If you promise to get my mother out when you get her out, I'll help you."

"How can you help?" Henry demanded.

The girl rolled her eyes. "Because I know everything, duh."

"Tell us who *he* is," Landon demanded.

"My father. Rob Currington."

"Currington. He was a ranch hand for us when I was a kid," Zara said. "With Hamilton Chinelly."

"Hamilton's a pawn in all this. Everyone's a pawn. That's what he always says, anyway," the girl said. "We have to hurry. He wants this over tonight. He promised me if I gave him the lady, he'd let me and my mother go. But he lied. He's going to kill everyone once he gets what he wants. I'm not going to let him kill my mother."

And I'm not going to let him kill Hazeleigh.

"What does he want?" Cal had the presence of mind to ask the question, when all Landon could think of was retribution.

"He found some of the bank-robbery gold, but some of it's still missing. She's the only one who knows where it is now that he killed his father."

Mr. Field. It still wasn't making a ton of sense, but it sure all connected a little clearer.

"She's in the house?"

"He has my mother chained up in the basement with one of his cousins watching her. I think that's where he'll take Hazeleigh. But you have to be careful. The house is falling down. You can't just run in. You have to follow me."

Landon could tell that his brothers didn't like that idea, but he didn't see as they had much of a choice. "All right."

The girl swung down from the horse. She didn't have her guns anymore, but when she stepped into the small circle of light Landon's flashlight made, he could see her nose was bleeding.

"I'll do everything I can to get your mother out," he promised, wanting to give her shoulder a reassuring squeeze. She shifted away, the movement sharp enough that he had the sneaking suspicion she also knew what it felt like to have her father rough her up.

"You'll follow me. You'll listen to me. Or we're all dead." She was so serious. So fierce. Landon didn't want to think of what had made a girl of ten that hardened.

"Looks like we've got ourselves a mini Cal," Henry said. "Lead the way, kid."

They set out, six full-grown military men and one ranch woman, following a little girl into danger.

Chapter Twenty-Three

The house was in ruins. The man dragged Hazeleigh out of the utility vehicle and toward it, like they were going to go inside, when she couldn't imagine the house being able to stand the weight of much of anything. The roof was caved in at spots, the walls had buckled in others.

But he walked straight for the front door and kicked it open, dragging her behind.

"Be careful now. One wrong step and *whoops* you'll find yourself bloody and broken, nine feet down onto the hard concrete below."

Hazeleigh swallowed. She eyed the floor. All was dark except there was a little beam of light coming up from the floorboards. She believed him. If the floor had this many cracks that it showed off the light below, she might crash right through.

He led her through the house, and she could tell that he was being very careful of where they stepped. This house was definitely not safe to be in. She hoped Landon and everyone would recognize that before they came in guns blazing.

Because they would come. They would save her. It would all be okay. She had to believe that. It was the only way to get through this.

He finally made it to a cellar-type entrance in the back of

the house, though whatever door had once been there was long gone. He pulled her down rickety stairs, now much less careful about where and how they stepped.

In the basement, lamps were lit. One man stood there, beefy arms crossed, many guns strapped to his person. A woman sat in a corner, tied to a chair.

Hazeleigh didn't recognize either of them. But the woman's face made her gut churn with anxiety. She was severely bruised, with dried blood coming from her nose and mouth and ear. She didn't even look up when they entered the room.

"Sarabeth came through, huh?" the man said, sounding surprised.

"That she did. Get another chair and some zip ties."

The man rushed to do as he was told and pulled an old metal folding chair to the center of the room. "Gonna let Jessie go, then?"

The man let out a nasty laugh. "Like hell. Once we have what we need, everyone is going up in flames. *Everyone.* And no one will ever know I was here."

The man roughly grabbed Hazeleigh and tied her to the metal chair. She didn't fight him. There didn't seem much point. Even if she could get away from them, she couldn't run upstairs. She'd just fall right through.

Besides, Landon knew she was here. He'd figure it out. She was trusting him to do what needed to be done, all so they could help save that little girl.

Please be okay, Sarabeth.

"Now, where's the rest of it?"

She looked at the man, who looked so much like a young Mr. Field it was disorienting. "I don't know what you're talking about."

The backhanded slap was so sudden, she hadn't even flinched before the pain exploded across her cheek. She nearly toppled to the side, chair and all, but the other man must have grabbed the chair, and she was yanked back with a jarring thud.

"I want to know where the rest of the gold is. It was supposed to be in that stupid schoolhouse, but there was only a quarter of it. That dumb old man kept babbling about a lot more than what we got."

So it was true. "You killed Mr. Field over some fake gold?"

"Fake? Fake." He stormed over to a duffel bag and undid the zipper, tipping it so she could see inside. Coins jangled together. "This isn't fake." He stormed back over to her. "Where's the rest of it?"

"I don't—" The slap was on the opposite side this time. Her skin was on fire. She felt rattled and tears formed in her eyes—from both emotion and pure pain.

"He told you everything. You organized *everything*. That stupid old man told me that if there was something to know his assistant *knew* it. Begged me to let him live so he could call you. He was my father and he trusted *you*."

"Your father? You killed your father?" Mr. Field had a son he'd never told anyone about.

"He was never a father to me. Paid off my mother, sent her away, all so he could look for gold. Well, I found the damn gold, didn't I? But there's supposed to be more, and I want it."

It was more than greed. Something twisted up in his relationship, or lack of one, with his father. "I didn't know everything, because I didn't know about you."

That seemed to stop him for a second. But only a second. Another blow landed and this time she couldn't hold back the sob of pain. She understood why the other woman in the room just sat there, unmoving. There was nothing to do but absorb the pain and hope—hope that help would come.

LANDON CAME TO a stop when the little girl leading them did. They stood just off the porch that was now little more than splintered boards and rubble.

"The floor inside isn't stable," she whispered. "They've been hiding in the basement, and there's only one way to get down there. You have to be careful."

"You're sure there's only two men in there?" Cal asked in a low tone.

"There only have been this whole time. Hamilton would come sometimes, but he was too scared to go in. Dad's cousin, Ben, almost never leaves. Dad comes and goes."

"He lets you come and go?" Landon asked gently.

"He doesn't care what I do as long as I keep out of his way and do what he asks right when he asks."

"Okay. So what do we call you?"

"Bigfo—"

"What's your name?" Landon said, firmly but gently.

"Sarabeth," she muttered. "If you don't get my mom out, I am going to kill you. I swear it."

"I believe you." And he did. Maybe he wouldn't *let* her kill him, but he had no doubt she would try. "You're a brave one, Sarabeth. Your mom's going to be very proud when we get her out of there. But you're going to have to—"

"I have to lead you. If you don't follow me in, you'll fall through the floor. Even if not, he's going to hear you and start shooting." She sucked in a deep breath. "The less people that go in there, the better chance we have of making it through."

"A shooting gauntlet. Fun," Henry said.

"No." Landon straightened, eyeing the house. "If just Sarabeth and I go in, we might be able to avoid being heard. Or if he thinks it's just her, we might not get shot at. You guys can wait out here—"

"Landon—"

"No, hear me out, Cal. Someone starts shooting, you can all rush in. But if we can sneak in, element of surprise works in our favor. Two guys? I can take out two guys. You know I can."

"Even all burnt up like that?"

"I'm fine," Landon insisted. "Sarabeth and I go in and see what we can do. You guys are backup. Deal?"

There was a gradual assent, though no one seemed too happy about it. But they didn't have time for options everyone loved.

"All right, Sarabeth."

"You're going to need this." She shrugged off her backpack and then held out his gun, which she'd made him put down back at the schoolhouse.

Landon took it and put it back in its holster. "Thanks. You still got yours?"

She pulled it out. "Yeah."

"Can you aim?"

"Missed you on purpose earlier."

He didn't know if it was true or if she was trying to make herself feel better, but hopefully they got out of this without her needing to shoot.

"Go on, then. Lead the way."

She crept over the rubble of the porch, barely making a sound. Landon did his best to copy her every move. She got to the door, paused and then pushed it open slowly—so slowly, no noise was made.

She slid into the opening she'd made. Not big enough for him, but he copied her, moving the door with minuscule pressure so as not to make a sound.

He heard the low rumble of voices and then a *thwack*. The sound of flesh hitting flesh, and the muted whimper of a woman.

He might have leaped forward, but Sarabeth put her

hand on his. Her little fingers curled around his hand, and she led him forward. Inch by inch.

He followed her steps exactly, but something rattled next to them—probably a mouse, and Sarabeth jumped and stumbled a little bit, making enough noise with splintering wood to attract attention.

Landon reached out and grabbed her as her ankle went through the floor. He steadied her back on the good part of the floor, but someone would be coming. He lowered his free hand to his gun.

"Rob?" Sarabeth called out. "It's me. I'm okay."

"Damn it," someone rumbled from below. "She really is a cockroach. Get your butt down here, then."

Landon let out the quietest breath he could manage. She might have stumbled, but she'd just saved the day. No one seemed to suspect she might be with someone.

She started moving forward again, slower this time. Landon followed, trying to make his foot land at the same time hers did so it didn't sound like two pairs of footsteps, but it was too risky to keep going that way.

He reached out, stopped Sarabeth's progress. "Let me pick you up," he said, barely disturbing the air he'd spoken the words so quietly. He didn't wait for assent. She stiffened as he put his hands on her waist, but let him lift her off the ground. "One set of footsteps," he said into her ear.

He felt her nod against him. Then he moved forward the last few steps in the line they'd been following. There was an opening, light shining through. He set her down at the top of the stairs.

She looked back at him, held up her hands. Ten fingers. *Ten seconds.*

He nodded. She scrambled down the stairs, making a ruckus as she did. Landon could hear the grumbles, but thankfully there were no more blows.

He counted in his head. Ten seconds. He didn't know what she planned to do with ten seconds, but he trusted her. He had to trust her.

Once he hit ten, he snuck down the stairs. He ducked into the basement just in time to see Sarabeth go flying, her gun clattering out of her grasp and her head hitting the concrete hard and going still—far too still. Hazeleigh let out a gasp of pain—her face was red and bruised. Another woman, bloody and bruised, was tied up in the corner.

In the span of only seconds, Landon was across the room—one hand grabbing the gun moving toward him and his other a fist going into the shorter man's neck.

The gun clattered to the ground, and the man who'd been throat-punched choked out a gurgled gasp.

Then it was a melee. Punches, kicks. He dodged blows, landed them. Two against one, but he'd beaten these odds before, and he wasn't about to let either man lay another hand on any of the women they'd abused.

The shorter guy managed to get an arm around Landon's neck, but that gave Landon the leverage to flip him over. He knew it left him vulnerable to the other man, but if he could take out this one—

He stepped on his throat, the man struggling but fading fast. When he looked behind him, he saw it was a mistake. The other man had grabbed his gun and was moving it in Landon's direction.

The gun went off—an echoing boom in the basement—but not *that* gun. The man—this Rob Currington—jerked once, the gun sliding from his grasp as he fell to the floor. Lifeless.

Landon whirled toward the new shooter who'd just essentially saved his life.

But it wasn't one of his brothers.

It was Sarabeth.

Chapter Twenty-Four

She didn't fall apart. After a few moments, Sarabeth carefully put down the gun and went and untied her mother's bonds, which spurred Landon into action, and he'd come to untie Hazeleigh.

"You're hurt," he murmured, gently undoing the ties.

"I'm alive." Hazeleigh turned to look at the little girl trying to help her mother to stand as the cavalry rushed in. The Thompson brothers. Zara.

Zara made a beeline for Hazeleigh.

"Everyone's okay," Landon assured her, helping her to her feet.

"Oh, Landon, you're burnt." His shirt was torn and the nasty blisters... It must have happened in the explosion, and he hadn't let on all this time.

"And your face looks like it was used as a punching bag," Zara said flatly.

"He thought I knew where this other gold is, but I don't."

"Other gold?"

Hazeleigh pointed to the bag. "He found some of the bank-robbery gold."

There was a moment of silence. "Mr. Field was...right," Zara said.

Emotion clogged Hazeleigh's throat. Poor Mr. Field. All that work. All that time. And it had been there. He'd never get the chance to see it.

"He found out that old guy was his father, and thought he'd know where the gold was," Sarabeth said.

"Since I'm connected to the Petersons," the mother said, leaning on Henry, who'd helped Sarabeth get her out of the chair. Her eye was swollen shut and her voice was weak, but she seemed determined to explain. "This land where Mr. Field thought the gold was—Rob came and got me from where I'd been hiding Sarabeth from him."

"You pretended to be hurt," Landon said, crouching down to study Sarabeth's face. "When your dad threw you, you pretended to be hurt." He sounded amazed.

Sarabeth looked toward her father's body, but the Thompsons had made themselves into a kind of shield so neither the body nor the blood could be seen. She shrugged. "Yeah, figured you could use some help."

Landon kneeled in front of her. He reached out but dropped his hands before he touched her. "Thank you," he said sincerely.

"Yeah, well. Thanks to you, too, I guess. You helped. I couldn't do it myself." She leaned into her mother, who seemed shaky at best. "I couldn't get her out myself."

"But you helped," Hazeleigh said, her voice sounding raw even to her. Her face throbbed, but everything was...

Well, not okay. People were dead. But answers had been found.

Even when the police came, thanks to Dunne calling them in, Sarabeth didn't fall apart. She held her mother's hand, and let Hazeleigh hold her other, and she told the cops everything.

From her father kidnapping them from their house in

Arizona, to what Rob had told her about Mr. Field and the gold over the course of the last few weeks, down to her shooting her own father to save Landon.

Hazeleigh was no longer a person of interest, and the man who'd killed Mr. Field was no longer a threat.

The ambulance took away the body of Rob Currington and the wounded cousin, the Thompson brothers once again making sure Sarabeth didn't see the body. When the EMTs came, they insisted that Landon, Hazeleigh, Sarabeth and her mother, Jessie, go to the hospital.

The rest got a little fuzzy. By the time Hazeleigh was home again, with painkillers and ice packs but luckily no broken bones, she hardly remembered the trip. But Zara bundled her inside, tucked her into her old room in the main house and Hazeleigh slept for what felt like days.

When she woke up, she was disoriented for a moment. Because it was her old, childhood room, but the bed was bigger and the decor was different.

And there was a man in it. Snoring softly.

She looked over at him, her heart swelling painfully. They'd survived. Figured it out. He'd been by her side, he'd trusted her, and in the end he hadn't just saved her, he'd made sure to save that little girl. Who'd been brave enough to save them both.

His eyes blinked open as if he could sense her looking at him even in a deep sleep. He shifted. "You're up," he rasped.

"I am." She looked around the room. It looked like daytime, but she didn't have the foggiest idea when she'd gone to sleep. "I don't know what day it is, but I am up."

"Wednesday," he said with a yawn. He glanced at the clock. "I think."

Then he carefully wrapped his arm around her, and she snuggled in. Relief. "Everything is going to be okay."

"Yeah, it is." She was tempted to fall back asleep. "Sarabeth?"

"Her and her mother are with family services figuring everything out. They're in good hands, and they'll be okay. We'll make sure of it."

We'll make sure of it. Hazeleigh smiled and sank into him again, relaxing. Sarabeth and her mother might not know it yet, but they'd just joined their cobbled-together family. "Really good." She sighed heavily. "She saved us. Well, you both saved us and—"

"I think we worked together to save each other," he interrupted. "A team."

"A family," Hazeleigh corrected.

He chuckled, though it seemed a little sad, and he stiffened underneath her cheek. "Speaking of family... Look..." He cleared his throat. "There's more than just the military thing you should know, Hazeleigh. Now that everything is going to calm down... The thing is, the six of us were in the military together. But we're not actual biological brothers. Because of a military mistake, we had to have our identities wiped and disappear. Start this new...fake, quiet life."

"I guess Wilde seemed like a good place for a quiet life on paper."

"Seemed like indeed." He chuckled, then winced a little. But he kept her hand in his, as if inspecting her fingers. "I'm sorry if that feels like a lie."

"Did you lie?" It didn't feel like a lie. An omission maybe, but nothing...horrible. Nothing that changed how she felt about them.

"I'm not related to them. My last name isn't Thompson. These are lies."

Hazeleigh rolled to face him, studying all that guilt. So serious. So frustrated with himself. She understood it well. She understood *him* well. And she was pretty confident they'd grow to understand each other even better. In all that love they had for one another.

"But they're your brothers, blood or not. They're your family, even if you chose the name Thompson rather than having it handed to you at birth. And you're telling me now, when it's important. I'm not going to hold it against you, Landon. And I'm not going to let you be a martyr about it."

"I guess we're pretty good at that—not letting each other martyr ourselves." He smiled and touched her cheek.

"Yeah, we are. I think we're going to be pretty good at loving each other."

"Yeah, I think we are."

In that moment she realized she didn't *think* they were going to be good at it.

She knew.

* * * * *

MILLS & BOON

THE HEART OF ROMANCE

A ROMANCE FOR EVERY READER

MODERN

Prepare to be swept off your feet by sophisticated, sexy and seductive heroes, in some of the world's most glamourous and romantic locations, where power and passion collide.

HISTORICAL

Escape with historical heroes from time gone by. Whether your passion is for wicked Regency Rakes, muscled Vikings or rugged Highlanders, awaken the romance of the past.

MEDICAL

Set your pulse racing with dedicated, delectable doctors in the high-pressure world of medicine, where emotions run high and passion, comfort and love are the best medicine.

True Love

Celebrate true love with tender stories of heartfelt romance, from the rush of falling in love to the joy a new baby can bring, and a focus on the emotional heart of a relationship.

Desire

Indulge in secrets and scandal, intense drama and plenty of sizzling hot action with powerful and passionate heroes who have it all: wealth, status, good looks...everything but the right woman.

HEROES

Experience all the excitement of a gripping thriller, with an intense romance at its heart. Resourceful, true-to-life women and strong, fearless me face danger and desire - a killer combination!

To see which titles are coming soon, please visit

millsandboon.co.uk/nextmonth

LET'S TALK
Romance

For exclusive extracts, competitions
and special offers, find us online:

 facebook.com/millsandboon
 @MillsandBoon
 @MillsandBoonUK

Get in touch on 01413 063232

For all the latest titles coming soon, visit
millsandboon.co.uk/nextmonth

JOIN US ON SOCIAL MEDIA!

Stay up to date with our latest releases, author news and gossip, special offers and discounts, and all the behind-the-scenes action from Mills & Boon...

 @millsandboon

 @millsandboonuk

 facebook.com/millsandboon

 @millsandboonuk

It might just be true love...

GET YOUR ROMANCE FIX!

Get the latest romance news, exclusive author interviews, story extracts and much more!

MILLS & BOON
Desire

Indulge in secrets and scandal, intense drama and plenty of sizzling hot action with powerful and passionate heroes who have it all: wealth, status, good looks…everything but the right woman.

MILLS & BOON

MODERN

Power and Passion

Prepare to be swept off your feet by sophisticated, sexy and seductive heroes, in some of the world's most glamourous and romantic locations, where power and passion collide.

MILLS & BOON
MEDICAL
Pulse-Racing Passion

Set your pulse racing with dedicated, delectable doctors in the high-pressure world of medicine, where emotions run high and passion, comfort and love are the best medicine.

MILLS & BOON
True Love

Romance from the Heart

Celebrate true love with tender stories of
heartfelt romance, from the rush of falling in
love to the joy a new baby can bring, and a
focus on the emotional heart of a relationship.